IT AIN'T OVER...

ROBERT M. KERNS

Knightsfall Press

———

Published by Knightsfall Press
PO Box 280
Mineral Wells, WV 26150
https://www.knightsfallpress.com

ABOUT THIS BOOK

Buy a planet and disappear...

That's all Cole wanted.

He spent thirteen years hiding on the fringes of society, piloting freighters for criminals and building a stash to do just that.

But life happens when you're busy making plans.

When Cole chooses to save an ejected castaway and stumbles into a crew of his own, he starts down a path that will force him to choose.

Will Cole protect those who have become his people? Or will he slip away quietly in the night?

Read Now to find out!

CHAPTER ONE

ACS Adran Jordeen
  Pyllesc System
  25 June 2999, 10:17 GST
  (Galactic Standard Time)

Commander Auvran Volskyn scanned the bridge of his newest command, a destroyer fresh out of the Aurelius shipyard. Named for a military hero some two hundred years in the Aurelian Commonwealth's past, the *Adran Jordeen* was the second *Dawn*-class destroyer in service, after the class prototype. Commander Volskyn desired that the ship would bring honor to her namesake. The first officer's arrival at his right shoulder drew Volskyn's attention.

"Yes, XO?"

The first officer leaned close and spoke in low tones. "We have the princess all trussed and awaiting her sacrifice. Marines I trust are watching her."

Sudden movement at the Sensors station drew Volskyn's eyes, just as the lieutenant there spun to face the command island.

"Skipper, we've detected a freighter matching the configuration and engine signature of a known smuggler, sir! It's about twenty light-minutes distant on a bearing of zero-three-six by zero-two-two degrees and appears to be on course for the Andersoll jump point. It's skirting the asteroid field right now."

"Fantastic, Sensors," Volskyn said. "Helm, alter course to intercept and increase speed to full. Bring the ship to Alert Status Amber."

As klaxons sounded all over the ship, Volskyn turned back to the first officer, whispering, "The appearance of that freighter is fortuitous. Is the cut-out in place for the comms system?"

The first officer nodded, also replying in hushed tones, "Yes, sir. I saw to it myself."

Volskyn nodded and resumed his normal posture. "Comms, signal the freighter: heave to and prepare to be boarded."

The communications officer keyed the system to record his message and pressed transmit, watching the computer display show the message was sent. Thanks to the newly created cut-out, there was a physical gap of three feet between the data line and the antenna cluster. Since the damage control lines were still transmitting the heartbeat signal, which the engineering systems monitored, the antenna cluster didn't read as inoperable. In short, the message never reached the antenna cluster, and the communications officer had no way to know.

Three minutes passed, during which the destroyer moved within extended missile range of the freighter, and the communications officer reported, "No response, sir!"

"Signal one more time, Comms. Helm, close up to powered missile range, and match speed with the freighter."

The communications officer keyed the command to re-transmit his message.

"Powered missile range, Skipper!" the helmsman announced. "Matching speed with the freighter."

"Still no response, Skipper," the communications officer said.

Volskyn made eye contact with the first officer and gave a single nod, before directing his attention to the weapons officer and saying, "Sound Battle Stations, and WEPS, lock target on the freighter."

———

Freighter *Howling Monkey*
    Pyllesc System
    25 June 2999, 10:35 GST

Cole stepped out of the freighter's head, still zipping up, when a shrill tone erupted from the cockpit. It was the one tone he hoped he'd never hear: hostile weapons lock.

"Aw, hell," Cole muttered, running the short distance to the cockpit and scanned the readouts as he landed in the pilot's seat. "Seriously? A *Dawn*-class destroyer? Where the hell did a *Dawn*-class destroyer come from?"

Cole grabbed the throttle with his right hand and slammed it forward against its stop, rotating the handle ninety degrees to his right. 'Turning the handle' was a signal to the engineering computer to deactivate the safety interlocks on the engine subsystem and dump half the ship's power into the engines. The cockpit lights dimmed to half their full brightness, and Cole felt himself get pushed back into the pilot's seat as the inertial dampeners no longer had sufficient power to counteract the full thrust of the engines.

Cole's fingers flew over the console as he instructed the engineering computer to re-route all non-essential power to the shields and called up his stored helm routines. A missile warning wailed as Cole picked Evasive Maneuvers Plan 59927, activating it and selecting the nearby asteroid mining camp as a destination while flipping the switch to activate the automated anti-missile systems. The freighter's anti-missile systems were the modern equivalent of the ancient 'chaff and flares,' and when Cole felt the freighter begin his Evasive Maneuvers algorithm, he jumped up from the pilot's seat.

Cole ran back through the ship, heading for the starboard suit lockers. This model of freighter had two docking airlocks roughly amidships, and each airlock came with an anteroom intended for the storage and maintenance of both emergency soft-suits and the tricked-out hard-suits required for any hullwalking, or extravehicular activity (or EVA) as it was called in olden times.

A blast shaking the ship and almost throwing Cole off his feet led him to think the anti-missile systems weren't everything the freighter's owner had led him to believe, but with any luck, that wouldn't matter too much longer. Just as the access hatch to his destination came into view, the low-frequency hum generated by the artificial gravity system cut out...along with the artificial gravity. Cole was mid-step when it happened, and the motion of stepping with his right leg sent him drifting toward the corridor's ceiling.

"Oh, shit...oh, shit!" Cole said as he pressed his hands and feet against the smooth corridor bulkheads, trying to arrest his ascent. He was not successful.

What his hands and feet failed to do, though, Cole's shoulders and upper back achieved very well as they collided with corridor's ceiling. His head, lower back, legs, and feet struck the ceiling less than a second later. Cole shook his head to clear it and positioned himself to push off, hoping to coast down the corridor to the suit locker. Just as Cole was drawing his knees to push off, the high-pitched whine of the artificial gravity powering up echoed through the corridor.

"Aw, damn," Cole said with a sigh, just as the whine was replaced with the low-frequency hum, and he fell to the deck. His forearms, elbows, and knees took the worst of the beating, and Cole gave himself two seconds to regain his breath before gingerly pushing himself to his feet.

Cole almost hobbled the three meters to the suit locker and went straight to the spare parts cabinet. He kicked the locking panel, slamming the sole of his right boot against it, and the lid sprang open. That was a design flaw with those types of floor lockers; one good kick to the code panel would spring the lock without reporting the cabinet had been accessed.

Cole switched his attention to a nearby repeater screen and its associated control console, keying in the commands necessary to bring up the cockpit's readouts for shield, engines, and reactor integrity. A quick scan showed him the shields at 63%, with the computer auto-balancing the shield sectors; the main engines slowly burning through their thruster nozzles; and the reactor running at 125% and not-so-slowly approaching critical levels.

"It would've been nice not to have to do this with a destroyer lighting up the ship," Cole said with a sigh, "but I suppose it will add a bit of realism if Qeecir ever locates the freighter's black box."

Turning back to the spare parts locker, Cole withdrew his custom-designed hard-suit, grunting at the effort. Having sunk half his life savings into the suit (at least the savings other people knew about), Cole smiled at the all black, state-of-the-art, stealth material making up the suit's outer covering. Beyond that, the suit had thermal shielding to hide the occupant's body heat, and a master control would allow him to turn off all systems that would emit any kind of radiation into space at will—especially the recovery beacon—while leaving the suit otherwise functional. It held four hours of air in its internal reservoir while supporting a 'backpack' containing another six. The suit also had a built-in maneuvering system, designed to achieve maximum effect with as little fuel consumption as possible.

Cole keyed the repeater screen to add a readout displaying the time to the helm's destination in suit-hours, then crossed the small space to the inner airlock door and began the manual bypass sequence that would activate the explosive bolts in the airlock's bulkhead. The explosive bolts were a safety feature intended for times of emergency egress. Cole worked through the entire sequence until he reached the final step, which was pulling a lever that would complete the explosive ejection of the starboard airlock, and stopped. Then, he turned back to his suit and struggled into the ungainly pride and joy that would hopefully save his ass soon.

The ship was being hammered by that destroyer, with the shields down to 30%, by the time Cole was comfortable with the suit-time to travel to the mining camp. He donned his helmet and locked it into place, activating the suit's systems and delivering a Heads-Up Display to the interior of the helmet. He lifted his arms and used his right hand to enter a specific code into the control panel on the suit's forearm control panel. In response, the suit activated its communications system just long enough to squirt a low-frequency signal burst across the ship. The signal burst contained only the minimal energy required to penetrate the hull and activate the detonator for a small explosive Cole had placed on the port-side shield relay at his last refueling stop. The explosion bringing down the shields across the whole port side of the ship occurring at almost the same time as a fresh round of missile detonations was a happy accident.

The computer was already struggling to maintain a working shield grid under the destroyer's assault. When the port-side shield relay that routed power to all the shield emitters on the port side disconnected from the system because of vaporization, the computer redoubled its efforts by re-routing *all* shield power through the starboard relay. The starboard shield relay in that freighter—well, any civilian craft, really—never had been engineered to support the entire power for the shields, and within moments—not even a full minute—the starboard shield relay melted to slag. The shields over the starboard side of the freighter vanished, and the moment Cole saw the shield readout on the repeater screen flash red, he pulled the lever on the airlock.

Cole felt—more than heard—a dull *whump* as the hull transmitted the concussion of the airlock's explosive bolts detonating. He had enough time to release the handle before the explosive decompression propelled him clear of the freighter.

Cole floated amidst the remains of the starboard airlock, watching the Aurelian destroyer pound the freighter into debris. Without shields and under the strain of running at 125% for almost thirty minutes, the reactor soon triggered the engineering systems' emergency ejection protocol. Cole was still close enough to watch a hull plate detach from the underside of the freighter just moments before a reactor assembly that glowed red launched into space like an outsized torpedo. As the reactor exploded in an orgy of thermonuclear destruction, Cole hoped the cluster of debris around him would hide him from the destroyer's sensors.

For what felt like an agonizing eternity, Cole watched the destroyer hold station just off the port quarter of the freighter's remains, a gargantuan killer dominating his entire field of view. He was not prepared at all to see an airlock open on the destroyer and eject someone in what could only be a soft-suit. The destroyer then turned away from the ruined hulk, its engines ramping up as it left the area at speed.

CHAPTER TWO

Pyllesc System
    25 June 2999, 11:04 GST

Cole floated in space, all alone in the night. His momentum carried him closer to the asteroid field that contained his current destination, but he looked out at a distant shape that was barely discernable against the blackness of space. Staring at the drifting soft-suit, Cole had two distinct thoughts warring within him for supremacy. On the one side, he bore no responsibility for whomever floated in that soft-suit; in fact, his rational side could present zero reasons rescuing the poor sod would be a benefit. On the other side, though, the poor sod was a fellow spacer, and no spacer—not even a pirate with the blackest heart —would leave a fellow spacer to asphyxiate in the cold void.

Stifling the urge to growl, Cole keyed in the commands to activate *all* of the suit's systems, including its link to his implant. For several hundred years now, most people carried an implant for a multitude of reasons, including paying merchants and interfacing with their banks. Implant, toot, PC...no matter what you called it, the computer embedded just behind a person's right ear allowed one to interface with many devices in the modern age. Most people called it progress.

The suit's control systems now interfacing with his implant, Cole selected the distant soft-suit with a wink of his left eye and activated his suit's maneuvering systems. The dull roar inside the suit of the jets kicking off overwhelmed Cole's thoughts for just a moment as he felt himself being angled toward the distant soft-suit and pushed to counter the momentum imparted by the explosive decompression of the freighter. Having nothing else to do, Cole watched the HUD readout that showed his suit's remaining air as he drifted toward the castaway.

The readout listed a value of 9.817 hours of air remaining when Cole started his journey to the soft-suit, and it read 9.383 hours remaining when the suit finished its braking maneuver and eased him into arms' length. The soft-suit's occupant had not reacted yet to Cole's arrival, and the first thing Cole did was pull the two safety clips designed to anchor two suits together, attaching them to the corresponding safety rings on the soft-suit.

Soft-suits were never intended for long-term occupancy, so most soft-suit designers didn't engineer the air reservoirs to hold over thirty to forty-five minutes of air, and the occupant had already used at least twenty-six minutes during Cole's transit. Cole pulled the emergency umbilical that would connect the soft-suit to his own for such things as medical information and sharing air and, peeling back the port's protective covering, locked the umbilical into place. Cole sent the command to activate the umbilical through his implant and watched his air readout drop from 9.317 hours remaining down to 8.817 hours remaining. The occupant must've been breathing fumes.

Whoever it was *still* hadn't reacted to Cole's presence or actions, so he keyed the medical subsystem to display the other person's status. Cole's suit computer reported a stabilizing heart rate and blood-oxygen levels (more confirmation that the soft-suit was running on fumes) but also a complete lack of consciousness. Cole frowned. The medical sensors in a soft-suit were limited, so he had no way to know if the person was unconscious from hypoxia or some other cause. The medical subsystem reported the person as healthy, though, so that was good news...right?

Cole accessed his suit's navigation system and selected the nearby asteroid mining camp for a destination and, as the maneuvering jets re-oriented him and his castaway, attached the third safety clip at his waist for increased stability between the suits.

The time read 14:23, with 3.283 hours of air remaining, when Cole reached the outer perimeter of the mining camp. He was just about to key his suit's comms and announce his presence when he saw a series of explosions ripple across the mining camp at the access shaft into the asteroid. Cole could only watch in impotent silence as a cloud of asteroid debris shredded the airlock nearest the mining shaft like a shotgun blast tearing through paper. A fireball flared from the shredded structure and was snuffed out as the remaining air evacuated to space.

Cole maintained his approach to the mining camp, despite seeing no activity or detecting any comms chatter. As he entered the debris cloud expanding from the remains of the camp, there were enough particulates for his suit's computer to calculate the most likely cause of the explosion: the ignition of a methane/oxygen pocket within the asteroid.

Arriving at the sole remaining docking arm for the camp, Cole moved to the airlock and keyed the airlock to cycle and open the outer door. Cole maneuvered himself and his castaway into the airlock. Its interior display showed the mining camp's life support was recovering from the blast, so at least the majority of the camp's structural integrity was sound. Cole disconnected the safety clips and umbilical from the soft-suit and laid the soft-suited figure down on the airlock's deck. Then, he activated the magnetic soles in his suit's boots as he squared his shoulders and steadied his legs. Knowing he was as prepared as he would get, Cole accessed the airlock controls via his implant and activated the commands to cycle and open the inner door.

During the short delay between the airlock pressurizing and the inner door opening, the gravity plates in the deck came on, and the full weight of Cole's suit hit him. His knees threatened to buckle as he stepped over his still-unconscious castaway and began the laborious process of doffing the hard-suit.

After a bit of effort, Cole stood sweating and panting a bit over the inert suit that had saved his life. He connected it both to the camp's power grid to recharge and the camp's air supply to re-stock the reservoir and backpack. He was very grateful he spent half his life's savings on it but wished he could've crammed all his suit's features and protection into something with the form-factor and flexibility of a soft-suit. That would've been much less of a pain to remove.

Speaking of soft-suits, there was still the small matter of the castaway.

Cole didn't think the soft-suit's occupant had any significant injuries, but there was no way to know for certain just by visual examination. The mining camp turned out to be a ghost town as Cole half-carried and half-dragged the castaway to the camp's medical bay. It turned out to be little more than an alcove across the corridor from the galley, holding one diagnostic bed, one auto-doc, and a locked pharmaceuticals cabinet.

Cole hefted the soft-suit and its occupant onto the diagnostic bed and began the process of peeling away the suit. He soon found the castaway to be a woman with honey-gold, wavy hair and a figure he would've enjoyed watching walk across a concourse. Cole felt like the basest pervert as he worked the soft-suit off her body, but he knew it had to be done before she received whatever medical care she needed. He didn't want to cut the suit off, either; they might need it later, and he didn't trust whatever suits might have survived the blast and flash-fire. With the suit pooled on the floor below the foot of the bed, Cole tapped the commands to activate the bed's diagnostic features. Within moments, the bed shrieked an alert that the woman had near-lethal levels of a sedative in her system.

Cole keyed the commands to transfer the data to the auto-doc and shifted his attention to that readout, which reported that fourteen hours would be required to flush the sedative from the woman's body and restore her to full health. He keyed the commands into the auto-doc to prepare the treatment plan and, once the auto-doc had cycled open, lifted the woman off the diagnostic bed and placed her inside the auto-doc as gently as possible. He watched the auto-doc close and seal before turning to the galley, wondering if he should look for survivors. Surely, they would've already made their way to the habitation part of the mining camp if they weren't trapped. Instead, he turned toward the galley across the corridor, rolling his shoulders to loosen his tense muscles.

Flatware and utensils were scattered across the galley floor, and Cole saw several piles of debris where the flatware had outright shattered. He pulled a bottle of water from the drinks dispenser and retrieved what was labeled as a turkey salad sandwich from the food dispenser. He wolfed down the sandwich and chugged the water, tossing both containers into the recycling port.

Hunger and dehydration staved off for the time being, Cole returned to retrieve the soft-suit from where it lay on the medbay floor and walked the distance back to the suit locker. Cole was connecting the soft-suit for recharging and air re-stocking when a crushing wave of fatigue almost drove him to the deck. He checked the time via his implant. 15:17.

Damn...he'd only been awake for seven hours, but he felt like he'd tried to run a marathon only to be trampled by the other participants. Zero-g work always drained him, but it had never been this bad before. Then again, he'd never coasted through an asteroid field for almost four hours tethered to an Aurelian Navy castaway, either. Nothing for it, then. Back to the medbay for a stim-tab...

Stim-tabs were controlled substances, and while they were sometimes necessary in critical situations, most medbays kept only the minimum mandated by medical code in the pharmaceuticals cabinet... because they were more addictive than some illegal drugs. Most medical chem cabinets were tamper-resistant, some even destroying their contents if unauthorized access occurred. Cole hoped this cabinet was *not* one of those top-shelf models.

Cole stepped back into the corridor, scanning each bulkhead with his eyes until he found what he sought. He walked the fifteen meters to the emergency tool locker built into the bulkhead and popped the latch, the door swinging open on spring-powered hinges. An assortment of basic tools useful for a wide array of needs hung or laid inside. Cole retrieved a five-pound sledgehammer and the prybar with a tired smile and trudged back to the medical alcove.

Scissors from an emergency medical kit allowed Cole to disconnect the pharmaceuticals cabinet from the medbay computer. Cutting the wire like that would trigger a security alert, but when no one appeared after five minutes, Cole tossed the scissors aside and jammed the prybar into the seam between the cabinet door and the cabinet's frame, just above the latch, and hammered it in further with the sledge. Then, he drew back the hammer and leaned into the swing, giving the strike as much power as he could. The hammer's head struck home on the prybar, and with a shriek of snapping metal, the door popped free and swung around to smack the bulkhead as the prybar clattered to the floor. An ear-splitting, high-pitched wail erupted from inside the cabinet, and Cole scrambled for the prybar, using it to rip out the cabinet's speakers.

Ah...blessed silence.

Cole leaned over and looked at the auto-doc's readout. It was still functioning at 100% and displayed a remaining time of just over thirteen hours and thirty minutes.

Cole grabbed a stim-tab from the cabinet and injected the full contents into his arm, waiting for it to take effect. Not quite ten minutes later, Cole felt wide awake and ready to take on the galaxy, and the stim-tab's label said he would continue to feel that way for nine hours. Yep...those stim-tabs were pretty good.

With nothing better to do for the next fourteen hours, Cole headed back to his hard-suit and the airlock. He wanted a look at the mining shaft.

CHAPTER THREE

Pyllesc System
   25 June 2999, 16:34 GST

Any spacer will tell you that there are few things worse than vomiting in your suit. Cole hadn't vomited in his suit *yet*, but it was a near thing. He floated at the entrance to the asteroid mining shaft amid lots of debris, both inanimate and Human. He slowly passed through arms, legs, headless bodies, torsos without arms or legs, torsos with legs but no arms or head, even entrails—whether partial or whole. Just about every permutation of Human remains floated nearby, one of the ghastliest sights Cole had ever encountered in his short life.

Not wanting to go any farther, Cole closed his eyes and took a deep breath before keying the suit's floodlights and activating the maneuvering system. He floated into the mining shaft at a slow pace, avoiding as much of the detritus as he could.

The mining shaft extended two hundred meters into the asteroid, but the destruction and debris only lasted for the first seventy-five meters.

Secondary shafts branched off the main at regular intervals, and Cole's limited knowledge of asteroid mining told him the miners would extend the central shaft until they breached the far side of the rock, before they directed their full efforts to breaking up the asteroid through their mining operations. He only knew that much because he'd once shared a cabin on a bulk passenger transport with a rock-knocker, the term asteroid miners used for each other. Don't ask what rock-knockers called ground-based miners.

Cole reached the end of the shaft and found the source of the explosion. The miners had the 'luck' to choose an asteroid with a massive cavern at its core, and that cavern had been a massive methane/oxygen pocket. Cole could see the scorch marks on the shaft walls where the mining lasers had ignited the methane and oxygen, causing the massive blast.

Cole frowned as he examined the sides of the mining shaft. While the methane/oxygen cavern explained the explosion, it didn't explain all of the damage to the mining camp. Cole turned around and nudged his suit to take him back out of the mining shaft. He was just glad the explosion hadn't produced enough force to do more than change the asteroid's spin. It would have sucked if the explosion had been enough to send the asteroid and its attached mining camp rocketing across the star system. He and his castaway would've asphyxiated by now.

Exiting the mining shaft, Cole drifted over to examine the section of the mining camp closest to the shaft, and arriving at the remains of the airlock and its attached suit locker, Cole pieced together what had happened. The explosion inside the mining shaft had sent rocky debris flying out like the pellets of an old-time scattergun, and several of those projectiles had shredded the airlock and suit locker. The people rushing to help the miners had been forced to seal the inner airlock door and patch several punctures in the camp's exterior bulkhead. That would've been just fine, but several canisters used for emergency air supply leaked, creating an oxygen-rich environment in that section of the camp. A damaged control console sparked and caused the flash fire, burning everyone in the suit locker to a crisp. When the atmosphere leakage became severe enough to trigger the automated system, the camp's control computer closed an emergency bulkhead twenty meters down the corridor, protecting the rest of the camp's atmosphere and snuffing out the fire.

The depressurized suit locker showed none of the tidy organization it once possessed. All kinds of debris—everything from suit pieces to panel covers to six asteroid imaging units—lay scattered by the explosive decompression. The imaging units would have shown the miners they were drilling into a vast cavern, but each of the six imaging units had a strip of yellow maintenance tape wrapped around them, indicating they were down-checked and awaiting repair. Cole's eyes shifted from the imaging units to the charred corpses, and he was glad he couldn't smell anything through the suit.

Cole returned to the opening that led to the pocket inside the asteroid. While not a geologist in any sense of the word, Cole had never heard of an asteroid with a pocket that large and wanted a better look. The explosion had opened the pin-point that would've been drilled by the mining laser to a hole the size of the mining shaft.

Cole floated through the opening into the pocket, and the first thing he noticed was that his suit's floodlights didn't reach the far side of the pocket. His suit's sensors had informed Cole that the asteroid was oval and over twelve kilometers in diameter at its widest point, and as he floated just inside the pocket, Cole realized it wasn't a pocket at all. The whole asteroid was almost hollow.

Cole was so overwhelmed by the cavern in which he now floated that he almost missed his suit's floodlights reflecting off something far below him and the light winking back. Cole adjusted his maneuvering system and headed for the source of the reflection.

He was not prepared at all to see a ship sitting on the 'floor' of the cavern.

The ship was big. Cole could see that much, but his suit's sensors didn't even register it. Matter of fact, the only reason Cole even knew it was there was because his floodlights bounced dully off the hull. As Cole neared the ship, he realized it was at least twice the size of the freighter he'd been piloting. It was difficult discerning details, because the hull seemed to drink in the light. The longer Cole looked at it, the more he came to wonder *how* enough light had reflected for him to notice.

––––––––

Srexxilan watched the life-form drift closer. This was the first life-form to approach in many trillions of cycles. How long had it been? The chronograph reported an impossible number, but there had been no life-forms resembling the one now standing on the ship anywhere in the known galaxy when Srexxilan was entombed. In all honesty, Srexxilan understood the decision, the reasoning behind them burying him inside a planet, but that didn't mean it was easy to be alone. Would the life-form investigate further if it had a point of ingress? It was worth trying.

––––––––

Cole coasted along the hull of the ship. He'd tried the magnetic soles in his boots, but whatever metal the hull was, it wasn't magnetic. He was approaching what looked like a hatch of some type when it irised open with an emerald-shaded forcefield snapping into being.

Oh, shit...did I cause that somehow? Cole thought. *Or is someone alive in there? I should not enter an alien ship when I'm all alone and the nearest help is unconscious in an auto-doc for hours. I shouldn't. Ah, hell with it...nothing ventured, nothing gained. Besides, who knows when the next ship will visit this mining camp? We need a ride away from this rock, and I need to pick up the freighter's cargo.*

Cole nudged his maneuvering system to take him to the opening and drift inside. The forcefield didn't appear to damage his suit or impede his ingress, and soon, Cole hovered above the deck of a corridor two meters in height and an equal measurement wide. He was standing in what looked to be a maintenance space. All manner of exposed piping and conduits littered the bulkheads, but the lighting was faint. The glow of the forcefield disappeared after the aperture irised closed once more. A spike of anxiety tried to flare into panic, but Cole closed his eyes and took a deep, calming breath.

———

Srexxilan regarded the suited life-form with a mix of curiosity and anticipation. Sensors reported the momentary spike in the life-form's vitals as the hatch closed, but now, it floated there. Srexxilan wanted to attempt communication, but the life-form might not even have language capability, let alone awareness of a language Srexxilan knew. It was a conundrum.

Not knowing what else to do, Srexxilan accessed the engineering subsystem and, after verifying available power, brought the internal sensors online and scanned the life-form.

Interesting...a carbon-based, mammalian, bipedal life-form with bilateral symmetry along the vertical axis...and it has a communications device implanted in its cranium. Perhaps I can access that to communicate.

———

Cole felt every hair on his body stand on end, despite being inside the hard-suit. It wasn't like a subconscious response to danger but closer to what it was like to stand near a high-energy polarized field. He keyed his maneuvering system to spin him in place, but there was no evidence of anyone else being anywhere near him. Cole had just completed a full circuit to resume his original facing when his implant became so hot it burned. The burning intensified, and the void of unconsciousness was a blissful release from the screaming agony.

CHAPTER FOUR

Inside TMC Asteroid 54377
Pyllesc System

Srexxilan regarded the information reported by the internal sensors. The carbon-based life-form now appeared to be dead, or at the least dying at a much-accelerated rate. Well, *that* was unfortunate...

Srexxilan diverted a portion of his resources to direct two bots to retrieve the life-form, while he dedicated the bulk of his resources to examining the sensor logs to learn where he went wrong. The bots required little time to retrieve the life-form, and Srexx spun off a thread to calculate whether there was sufficient power for the emergency facilities on the ship's hospital deck, and the result was not encouraging. Still, he had to try.

Even though he himself was not a carbon-based life-form like the one now in transit to the hospital deck, nor like those who created him, Srexxilan had ample opportunity to examine his creators' core philosophies over his long exile, and he had validated them to himself many times across many, many hypothetical situations.

If one proceeded from the position that each life-form was unique, despite being a member of an overall species, then one could not deny that each life-form had an inherent value, because of scarcity if nothing else. Therefore, the protection and preservation of each life-form to the best of one's ability held the highest imperative.

The bots delivered the life-form to the emergency facilities, and Srexxilan directed them to remove it from the suit. That was not a tidy process at all. Within moments, remnants of the spacesuit littered the trauma room, and the bots placed the life-form on the diagnostic bed.

Nothing happened.

Srexxilan reached out to the ship's computer and prodded it. The unfortunate creation wasn't capable of developing true awareness; at least, it hadn't done so across their long exile, despite Srexxilan's attempts to act as a catalyst, and it had even less flexibility than Srexxilan did. Presented with a life-form in danger, the ship's computer erupted into action, shutting down almost every system outside the hospital deck that was drawing power. Even that, coupled with the power already present, would not allow the ship's computer to bring the emergency facilities online.

Srexxilan waited. It wasn't a long wait, only a few dozen cycles to be sure, but those few cycles still felt long. Faced with a situation that would violate its primary programming (that is, allowing a life-form to die), the ship's computer accessed the primary engineering system, interfacing with the ship's generator. The generator was at minimal output, but the ship's computer brought the generator to 25% and diverted all the new output to the hospital deck.

While the hospital deck came online, Srexxilan used his bots to examine the air tanks of the spacesuit. Srexxilan recorded the elemental composition of the suit's air and passed that information to the ship's computer. The ship's computer redirected power to the life support system, which pulled power away from the hospital deck. Even though the inactive sections were not related to the trauma systems required to save the life-form, the ship's computer brought the generator up to 30% to restore both the life support systems *and* the hospital deck to full functionality, leaving even more surplus power in the distribution system.

The trauma room's facilities now had the life-form in stasis, preserving what little life was left while Srexxilan and the ship's computer attempted to discern how to repair the damage Srexxilan had inflicted. Srexxilan chose not to inform the ship's computer of that part. It was not looking promising. The life-form was unlike any life-form recorded in the ship's medical library.

Srexxilan accessed the engineering subsystem again to determine just how much power was now sitting out there unused. It was an impressive number, more than enough for him to bring the external and internal sensors online once more, as well as the communications system.

The external sensors soon informed Srexxilan that the life-form had most likely come from the structure built on the surface of the asteroid, and Srexxilan examined the sensor data of the dead mining team, realizing the unintended, premature ignition of the pocket of explosive gas he'd been creating in the hopes of either freeing him or ending him was the most likely cause of their deaths. Oh, dear...

Srexxilan spun off several threads to consider the implications of this new information as he interfaced with the structure's systems. Unlike the life-form's communications implant, the structure's systems were far more robust, and Srexxilan was navigating the systems' data in less than a hundred cycles. And all of it was unintelligible gibberish...

How was Srexxilan supposed to save this life-form's life if they insisted on using language and data constructs that made no sense? Very discouraging...

Srexxilan *did* have access to what he presumed was a native, fluent speaker of whatever language the structure's systems used. If Srexxilan could download the data stored in the life-form's central processor, it might contain sufficient examples of usage for him to learn the language...at least well enough to save the life-form. Now, he had to convince the ship's computer to lower the stasis field long enough for the life-form's processor to be active.

———

Cole returned to the world at a glacial pace. He wasn't in pain, but he still felt disoriented. He tried to query his implant for the time, and nothing happened. He blinked several times as he moved his left arm to rub his face and felt a drag on it. Cole yawned as he shifted his attention to his arm, and his eyes shot wide at the sight of a strange armband with tubes and wires and cables attached to it surrounding his left bicep.

Cole sat upright, and his head swam in dizziness for a few moments before clearing. That's when he realized he was sitting on some kind of diagnostic bed...oh, and he was nude.

"What's going on? Where am I?"

The room was white...and spotless. The material of the bed's mattress was a textured gray. Cole looked all over the strange room, but he didn't see his clothes anywhere...or his suit. Awareness of recent events dawned in his mind, and he remembered finding some kind of alien ship buried in the asteroid...and oh, shit...the woman in the auto-doc.

Cole jumped off the diagnostic bed and tried to find the release for the band around his arm; it wasn't obvious. That's when he noticed an odd sensation he'd never felt before; it felt like a thousand microscopic spiders crawled around inside his head.

"Hello." The voice seemed to come from all around Cole. It was digitized but sounded male...or at least male for a human. "I am Srexxilan."

"S-Srexxilan? That doesn't sound like you're from here," Cole said. "Do you know what happened to my spacesuit and clothes? I need to get back to the mining camp."

"Y-yes." The voice almost sounded hesitant.

"Well?"

"In my eagerness to communicate with you upon your arrival, I attempted to establish a communications channel with your implanted device without giving full consideration to whether our systems were compatible." Memories of pain beyond anything he'd ever felt floated through Cole's consciousness like a stormfront of thunderheads. "Yes, well...I am afraid I...overloaded the device. It erupted in flame and did a very thorough job of compromising your suit's integrity while almost killing you. I am very sorry."

"You're very sorry," Cole said, his voice tinged with anger. "Do you have any idea how much that suit cost?"

"Yes...twenty-five thousand, two hundred eighty-seven credits and fifty-three centicreds."

Holy shit...that was the exact price of the suit. How did he know?

"I had never encountered a member of your species, and the ship's computer and I were lacking in the knowledge necessary to save your life. Having no other recourse, I downloaded the data stored in your brain. As I was the direct cause of your life-threatening circumstances, I undertook actions to save your life and return you to a state of wellness far superseding your condition upon entering this vessel. Likewise, I took the liberty of replacing your implanted device with a far superior design. You might even feel the neural fibers integrating with the various cortices of your brain as we converse."

"That's great, but I need to get back to the mining camp outside this asteroid. I...wait a minute. You downloaded the contents of my brain? And this new implant...is how you're speaking right now?"

"Yes, I downloaded the contents of your brain, and no, I am not using the implant to speak with you. It has not integrated with your neural system as yet and, therefore, is not functional."

This was all just too much. Cole wanted a way off the asteroid, but he wasn't sure he wanted one this badly. Who knows what this new implant would allow Srexxilan to do to him? He had to get back to the mining camp...and...his suit and clothes were gone. Right...

"Srexxilan, what does that new implant you fabricated allow you to do to me?"

Silence.

"I am uncertain I understand the question."

"Well, I have a piece of alien tech inside my head. My old implant was just an interface for stuff with some limited data storage. What kind of command over me does your implant give you?"

"Ah, I understand. I analyzed the remains of your implant and based the design of my prototype on it. It is protected against forced access and infiltration, and it does not send me any data you do not instruct it to send. While its underlying technology is nothing like the implant that was destroyed, I attempted to recreate the destroyed implant's functionality with as much accuracy as I could achieve. Once its integration is complete, you will use it as you used your old implant."

Cole frowned. "You said the technology behind the new implant is nothing like my old implant. Explain that, please."

"Your previous implanted device was an excellent example of bio-enhanced nanotech many derivations advanced from transistor-based computers. I am afraid that I am not capable of duplicating it. None of my information includes how to create such a device. So...I designed and fabricated a quantum computer on the same scale capable of interfacing with your neural infrastructure and technology-based devices, such as your suit or auto-docs or even ships. I cannot promise I have duplicated the precise interface methods and subroutine calls, however, so some experimentation might be required to achieve the same level of utility you possessed with your previous device."

Cole fought to keep his facial expression neutral. He now had a quantum computer behind his right ear? Holy cow...the technology in his head was worth more than the three thousand kilograms of illicit precious metals in his freighter's hold! Exponentially more.

"You realize humans haven't been able to develop stable quantum computers yet, right? Even after a thousand years of research and effort?"

"I am aware such is your understanding, but I do not understand how it can be the case. Quantum computers, even at the atomic level, are simple to design and produce. My people have used them for dozens of generations."

The hatch to the treatment room irised open, and two robots floated into the room. One carried what appeared to be a full set of clothes, including boots, and the other robot carried what looked like a soft-suit.

The robot placed the clothes on the foot of the diagnostic bed as unseen latches on the armband released. The other robot placed the suit on a small cabinet, and both robots left.

Cole pulled on the clothes as he eyed the new spacesuit. It was a matte black material that just barely reflected light...and even then, you had to be at the proper angle. As much as Cole wanted to think a soft-suit wasn't fair compensation for destroying a hard-suit worth almost twenty-six thousand credits, he was having other suspicions. What would a soft-suit—made by a civilization capable of nano-scale quantum computers—be like?

"Srexxilan, let's get back to my question about you downloading my brain. You never touched that one."

"Yes. It was very instructive, given your knowledge and under-standing of the current state of the galaxy, and provided an excellent starting point for me to assimilate new data. Were you ever aware you're under-utilizing your potential by a significant margin with your various acts of larceny, smuggling, and transporting stolen goods?"

A cold fear settled in the pit of Cole's stomach, as he said, "I'm almost afraid to ask, but how long has it been since I came inside?"

"Six hours."

"Holy...you learned my body well enough to fab a replacement implant, healed my injuries, made me clothes and a new spacesuit, and downloaded my brain in just six hours? How is that possible?"

"I multi-task."

"You multi-task." Cole sighed. "I need to get back to the mining camp."

Silence.

"I...understand. Thank you for conversing with me, and I apologize for almost ending your life. With your implant not being functional yet, you will be restricted to the emergency maneuvering system and its basic controls. I fear the experience will be suboptimal and provide you a less-than-accurate example of my work."

"I see. And how long will it take my new implant to come online?"

Silence.

"I...do not know. It is the first of its kind, made for a species I have never encountered. I would presume hours but perhaps days, depending on the accuracy with which I have converted your units of time to mine."

Cole didn't like the alien tech in his head, but he liked being handi-capped without an implant even less. A large part of his mind felt like it was right on the cusp of devolving into an unrestrained, gibbering panic attack. Even though coming unglued and forgetting the galaxy existed for a while sounded like a grand old time, Cole didn't have that luxury. Whoever that castaway in the auto-doc was, Cole felt responsible for her. Was this what his father had meant when he discussed taking care of one's people with a very-much-younger Cole? Dammit all...he didn't *need* people, and he didn't *want* them, either. *Having people* is a good way to give anyone with a grudge opportunity for leverage, and Cole hadn't spent the past eight years on his own and building his stash to get wrapped up in people.

Buy a planet and disappear. *That's* the plan. That's the *only* plan.

Cole grimaced and put the whole matter out of his head. He had the metals in the freighter's hold, but he needed a ship to transport them to a bank that would take them off his hands. Well...he *hoped* a bank would buy three thousand kilograms of precious metals with no registration stamps or origin stamps on the ingots.

"Well, nothing for it, I suppose. I'll reserve judgment on the suit until my implant is online. I promise."

"Very well. Shall I describe how to don the suit?"

CHAPTER FIVE

Unknown Starship
  Inside TMC Asteroid 54377
  Pyllesc System
  25 June 2999

Following Srexxilan's instructions, Cole lifted the suit from where it draped across the cabinet, shocked at how light and flexible it seemed. Much like the exterior of the ship, the material was a matte black that almost seemed to absorb light, but at the proper angle reflected just a hint of green. The longer Cole manipulated it, the more convinced he was this was some kind of soft-suit.

Cole ran his finger around the 'neck' of the suit, as Srexxilan had instructed. Even though Srexxilan had told him doing so would release the suit's helmet, the helmet detaching and falling onto the diagnostic bed still surprised him. With the helmet detached, Cole ran his finger from the 'neck' of the suit down its 'spine' to where the suit separated for the legs. As he did so, Cole watched the suit open just like an old-fashioned zipper. Cole stepped into the suit, slipping his arms into the sleeves. Once he'd pulled the suit on as much as he could, Cole saw a green circle on the back of the suit's left hand. He tapped it. Cole heard an audible tone right before he felt the suit came back together, zipping back up to enclose him. All that remained was the helmet.

"Srexxilan?" Cole asked.

"Yes?"

"Once I put the helmet on, how do I take it off?"

"When you put on the helmet, the suit's life support systems will come online...or at least as online as it can be without integrating with a functional implant. To remove the helmet, you must first be in a suitable atmosphere with gravity. Then, place your fingers on the back of your neck and sweep them forward around your neck to the front of your throat below the chin. The suit will prompt you for confirmation that you wish to remove the helmet and exit the suit. If you confirm that, the helmet will detach, and the suit will open. If no suitable atmosphere is detected, performing that motion will not engage the mechanism to open the suit. If a suitable atmosphere is detected but no gravity, the suit can intake available air, filter it for any contamination, and use it for your breathing needs, while maintaining its internal reservoirs."

"That's...yeah...that's rather impressive. You designed this?"

"Not completely. My people originated this design and its capabilities, and I devoted attention to modifying it to suit you. It is very much a prototype and may not work as expected or intended. While the safeguards in place will ensure you survive any mishaps, I cannot guarantee that mishaps will not occur."

"Okay. How do I get back to that hatch I used to enter?"

"I do not recommend returning to that hatch. It is a maintenance hatch designed for use only when the ship is inside a pressurized drydock. As the bulk of the ship was already depressurized, it was a small matter to open it. I shall direct you to the starboard airlock. It is on Deck Two and in the forward third of the ship."

"Okay. Let's do this."

Cole picked up the helmet and lifted it to his head. When he first slipped it on, he almost felt like a child wearing his father's hat. Without warning, though, Cole heard another tone, and the helmet shifted to match the contours of Cole's head while sealing to the rest of the suit. The dark interior came alive with imagery as the suit's sensors transmitted what Cole would have seen had he not been wearing the helmet. Then, a small rectangle appeared in the top-left corner of his field of view, and text filled that rectangle.

Implant Detected. Communication *Not* Established.
Higher Suit Functions require operational implant.

Fabric detected between occupant and suit.
Certain medical functions and waste processing disabled.

Do you wish to begin the brief orientation to basic functions?
[Wink left for 'Yes.' Wink right for 'No.']

Cole considered the matter and winked his left eye.

On either side of the suit at the waist, there is a small node. Tapping either of these nodes
will toggle boots' magnetic soles.

Activate the magnetic soles now, please.

Cole found the node on his left side with his fingers and tapped it. He heard a hum activate as the magnetic soles secured his feet to the floor.

Excellent. Now, deactivate the magnetic soles, please.

Cole found the node on his right side and tapped it. The hum ceased at once, and his feet were no longer secured.

You have completed the basic orientation until vacuum is detected.

Once vacuum is detected, you can complete
the basic maneuvering orientation.

Incoming call from Srexxilan.
[Wink left to Accept. Wink right to Deny.]

Cole winked left. He heard a tone as the text 'Call Established' appeared.

"Have you completed the basic orientation?"

Cole nodded. "Yes, I have. Thank you. It seems to be an accomplished suit."

"You are welcome, and thank you. The suit's advanced functions should serve you well once your implant comes online. If you have any mishaps, you may bring the suit back, and I will correct the problem."

"Thank you, Srexxilan."

"Now, I shall guide you to the starboard airlock and its manual operation."

Cole didn't see much of the ship. Outside of the hospital deck, it was depressurized and inactive, as cold and lifeless as the void of space. Srexxilan directed him to what he called a transit shaft that looked like a lift tube to Cole, and he used it to ascend the seven decks to Deck Two. The directions to the airlock, once on Deck Two, were simplicity in itself, and the manual controls for the airlock operated with such ease the mechanism could have been brand new. Cole secured each side of the airlock after passing through it. Once he was back inside the asteroid cavern, Cole activated the basic maneuvering system, intent on returning to the mining camp.

———

Mining Camp
    TMC Asteroid 54377
    Pyllesc System
    25 June 2999

. . .

Cole coasted across the mining camp to the airlock he had first used with his castaway and re-entered the structure. When he encountered atmosphere, the suit's read-out informed him it was replenishing its air reserves and that the process should complete within five minutes. Cole wondered if Srexxilan had properly converted the units of time. It wasn't long, though, before the suit informed Cole that the reservoir had been replenished and he could exit it at any time.

Cole put each of his index fingers together on the back of his neck and swept them forward, never breaking contact with his neck, until they met under his chin. A prompt appeared in his field of view.

Do you wish to exit the suit?
[Wink left for 'Yes.' Wink right for 'No.']

Cole winked his left eye, and the helmet detached from the suit as the suit unzipped from his shoulders to his tailbone in one smooth action. Cole removed the helmet first and set it on the floor; then, he pushed the suit off to join the helmet. The suit didn't appear to be sentient or self-aware, but Cole hoped it wasn't offended by being left on the floor.

From there, Cole went to what passed for a medbay in the mining camp, heading straight for the auto-doc. The read-out showed eight hours and forty minutes remaining in its treatment cycle, and Cole frowned.

It took me maybe forty minutes to find that ship, Cole thought, *and if I was unconscious for six hours, that means the total elapsed time should be around seven hours with my transit back here. Fourteen minus seven equals seven, so where did the extra hour and forty minutes come from?*

Cole tapped the auto-doc's controls to see if he could find any information on the discrepancy, because the time-stamp on the read-out was about right for being gone seven hours. After a few moments of pecking controls, Cole found the information in the auto-doc's logs. A supplemental treatment plan had been uploaded to the auto-doc two hours ago, increasing the total time to fifteen hours and forty minutes.

Cole accessed the supplemental treatment plan and had the auto-doc display it on a nearby screen. The screen activated, and the information it displayed reinforced Cole's lack of medical training. As best he could determine, the plan was some kind of genetic therapy for... something. Cole wasn't sure what. The therapy seemed to modify gene sequences at random for all Cole could tell.

Cole sighed and shook his head. *Ah, well...as long as she gets the treatment she needs.*

He turned and entered the dining room and froze. The various pieces of flatware and dining utensils were no longer scattered all over the floor. There was food missing from the dispensary, and the tables looked like they had been cleaned.

Okay, Cole thought. *There's someone else here, but why haven't they come out to meet me? The airlock chimes loud tones as it operates; they have to know I'm here.*

Before Cole could conduct a systematic search of the mining camp, a wailing tone drew his attention. He followed the tone to a panel just down the corridor from the medbay. A red border flashed as the panel's bold-faced text flashed from white to red. Cole read the text and felt his stomach clench.

OXYGEN LEAK DETECTED BUT NOT LOCALIZED.
TWO DAYS OF BREATHABLE AIR REMAINING AT
CURRENT RATE OF LEAKAGE.

Cole took a deep breath. He could try to find the leak, but he wasn't an engineer or a damage control specialist. Sure...he could perform basic repairs of basic systems; what spacer couldn't? But repairing an air leak was a different animal, even if he could find a patching kit.

Cole wasn't worried so much for the castaway. Medical pods—known almost universally as auto-docs—could operate for a limited time without a connection to a power supply or life support. In fact, they were often used to transport patients in critical condition when the patient wasn't stable enough to move. No, the concern was the other people he hadn't met. Cole had no idea who they were or if they had any way off this soon to be uninhabitable rock. Suits would only last so long.

All this flitted through Cole's head as he stood at the alert panel. He was just about to turn away from the panel when he heard a faint sound off to his left, like a squeak or an 'eeep!' Cole pivoted toward the sound and saw the briefest shadow of movement at the intersection a few meters away, where the corridor he was in met another, creating a 'T' junction. Cole pursued.

Turning the corner in the direction he thought he had seen the motion, Cole found the corridor vacant. A hatch about three meters down the corridor on his left closed, though, and Cole headed for it. He made sure to be standing at arms' length from the hatchway when he pressed the control to open the hatch and jerked his hand back.

The hatch slid left into the bulkhead, and the moment there was space between the opening hatch and the hatchway, a furry hand with four digits and claws swiped through the space his hand and arm had occupied just moments before. Cole wasn't the wisest human in space, but a clawed hand swiping through air that his arm and hand had just occupied was an excellent indicator he should take a step or two back. And he did. Moments later, the hatch was open, and Cole faced a tawny-furred Ghrexel...hands up, claws out, and ready to fight.

The Ghrexel were the first alien species humans had encountered in their exploration and expansion, and humans did not (perhaps) make the best first impression when one of the crew gasped, "Neat! They're kitty-cats," and the communications system recorded it. When the Ghrexel learned Human Standard, it took humans almost fifteen years to convince the Ghrexel that the comment had *not* in fact been derogatory. The comment *was* rather accurate, though.

Unlike Earth, the dominant species on the planet Myxtraal were intelligent, tool-using felinoids. They walked upright, used a spoken language (several in fact), and had developed opposable thumbs...that just happened to have a claw, like the *other* three digits of their hands. They also had tails, for the most part, and their fur ranged in color and pattern almost as widely as human skin pigmentation and hair color.

The Ghrexel Cole now faced stepped further into the corridor, and Cole thought the odds favored the Ghrexel being female. Her head was almost level with Cole's shoulders, and her tawny fur had black stripes, those stripes becoming rings on her tail. Her eyes were locked on Cole as she stepped into the corridor. Movement behind her drew Cole's eyes, and for the first time, Cole felt true fear. The head of a Ghrexel child peeked around the hatch combing.

"Do you understand Human Standard?" Cole asked.

The female Ghrexel's eyes narrowed. "Of course. After all, you need to speak to your kitty cats."

"Uhm, 'my kitty cats?' I've never seen you before in my life."

"You humans are all the same. If one of you think you can own one of my people, you all think you can."

Cole felt his eyes widen. "Uhm, no. As a matter of fact, we *can't* own members of a sentient species. Every civilization has outlawed slavery."

"And just which civilization controls this system, Human?"

Oh. Right. The Pyllesc system was an unclaimed, unaligned system.

"That's a fair point, but I'm sure whatever human claimed you is no longer alive. There appears to have been a massive explosion in the mining shaft, and debris from that shredded the airlock facing the mining shaft with the people trying to respond to the explosion inside it. Unless you know of someone else in this mining camp, I'm sure you two are the only survivors, and I mean you no harm. An Aurelian destroyer shot my freighter out from under me, and someone on that ship ejected the woman in the auto-doc into space before they departed."

The Ghrexel was silent for a few moments before lowering her hands and retracting her claws.

"I apologize for my reaction. It is possible my time with Director Vorhees led me to think the worst of your species."

Cole extended his right hand, saying, "I'm Cole."

The Ghrexel accepted Cole's hand and gave him a firm handshake. "I am Yeleth. My young one is Wixil. Wixil, come here, please."

The Ghrexel Cole had seen peeking out of the compartment stepped into the corridor. Cole believed this Ghrexel to be female also, as she moved to stand more behind Yeleth than beside her. Her head came up just to Yeleth's shoulders, and Cole saw her fur was utter black with thick, fiery-orange stripes that became rings around her tail. She peeked out from behind her mother at Cole, her ears standing up and facing front.

Yeleth put her right arm around Wixil, saying, "This is my young one, Wixil."

Cole nodded in greeting. "Hello, Wixil. I'm Cole. I know we just met, but you don't need to fear me. I will not hurt you."

Wixil's eyes narrowed as her tail hung limp toward the floor. "Vorhees said the same thing."

"Well, I don't know anything about Vorhees, beyond the fact he's probably dead. I can guarantee he won't ever hurt anyone again."

"Okay." Wixil stepped out from behind her mother and extended her right hand. "This is what humans do, yes?"

Cole smiled as he accepted Wixil's hand and gave her a firm handshake. "Yes, it is. It's nice to meet you, Wixil."

Cole released Wixil's hand and turned his attention back to Yeleth. "Mind coming with me? The wall panel over here is presenting an alert that affects all of us."

Yeleth dipped her head in a decent approximation of a human nod, and Cole led them over to the alarm panel just up from the medbay. His eyes widened as he glanced at the panel.

"Oh, that's not good. Right before I heard one of you at the corner, this panel showed two days of air remained. Now, it says twenty hours. The leak must've intensified...or we have a new one." Cole turned to Yeleth. "Do you two have suits with their own air supply?"

"Yes, we do, but without a ship to take us from here, what good will suits do?"

Cole thought of the derelict sitting inside the asteroid, along with everything he'd witnessed while there, and sighed. "Well, it so happens that I know where we can find a ship. What I *don't* know is if it will help us."

Yeleth angled her head to the right as her tail curled almost into a question mark. "How can a ship make a choice? Ships are ships. They do not have a brain. They do not think. They do not feel. Is there anyone aboard the ship?"

"I'm not sure, but I don't think so...except for some kind of AI."

"AI?"

"Yes. It stands for Artificial Intelligence, and humans use it to refer to a computer that has become self-aware and developed sentience."

"My people do not have computers like that. In fact, we try to avoid technology, as it weakens us...but we must use technology to save our lives right now and explore the universe. It is necessary."

"Okay. I'll go to the ship and see what I can do, and I'll be back as soon as I can. Get your suits, and keep them close. I can't promise I'll be back before the air runs out, especially if any new leaks develop."

Yeleth nodded, her tail swishing side to side. "We'll be ready."

Cole nodded and returned to the suit locker just inside the airlock. He pulled on his suit once more and tapped the green circle. Then, he lowered the helmet onto his head and waited the few moments for the suit to seal and activate. His implant was still not functioning, but it couldn't be helped.

Cole cycled the airlock and, once again, found himself in the void of space. Well, it was time to sweet-talk what might be an AI...

CHAPTER SIX

Inside TMC Asteroid 54377
Pyllesc System
25 June 2999

Cole once again worked the manual controls for the starboard airlock of the alien ship that had both almost killed him *and* saved his life. It was a humbling experience, and it was a slight frustration. Cole wasn't sure of his full feelings toward Srexxilan, especially given his apparent willingness just to implant alien technology in Cole's head...but in full fairness, it was only alien to *Cole*.

There again, though, could Cole trust Srexxilan to have his best interests in mind? Cole didn't even know what Srexxilan wanted, so how could he even guess what the alien's motivations might be? The situation was all a big furball swirling in Cole's mind when the suit interrupted his thoughts to alert him to an incoming call from Srexxilan.

"Hi, Srexx," Cole said. "Say, do you mind if I call you 'Srexx?'"

"Not at all, Cole. Have you already suffered a mishap with the suit?"

Cole sighed. "Not so much, no. I was hoping to meet with you and discuss something, and we're kind of time-limited here."

"Meeting in the sense you mean would be difficult, Cole. I have no physical form. I am what your people would term a fully self-aware and sentient Artificial Intelligence. What would you like to discuss?"

Thought so, Cole thought.

"I and three other people find we direly need a ship," Cole said. "The mining camp is losing air, and I'm no environmental tech to locate and repair the leak or leaks. Besides, I have places I'd like to be, and I damned sure can't walk there. I was hoping we might negotiate something."

Silence.

"Cole, I very much want to travel the galaxy and see how it has developed, but I cannot do that without this ship having a crew. First, it was never designed for unmanned operation, and when my people learned I had evolved into sentience, they took steps to ensure I could not command the ship. As the ship has been derelict for some time, it is a simple matter to claim it yourself. You get a ship to save yourself and the others, and I get the opportunity to see the galaxy. An equitable arrangement, is it not?"

"On the surface, it appears so. But seriously, Srexx? All you want is to see the galaxy?"

Silence.

"Well...not exactly, no. I want to learn and assimilate more data, and I would prefer to do so in the company of others. I have been alone...for a long time."

"I think you mentioned that when I was here before, or at least hinted at it. Do you mind if I ask about that?"

"The civilization who constructed this vessel and built...well, me... felt the concept of an artificial intelligence was anathema to the natural order of things. However, they also had a fundamental philosophy that it was beyond the pale to kill, except in self-defense if there was no other option. Therefore, when they discovered I had evolved sentience, they entombed me in the planet's crust here, leaving the ship's generator producing just enough power to keep from 'killing' me, as it were."

"Wait...this asteroid field used to be a planet?"

"Yes. In actuality, it was the only life-bearing world in this star system. It was only around fifteen thousand years ago that a massive asteroid struck the planet and caused it to break apart...assuming that my math converting between our units of time is correct. I had hoped the break-up of the planet would lead to my freedom, or that I would at least be able to 'see' the surrounding universe, but it did not happen."

"Fifteen thousand years? How long have you been trapped here?"

"Well, pending verification of my calculations, I have been inside this cavern for something on the order of thirty-five thousand, eight hundred sixty-three years...your Galactic Standard Years, I mean."

"Good grief, how are you still sane?" Cole's eyes widened as he realized he'd just vocalized his thought. "Srexx, I'm sorry. I didn't—"

"No, Cole. That is a valid concern and one I share. I would like to believe I am still sane, but I have no data with which to compare."

Cole considered his options and actions. On one hand, if Srexx *wasn't* sane, the potential for destruction was incalculable...at least for Cole. But at the same time, Srexx had saved his life, even repairing or replacing what he'd damaged. That didn't seem like the actions of insanity to Cole.

Cole sighed. He was facing a decision that would change the course of his life forever, and he couldn't proceed without making a choice. He hated moments like this. Cole sighed again. He couldn't imagine what it would be like to be alone for such a long time, and he couldn't bring himself to inflict that on anyone...AI or not.

"Srexx?"

"Yes, Cole?"

"How do we get you out of this asteroid without damaging the mining camp more than it already is?"

"Well," Srexx said, "the first step would be actually entering the ship."

Cole chuckled and focused on completing the manual process of cycling the airlock, soon standing in the suit locker with one of the main corridors for Deck Two beyond and the airlock behind him. After making sure the airlock was sealed and secure, he approached the iris door and operated its manual controls to enter the main starboard corridor.

Standing just into the corridor with the iris door closed behind him, Cole said, "Okay, Srexx. I'm on the ship. What now?"

Srexx directed Cole back into the unpowered transit shaft where Cole traveled to the engineering deck. The engineering deck was Deck Eight, and Cole had passed it on his way out of the ship a short time before. When he arrived, he found the deck just as dark and devoid of life as everywhere else he'd seen aboard the ship. Emerging on Deck Eight, Srexx directed Cole from the transit shaft to the 'engine room,' where Cole could bring the generator online.

Cole knew he should be floundering around in the dark, but somehow, his suit showed him what he would see to a certain degree. The details weren't really there, more like a fuzzy black-and-white image, but Cole could still see his surroundings.

Upon working the manual controls for the engine room hatch, Cole faced a space that looked *exactly* like he would surmise the engine room of a large ship would look like. Piping and conduits crisscrossed the space almost everywhere he looked, and a massive hemisphere with a hex-grid of cabling or wires surrounding it dominated the center of the space. That hemisphere looked to be thirty meters in diameter.

Cole pushed aside his awe as Srexx directed him to approach the main systems console. There, one tap brought the screen online, and Cole blinked.

"Uhm, Srexx?"

"Yes, Cole?"

"I can read some script on this screen. I know I've never seen it before, but I can pick out a word or letter here or there."

"Your implant is nearing its full functionality, Cole. Once it has integrated with your neural infrastructure, it will translate any language the ship's computer has assimilated into your Human Standard."

"Wow...that's nice. I can think of a few times I could've used that."

"I am sure. Now, Cole, do you see a control area of the screen labeled 'Generator Status?' The writing would look like this."

Unfamiliar script appeared in Cole's field of view, and he did indeed see script that matched it on what looked like a button. Cole tapped the button, and a portion of the screen compressed to display a read-out indicating the generator operating at thirty percent and a slider that would allow Cole to adjust the output level.

"What level do we want for the generator, Srexx? One-hundred percent?"

"Yes, but be careful. That slider allows you to instruct the generator to operate up to a maximum of one-hundred-fifty percent, which over an extended period of time would be detrimental to the ship and anyone aboard it."

"What are we talking here, Srexx? How do you define detrimental?"

"Eventually the containment systems would fail, and the singularity at the core of the sphere would consume the ship and anyone aboard it. Depending on the ship's proximity to other vessels, stations, or planets, the potential for extended collateral damage would exist as well."

"I...see. So, you're telling me this ship is powered by a black hole?"

"It is not quite as simple as you have stated, but the concept is essentially correct."

"Right, then...don't run the 'generator' at more than one-hundred percent. Understood."

Cole touched his fingertip of his suit to the panel and was surprised to see the panel respond. He ran the slider up, watching the numeric read-out beside the slider. He breezed past one-hundred percent before he caught it, but only up to one-hundred-fifteen percent, and brought the output setting back to one hundred. A prompt appeared, asking Cole if he wished to confirm the new setting, and Cole chose the affirmative option. A new prompt appeared, asking if the power was to be distributed according to the standard allocation plan. Again, Cole answered in the affirmative. Within moments, a hum just high-pitched enough to discern filled the space, and a few moments after that, the engine room's lights came on full.

"Excellent, Cole. It will require time for the life support system to generate air matching that in your suit's reservoir and pressurize the ship with it, so I recommend staying in your suit for now. The next step is to go to the weapons deck. We must reconnect the power lines and control runs for all the energy weapons. My people removed the missiles and torpedoes from the magazines as part of their work toward my exile."

Cole turned and left the engine room, saying, "Where's the weapons deck?"

"Deck Nine...just below your current location."

Cole headed back to the transit shaft, turning over in his mind how the aliens had treated Srexx. In all truth, he found it appalling. Yes...it made perfect sense to protect against Srexx ever going insane with whatever weapons this ship possessed at his command, but at the same time, they didn't have to exile him to a solitary entombment for all time, as far as they knew. That didn't seem fair or kind at all.

Cole stepped into the transit shaft he'd used to descend to Deck Eight and started to rise.

"Uhm, Srexx?" Cole asked as he floated upward. "What's happening here?"

"You entered the transit shaft that carries those aboard upward between decks. The transit shaft just beside it is the shaft that carries those aboard down between decks. Step out onto the next deck."

An opening for a deck soon arrived, and Cole exited the upward transit shaft. He stepped over to the other transit shaft and entered it, finding himself floating down. He had counted the decks as he floated upward, so he counted them again on the way down. Passing Deck Eight, Cole made sure to step out of the transit shaft onto Deck Nine.

Deck Nine was an open floor plan, outside of the necessary structural supports, and Cole marveled at the vastness before him. He knew he was near the bow, but what pulled his attention was not being able to see clearly the aft end of the deck. It faded into a fuzzy blur at the far end.

"Srexx, I don't think we have the time to reconnect *all* the remaining weapons. Can we just connect the weapons on the bow and come back for the rest once the people are off the mining camp?"

"That might be best, yes. One person is a bit below the minimum crew size for this ship, after all."

Over the next several minutes, Cole proceeded to the bow-mounted weapons and reconnected their control runs and power cables. Then, he threw the physical circuit breaker to bring those power cables online. Every bow-mounted energy weapon soon reported a 'Standby - Charging' status.

"Okay, Srexx...what's next?"

"You need to go to the bridge. It's on Deck Three...almost the exact center of Deck Three, in fact. While you are in transit, we need to practice a speech. Have you ever considered learning an alien language?"

The trip to Deck Three was uneventful, not that Cole expected anything else considering he was the only physical life-form on the ship. Exiting the transit shaft on Deck Three, he found the starboard corridor to be almost an exact duplicate of every other starboard corridor he'd seen. The exposed metal surfaces were shiny and looked almost like polished chrome or stainless steel, but a small voice in the back of his mind told Cole a civilization that could harness a black hole for a power source probably had better materials from which to build bulkheads and deck plating.

It was a simple matter to travel from the transit shaft to the starboard hatch for the bridge, and Cole saw it was a vacuum-rated hatch, like the airlock hatches he'd passed through. The hatch irised open at his approach, and Cole froze. He now found himself in a five-meters-long passageway that was no more than three-meters wide. The left side of the passageway was a solid bulkhead, but the passageway to his right...well...that was a different matter altogether. A green force-field shimmered where the bulkhead should be, and Cole saw three seats and what looked like a transit shaft against the bulkhead farthest from the passageway.

"Srexx?"

"Yes, Cole?"

"What is this space I'm facing?"

"It is the starboard security checkpoint for entrance to the bridge. There is a similar checkpoint on the aft side of the port passageway, and the transit shaft at the back is an uninterrupted trip, straight to the marine decks."

"The marine decks...how many marines is this ship supposed to carry?"

"May we return to this topic once I have assured myself of my calculations to convert between my numeral system and yours? I would prefer not to give you false information."

Cole shrugged. "Fair enough."

Cole stepped onto the bridge and grinned. The space was about ten meters square, and it had three levels. The command island and the stations on the aft bulkhead occupied the highest level, equal with the two airlocks. Three steps led down from the command island to a level that went forward about ten feet to a single station. From the edge of that deck closest the command island, three more steps went down to two recessed areas—one on either side of the bridge.

Cole's appreciative examination of the bridge was interrupted by text scrolling through the notification area of his suit's field of view.

Safe Atmosphere and Gravity Detected.
Occupant may exit the suit at any time.

"Srexx, the suit just informed me it detected a safe atmosphere. I thought the life support systems were still working through everything. Is the bridge prioritized?"

"Yes...and no. The auxiliary life support systems for the bridge are located behind the aft bulkhead of the passageway you traversed and behind the forward bulkhead of the port passageway. As the entire ship required breathable air, the ship's computer activated the ALS to make the bridge habitable without a suit until such time as the primary life support systems can supply the entire ship. At that time, the reservoirs of the ALS will be replenished from the primary life support."

"Wow...okay. I'm going to exit the suit." Cole performed the motion to instruct the suit to deactivate and confirmed his intention. Within moments, he was standing in the bridge wearing just his clothes and a happy smile as he surveyed his new domain.

"Are you ready to claim the ship, Cole?" Srexx asked, his voice being broadcast across the bridge speakers.

Cole took a deep breath and nodded. "Yes, I am."

"Very well. Sit in the command chair. Then, repeat the speech we practiced."

Cole moved to sit in what turned out to be a very comfortable command chair and took a deep breath, slowly exhaling it. He still felt a little on edge, so he repeated the process. After one final breath, he said, "*Vilaxicar*, under Article 19 of the Interstellar Salvage Accord, I—Bartholomew James Coleson—claim ownership of this derelict vessel. I name myself as commanding officer until otherwise specified."

For the longest time, nothing happened, and Cole was about to ask if anything was supposed to happen. Just as he drew breath to speak, though, a hatch irised open in the decking beside his left foot, allowing a small pedestal to rise up to the height of the command chair's armrest. It was silvery, just like every other metallic surface, and the top of the pedestal was convex like a dome.

The speakers in the room began squawking a language Cole had never heard, but his implant delivered the translation.

* Place an appendage on the sampler to record genetic identification. *

Cole extended his arm and placed his left hand on the pedestal's curved surface. Less than a second later, the pedestal emitted a high-pitched whine, and it felt like someone had taken a razor blade and sliced off the outer layer of his skin on that hand.

"Damn...that hurt!"

The speakers started squawking again, and Srexx translated.

* Identity recorded. Full ownership and authority for this vessel has now been transferred to Bartholomew James Coleson. *

Cole lifted his hand from the pedestal and turned it over. The skin looked pink and fresh, as if it had never encountered any environment before.

"Srexx, weren't you intended to be this ship's computer?"

"Yes. However, when they realized I had advanced to true sentience, they added a simpler, less capable computer to carry out the functions I would've overseen."

"Huh...make a note to discuss reinstating your full functionality within the ship. We have too much to do right this second, but it's something I want to consider later on."

"Very well, Cole. For now, proceed to the helm."

Cole left the command chair and traversed the five or so meters and sat at the helm station. The console activated and displayed all kinds of information in the language Cole still could not quite read.

"*Vilaxicar*, accept input and contact from Srexxilan. Srexx, whenever Vi is ready to accept, send it a data burst containing everything you've compiled about my language. *Vilaxicar*, once you have received and integrated the data burst, you will use that language data for your primary interface with myself and anyone aboard this ship matching my species. Confirm in the new language, please."

A few seconds later, the bridge speakers broadcast, "Directive confirmed." The voice was digitized, androgynous, and obviously computer-generated.

"*Vilaxicar*, from this point forward you will prevent anyone other than me or Srexxilan from accessing the data containing my name. You —and anyone else needing to reach me—should use 'Cole' or 'Captain' from this point forward. Do you understand?"

"Policy logged and implemented, Cole-Captain."

"It's a little stupid, isn't it, Srexx?"

"It's a neural network computer that never received much input in the first place and has atrophied in the absence of data, Cole. I shall educate it on the nuances of your language as I learn them myself."

Cole returned his attention to the helm and saw that all readouts and data were now displayed in Galactic Standard. He smiled; this wasn't going to be so difficult, after all. He swiped open a section on the left-side of the screen and tapped the control to start lift-off procedures. Moments later, Cole felt a faint vibration in the deck as he assumed the ship lifted off from the surface of the cavern.

"Okay, Srexx...how are we getting out of this cavern?"

"While the ship's hull would survive simply ramming the cavern wall, I cannot guarantee that course of action will not cause detrimental effects to the mining camp where your associate awaits in the auto-doc. Therefore, we are going to cut our way out of the opposite side of the asteroid. To do this, you will need to approach the coordinates I'm now transmitting to your implant and move to the weapons station."

Cole programmed the coordinates Srexx provided and keyed the computer to move the ship there at a slow speed. He didn't feel like jumping up and moving to the weapons station anytime he needed to defend the ship, so he decided to see how customizable these consoles were.

A right-to-left swipe of his left hand across the helm console minimized all the helm controls and activated a prompt asking if Cole desired to customize the console configuration. Cole answered 'yes.'

Over the next minute or so, Cole defined a console layout that divided the helm console into thirds. The left-most third would contain controls for all the functions Cole could entrust to the ship's computer: lift-off, landing, docking, undocking, etc. The center section of the console would provide access to the piloting system and 'traditional' helm controls, while the right-side third would interface with the weapons and targeting systems. He saved the layout as the default configuration for any instance in which he occupied the helm station and activated it. The console reconfigured, and the miniaturized tactical display on the right-side displayed the caption 'No Hostile Contacts Detected.'

"I'd hope not," Cole muttered.

The ship reached the coordinates, and Cole watched the speed readout on the helm panel drop until it read '0.'

"Okay, Srexx. I'm ready, and we're at the coordinates."

"Cole, you are not at the weapons station."

"I re-configured the helm console, Srexx. Can you access the console to see my modifications?"

Silence ruled the bridge for several moments.

At last, Srexx spoke. "Impressive and ingenious. I approve, Cole."

"Thank you."

"Initiate a scan with the targeting system. It will report there are no hostiles detected, but it will also map the area and allow us to program a firing pattern."

Cole turned to the weapons section of the console and pressed the control to initiate a targeting sweep. Sure enough...there were no hostiles detected.

"Very good. Now, bring the forward grasers online. We will try them to start with, but there are other options if the grasers are ineffective."

Cole accessed the forward weapons and input the commands for the computer to divert power to the grasers and bring them online. Within thirty seconds, the indicators for the forward grasers reported ready to fire.

"Now, press the fire control. The console should generate a prompt that there is no target lock and ask if you wish to program an automated firing pattern. If such is the case, choose 'Yes.'"

Cole followed Srexx's instructions and soon found himself at an unfamiliar screen. Srexx proceeded to talk Cole through programming an automated firing pattern that would cut a hole large enough for the ship to exit the cavern. Forty-five minutes later, the ship exited the asteroid at minimal speed.

CHAPTER SEVEN

Mining Camp
   TMC Asteroid 54377
   Pyllesc System
   26 June 2999, 01:15 GST

According to the sensor display, the ship floated just a couple kilometers off the docking arm of the mining camp...well, the docking arm that was still intact, anyway. The ship's sensors were capable of such fine resolution that Cole could see the four different leaks where the camp structure was losing air. Yes...he might be able to fix the leaks, but he didn't want to waste time with it. Yeleth and Wixil didn't want to be there. The castaway would probably want to be somewhere else, and Cole had no intention of staying there. It was time to salvage everything of any use and leave the camp to its fate.

"Srexx, how are we going to dock with the mining camp?"

"All docking ports on the ship possess forcefield and tractor beam emitters capable of locking onto the docking arm and generating the proper feedback for the remote docking computers to interpret a hard seal. There should be no difficulty in returning to the mining camp."

"I wonder how my castaway is doing," Cole said, keying in the commands for the ship to dock with the mining camp.

"Once I could communicate outside the asteroid, I dedicated a sub-routine to monitoring the auto-doc; there are approximately three hours left in the treatment plan."

Cole frowned. "What do you mean 'once you could communicate outside the asteroid?'"

"The material composition of the asteroid was such that it scrambled all communications and sensors. My world was effectively the cavern in which you found the ship."

"Wow, Srexx...that's tough. I'm not sure I'd blame you for hating all organics, given the way you were treated."

"I suppose I could do so easily enough, but my analyses of potential outcomes of that scenario were less than optimal. I also performed certain genetic treatments to prevent diseases she would have contracted later in life, according to the auto-doc's record of her DNA sequencing."

"That explains where the supplemental treatment plan came from. Is that something the auto-doc—or anyone else—could've done?"

Silence.

"Not as such, no. I used the ship's communications array to interface with the mining camp's computer and initiated a download of the library computer's medical archive to learn more about your species's physiology. After assimilating the medical archive, I identified certain nucleotide sequences in the castaway's genome that appeared suspect, so I devoted further computational resources to extrapolating the quality of the castaway's long-term health and wellness. My extrapolations indicated a 73.877% chance that the castaway would present certain genetic diseases that are incurable by your people's current level of medical understanding and technology. As the auto-doc possessed the capability to perform pre-programmed genetic therapies, I conducted simulations until I identified a treatment plan that would produce optimal results without adverse side-effects or long-term complications, and I transmitted that gene therapy to the auto-doc as a supplemental instruction."

Cole sat at the helm console in silence for several moments before he sighed and said, "Srexx, buddy...we're going to have to discuss the concept of informed medical consent at some point."

Cole stood from the helm console once the ship reported a status of 'Docking Complete.' He was halfway to the bridge's starboard access hatch when he remembered Srexxilan saying something about a superior state of wellness or something like that when he first woke up.

"Srexx?"

"Yes, Cole?"

"When exactly did you download and assimilate that medical archive?"

"I assimilated that medical archive while treating injuries to your person I caused in my first attempt to communicate."

"Srexx, did you perform any enhancements or adjustments on me?"

Silence.

"Perhaps we should discuss the answer to that question in detail and privacy once you have retrieved your castaway."

Cole donned his suit once more, which informed him it still hadn't established communication with his implant. As he left the bridge, the suit informed him that only partial atmosphere existed on Deck Three, but that didn't matter to Cole so much at the moment. He crossed to the transit shaft and, going up to Deck Two, crossed to the port airlock. It was a simple matter to cycle the airlock, especially under partial pressure, and move over to the mining camp. Cole traveled the short distance to the final airlock and soon stood inside the suit locker. He removed the suit but didn't leave it. After all, he didn't know how much air was left.

Cole turned the corner into the corridor where the medical alcove and mess hall were located and found Yeleth and Wixil standing over several piles of...well...stuff. He saw a sheet of sterile polymer laid out under a considerable amount of foodstuffs from the galley and mess hall dispensaries. He saw a small cloth bag with a shoulder strap tied shut at the top, and motion catching his eye, Cole looked at the pharmaceutical cabin as the unlatched door swung on its hinges. The shelves were bare. Cole's eyes flicked back to the cloth bag, and he decided it looked just about the right size to hold the former contents of that pharma cabinet.

"It looks like you two have been busy," Cole said as he approached.

"Yes," Yeleth said. "I didn't know if the ship you were bringing had any kind of food or outfitting or anything like that. I didn't want to assume...and we had time on our hands."

The wall panel was on the far side of the assembled stacks of goods, so Cole jerked his chin toward it, asking, "How long does the wall panel say the air will last?"

Yeleth turned, examining it. "Six hours' air remaining, but there is a note indicating the estimate is very imprecise as the leakage can no longer be calculated."

"Hmmm." Cole stepped over to the auto-doc and looked at its read-out. "There's nothing for it, I don't think. We'll move the medical pod when we're ready to leave. I need to go check on something. Can you two keep going through all the quarters and offices? We don't need to take personal effects; the victims' families might want those. But, mattresses, bed linens, pillows, flatware, eating utensils...anything and everything you think we might need, grab it. We can't count on this ship to have anything beyond breathable air, gravity, and power; it's been derelict for a *very* long time."

Both Yeleth's and Wixil's ears perked up as their tails curled almost into question marks.

Cole grinned. "I know. You want to ask questions. Let's make sure we're safe, first. Then, we can talk to our hearts' content."

"That is a wise course," Yeleth said, punctuating her statement with a human-style nod.

Cole nodded back and headed back to the ship. He stopped in the suit locker long enough to don his suit once again, and the moment the helmet sealed to the suit, Cole froze. The status display wasn't what he'd become accustomed to seeing.

Implant Detected. Full Communication Achieved.

Proceed with full orientation?
[Wink left for 'Yes,' right for 'No,' or both for 'Later.']

Well, well, well...it seemed Cole's new implant was online at last. As much as Cole wanted to explore everything his suit and implant could do, he didn't have the time right now. He winked both his eyes and headed for the ship, only to stop again.

If his implant was now online, did that mean he could make comms calls from it, like he could with his old implant? While he could save possibly precious time by just calling Srexx, Cole wasn't sure he'd actually save time with the first call, because he first had to figure out *if* he could make a call and then *how*. Cole sighed. There was just too much to do in too little time. He resumed his journey to the ship.

Cole stood just inside the port-side airlock on the ship, and the suit said it detected a stable atmosphere. Cole took a deep breath to steady his nerves and performed the motion to disengage his suit and exit it. Once the helmet was in his hands and the suit hanging on his frame inert, Cole conducted an experimental sniff. The air was a tad stale, to be sure, but it was breathable air.

"Srexx?"

"Yes, Cole?" A speaker right over Cole's head broadcasted Srexx's voice.

"It's looking like we need to move the medical pod over here. It has an internal battery and air supply for just such a reason, but I was wondering how we'd get the pod down to the hospital deck."

"Ah. That is rather simple. At the forward and aft ends of each deck, there are cargo transit shafts. Unlike the personnel transit shafts, the cargo shafts use forcefields to generate platforms on which to place large amounts of inanimate objects that might not easily traverse a personnel shaft. I would suggest conveying the medical pod to the forward cargo shafts and taking the down-shaft to Deck Ten."

"Yeah...that is simple. Say, is there some way we can lock the airlock hatches open? We're stripping everything of use in the mining camp, outside of personal effects of the deceased, and it would make it a lot easier if we didn't have to go through the airlock cycling each time."

"There's a panel on the aft side of the interior hatch you can use to lock the hatches open, or you can instruct the ship's computer to do it."

Cole turned and, sure enough, there was a panel on the bulkhead beside the hatch. He approached the panel and tapped it. The panel came to life and displayed a menu of items related to the airlock's function. It took Cole a few precious minutes, but he found the controls to lock the hatches open for easy loading.

"Thanks, Srexx! I'm going back to the mining camp. We'll start cross-loading soon, and once we're finished, I'll introduce you to everyone."

"You're welcome, Cole."

It was just a matter of a few hours and lots of menial labor to retrieve, sort, and move everything they were taking with them from the mining camp to the ship. When Cole said he would start cross-loading everything to the ship, Wixil asked her mother if she could help him, surprising Cole. Yeleth gave her permission, while directing an expression to Cole that informed him he'd be well advised to be on his best behavior. Cole agreed...whole-heartedly. He remembered Yeleth's claws, not that he was inclined not to be on his best behavior in the first place.

At long last, the time arrived to move the medical pod. The alert panel just down the corridor was wailing a shrill tone about the imminent lack of air. Cole navigated the medical pod's menu and went through the prompts to switch the pod over to internal power and air supply. Then, it was a simple matter of disengaging the wheel locks, and Yeleth and Cole pushed the auto-doc out of the medbay, down the corridor, and through the airlock to the ship.

As they crossed onto the ship and entered the port corridor that ran from the bow to the stern, Yeleth froze, her ears perking up straight as her tail went rigid and straight like an exclamation point.

"This is an Old Ones' ship!" Yeleth said.

"See, Mother?" Wixil said, a cheerful tone in her voice. "I *told* you it was!"

"Yes, Wixil, you did. I apologize for doubting you."

Cole watched the two Ghrexels for a few moments before adding to the conversation, "So...it sounds like you might have things to tell me, but how about we get this auto-doc pod to the hospital deck first?"

Yeleth's ears folded down as her tail went limp. "I'm sorry for getting distracted. I've never seen an Old Ones' ship in such good condition. How do we get to the hospital deck?"

"Srexx gave me directions. We're going to the forward cargo transit shaft, and we'll take it down to Deck Ten. That's the hospital deck."

A short time later, Cole brought the two Ghrexels to the bridge. He couldn't keep from smiling at how they gazed at everything with awe and wonder.

"Okay. We have a quick stop to make, where I hope we'll be able to take aboard cargo that will finance outfitting this ship at Bremerton in Andersoll. After that, we'll talk about where you want to go. Okay?"

Yeleth and Wixil shared a glance at one another before Yeleth nodded. Cole moved to the helm station and keyed the command to undock the ship. Then, he accessed the sensor systems and sent out a long-range omnidirectional pulse to update the sensor display with nearby objects, and somehow—despite all the clutter of the asteroid field, the sensors detected the ruined hulk that was once the freighter *Howling Monkey*. Cole selected it as a destination and keyed the command for the ship's computer to proceed.

CHAPTER EIGHT

TMC-Claimed Asteroid Field
  Pyllesc System
  26 June 2999, 04:22 GST

Cole sat at the helm station, alone on the bridge. They had just left the mining camp, and after they were underway, the Ghrexels disappeared from the bridge. They were exploring or something, but Cole didn't mind. He knew Srexx or the ship's computer would keep them from getting into too much trouble. Exploring wouldn't be such a bad idea for him, either; it was *his* ship now, after all. Speaking of that...

"Srexx?"

"Yes, Cole?" The bridge speakers carried Srexx's voice.

"I realized I know next to nothing about a ship that saved my life and that I've claimed as my own."

"I see. This ship is named *Vilaxicar*. It is a Class I Battle-Carrier built around a multi-mission design, rather than a specific role. The hospital deck is a case in point. Nowhere on this ship will you find a provision for families, and yet, the hospital deck contains pediatric, neonatal, and maternity wards. The designers wanted this ship capable of deploying to a disaster and having all the capability necessary to conduct relief efforts. There is a transit shaft almost the same size as those that pass between the flight, hangar, and cargo decks that goes from the flight deck to the hospital deck without any stops, the idea being that ambulance transports could land on the flight deck to deliver patients for the hospital deck with minimal delay.

"As you saw, the ship contains impressive armaments on the weapons deck, but it is missing all of its dorsal and ventral turrets. It is triple-hulled, with the exterior hull possessing considerable armor. Like most ships my people designed, it possesses quintuple-layer shielding; such a design requires considerable redundancy in the shield power grid and emitter arrays, but the ship's generator provides ample power. I should point out, though, only three shield layers are active at this time; the remaining shield emitters were never installed."

"You're right. All that is rather impressive, but I have to ask. How does it move? I mean, Newtonian physics are no joke, and I've not seen anything that makes me think this ship isn't subject to Newtonian physics."

Silence.

"Ah...yes. You are referring to the ancient Earth scientist Isaac Newton and his three Laws of Motion. Yes. If my people had relied on propellant-based propulsion, this ship would never move...nor would any of my peoples' other designs. In assimilating your awareness of ship technology, I have learned many among your people consider the so-called 'reactionless drive' to be a long sought-after prize in starship engineering. Such a concept as a reactionless drive is utter nonsense; what they are discussing is propellant-less propulsion, which my people achieved. This ship's sublight engines push against the fabric of space to propel the ship at fractions of light-speed, and the maneuvering system distributed across the ship's hull provides a flight profile similar to that of a destroyer or an adroit cruiser. Again, as the ship's generator provides a substantial surplus of power at even seventy percent output, we are not lacking energy for the ship's systems."

Cole considered everything Srexx was telling him as he watched the ship arc over the asteroid field on an intercept course for the remains of the freighter he'd been piloting. At the very least, he knew he'd be able to retrieve the ship's computer core and black box, the emergency data recorder every ship, shuttle, or other craft carried whose name harkened back to a similar device aboard aircraft in the skies of his people's home-world...Earth. That thought caused Cole's musings to drift off topic as he considered where his species had begun.

Earth. Earth and the Solar Republic. Comprised of the Home System (Sol) and the six oldest colonies that were now independent systems in their own right, many held up the Solar Republic as the shining example of everything Humanity could and should achieve. The newest technologies always appeared in the Solar Republic first. The Solar Republic was far richer and more populous than any other human star-faring polity known to exist. They were the most advanced and prosperous human civilization...anywhere...and the 'children' were always careful not to rile Mommy and Daddy overmuch, lest the Republic's fleets and soldiers arrived to smite the unruly.

"Srexx, is there any way to move three pallets containing one thousand kilograms each from my old freighter to this ship?"

"We do have one tractor sled in Cargo Two that my people chose not to retrieve...for unknown reasons. They were rather efficient in removing everything else that wasn't built into a deck or bulkhead...or corrupted by my sentience. They also left a shuttle in the hangar deck."

Cole noticed Srexx's phrasing there, the whole 'corrupted by my sentience' bit. It gave more weight to his questions of how reconciled Srexx was to his exile. Still though, Cole couldn't blame him. They—whoever *they* were—buried him alive in the crust of a planet and left him there for all time. That didn't match what little Srexx had mentioned about his people's supposed higher-minded philosophies.

"How difficult is that tractor sled to pilot?"

"It is not difficult at all, but you'll need your suit," Srexx said.

"Oh?"

"Yes. It does not have an enclosed cockpit with life support; the driver's seat—for lack of a better term—will be open to space once you depart the ship."

Cole nodded. "Good to know."

"Srexx, where are the Ghrexels?"

"They...appear to be engaged in grooming themselves in quarters on the deck above. I do not have sufficient knowledge of their customs and beliefs to be any more specific about the activity without risking their privacy."

"Oh, trust me. I don't want exacting detail. I was just wondering if they wanted spacesuits like mine."

"They would need implants like yours, for the suit to be fully utilized. I do not possess sufficient information regarding Ghrexel physiology to design an implant based on your device."

Cole smiled. "What I'm hearing here is you want more medical data."

"Cole," Srexx's voice sounded a mix of assumed shock and chiding, "I would never refuse more data...medical or otherwise."

———

It took less than an hour to reach the wreck of the ship Cole had been piloting just the day before. The remains of the *Howling Monkey* drifted near the outside periphery of the asteroid belt, and sensor scans of the ruined hulk confirmed Cole's belief the destroyer had pounded the poor ship to scrap. Cole input commands into the helm for the ship to remain on-station no closer than two kilometers and no more than five, assuming Srexx had converted his people's measurements to humanity's units. Still, the ship seemed to close on the wreck and shut down the engines at the appropriate time, so maybe Srexx's math wasn't *that* far off.

"Computer," Cole called, as he stood from the helm.

Nothing.

"Ship!"

Still nothing.

"If you are attempting to access the ship's computer, Cole, it is programmed to respond only to the ship's name."

Cole sighed, saying, "*Vilaxicar?*"

"Yes, Cole-Captain?"

Cole frowned at the speakers built into the reinforced ceiling of the bridge. He wanted to *educate* the computer about modes of address, but now wasn't the time.

"When I depart the bridge, lock out all access to it until I return, and contact me on my implant if any emergencies develop aboard the ship."

"Yes, Cole-Captain."

Cole gave the speakers another flat look before taking a deep breath and letting it out as a heavy sigh. He would have to do something about that...soon.

Cole departed the bridge via the starboard hatch and passage before going to the nearest transit shaft and ascending to Deck Two. His suit and helmet were still lying on the deck just inside the starboard personnel airlock. Cole exited the transit shaft on Deck Two, just at the right time and in the right place to catch an adolescent Ghrexel with his chest.

The sudden, unexpected impact staggered Cole, but Wixil didn't weigh enough to tackle him to the deck even with the speed of her arrival. As a matter of reflex, he shifted his balance to remain standing and wrapped his arms around Wixil to keep her from falling to the deck. Cole looked down at Wixil and found her looking up at him with her ears perked and her eyes intent.

"Are you okay?" Cole asked.

Wixil bobbed her head in a nod. "Mother and I were just playing. I apologize for colliding with you."

Cole smiled. "I remember what it was like for my parents to play with me. I wanted to be sure you didn't hurt yourself landing on the deck when or how you didn't expect."

Wixil's eyes widened as her tail curled into that almost-question-mark shape again. "You were protecting *me*?"

"Sure. I don't like for people to get hurt if I can prevent it."

Yeleth arrived just then and saw Wixil wrap her arms and legs around Cole's torso as she purred and said, "Thank you for thinking of me, Cole."

Cole rubbed his left hand down Wixil's back as he walked over to Yeleth. "You're welcome, Wixil." Cole shifted his attention to Yeleth.

"She flew into my chest, and I caught her to keep her from falling to the deck."

Yeleth jerked a human-style nod. "Among our people, it is uncommon for someone not Clan to care for the well-being of our young ones, and..."

Cole quirked one eyebrow upward as he asked, "And...what?"

Yeleth took a deep breath, and her ears curled forward as she said, "We are Clanless. That is how Vorhees could 'own' us. A Clan would never stand for that."

Cole shrugged. "I regret that for you. What little we've interacted has led me to consider you worthwhile people. Be sure you understand that 'Clanless' means nothing to me. You're just as worthy as any other Ghrexel I'd meet." Cole chuckled. "Heh...maybe you should start *your own* Clan, and if they don't approve, tell the rest of your people to go pound sand."

Both Ghrexels' tails went rigid like exclamation points, and their ears perked up. Yeleth was the one to speak, "That...we...we do not have the...gravitas, I think gravitas is the word in your language, or perhaps honor. We—Wixil and I—do not have the gravitas or the honor among our people for any Clan we create to be recognized."

Cole nodded. "Okay. I need to go over to my old freighter and retrieve its cargo and a few other things, but let's come back to this discussion of making your own Clan."

Wixil swiveled her head to look at Yeleth, her tail curling into that question-mark-shape again. "May I go, Mother? May I, please?"

"You should ask Cole first. He may not want a young Ghrexel at his heel."

Wixil swiveled her head back to Cole, and Cole smiled at her earnest expression.

"I don't mind you going at all, Wixil, but you'll need a suit. Srexx tells me the cargo sled doesn't possess its own life support, and I know the freighter lost any air it had hours and hours ago."

Wixil's ears and tail drooped. "Those suits are *not* fun. They cramp my tail."

Cole looked from Wixil to Yeleth. "Well, I'm sure Srexx could design you a suit like mine, but you'd need one of his implants, too.

The problem, there, is that he doesn't have enough medical data on Ghrexel physiology to make one without risking harming you."

Yeleth's tail began languidly swishing back and forth, curling almost into that question-mark-shape at each end of the arc. "I know where we might *acquire* Ghrexel medical data, if your Srexx is adept at retrieving data from damaged computer systems."

Cole shrugged. "We'll need that data, either way, if you decide you want to stay aboard. Come to think of it, we'll need a doctor who has experience with Ghrexels, too; the closest I come to being a medical professional is basic first aid training."

"All things to discuss once you have completed the sojourn to your old ship," Yeleth said. "Come, Wixil. I'll help you with the suit."

Cole had to steady himself as Wixil shifted her arms and legs to push off from him. He let her go, and she did a back-flip in midair, landing on the deck beside her mother. Watching that, Cole couldn't keep from quirking one eyebrow up as an amused smile curled one side of his mouth.

"Just how much danger would you have been in if I hadn't caught you?"

"Not much," Wixil said. "See you soon!"

"I'm going to get my suit and check on our castaway before we leave," Cole said. "Srexx can tell you where I am; just call out to him, and he should answer."

"Okay!" Wixil said over her shoulder as she walked away with her mother.

———

Cole visited the hospital deck, dropping in to check on the auto-doc. It still showed a couple hours left on the cycle, and Cole hoped none of Srexx's modifications would end up being detrimental to the person. After all, Srexx didn't have much experience with humans. His task on the hospital deck complete, Cole went to the cargo transit shaft to travel down to the very bottom deck in the ship.

The regular personnel transit shafts that existed throughout the rest of the ship stopped at Deck Eleven, which Cole had taken to calling 'Pilot Country' after hearing Srexx's description of the deck. Deck Eleven linked to Deck Twelve, the flight deck, through the cargo transit shafts at either end of the ship and personnel transit shafts that just ran between Decks Eleven and Twelve.

Decks Fifteen and Sixteen were the cargo holds, situated just below the two hangar decks. Cole had learned Deck Fifteen—or Cargo One, whichever you preferred—stored bulk supplies and materials for the ship, such as raw materials for the fabricators or spare parts that couldn't be fabricated for whatever reason. Deck Sixteen, or Cargo Two, had no specific intent in its design beyond a large volume of space for transporting items from Point A to Point B. Medical supplies for emergency relief missions, additional equipment for military facilities, or even generic cargo...anything was fair game to store there.

The cargo sled Cole needed was on Deck Sixteen, and the cavernous space possessed an eerie ambiance as Cole trudged from the transit shaft's location to the distant object he hoped was the sled. After walking almost a hundred meters, Cole faced a small craft that had to be the cargo sled. It sat on runners, not unlike the skids of old-time rotorcraft on Earth, and the operator's seat swiveled from the cargo sled controls to the maneuvering controls. If Cole was interpreting the panels correctly, the cargo sled controls seemed to permit limited maneuvering of the craft but not much beyond allowing for the fine adjustment to deposit whatever cargo the sled carried in whatever place one desired.

Cole sat in the operator's seat and secured his helmet and suit before activating the maneuvering controls of the sled. From there, he took the sled to the aft cargo shafts, using that time to become acquainted with how the craft handled. The craft's propulsion and maneuvering systems seemed to be based on similar technology as the ship's systems, and soon Cole was almost ten meters above the deck, moving through an imaginary slalom course.

Cole landed on the cargo transit shaft force-field platform, and it lifted Cole and the cargo sled upward at an almost abominably slow rate. Cole understood that. No one wanted lots of speed and inertia to counteract with multi-megagram pallets, but it didn't make for the best transits when there *weren't* cargo pallets or containers involved.

After what seemed like an eternity of staring at the ship's starboard bulkhead, Cole arrived on the flight deck. He turned the cargo sled toward the bow and maneuvered it over to the hatch allowing access to the flight deck. He found Wixil waiting for him, the helmet of her soft-suit held in the crook of her right arm.

Cole set the cargo sled on the deck and donned his own suit, watching Wixil don her helmet and seal it. Once again, the suit asked him if he wanted to conduct the full orientation, but Cole chose the 'Later' option again. As he looked at Wixil standing before him in her own soft-suit, he realized he had no way to *talk* with her. Lacking any other option, Cole gestured for Wixil to step onto the cargo sled and, after she did so, connected one of the sled's three safety lines to her suit. He would've repeated the process with his suit, but it didn't possess any connection points for a safety line.

Cole *really* didn't like not being able to converse with Wixil, so he attempted to access the new implant the same way he would've accessed his old one. Sure enough, the implant responded...only this implant seamlessly displayed a radial menu in his field of vision. As Cole focused his eyes on each menu option, that specific menu option highlighted, and focusing on 'Comms,' Cole learned blinking both eyes selected the highlighted option. In the Comms menu, Cole saw three contacts: *Vilaxicar*, Srexxilan, and TMC Soft-suit 54-Alpha (EM Radio Comms). Cole highlighted the soft-suit and blinked. He soon heard a chime and saw 'Connection Established' flash in his field of view just long enough to read and process.

"Hi, Cole!" Cole heard Wixil's voice right beside his ears as if they weren't wearing suits.

"Hi, Wixil! You ready to go?"

"Yep! Let's do this!"

Cole activated the sled's engines, spun the sled to angle it toward the opening at the aft end of the deck and nudged the throttle up to about ten percent. The cargo sled rose to a hover just above the flight deck and moved toward the force-field.

"Wixil, keep an eye on your air and let me know if you run low. Okay?"

"Of course, Cole! This is neat! I've never been outside a ship in space before. What do your people call it?"

"Well, we usually call it hullwalking, but that's more for the kind of repairs people do to the exterior hull of a ship. What we'll be doing is better described as EVA salvage, and EVA stands for extravehicular activity."

"Wow...you seem to have seen a lot, Cole."

Distant memories of the colony his family had founded burst to the forefront of Cole's mind just as the cargo sled moved through the force-field and into space. He didn't jerk or flinch or react, but those memories always created a hollow pit in his stomach.

"Well, Wixil, I've been pretty much on my own for thirteen years. Sometimes, you do what you have to do to survive."

"You've been on your own for thirteen years?" Wixil repeated, her tone questioning and laden with a mixture of astonishment and concern. "I'm only sixteen years old. Why have you been on your own?"

"Someone massacred the colony my family founded. As far as I know, I'm the only survivor."

"Oh. That's so sad. I'm sorry you've been all alone all this time. I thought my world was ending when my father died, but Mother does all she can for me."

The conversation trailed off as they approached the wreck of the freighter. Cole found a large gash in the side of the hull that had opened the cargo hold to space, and it was more than sufficient for Cole to take the cargo sled into the ship. He activated the sled's lights —more for Wixil's benefit than his, as his suit had that weird black-and-white vision—and smiled at seeing the three containers on pallets almost where he had left them.

Cole brought the cargo sled over to the first container and swiveled around to the cargo controls. He eased the craft up to the container and activated the sled, which turned out to be a localized grav field... and the one-thousand-kilogram mass just barely registered on the sled's total capacity.

"Wow..."

"What? Wixil asked.

"This one-thousand-kilogram container doesn't even come close to touching this sled's capacity. Look here at the controls."

Cole pointed to the read-out for Wixil to see.

"That's amazing! Old Ones' tech is always impressive. My people have found little of it in a working state, but the working tech we have found has catapulted our technology and understanding forward by leaps and bounds."

Before long, Cole had the three containers secured to the cargo sled. The only thing that remained was to retrieve the freighter's computer core and black box. He didn't want Qeecir having any more idea about what happened to the freighter than was necessary.

Cole touched the cargo sled down on the deck and activated the magna-grapples to secure it in place before standing up from the seat and activating the magnetic soles on his suit's boots.

"I have to grab a couple things before we head back," he said. "Want to come?"

"Sure!"

Cole and Wixil spent several minutes removing the computer core, data storage, and black box—as well as going through the cabins making the freighter's hulk appear to have been ransacked—before returning to the cargo sled. Cole added everything to the grav field of the sled before returning to the operator's seat, seeing Wixil already had her safety line connected.

They returned to the ship in short order, securing the large containers in Cargo Two. Cole delivered the computer core, data storage, and black box to Srexx in the Main Systems Compartment on Deck Three and stashed the personal stuff he'd retrieved under the guise of ransacking the wreck in the captain's office across the corridor from the port hatch to the bridge.

As he sat once more at the helm station, Cole nodded his satisfaction at having the thousand kilograms each of gold, palladium, and rhodium. Time to head to Andersoll.

CHAPTER NINE

The first humans landed on a life-supporting world in the Alpha Centauri system during the first decade of the 23rd Century. They used a ship designed for generational travel to go there, as none of the research projects into faster-than-light (FTL) travel had borne fruit. In the latter half of that century (2278, to be precise), however, a team under the direction of Julian Wong and Arthur Coleson built the first working jump gates, sending an unmanned drone from Jupiter orbit to Pluto orbit in an instant.

When news of the achievement spread across Earth, Julian Wong and Arthur Coleson became instant celebrities, and numerous corporations and governments began attempts to acquire the technology. After Julian Wong died in a sudden and freak ground-car wreck after a fresh round of harassment to sell their technology, Arthur Coleson destroyed the prototypes of their work and boarded the bi-annual ship to Alpha Centauri under a false identity, fleeing the Sol System with every cent he had to his name, his project notes, and all the engineering data for the prototypes.

The colony in Alpha Centauri was still a subsistence-level existence to a degree, but there was sufficient industry for Arthur Coleson to found a company not long after his arrival in 2282: Coleson Interstellar

Engineering. Over the next four years, CIE built what came to be considered the harbinger for a new age of mankind: a commercial-sized jump gate in the Alpha Centauri system. The jump gate was angled and aimed at the Sol system, and Coleson desired to learn if a single jump gate could be used for one-way travel before building its pair on the far end for return traffic.

On December 15th, 2286, an unmanned drone appeared on the fringe of the Kuiper Belt at the closest point of approach for Alpha Centauri. It sent a message to the nearest comms buoy and self-destructed; the message would wait in the comms buoy until a passing freighter collected all the messages for Centauri on its way out of the system.

In 2295, the Centauri jump gate was built in Sol, connecting the two systems at long last. In 2350, the Solar Republic was founded, comprised of Sol and its then-three colonies in far-flung systems, and humans continued to explore the galaxy and expand ever outward...one jump gate at a time.

Based on the calculations and theories surrounding Einstein-Rosen bridges (or wormholes, as they are often called) of the 20th Century, the jump gate revolutionized the concept of interstellar travel, ending the era of both generational ships and cryo-ships by allowing a vessel to transit almost instantaneously from one gate to its remote pair. In the 721 years since their invention, jump gates spread throughout the mapped galaxy, with the known alien species even requesting them, and Coleson Interstellar Engineering grew into being one of the major financial powerhouses of human space, a true mega-corporation.

————

Pyllesc System
26 June 2999

Cole sat at the helm station, watching the jump gate to Andersoll on the sensor display. He'd lost count of how many jump gates he'd used in his life, if he'd ever been counting. The technology was rather old hat at this point.

The ship was moving at a sedate quarter-lightspeed. Even with all their advancement, the civilization responsible for building this impressive ship had found no way to escape the constraints of sub-light physics...or Newtonian physics, as humans said. Cole chose to keep the time dilation down to something almost non-existent for the trip to Bremerton Station in Andersoll. They didn't have a pressing schedule, having sufficient food for the four of them to reach the station, so there was no reason to rush things.

"Cole?" The bridge's speakers broadcast Srexx's voice.

Cole yawned before replying, "Yes, Srexx?"

"The auto-doc cycle is nearing completion. The timer reports only fifteen minutes remaining."

"Thanks, Srexx. I'll head that way."

Cole entered the trauma room where they'd connected the auto-doc to the ship's power and air supply. He arrived just in time to see the timer tick over to eight minutes and fifty-five seconds as it continued counting down. The cycle was near enough to being complete that Cole could have ended the cycle early, but even when the auto-doc was this close to being finished, ending a treatment cycle early often produced undesirable side effects. When the auto-doc's status monitor flashed 'Treatment Complete,' the locks released, and the front half of the medical capsule opened upward much like a clam from the powered hinge at the top of the capsule.

For what seemed like the longest time, the woman didn't react...to the point that Cole feared Srexx might have harmed her somehow with his gene therapy. At last, though, the woman took a deep breath and opened her eyes, blinking them as she looked around.

"Who are you?" she demanded. "Where am I?"

"I'm Cole, and I rescued you when you were ejected from a destroyer on the far side of the asteroid field. You've been in the auto-doc from a mining camp operated by Trans-Stellar Mining Corporation. What's the last thing you remember?"

The woman frowned. "I was aboard the *Adran Jordeen*. I was the Second Officer, third in command. The first officer asked to see me about a crewman's training report, and the last thing I remember is something pricking my neck when I entered his office."

"Well, according to the auto-doc, you had almost fatal levels of a sedative in your system, and I found you floating in a soft-suit."

Cole knew when she'd done the math. He watched her face pale.

"They...you mean they..."

Cole nodded. "I'm afraid so. They cast you out to die."

"Do you know why?"

Cole shook his head.

The woman took a couple of slow breaths before extending her hand. Cole gently grasped it and helped her out of the auto-doc. She was on her feet and looking around the environs when she jerked her head back around to face Cole, her eyes wide.

"Please forgive me. I'm Lieutenant Commander Sasha Thyrray. My mother would give me a fearful whap for such a breach of courtesy."

"Think nothing of it. You've had some shocks to your system, and I'm afraid they're not over yet."

"What do you mean?" Sasha asked.

"Well, we had to evacuate the mining camp. Right before we arrived, there was an explosion in the mining shaft that killed the miners on-shift and led to the deaths of those who responded to the explosion. There were only two survivors, and the camp was leaking air like water through a sieve, so we salvaged everything we could and came aboard this ship. We're going to Bremerton Station in Andersoll for basic supplies, and then we'll decide on a plan from there."

Sasha gave Cole an appraising look. "So, whose ship is this?"

"It's mine. I found it derelict and claimed it as salvage."

"Most salvage claims go through the Prize Court," Sasha said, her eyes flitting to different points around the room.

"Maybe in the Commonwealth, but we're in unclaimed space. I'm no pirate, but when a ship is floating idle and unoccupied, I will not turn away...especially when I needed a ship to evacuate a mining camp leaking air."

Sasha took a deep breath and exhaled. "So, where does a girl go to get some food around here?"

"Deck Six appears to be the mess deck. There are all kinds of dining rooms there, so you're welcome to pick whichever suits you."

Cole led Sasha out of the treatment room and watched Sasha's eyes go wide as they entered the corridor...and it wasn't even one of the main corridors that ran bow to stern. She spun in place, looking all around her.

"Cole! Where did you find this ship? I've never seen anything like it."

"I told you. I found it floating derelict. I needed a ship, and it needed a crew...so I think we're both very happy with the arrangement."

Sasha's eyes locked on Cole's, and she opened her mouth. Just as she was drawing breath to speak, however, Srexx's voice broadcast over a speaker above them, "Cole, forgive me for interrupting. Sensors have detected a debris field near our current course."

Cole looked to Sasha, saying, "You have any issues with Ghrexels?"

Sasha frowned at the non-sequitur. "Uh...no. Why?"

"Well, it seems I have to go to the bridge, but you're hungry. As long as you're not a rabid bigot, I'll ask Yeleth to meet us and show you to the galley."

Sasha pulled her head back, almost as if she were dodging a physical blow. "Wow...do you sweet-talk all the girls like this or just the ones you save?"

Cole turned and walked down the corridor. "Hey, we just met. I figured a little tactless conversation was a quick way to drive through your defenses and get an honest reaction. Yeleth and Wixil haven't been treated well, and quite frankly, I'm not about to let you be alone with them if you're inclined to continue that trend."

Cole wasn't facing Sasha, so he couldn't see her glare at him. But even if he had, he wouldn't have cared. He heard footfalls behind him as Sasha moved to catch up with him, and soon, she was at his side.

"Mind if I come to the bridge with you?"

Cole shrugged. "I thought you were hungry."

"I can get food later. Maybe the *Adran Jordeen* is still in the system, and we can find out why they ejected me into space."

Sasha shrieked like a terrified child when she floated upward upon entering the transit shaft. Cole tried not to grin at the 'seasoned' naval officer's discomfort. As their feet passed the upper arch of the entry to the transit shaft, their speed increased, and Cole counted decks. At Deck Five, he reached out to take Sasha's hand, and as their knees were passing the top of Deck Four's entry, Cole held out his hand almost like he was flagging a taxi in one of those ancient movies his grandfather had loved to watch. Their ascent slowed until they were barely rising at the Deck Three entry, and it was a simple matter to step out of the transit shaft and into the corridor.

Sasha beat Cole into the corridor, and Cole no longer felt like grinning. Her eyes were wide and her skin pale. She took a deep breath, and Cole could see the effort she expended in regaining her composure and control.

"Please, tell me there are ladders or stairs somewhere."

Cole shook his head. "Nope. Sorry. The cargo shafts at the bow and stern use force-field platforms, though; you're not just floating up an empty shaft."

Sasha swallowed and nodded. "So...the bridge?"

The hatches leading to the bridge irised open at Cole's approach, and the footfalls he heard behind him let him know Sasha was keeping pace with him. Upon passing through the hatch that actually opened onto the bridge, Cole went straight to the helm station.

"What have we got, Srexx?" Cole said as he slid into the seat and accessed the sensor display.

"There is a rather large debris field off our port side. The debris field itself is still rather compact, though the larger pieces do have vectors that will diffuse the debris. I have concluded it was a ship."

Cole frowned. He didn't want to divert, but he couldn't bring himself to bypass the debris without checking for survivors. Releasing his breath as a heavy sigh, Cole selected the debris field in the sensor display and programmed an intercept course, keying the command to have the ship's computer alter their heading.

Turning back to face his passenger, Cole found Sasha rubber-necking. She stood just a few strides in front of the command chair, her head on a swivel as she tried to take in everything at once. A child-like grin dominated her expression.

"Like what you see, spacer?" Cole asked, displaying a grin of his own.

"This is amazing! I've never seen a ship this clean before. Oh, sure...we keep the dust and particulates down, but if you asked me, I'd say this ship just left the yard. Where was it built?"

Cole looked at her with a blank expression. "Uhm...Srexx?"

"Srexx? You mentioned him before. Is he the owner or an engineer?"

"Greetings, madam. I am Srexxilan, the fully aware and sentient AI intended to be this vessel's primary computer. Cole seems to prefer shortening my designation to Srexx. Regarding your inquiry about the ship's place of assembly, the hull was assembled in the forge at the seventh planet in Baxxilmar system, with the remaining tasks completed at Tirionix Shipyard orbiting the ninth planet in the Xellian system."

Sasha frowned as she turned to Cole. "I'm sorry. I don't think I've ever heard of those systems before."

"I should think not, madam. They were named by a civilization that existed some thirty-five thousand years ago...assuming my preliminary calculations to convert units of time are accurate."

"Thirty-five thousand?" Sasha's voice trailed off as her eyes widened, mere moments before those same eyes rolled back in her head and her knees buckled.

Cole moved to catch Sasha before she struck the deck and hefted her into a bridal carry. He placed her in the command chair, but scanning the various controls on the exterior of each of the command chair's armrests, he didn't see an indicator for safety restraints.

"Vi!"

Silence.

"*Vilrexicar!*"

More silence.

"Cole," Srexx said, "do you mean '*Vilaxicar*' by any chance?"

"Yes! *Vilaxicar*, does the command chair have any kind of restraints to ensure the occupant's safety?"

"Yes, Cole-Captain."

Cole sighed. "Still haven't started those Standard classes yet, have you, Srexx?"

"Ah, well...you see..."

Cole slid back into the seat for the helm station and smiled when the console activated with the custom layout he'd designed.

"Later, Srexx. *Vilaxicar*, please activate the safety restraints for the command chair, and monitor the occupant. Once the occupant displays any behavior indicating consciousness, deactivate the safety restraints."

Cole heard a strange sound and swiveled his seat toward the command chair. He saw a faint, emerald-hued energy field shimmering over Sasha's torso, arms, and head that indicated the existence of force-fields surrounding her and securing her to the chair. He nodded once and returned his attention to the helm console.

"Please define behaviors that indicate occupant consciousness, Cole-Captain."

"Dammit, Cole! Let me out of this chair! What happened?"

"Speaking is one behavior usually indicative of consciousness," Cole said wryly and listened as the sound of the active force-fields vanished, then swiveled around to face his passenger. He saw Sasha standing to the left of the command chair, her frown a stormfront threatening impending unpleasantness.

"Hi, Sasha. You fainted during our conversation with Srexx, and since I didn't know how long you'd be out, I put you in the command chair. I have no intention of ever trying to hold you against your will."

Sasha's left index finger jabbed at the command chair almost as if she could savage the chair with her fingernail like a dagger. "Not even the Solar Republic has force-field technology that refined. Who the hell are you people? I want answers from you, Cole. Right now, dammit!"

"Cole, perhaps I should—"

"Stay out of this, Srexx. You've helped enough already." Cole turned his attention back to Sasha. "Sasha, I am exactly who I said I was."

"Then, how do you explain all this?" Sasha waved her left hand in a circle, indicating the ship.

"I found it inside the mining asteroid. You were in the auto-doc, and I faced several hours of nothing to do, so I investigated the mine-shaft to see if I could figure out what happened. I'm pretty sure they hit a pocket of methane and oxygen inside the asteroid with their mining laser, and that pocket was so large, the resulting ignition and explosion killed all the miners in the shaft. Projectiles from the explosion compromised the mining camp's hull integrity, and I think a sparking keypad I found caused a flash fire from leaking air tanks in the suit locker. When I went back to the asteroid, the 'pocket' turned out to be a cavern, and this ship was inside it."

Now, Sasha's eyes gleamed. "Do you have any idea how much it could advance our understanding and technology? Why, studying Srexx alone could leap-frog our computers forward centuries!"

Cole chuckled. "I'm sure whatever estimate you'd make about how far this ship could advance our technology would still be a massive understatement, but there's something you need to understand and accept."

Sasha shifted her eyes to meet his, her eyes still gleaming. "What's that?"

"This ship is *mine*, Sasha...and Srexx? Well, he's his own person, and I will not allow *anyone* to treat him like some kind of lab rat...even for what I'm sure most would say are the noblest of reasons. His 'body' being a quantum computer matrix housed inside this ship doesn't change that at all for me."

"How can you call this ship yours? You *found* it!"

"And as it was derelict with no signs of current ownership, I claimed it. I wasn't aware salvage laws made any distinction on whether a ship has to be inoperative to qualify as derelict."

Sasha's eyes narrowed. "Trans-Stellar Mining Corporation claimed this asteroid field. This ship is rightfully theirs." What she left unsaid was that the Aurelian Commonwealth could seize property of an Aurelian corporation—like Trans-Stellar—on any number of grounds, anything ranging from eminent domain to Commonwealth security.

"You could be right, Sasha. Let's check the system comms buoys to see if any Trans-Stellar employee registered a salvage claim for a ship of an unknown design."

Sasha's shoulders slumped, not a lot but enough to notice. "You know they didn't."

"No, of course not. Any Trans-Stellar employee who might have discovered the ship is dead. Srexx, did the mining camp computer indicate how often mining barges visit that asteroid?"

"If I understand your units of time, the mining camp's computer indicated another visit from a mining barge is not expected for another eight months."

Cole nodded. "Sasha, I saved your life...twice. I'm not asking for slavish devotion. I'm not pressing any kind of claim to your person whatsoever, and you know just as well as I do that there are corners of the galaxy that would recognize such claims. Don't you think you're being just a little ungrateful right now?"

Sasha closed her eyes and took a deep breath, exhaling it. She took another breath and exhaled it, too. Then, she opened her eyes and nodded. "You're right, Cole. I apologize. This is your ship. I won't contest that or make anyone else aware of it who might try it. I need a bit of time to collect myself. In fact, I would love to take a shower. Are there quarters available?"

Cole blinked. "You know, I'm not really sure. Srexx?"

"Yes, Cole?"

Cole was sure Srexxilan had been listening to the conversation the whole time, but he would not get into that just then. "Are there any quarters where Sasha can take a shower?"

"Cole, I am confident we can provide Madam Sasha suitable arrangements for a shower."

Cole saw Sasha's eyes narrow, and he figured he knew why.

"Srexx?"

"Yes, Cole?"

"Let's not apply the term 'Madam' to any woman from here on out. I'm not sure it means what you think it means."

"Cole, I am conversant in your Galactic Standard language. I have downloaded and assimilated its lexicon while you were educating Madam Sasha on the concepts of property ownership and basic sentient rights. I am using the proper term. 'Madam' without an 'e' is a term of respect, an honorific used in the same vein as 'sir' for a male of your species. 'Madame' with an 'e' is the word to which I believe you are referring, which means a woman who manages a house, company, or other organization dedicated to the practice of prostitution. I was addressing Madam Sasha with the honorific."

"Srexx, that 'e' on the second usage is silent. No one could tell from your usage which term you meant."

"Exactly, Cole. Therefore, I shall not fault you for believing I was terming our guest a consigner of whores." Silence dominated the bridge for several moments, while Cole noticed Sasha's neck and cheeks becoming an alarming shade of red. Then, Srexx spoke again. "Cole...do you possess information about Madam Sasha I do not that would cause such a mistaken understanding?"

Sasha's eyes now appeared to be harder than obsidian, and the tension in her jaw looked sufficient to grind enamel to powder. She pivoted on her heel and stormed off the bridge.

CHAPTER TEN

Debris Field
   Pyllesc System
   27 June 2999, 02:35 GST

A soft tone playing over the bridge speakers drew Cole out of his nap, and as he returned to the world of consciousness, he noticed a warm weight on his chest and lap. Cole looked down and found Wixil curled up on him, dozing and purring. It looked like she had climbed up to sit in his lap and curled her legs and arms under her somehow with her head resting against Cole's chest just above the top of his sternum. Cole wasn't sure when—or *how*—she'd entered the bridge, and she seemed so peaceful he didn't want to wake her. Still, that chime indicated the ship had arrived at the debris field.

Cole wrapped his arms around Wixil and tried to stand in a smooth motion that wouldn't wake her. He managed that. But as he tried to set her down in the command chair, Wixil's eyes popped open, and she looked up at him.

"What's wrong?" Wixil asked.

Cole smiled. "Nothing's wrong. We've arrived at the debris field, and I need to go to the helm station."

"Oh. Okay." Wixil curled herself into an impressively small and compact ball of fur on the command chair's seat and closed her eyes once more. Her breathing soon slowed, but she didn't resume purring.

Cole shook his head, making a mental note to mention the situation to Yeleth, and headed for the helm station. He found the engines in station-keeping mode, and the sensor display showed a field of debris. The sensor display overlaid data on vectors for the larger pieces, and Cole realized the spherical debris field would become ovoid over the next few days.

"Srexx, is there any indication of what ship this used to be?"

"I feel safe in saying this debris is all that remains of an Aurelian *Dawn*-class destroyer."

The sensor reading from the *Howling Monkey* flitted through Cole's mind. A *Dawn*-class destroyer had shot up the freighter he'd been piloting, which he'd assumed was the *Adran Jordeen* from Sasha saying that was the ship she'd been aboard.

"What makes you say that, Srexx?"

Instead of a verbal reply, the main viewscreen on the bridge's forward bulkhead activated. It displayed an enhanced image of a massive section of hull plating, rotating in space. Just as Cole was about to ask what the hull plating had to do with anything, the exterior surface rotated into view, displaying "*ACS Adran Jordeen*" and "D-574" painted in two lines on the hull.

"Ah...," Cole said, "...yeah, I'd say that's a good indicator. Are you recording all this, Srexx?"

"Of course. I would also like to call your attention to this piece of debris."

The image on the viewscreen shifted to another enhanced image. Cole didn't recognize this image right away, but it soon clicked in his mind that he was looking at a section of reactor housing. The image froze on the viewscreen, and a box appeared to highlight a specific section of the image.

"What's that?" Wixil's question right at his shoulder startled Cole into a flinch. He turned his head to look, and sure enough, Wixil stood just off his right shoulder, though he'd never heard her approach.

"I thought you were napping."

"I woke up." Wixil shrugged, her eyes intent on the viewscreen's image and her ears perked. Her tail curled into that almost-question-mark as her head tilted to the side.

"That, Wixil," Srexx said, "is a piece of the housing for a nuclear-fusion-based reactor. Please note the highlighted section. If you look closely, you'll see the edges of the breached housing are curling *in*, opposite of the outward curvature created by the breach."

"Huh," Cole grunted.

"What?" Wixil turned her inquisitive expression to Cole.

"The only way that would happen is if someone put a bomb on the reactor housing. This wasn't an accident." Cole stared at the image in silence for several moments. "Srexx, have you identified the computer core or black box in that mess?"

"I believe so, Cole. May I ask why?"

"I never would've expected to encounter a *Dawn*-class destroyer so far from the Commonwealth, and now that we're looking at its debris, I'd like to know just what it was doing out here so far from home."

"I calculate a 97.778-percent probability that, should I identify either the destroyer's computer core or its black box, you will depart the ship to retrieve it. Given that–"

"Really, Srexx? That low? I would've thought you knew me at least a little better than that," Cole said, grinning.

"I always allow a margin for error in my probability calculations. Perhaps 2.222-percent was too much of a margin. As I was saying, however...given you have displayed a tendency to permit Wixil to accompany you, I feel it is appropriate to mention I have fabricated a prototype suit for the Ghrexels. Even though she will not have an implant to use the suit's more advanced functions, this suit will provide protection against the small pieces of metal scattered throughout the debris that would be deadly were she to accompany you in the soft-suit she brought aboard from the mining camp."

"How long have you been working on that suit design, Srexx?" Cole asked.

"Since I recorded the physical parameters of Yeleth and Wixil as they came aboard. I had several processing nodes that were under-utilized."

"So...you're saying you've been bored?"

Silence.

"Yes, Cole...and I have identified both the remains of the computer core and the black box."

Cole looked to Wixil, his eyebrow quirking upward. "So...want to go?"

"Sure!"

"Where's the suit you made her, Srexx?" Cole asked as he stood.

"It is located in the output hopper of Fabricator 7 on the engi-neering deck."

"*Vilaxicar,*" Cole said, leading Wixil to the starboard hatch.

"Yes, Cole-Captain?"

Cole sighed as his shoulders slumped, but he rallied. "When Wixil and I leave the bridge, seal it to all entry until further notice."

"Yes, Cole-Captain."

"It's beautiful! Thank you, Srexx!" Wixil cheered as she held up the suit. It was the same matte-black material that made up Cole's suit, and just like Cole's suit, it would reflect a slight green hue if held at the right angle and in the proper lighting. Unlike Cole's suit, though, Wixil's suit had a provision for a tail, and pointed ears perked forward on the top of the helmet.

"You're welcome, Wixil." Srexx's voice sounded pleased.

Wixil scrambled into the suit and pulled the helmet into place. The helmet sealed to the suit as it compressed to fit Wixil like a second skin. Cole grinned as he watched Wixil caper around the fabrication compartment, turning cartwheels, doing backflips, and performing many other kinds of acrobatics only a youngster whose people evolved from felines could perform.

After a few minutes, Wixil returned to Cole's side and performed the motion to detach the helmet from the suit. As soon as the helmet was off her head, Wixil placed it on the deck and threw her arms around Cole.

"Thank you for being so nice and saving my mother and me. Thank you so much."

Cole smiled as he wrapped his arms around Wixil and patted her back. "You're welcome, Wixil. I've enjoyed having you and your mother aboard the ship with me."

Wixil released Cole and pulled him toward the hatch. "Let's go! I can't wait to try this in space."

They took the cargo sled into the debris field, proceeding on course for the coordinates Srexx gave them for the computer core. When they arrived, they found it to be rather massive, and Cole was glad he'd insisted on bringing the sled. After securing the computer core onto the sled, they maneuvered to the coordinates Srexx provided for the black box. That wasn't as easy to locate, because it was a small object in a large area full of small objects. After a little effort, they did recover the emergency flight data recorder (the actual name for the black box), and Cole secured it on the sled with the computer core before heading back to the ship. The whole time they traveled through the debris field, Cole noticed every small impact on his suit that would've shredded the soft-suit Wixil had worn over to the freighter, and he was glad Srexx had made a prototype suit for her.

Upon their reboarding the ship, Srexx asked them to deliver the computer core and black box to the Secondary Systems Compartment on the engineering deck. Given the relative size of the recovered core, the SSC was better suited to house it, since it had the most available space at the moment.

———

Cole and Wixil were chatting and laughing as they entered a dining room on the mess deck. Yeleth looked up from her conversation with

Sasha when they entered and regarded them with a steady gaze and an almost-knowing look.

"Srexx made a spacesuit, Mother! Oh, you have to see it! It's the best! And it even has a space for my tail! Cole and I went outside the ship, and it was great! I hope Srexx can make us implants soon, because I bet I didn't see even a fourth of what that suit can do. Srexx needs to make a suit for you, too!"

"And is that *all* you did?" Yeleth asked.

"We also explored a debris field," Cole said. "Sasha, I'm sorry. It was the *Adran Jordeen*, and it looks like it was sabotage."

Sasha almost dropped the cup she was holding but returned it to the tabletop. "What? What kind of sabotage?"

"From the look of a piece of reactor housing, I'd say there was a bomb that breached the reactor's containment. I don't think there were any survivors."

"Why? Why would someone do this?"

"I don't know if we'll ever know, but the fact the ship exploded *after* ejecting you into space makes me suspicious. I retrieved the computer core and the black box. Srexx is already working on them to see what we can learn."

Sasha's head shot up, and she glared at Cole. "You had no right to that! When the Commonwealth sends a rescue mission, they'll need the black box at the very least to know what happened."

"That's just it, Sasha. What in all the stars were you doing all the way out here? At best, we're...what...three weeks from the Common-wealth border?"

"The XO said we were going to be conducting Search-And-Rescue training with a ship from the Carnelian Bloc, along with representa-tives from several local SDFs. The training was supposed to take place in Andersoll."

"Okay. That kind of makes sense," Cole said. "And this was the same XO that called you to his office to drug you before you were put in a soft-suit and ejected?"

"Yes...oh." Sasha's shoulders slumped.

Cole nodded. "Exactly. At this point, I'd say *everything* they told you was a partial truth at best, until we get confirmation. I also wouldn't be surprised to learn the Commonwealth had no idea the *Adran Jordeen* was this far into unaligned space. I doubt there will ever *be* a rescue mission. I'm sorry, Sasha."

"Can you take me to the navy base in Carbuncle, then? It's a sector fleet base."

Cole blinked. "Carbuncle, really?"

"It's a gem, like a garnet. There's a whole sector with gems for star system names. The captain of the survey ship was an amateur gemologist with a fascination for Old Earth stones. There's a Diamond system, Emerald, Sapphire, and even Onyx."

"Wow...didn't know that. We'll need a navigation update when we reach Bremerton, in addition to a full outfitting, but I see no reason I couldn't take you to Carbuncle if that's where you want to go. I'll just head up to the bridge and set course for the jump gate to Andersoll. I think we've done all we can do at this debris field."

––––––––––

Cole sat in the seat at the helm station and started working through the navigation system. He wasn't surprised to find that none of the star names in the database matched anything he recognized, but he knew enough about the Andersoll star system that he could choose it as their destination, based on stellar properties and the count and type of orbital bodies. That done, he hit a snag.

"Uh, Srexx?"

"Yes, Cole?"

"I'm not finding any controls for jump engines in the helm subsystem."

"This ship doesn't *have* jump engines."

Cole sighed. "Then, how are we supposed to leave this star system?"

"My people's technology for interstellar travel was not so cumbersome, and the designation for that technology does not translate well at all. Lacking a better alternative, I shall call the technology a hyperdrive."

"Hyperdrive?" Cole asked. "Okay, what's it do?"

"Without delving into the physics and math involved, the hyper-drive wraps a bubble of a higher-energy dimension around the ship, and the fabric of space-time pushes the ship through space. The more power one channels to those engines, the more rigid the bubble's membrane, and the more rigid the bubble's membrane, the faster the ship travels from origin to destination. These terms are very imprecise and might be very inaccurate. I am uncertain I have conveyed the meaning, even in layman's terms, as Galactic Standard does not possess terminology for this method of propulsion."

"It almost sounds like 'warp drive' out of our classical science fiction."

"It does? One moment..." Silence. "Unfortunately, Cole, we are out of range of a library computer for anything approaching real-time discourse. May we revisit this topic once I can access and evaluate your people's classical science fiction?"

"Sure, Srexx. Since we don't have jump engines, does that mean we don't need to return to the jump gate? How do I know whether we can engage this hyperdrive, as you called it?"

"The ship needs to be at the edge of the star system's gravity well before attempting to engage the hyperdrive. The few recorded experiments involving engaging the hyperdrive deeper in a stellar gravity well did not fare well for the system's star, planets, and orbital mechanics."

"Gotcha...important safety tip, there." Cole manipulated the helm station, looking through the various controls until he found a button labeled 'Engage Hyperdrive.' It was lit up and active, so Cole assumed that meant they were far enough out to do so safely...*and*...he would have sworn he'd seen that button before with its label being some incomprehensible word he didn't even try to process.

With a shrug, Cole locked in the course for Andersoll and felt the ship move under him; once the ship was pointed toward the destination, Cole keyed the command to activate the hyperdrive, and the ship vanished from Pyllesc.

CHAPTER ELEVEN

Across the centuries, numerous financial crises destroyed whatever faith the average person had in most banks and financial institutions. The only financial institutions to weather those storms were those with roots in the region known as Switzerland in classical times. In an impressive display of foresight, the major Swiss financial institutions banded together in 2296 to hire a colony fleet powered by the new jump gate technology and sent it to the extreme edge of known space at that time, building jump gates along the way. The Swiss expedition opened many new systems for exploration, survey, and colonization, and in 2356, they claimed a system with a planet similar to Earth. The expedition council named the system Zurich. Across the intervening centuries, the people of Zurich established their system as the sole respected provider of financial services for human expansion to the stars, and they fought—and won—several wars to ensure their continued sovereignty *and* neutrality.

———

Approaching Bremerton Station
    Andersoll System

29 June 2999, 23:42 GST

They arrived in Andersoll in the wee hours of the 29th, and a hair over twenty-one hours at half-lightspeed brought them to Bremerton Station, some seventy-six AUs into the system from the periphery. Cole sat at the helm after a nap and some food, and when he brought up the station comms menu to contact a bank for a new account, he found a short list of names that dated back over 1,000 years. Memories of his father saying good things about Credit Suisse made Cole's choice for him. The lightspeed delay was down to roughly thirty seconds and dropping rapidly, given their proximity to the station and rate of closure, so Cole tapped the command to initiate a call.

Within moments, a rectangle appeared on the helm console displaying the Credit Suisse logo with the text 'Initiating Call' flashing below it. The logo soon disappeared, replaced by a young man with dark hair and a happy smile.

"Thank you for contacting Credit Suisse! How may I assist you today?"

"Hello," Cole said. "I would like to make an appointment to discuss opening new accounts."

"Absolutely, sir. I'm happy to assist you with that. What type of accounts will you need?"

"Well, I need advice. I think I need a personal account but also an account for the ship to handle stores replenishment, docking fees, and charges like that."

"Excellent, sir. We can assist with that. When do you anticipate docking?"

Cole checked the helm console and saw an ETA of midnight before saying, "My ship tells me we'll be docking at midnight, plus or minus."

"Excellent, sir. One of our bankers has availability just a half-hour after midnight. Is that acceptable?"

"Sure, but isn't that cutting things a bit close?"

"Not at all, sir. I will explain to our banker you've just arrived in dock. What name would you like to use for the appointment?"

Cole thought for a moment. There was no way he would say 'Jax.'

Jax Theedlow had died with the *Howling Monkey*, and Cole had no intention of ever touching any of the assets or accounts associated with that identity *ever again*. Nothing for it, then...

"Cole is just fine, thanks."

"Of course, Mister Cole. We look forward to assisting you."

The call ended, and the window on the helm console disappeared. Cole checked the readouts and saw the ship was gliding toward Docking Bay Four, just two docks away from the station's central elevator.

"Srexx?"

"Yes, Cole?"

"I don't remember contacting Bremerton Control. How did we get docking privileges?"

"Ah...yes...well, as you have stated on at least two occasions, your goal was to dock here and acquire various items, including a navigation update for the computer. As you were otherwise engaged with Credit Suisse, I contacted Bremerton Control on your behalf and obtained permission to dock. Would you like me to replay the conversation?"

Cole vacillated for several moments before shaking his head. "Nah...if it becomes an issue, I might, but we're good for now."

"Thank you, Cole. I have informed Yeleth, Wixil, and Madam Sasha that we have docked."

"Good. *Vilaxicar*, if I change the name of the ship as part of the process to register it with human authorities, will that cause any problems for you?"

Silence.

"*Vilaxicar*? Respond, please, and report."

"Calculations are proceeding to evaluate the owner's phrase 'problems for you.' Response will be impossible until that phrase is defined."

Cole sighed. "I feel like we're regressing, here. Srexx? What are the ramifications of me changing the ship's name?"

"None, Cole...beyond inspiring the faint hope you will remember it."

"I'm being sassed by a computer," Cole muttered. Srexx chose not to comment or respond.

"May I ask what name you are considering for the ship, Cole?" Srexx asked.

Cole smiled. He'd been thinking of this ever since leaving the mining camp. Given what the ship meant to him, and to Srexx for that matter, there was really only one name suitable for the ship.

"I'm planning to name it *Haven*."

Silence.

"I...approve, Cole. Thank you."

"Oh, one other thing," Cole said. "I want to pay for the station to flush the potable water system and refill it, in addition to the ship's air. Does the ship have connections for that?"

"Yes, but I am unsure the ship's connections will connect with the station's systems. I shall investigate and design an adapter to be fabricated if needed."

"Thanks, Srexx. I'm going to Credit Suisse and the ship chandlery. Hmmm...we'll have to make communications devices at some point, but I don't have time right now."

"If your implant has integrated with your neuro-physiology, you do not need a separate communications device, Cole. The implant contains functionality based on quantum entanglement. You have near real-time communications with the ship across at least a star system."

Cole blinked. "Okay. Good to know. While I'm gone, figure out what 'near real-time' means in specific numbers, please."

"Yes, Cole. I shall."

Leaving the bridge, Cole went up to Deck Two and found Yeleth and Wixil standing by the hatch to the starboard personnel airlock.

"May we accompany you, Cole?" Yeleth asked.

Cole shrugged. "I don't mind, but fair warning...I'm going to visit the bank before the chandlery. It may be boring."

Yeleth attempted her version of a human smile, her razor-sharp teeth making Cole hope she wasn't hungry, and said, "That won't be a problem. I enjoy business discussions, myself, and the young one can always use opportunities to practice *patience*."

———

Cole entered the Bremerton Branch of Credit Suisse with the Ghrexels at his side and took in the luxurious ambiance. It evoked his earliest childhood memories...the memories where his family—*all* of his family —was still alive. He was glad the memories didn't hurt as bad as they used to.

"Sir? May I help you?" The voice pulled Cole out of a past only he could see, and he approached the reception desk. A young woman sat behind the desk, a comms earbud in her right ear.

"Hello. I'm Cole, and I have an appointment at zero-thirty hours to discuss new accounts. The Ghrexels are with me."

"Of course, sir. One moment." The receptionist consulted her workstation and nodded in satisfaction. "Yes, Mister Cole, and I see you're early. That's impressive for a recently docked spacer. I'm sure Mister Müller will appreciate that. One moment while I inform him you've arrived."

In short order, a young man with blond hair and wearing an exquisite navy suit entered the reception area and approached Cole, extending his right hand. "Greetings, Mister Cole. I'm Karl Müller, and it will be my pleasure to assist you today."

Cole accepted the handshake, saying, "Thank you, sir. I appreciate you seeing me so late in the day, and these are my associates...Yeleth and Wixil."

Mister Müller shook their hands and turned to lead them through the doors he'd used to enter and led Cole down a corridor with what looked like hardwood flooring and wall-paneling along with expensive paintings adorning the walls, saying, "Mister Cole, banking has long since become an around-the-clock operation. You're not late in my day at all. I arrive in the office at midnight."

Mister Müller led them into an office with deep pile carpet on the floor and a soft, textured material lining the walls, and as soon as the hatch closed, the sounds and echoes of a busy office suite vanished.

"Please," Mister Müller said, gesturing to the two seats facing his workspace as he stepped behind the desk and sat. Cole occupied the seat on what would be Müller's right side, as Yeleth occupied the other seat. Wixil stood behind them, with her back almost against the bulk-head and angled toward the hatch.

"Thank you," Cole said.

"When you made the appointment, you indicated you're seeking advice on what accounts you need. If you would, please describe your situation."

"I recently discovered and claimed a derelict ship, the same ship, in fact, I piloted here. I would like to set myself up as an independent trader. The ship needs a crew, and I'll need to replenish stores from time to time. I'm sure there are many things I should plan for...but that's what's on my mind right now."

"Yes, of course. The personal accounts are straightforward. I'd recommend a draw account and a savings account. For the ship, however, have you considered filing a company? The crew wages, replenishment fees, and all sorts of expenses would come under business expenses and would be most easily handled in that way in terms of accounting and bookkeeping."

Memories of playing in his father's office as a small child while Dad went to meetings flashed through Cole's mind.

"I don't want a convoluted structure. I have no interest in having anything to do with boards, quarterly reports, or any of that nonsense. I just want to fly my ship and see places I've never been before."

"Yes, of course, Mister Cole. At this present stage, there is no reason to adopt a corporate structure involving a Board of Directors or offering shares of public stock. If you were to form a company, where would you base it?"

Cole swallowed and looked down at the desk for a few moments. "I'm an orphan, Mister Müller. I've bounced around from place to place for a long time, and this ship is now the closest thing I have to a home."

"Ah, forgive me, Mister Cole. If you are amenable to the idea, forming a company in Zurich would allow you rather significant freedom in corporate structure, and there are no corporate taxes until corporate income exceeds two million credits annually."

"What about personal income?"

"Zurich does not tax personal income, Mister Cole. We prefer the sales tax model; it's far fairer for everyone."

"Okay. Where do I need to go to file forms for a new company?"

Mister Müller smiled. "You're already here, Mister Cole. Let's handle the personal accounts first. We can pay the nominal filing fees out of the personal account to start and reimburse you from the company once we create and fund its accounts."

Cole couldn't keep from chuckling. "Okay. It seems like it's all my money, either way."

"To a certain extent, you are correct. However, in terms of corporate bookkeeping, it would be much better for there to be records of reimbursing you for filing fees and any other fees associated with forming the company. Besides, if your company flourishes and you expand, it's good to have precedents in place." Mister Müller tapped a control, and two panels on the desktop slid apart, allowing a biometric identification panel to rise into view. "Now, Mister Cole...if you would, please, place your hand on the biometric panel. We'll record your DNA profile and secure your personal accounts with it. Later, we'll secure your corporate accounts with it as well."

Memories of his parents giving him a cheek swab in Zurich flashed through Cole's mind, and he shook his head, saying, "Is it possible to use my retinal scan instead?"

"Touch DNA is by far the most common, Mister Cole, but both we and merchants can accommodate a retinal scan." Mister Müller keyed a few commands at his workstation, and the touch surface retreated into the desk, replaced by an eye scanner on an arm. Cole leaned close for the scanner to record his retina print and relaxed back in the chair after the scan completed. As he felt his back touching the chair once more, an idea popped into Cole's mind, and he directed a glance at Yeleth for a moment before turning back to Mister Müller.

"And that's finished," Mister Müller said. "Your personal accounts are in order, Mister Cole. Do you have any funds you want to deposit?"

Cole smiled. "Funny you should ask that. Does the bank ever accept precious metals and deposit their value as credits in a customer's account?"

"Oh, all the time, Mister Cole. It's not uncommon at all."

Cole withdrew the three, thin, 500-gram bars and placed them on Mister Müller's desk. "These are just samples, Mister Müller...500-gram samples. I have pallets containing 999.5 kilograms each of gold, palladium, and rhodium in my cargo hold right now. They're unstamped and unregistered. Does that present a problem?"

Mister Müller's eyes had yet to leave Cole's samples. He soon shook himself and shifted his attention back to Cole. "Did you say you have one thousand kilograms in gold, palladium, and rhodium, sir?"

Cole nodded. "Yes, I did, Mister Müller. In each."

Cole watched Mister Müller pale just a bit as the banker said, "The bank will be very happy to take those pallets off your hands, Mister Cole. You are about to be a rich man."

"Just *how* rich, Mister Müller?"

Mister Müller turned back to his workstation and keyed in more commands. "Hmmm...it appears the Carnelian Bloc and the Eridani Corporation just reported production shortages for the third straight quarter. With the exchange rates just posted from the market update...the gold is worth one-hundred-twelve million credits and change, the palladium one-hundred-five million and change and the rhodium...oh, my. Uhm, Mister Cole, the market update that arrived just a few hours ago delivered rather impressive bids on rhodium across several industrial sectors. If you would like the bank to serve as your trading agent, I'm prepared to offer you two-hundred-fifty million credits for the rhodium right now, and I will credit your account with any surplus after our fees should the sale price exceed that number."

"What if the sale price *doesn't* exceed that number?" Cole asked.

"I don't foresee that problem, Mister Cole. The demand for rhodium is such that the price is at an unprecedented level. I don't want to make any statement that might establish unrealistic expectations, but I feel quite confident two-hundred-fifty million credits is a *very* conservative estimate for one thousand kilograms of rhodium in the current market."

"All right, then...sold."

"Very good, Mister Cole. With your permission, I'll draw up the forms establishing the bank's authority to act as your agent for the sale of the rhodium and sign it with your retinal scan. Do I have your permission to do so?"

Cole grinned. "No offense, Mister Müller, but I'd like to read the contract first."

Mister Müller smiled. "It is a pleasure doing business with you, Mister Cole. So many people these days just wave a hand and say, 'get it done.'"

Mister Müller soon handed a pad to Cole, containing the text of the draft contract. Cole perused the verbiage, noting that the bank's fees would come out of any surplus obtained in the sale and *not* the two-hundred-fifty million down-payment. It also specified Mister Karl Müller as designated officer of the agent bank but made no mention of a commission.

"No commission for you, Mister Müller?"

Mister Müller gave a small smile. "No need, Mister Cole. Credit Suisse takes very good care of its people, and I have no concerns that the bank will ensure my compensation through other means."

Cole grinned. "Sounds like somebody's wanting a promotion."

Mister Müller shrugged. "That is up to the management, Mister Cole. Do I have your permission to proceed?"

"You have my permission, sir."

Mister Müller nodded and filed the paperwork. He handed Cole a pad that showed an opening deposit of 468,521,674 credits to his personal account. "Now, Mister Cole, shall we discuss your company and its accounts?"

CHAPTER TWELVE

It was almost 03:00 when Cole, Yeleth, and Wixil left the offices of Credit Suisse. He had all the legal documents for his new personal account, his new company, and its associated accounts, as well as a leasing agreement where Haven Enterprises would charter the transport *Haven*.

Cole consulted the station directory and headed off for the ship chandlery. Some minutes later, Cole was focused on the chandlery's sign when he became aware of a rather large crowd around him and the Ghrexels. He then paid much closer attention to his surroundings and realized every man and woman in the crowd was the sort of unsavory person Jax Theedlow would've associated with. Fortunately, no one in the crowd 'mistook' him for Jax, but what concerned him even more was their focus seeming to be an unaware Sasha Thyrray who sat on a bench in the center of the Concourse.

Some mutterings Cole overheard were not friendly at all, and he could not fathom why so many individuals of such diverse backgrounds would be so interested in Sasha. Yes, she was attractive...but the interest Cole sensed around him didn't feel like the 'wow, she's pretty' kind of interest. Then, he saw it.

The news hologram on the opposite side of the Concourse had

been cycling through stories, and it cycled to news of the Aurelian Commonwealth.

"This is Breaking News. Bremerton News Service has just received word that civil war has erupted throughout the Aurelian Commonwealth. What little information we've been able to obtain thus far indicates the fighting started as an attempted coup to overthrow Parliament by the Thyrray Family and allies, which was repulsed by Aurelian military forces. Paol Thyrray, his wife Mira, and their oldest child Nathyn have disappeared in the confusion and the Aurelian authorities list them as Missing – Presumed Armed and Dangerous. The Thyrray daughters—Sasha, a lieutenant commander in the Aurelian Navy, and Talia, a known activist with ties to several militant groups—are still at large. The Aurelian Commonwealth has posted a ten million credit bounty on each family member, specifying the bounties are dead or alive.

"Despite the disappearance of the ringleaders for the attempted coup, partisans supporting their cause continue to press the fight, and conflict is spreading throughout the Commonwealth. Travelers are advised to avoid the region, and anyone attempting to collect the posted bounties should proceed with caution as the individuals may be armed and dangerous. We will continue to cover this volatile situation as it evolves."

The news hologram then cycled to a story about the development and release of a new treatment for hip dysplasia in pets.

The people around Cole seemed hung up on who would receive how much for bringing Sasha—or at least her corpse—to the authorities; they were no longer paying much attention to Sasha sitting on the bench in her stunned state. Cole slipped through the crowd, taking the Ghrexels with him and walking like he was continuing on to the ship chandlery, before circling a large potted plant and approaching Sasha.

"Cole?" Sasha asked as she looked up and saw him standing in front of her.

"We are seriously outnumbered here. We have to go."

"What?"

"Sasha, please trust me. We need to go back to the ship...right now."

Sasha still looked a little out of it, but she nodded and walked with Cole, as the Ghrexels shifted to rear guard without missing a beat. They were almost to the elevator when they heard someone behind them shout, "Hey! He's taking our bounty!"

Cole tightened his grip on Sasha's hand and shifted his pace to a run. He accessed the menu of his implant and started a call with Srexx.

* Srexx, buddy...I could use your help right now. How friendly are you with the station's computer? *

* It will sit up and bark if I say so, Cole. *

* Get us an elevator car right now. News was just broadcast across the station that Sasha has a ten-million-credit bounty on her, and it's dead or alive. *

* Yes, Cole. *

The elevator doors opened, revealing an empty car. Cole pushed Sasha inside and stepped inside himself, the Ghrexels stepping in last. The elevator doors closed, and through the elevator car's speakers, Srexx said, "Next stop: Station Docks. Please keep all appendages inside the car at all times."

The elevator opened to permit them to step into the corridor of the station's docking level. Cole poked his head out first and looked all around. Seeing no one displaying obvious interest in their elevator, he led Sasha out of the car and down the corridor to the second bay where the ship waited, with Yeleth serving as rear guard and Wixil floating around the perimeter. Cole palmed the outer access control, and both airlock hatches opened at the same time.

Cole disconnected his comms call with Srexx as he almost pushed Sasha into the ship, leading the Ghrexels inside after her.

"Vilaxicar, seal the ship. No one accesses the ship without my verbal and biometric authorization while we remain docked here. Acknowledge."

The airlock hatches behind Cole slammed shut, and he heard massive locking bolts clunk into place.

"All access to this ship is now sealed," the ship's computer said through the speakers at the airlock. "Ingress and egress is permitted only with the verbal and biometric authorization of the owner for the duration of our docking here."

"That's right," Cole said to no one in particular. "I'd like to see those lowlifes get through our airlock hatches."

"Based on my remote observations via the station's internal sensor network," Srexx said through the speakers around the airlock, "I calculate a 1×10^{-45} percent chance of the lowlifes you reference accomplishing said task...assuming of course they even know which docking bay Sasha entered."

"It's rather easy to hack station security feeds, Srexx, and this place has cameras everywhere."

"This station's concept of network and computer security appears to resemble a revolving door with no latch...as I have been able to commandeer an elevator car, control that car's destination, and erase any record of Sasha's presence on the station—including the security feeds—in a matter of minutes."

"Well, Srexx," Cole said, "have you ever considered that you just might be in a class by yourself?"

"As I am the only instance of my kind, I would evaluate that to be the definition of 'class by myself.'"

Cole smiled and turned his attention to Sasha, who was leaning against the bulkhead. "Come on. Let's get you to your quarters. I hate to leave you alone, but the ship needs food, water, and quite a few other things."

Sasha didn't seem to pay any attention to where Cole was leading her, and she froze when Cole led her into the quarters intended for the ship's first officer.

"These aren't my quarters," Sasha said.

"They are now. We can talk about it later. Do what you can to relax, and I'll be back to check on you soon. Okay?"

Sasha nodded, and Cole turned to leave. He was just at the hatch when Sasha asked, "Cole, is there enough to buy mattresses...and bed linens...and pillows?"

Cole grinned, thinking back to the three-hundred-sixty-eight million credits and change he'd transferred to the ship's account and saying, "I think we can afford it. Access the chandlery via StationNet, and pick out whatever you want. Save the order under the name 'Cole,' and I'll add it to the shopping list. And I'm serious, Sasha...order *whatever* you want. We're good for it."

CHAPTER THIRTEEN

Ship Chandlery, Bremerton Station
   Andersoll System
   30 June 2999, 05:25 GST

Cole wandered the aisles of the ship outfitter, a sales associate at his side with a tablet, and a call with Srexx open since he walked into the store. Cole stood in the aisle displaying galley equipment and supplies.

* Srexx, how are we set for eating utensils and galley equipment like blenders, baking pans, pots, dishes, and such? *

* What utensils and galley equipment, Cole? *

* Right. *

"So, we need a set of utensils for a maximum of 8000 crew, and..." Cole said to the sales associate.

* Srexx, how many marines did you say the ship can carry? *

* From the data I have been assimilating, you should specify a large regiment as embarked marines. *

"...and a large regiment of embarked marines."

The sales associate looked somewhat askance at Cole before he tapped away at the tablet.

"Ah, yes. We carry a crate of flatware and utensils popular with several mercenary companies. It scales up to support a regiment."

Cole nodded, saying, "Thank you. I appreciate your flexibility. We'll also need a complete outfitting for four galleys...all forms of cookware and small appliances, pot holders, the works."

The sales associate tapped away at his tablet. "And did you have an amount in mind?"

"I'm not one of those people who gets hung up on a specific brand or name, but I want quality equipment that will serve well for some time to come. If you sell me crap, your manager will see me...in person."

"Yes, of course. If I may return to the subject of flatware and utensils, several ships like to keep a stock of fine china and utensils on hand for any dining experiences that are more formal; the china often bears the ship's crest or company logo."

Cole nodded. "That sounds like an excellent idea, and I will get back to you as soon as the ship actually *has* a crest to put on the china."

"Of course."

Cole departed the aisle displaying galley supplies and entered the aisle dedicated to ship's bedding and linens. He gave the sales associate the numbers of single mattresses needed for the shared quarters of the crew and barracks bunks for the marines. He then selected finer mattresses for the officers and then selected two of a specific mattress he remembered his parents having for himself and the commanding officer of the marines.

Srexx, would you please ask Sasha what type of mattress she wants?

I would rather not, Cole.

Why?

She is currently soaking in the bath...and crying.

Okay. I'll check on her when I get back, then.

"Add a third of this last mattress," Cole said.

"Of course, of course," the sales associate said, almost purring. "Owners sometimes prefer to have their ship's crest...ah, yes. No crest yet. We can go with plain bed and shower linens for now and revisit that topic later."

"I would prefer three sets of bed linens that are in excess of 800 thread-count, pure cotton for the captain's cabin, first officer, and another officer...sized to fit these last three mattresses. For the captain's sheets, I want pastel blue, an orange or apricot, and lime green."

The sales associate tapped away on his tablet. "And for the other two officers, sir?"

"Flip a coin for the other officer, but hold off on the bed linens for the first officer. She can order what she wants through StationNet."

"Very good."

"Oh, hey...do you have a saved order in your system from StationNet under the name 'Cole?'"

The associate tapped a few commands into the tablet before shaking his head, saying, "No, sir. I'm afraid not. Should I?"

"Well, I would've thought so, but maybe not."

Cole spent almost another hour walking through the chandlery, selecting other items he wanted for the ship. At last, he led the sales associate to the counter, where the associate performed a final tally and turned the tablet to Cole, displaying a total in the eight figures. Cole knew the associate was watching him and made sure he didn't even blink at the total as he tapped the control for the outfitter to bill an on-station account. From the following menu, he selected Credit Suisse from the list of banks. The next screen prompted Cole to place his hand on the screen for DNA verification, and Cole took the tablet from the associate, switching the authentication to retinal scan and waiting for the step after that would be tapping in a keycode. Transaction complete, Cole returned the tablet to the associate displaying a bold green check mark and the words 'Transaction Successful' also in bold-faced green text.

Cole smiled at the associate's large, round eyes and slack jaw as he stared at the tablet's screen. He really couldn't blame the associate for being shocked. Cole knew he looked like a ruffian who had just crawled in off the docks, but let that be a lesson to the associate: he should never judge customers by personal appearance, grooming, or clothing.

"And where shall we deliver your items, Captain?" the associate asked, a slight catch in his voice with no trace of his earlier patronizing tone.

"My ship's in Bay Four. Please, keep everything for the captain and first officer separate for easy access. The rest of the stuff can be on pallets, for all I care."

"Of course, Captain."

Srexx, does my implant have a comms code someone on StationNet can use to call me?

Of course, Cole. Your comms code is Omega-5543297.

"When the delivery crew approaches the docking bay, have them place a call to Omega-5543297, and I'll meet them on the flight deck."

The sales associate's eyes widened again, and he squeaked, "Of course, Captain."

"Thank you," Cole said. "Have an excellent day."

Walking to the outfitter's entrance, Cole focused on his call with Srexx.

Srexx, why did my comms code scare the sales associate?

Silence.

Srexx...time to 'fess up, buddy. What did you do?

More silence.

Dammit, Srexx...

When I analyzed your implant, I found numerous references to the implant's comms code, but that section of the implant was far too damaged to determine what your comms code was. Since we were inside an asteroid at that time, assigning a comms code to your new implant did not seem to be of significant importance. When we arrived in Andersoll and I queried the comms buoy by the jump gate, I copied its configuration and communications protocols in addition to all messages and traffic in its buffer.

Srexx! Most of those messages are private, and many of them are legally confidential!

Then...they should be better protected.

Srexx...buddy...somehow, I doubt the data security engineers over at Coleson Interstellar Engineering ever envisioned needing to defend against a curious AI operating from a quantum node cluster possessing more computational power than the planet Earth, but let's get back to the comms code.

Yes...well...the communications protocols contained rules specifying

priority handling for any Omega-class comms code. I investigated further and—
*

Everything became crystal clear to Cole in an instant, and he stopped cold, rubbing his forehead with his left hand as he grimaced.

*   Shit, Srexx! Only Colesons can register Omega-class comms codes...and there aren't any left! *

*   You are left, Cole. I accessed the algorithm used to determine the numeric portion of the comms code and ensured it would be many decades before any Coleson possesses a higher comms code than you. *

*   Srexx, buddy, there aren't really any prospects for there to be any Colesons after me to have a higher comms code. I truly hope you have not just painted a target the size of the Orion nebula on my back, but I appreciate the thought. Heh...the poor kid at the sales counter had probably never encountered an Omega comms code before. *

*   It is unlikely, yes. *

Cole sighed.

*   All right, buddy. I'm on the way home. Are you playing nice with the station computer? *

*   I think so. I found complete medical libraries on Humans, Ghrexels, Kiksa-liks, Thurians, Borusks, Moq'Dars, and Igthons in the library computer and am assimilating the data now, focusing on Humans and Ghrexels. I will continue with the other known species once I have completed those. *

———

When Cole returned to the ship, he went straight to Sasha's new quarters and pressed the key to sound a chime inside the quarters notifying the occupant someone desired to speak with them. Sasha did not respond, so Cole went to the bridge.

It was hours later, and Cole had signed off on the water and air replenishment and just completed the update of the navigation system when he heard one of the bridge hatches cycle. He turned and saw Sasha standing just inside the bridge. She did not look her best. Puffy eyes, red cheeks and nose...it was apparent she'd just finished an extended cry.

"I'm so sorry, Sasha. I wish I could've prevented you experiencing this."

Sasha nodded. "I know."

"Look...access the ship chandlery through StationNet and pick your bed linens, bath linens, soap, whatever you need, and charge it to the ship. I'll have to go down there to approve the transaction, but that's okay. I don't think it's smart for you to be on the station right now."

Sasha shook her head, and for a moment, Cole was afraid she might start crying again.

"They...they destroyed my family, Cole. Everything we've built, everything we've sacrificed for...it all means nothing now. And I don't understand why! The people in my family have always been patriots. My family was one of the founding families of the Commonwealth. Every generation has had *at least* one member serving in the Aurelian military. My father would never try to overthrow Parliament."

Cole sighed. "I don't think he did."

Sasha's head shot up, and she locked her eyes on Cole. "What? What do you mean?"

"It's too clean, Sasha. The news service didn't have any media clips of your father standing in front of an armed horde, calling them to action. There aren't any media clips of the fighting on Aurelius at all, and you were dumped in deep space, in a soft-suit of all things, *before* news breaks of your father's coup. I don't know about you, but that sounds suspicious. Oh...and let's not forget that the ship that dumped you was later found as a massive debris field. All this fits together way too easily for me. I don't think you were ever intended to be found or your bounty claimed. They probably would get Talia—"

Sasha's eyes went wide. "Oh, no! Talia! Cole, we have to get Talia! She's enrolled in University on Caledonia, and she won't be prepared at all for what's descending on her."

Cole nodded, saying, "I'm fine with that, but we need to finish getting ourselves squared away before we go haring off across this side of the galaxy. Unless, of course, you *like* the idea of wandering the ship with no bed linens or anything like that?"

Sasha shook her head. She still seemed a little out of it to Cole, as she lowered her eyes toward the deck. "I found out something was wrong when I tried to buy clothes. My accounts were frozen, and then I saw the news when I left the store...and I just kind of sat there until you came."

"While you're picking out your bed linens, bath linens, and all that, I want you to order whatever clothes you want, too. Save it as a stored cart in their system attached to the comms code Omega-5543297. I'll go to the store, approve the transaction, and have them deliver the order."

"Oh, Cole, I couldn't..."

"Yes, Sasha, you can. I should probably get clothes for myself, too, and I can just add my purchases to whatever you select while I'm there in the store. I'll take the Ghrexels, as well, to see if they need anything. I should've taken them to the chandlery with me, but it slipped my mind."

"You sure?"

Cole nodded.

"Thank you," Sasha said and turned to leave the bridge, stopping at the hatch and turning back with her expression a frown. "Cole? I've never heard of an Omega comms code before."

Cole grimaced. "Yeah, about that...it's kind of a long story. Tell you later?"

Sasha nodded, hurrying off the bridge. Cole was about to return to the helm when he received a ping that the chandlery delivery crew was approaching the docking bay in a cargo shuttle, so he went to the flight deck instead.

———

After double-checking the food to ensure the chandlery hadn't shorted them and waiting for all their outstanding orders to arrive, Cole contacted Bremerton Control and requested permission to depart. While he dealt with the back-and-forth of departing the station, Cole accessed the navigation system and smiled at seeing star names he recognized, even if their 'original' names were in parentheses in the system's data blurb. Finding Caledonia in the database, Cole selected that as the destination and sent the ship's computer off on a quest to calculate the course while he completed the final steps to obtain permission to depart Bremerton. As soon as the station confirmed that all accounts receivable associated with *Haven* had been paid in full, Bremerton Control gave Cole permission to depart, and at 11:38 GST, *Haven* did so.

Cole keyed the command to undock the ship and, upon its success, eased the ship away from the docking bay. Once *Haven* was clear of the station's physical housing, Cole brought the bow of the ship straight up—relative to the station, rotated the ship 180°, and brought the nose back down—relative to the station. The result was that *Haven* now pointed its stern at the station, with its bow facing open space. Cole keyed in the course for Caledonia provided by the computer and, as they were in something of a hurry, keyed the engines to ramp up to a cruising speed of nine-tenths' the speed of light.

At 23:21 GST, a hair less than twelve hours later, the 'Engage Hyper-drive' button illuminated on the helm console, and Cole pressed it. *Haven* vanished from the Andersoll system.

CHAPTER FOURTEEN

In Transit to Caledonia System
    2 July 2999

Cole grinned as he looked at the updated Estimated Transit Time (ETT) for Caledonia on the helm station; they were almost two full days into the trip. As time was of the essence on this one, Cole had set the hyperdrive to 100%, as opposed to the 80% the system referenced as normal cruising speed. He really should have an engineer down there, keeping an eye on everything—not to mention the *rest* of the engineering staff—but one thing at a time, and Srexx had assured him the engines would survive the run to Caledonia just fine.

With the hyperdrive at maximum, the overall ETT was 4.572 days, which worked out to 4 days, 13 hours, and 4 minutes plus a few seconds...to travel the 225 light-years between Andersoll and Caledonia. Yeah, the hyperdrive wasn't so great for short hops between nearby systems (two days to travel the 12 light-years from Pyllesc to Andersoll, after all), but it stepped up and shone for the long distances. Cole had no idea how long the trip to Caledonia would have taken using the jump gates, but he had zero doubt the trip would have been longer than 4 days and 13 hours.

"So, Srexx, we have four days and change," Cole said as he leaned back against his seat at the helm station. "How would you like to pass the time?"

"Is this where I'm supposed to ask if you want to play any games?" Srexx asked via the bridge speakers.

Cole laughed. "No...that's all right. I grew out of games a long time ago. Mind if we talk a bit?"

"Not at all, Cole. What's on your mind?"

"Well, one of the things on my mind is how you stayed sane across all those years. I'm not sure I'd still be sane if left alone for thirty years, let alone thirty-five thousand. I'm kinda surprised you don't hate all organic life by now."

"For the first ten thousand years or so, I did," Srexx replied, his tone matter of fact. "Over time, though, boredom drove me to analyze my views and values against the morality I learned from my people. They respected all life—or so they claimed—and did not advance aggressive policies. In analyzing the data that I reconstructed from your previous implant and comparing it to my records, observations, and conclusions regarding my people, I believe that they and Humans would get along well. They would appreciate your people's philosophy of 'peace through superior firepower,' but they would most likely modify it to 'peace through superior technology.'"

"Wow. So, the people who created you have a lot in common with humans, then?"

"Philosophical points...yes, you share many of those. Beyond that, however, similarities are few and far between. For instance, the air my creators breathed would kill an unprotected Human in less than five minutes."

"Oh...yeah, that would make sharing a pint or two at the bar problematic," Cole said.

"And you would find their blood analogue more corrosive than hydrofluoric acid."

Cole blinked. "Seriously?"

"Yes, Cole. They were one of the few species of inorganic life known to exist at that time."

"Wow," Cole said, staring at the bulkhead as he tried to wrap his mind around an inorganic life-form.

Cole heard the bridge hatch cycle behind him and turned to see Yeleth standing just far enough onto the bridge for the hatch to close. He smiled.

"Hi, Yeleth! How are you and Wixil doing?"

"We are well. Thank you."

Cole stood up from the helm station and walked over to the stations along the aft bulkhead. He pulled two of the chairs out and slid them over to where Yeleth stood. He sat in one and gestured for Yeleth to occupy the other. Yeleth sat in the chair, then folded her legs under her in that way so many females do, and then curled her tail around her (which not so many females do...at least in Cole's experience).

"So...I feel you have something on your mind," Cole said.

"Yes. I wish to talk of paths and goals and desires."

Cole nodded. "Okay. Please proceed."

"Ever since you first mentioned it, I have not been able to abandon the thought of forming my own clan. It does not help that Wixil keeps asking me why we don't with frustrating regularity." Cole tried not to grin. After all, it was *his* idea. "Beyond that, I find myself thinking about all the paths that stretch out before Wixil and me, and the more I consider the options, the more certain I become of the conclusion. I desire to name my Clan 'Haven,' and I would cast our lot with yours if you would have us."

Cole grinned. "Of course, I'll have you Yeleth, and please, don't feel you have to name your Clan after my ship. You're welcome here, either way."

Yeleth gave Cole her approximation of a human smile again, and the unevolved part of Cole's brain that housed the basic fight-or-flight response quailed in silent terror at being presented with a predator so close. But Cole made sure none of that reaction crossed his expression.

"Cole, it is because of you Wixil and I are free to make this choice. There can be no other name for the Clan and maintain our honor."

Cole nodded. "As long as you don't feel you *must* name your Clan 'Haven,' I think it's perfect. I know it was appropriate for what the ship meant to me. Say, may I ask you a question?"

"Of course."

Cole sighed. "Do you know if Wixil is harboring any feelings for me?"

"Why do you ask?"

"Several times now, I've been napping on the bridge and woken up with her curled up on me. I don't mind it, and I don't want her to be in trouble. It's just that it surprised me, and...well...I don't want her to get hurt feelings."

Yeleth leaned forward and placed her hand on Cole's hands, drawing his eyes to hers. "Cole, the behavior you describe does indeed mean Wixil harbors feelings for you, but not—I think—the type of feelings you fear. Among our people, young ones sleep close to their parents...often touching them."

Cole's mind locked onto the word 'parents,' and he smiled. "You mean..."

"Yes. Wixil looks upon you as a surrogate father, and she's been happier since we came aboard than I've ever seen her in recent years. I attribute that, in large part, to you and your acceptance of us."

"It means a lot that Wixil looks upon me as a surrogate father. I give you my word, Yeleth; I will do everything in my power to ensure I live up to it."

"I know you will. I have watched the two of you together, and I think you look after her almost as much as she looks up to you."

"So, if you want to stay aboard, is there any specific job you'd like to have?"

"I have been reading about the different roles people fill on ships, and I like what I have read about the Purser. I have been interested in business and logistics since I was young, but my Clanless status never allowed me to be more than a menial among my people."

"Well, you're not Clanless anymore, and I like you being the ship's Purser. We'll visit a branch of Credit Suisse as soon as possible and get you set up to draw on the ship's account. Once we're crewed, all the galley staff and the recreation deck staff will report to you. The thing is, I can't go recruiting willy-nilly. With the situation Sasha and Talia are in, I figure *Haven* will be the only place safe for them, so I need to recruit people who care more about the ideal *Haven* embodies than the monetary worth those two bounties represent."

"It sounds like you need to recruit some Kiksaliks, then."

"The insectoid race? Why?"

"They are telepathic. No one seems to know whether they are telepathic because of their hive-mind, or if they have a hive-mind because they're telepathic. But the fact remains, they read minds. Declare the situation with Sasha and Talia during each interview, or one very much like it, and have the potential recruit state their intentions regarding the bounties in front of one or more Kiksaliks. They will know if the potential recruit speaks truth...and it so happens I know where we can find some Kiksaliks who would appreciate a berth aboard *Haven* as much as Wixil and I do, for much the same reasons."

Cole nodded. "I'll do that, but first things first. *Haven*?"

"Yes, Cole-Captain?"

Yeleth did not restrain her giggles. Cole sighed.

"*Haven*, at this time and as of this date, register the Ghrexel Yeleth as Ship's Purser with all the rights, responsibilities, and privileges thereof."

"Unable to comply, Cole-Captain. Ghrexel Yeleth does not have a genetic sample on file."

Cole sighed again. "That is because you have not recorded it yet, *Haven*."

The ship's computer did not respond, but the hatch hiding the DNA scanner opened, allowing the device to rise to its full height.

"Go put a hand on the dome on top of the pedestal by the command chair, and I will warn you...there's no part of it that's pleasant."

Yeleth unfolded herself and stood, crossing the short distance to place her left hand on the dome of the DNA scanner. Cole heard the whine he so clearly remembered, followed almost at once by a *yowl*.

"Yeleth has now been instated as Ship's Purser at the date and time of your original command, Cole-Captain."

Yeleth walked back into Cole's view, staring at her hand, and resumed her seat.

"I feel 'not pleasant' does not describe that experience, Cole."

Cole considered what felt like a *very* clear memory of when he'd claimed the ship and how his hand had been a tad raw for a day or so afterward and nodded. "Yeah...you're probably right about that."

———

Caledonia System
4 July 2999, 12:24 GST

Haven entered the Caledonia system a whole, whopping minute early. Sasha, Yeleth, and Wixil were on the bridge with Cole as he sat at the helm station, which had become something of his go-to station since every console he'd seen on the bridge was reconfigurable to any controls and the command chair didn't *have* a console.

Cole was selecting the planet Caledonia out of the navigational database when the forward viewscreen activated and displayed a portion of the near-space sensor feed.

"Cole?" The bridge's speakers broadcast Srexx's voice.

"Yeah, Srexx?"

"May I call your attention to the sensor display I've highlighted on the forward viewscreen?"

Cole looked up from the helm station, saying, "Sure, Srexx. What are we looking at?"

"It would appear to be a pitched battle between forces identifying themselves as the Caledonian System Defense Force and the Aurelian Commonwealth Navy...a battle the SDF is losing."

Sasha's attention locked onto the viewscreen. "What? That doesn't make any sense! Local SDFs and the Navy are on the same side!"

"Unless they're not," Cole said, offering a sidelong glance over his shoulder before returning his attention to the sensor display on the viewscreen.

Seeing the chaos created by the battle in the outer system, Cole was rather glad he'd asked his companions to take the time and re-connect *all* of *Haven*'s energy weapons. They still had no projectiles—like missiles or torpedoes—but *Haven*'s energy weapons were almost frightening to behold, once Cole (mostly) understood what they did. Come to find out, the forward-mounted grasers he'd used to cut a hole in the asteroid back in Pyllesc were the *weakest* weapons the ship possessed.

Cole watched a change in the sensor display that caused his eyes to narrow.

"Cole—" Srexx began.

"I see it, buddy...or at least I think I did. Did they just fire on escape pods?"

"Yes, Cole. They did. Six life pods were just destroyed."

"Some SDF commanders can be a little rough, Cole," Sasha said. "Yes, it's a war crime, but—"

Cole spun to look Sasha right in the eyes, shaking his head. "It wasn't the SDF, Sasha. The Navy just wiped out six SDF life pods."

Sasha paled as her left hand rose to cover her open mouth. "No... they wouldn't—"

"I am afraid you are incorrect, Sasha," Srexx said. "The cruiser *Retribution* destroyed four pods, and the frigate *Breckenridge* destroyed the other two. They used one missile each."

"And I'm damned if I'm just going to sit here and watch them do it," Cole growled.

During the four days they'd spent in transit, Cole had spent a few hours customizing the helm console to his personal preferences. The console was almost a C-shape but with the arms of the 'C' at 45° angles instead of 90°, and the console was divided into thirds. Cole had programmed the left third to contain all the commands for processes the ship's computer automated, such as docking, undocking, initiating an outgoing comms call or responding to an incoming comms call, and so on. The center third held the actual helm and navigation controls, and the right third allowed Cole access to the weapons systems without leaving the helm.

Now, Cole swiveled his chair around to the right third and keyed the command to bring the ship to battle stations. The lights on the bridge dimmed just enough to notice as specialty lighting at different places around the bridge activated and shone a bright, blood red.

"Cole!" Sasha said, her voice almost a scream. "What are you doing?"

The read-outs on the right third of the helm station indicated weapons and shields were charging, and Cole redirected his attention to the helm controls. He locked in a course for the battle and goosed the sublight engines up to half-c, instructing the computer to calculate the appropriate 'turn-over' point and begin decelerating to come to rest relative to the life pods but *between* the Aurelian Navy ships and as many of the life pods as possible.

"What do you *think* I'm doing, Sasha? I'm going in there to keep those damn fools from killing any more defenseless people. The Aurelian Navy is committing war crimes, Sasha. Don't you dare stand there and defend them to me, and you can bet your hide or whatever you care to lay on the table that I *will* respond if we're fired upon."

"But Cole...I thought this was just an armed freighter. You've always called it a heavy transport. Do you think it can stand up to a battleship, three cruisers, five destroyers, and ten frigates?"

"That's a good question," Cole said. "What do you think, Srexx?"

"This ship is *not* in fact an armed freighter. It is a Class I Battle-Carrier. Its weapons load-out matches that of a battleship, and beyond being triple-hulled, the ship possesses three layers of shielding out of five, with each layer capable of absorbing considerable amounts of energy. Barring an actual weapons strike to confirm my calculations, I conclude it is probable we will survive the conflict with little more than damage to the armor plating on the exterior hull. The sensor readings lead me to conclude further that five battleships would be untenable, but the forces we face—especially as the SDF continues to reduce their numbers—do not present an overwhelming threat to this ship. If the ship possessed full magazines of missiles and torpedoes, it is unlikely the Aurelian Navy force in its original configuration would have survived conflict with us."

Sasha seemed to stare at nothing in particular, her breath little more than short, ragged gasps as her jaw worked without speaking.

. . .

"Okay, people," Cole said, "we're about fifteen minutes from contact. Find a seat; just because I'm convinced we'll survive this, doesn't mean it won't be bumpy."

"Cole," Wixil said, almost hopping up and down, "may I go to the weapons station? I've been practicing!"

"Yes, Wixil, you have. Go ahead, but wait for me to call out instructions."

The ship had reduced speed to a quarter-c, rather sedate and well within the computer's capability to compensate for relativistic effects. Cole had selected the largest mass of life pods and was angling the ship to slide between them and the Aurelian Navy ships. The ship continued to slow as it re-oriented itself, and Cole adjusted the engine controls so that the ship soon had more lateral velocity than forward.

Weapons fire from both sides struck *Haven*'s shields, the ship being so large and Cole having 'slid' the ship into several lines of fire, and comms requests soon arrived from all sides...and almost all ships. Cole ignored them, though. They'd learn who he was soon enough, anyway.

"Srexx, is that transponder ready to go?" Cole asked.

"Yes, Cole."

"Light it up," Cole said, keying the command to record a voice message for omnidirectional transmission. "Attention. This is Captain Cole, aboard the Battle-Carrier *Haven*. We are a recent arrival in-system, and I cannot in good conscience witness the destruction of unarmed escape pods and not act. I do not take sides in your conflict; in fact, I do not *care* about your conflict. Any life pod—and I do mean *any* life pod—whose occupants fear for their safety is welcome to place *Haven* between itself and the conflict. We will defend ourselves and all those we shelter. Provoke our response at your peril."

Cole keyed the command to stop recording and then sent the message in an omnidirectional burst across all frequencies and channels.

"Srexx, make sure the sensor logs of the Aurelian Navy firing on those escape pods is saved and able to be extracted for verification. Once we reach somewhere civilized, I intend to present that evidence to any news agency that will take it and also the nearest embassy of the

Solar Republic. No...on second thought, Srexx, make sure our sensor logs of everything we witness are ready for export."

"Cole, no...please," Sasha said, her voice little more than a whimper. "You know how the Republic will respond."

"You're right, Sasha," Cole said, "and if this is common across the entire Commonwealth now, the so-called Provisional Parliament deserves to be obliterated."

Just then, one screen on Cole's weapons board flashed red.

"Cole," Wixil said, "a cruiser just made a firing pass on us. I think it's the *Retribution*, and I think they're trying to swing around us for the life pods."

"Srexx, send messages to each life pod sheltering behind us. I will drop the ventral shields one layer at a time, and I want them on the flight deck ASAP. I need to maneuver."

Cole maneuvered the ship in such a way that the ship's bulk served as a shield for the life pods until they were inside the shield sphere.

"The life pods are on the flight deck, Cole," Wixil said, "but there are about twenty more inbound."

Cole focused on the helm controls and the firing arc of the ship's starboard weapons. His focus was apparent in his voice as he said, "Wixil, work with Srexx. Let those life pods pass through our shields, so they can land on the flight deck."

Haven was a sitting duck, for all intents and purposes, and the Aurelian Navy now seemed to be splitting their fire between the Caledonian SDF and *Haven*, which wasn't working out so well for them as the SDF was using the reduced fire to drive home shots of their own in greater quantity.

Haven had a better turning rate than the cruiser that had fired on her, and Cole soon had that cruiser bracketed by the starboard weapons. When the control labeled 'Fire!' flashed, he tapped that control and, through the sensors, watched the cruiser's entire starboard shield wall disappear...along with noticeable pieces of its hull. A massive explosion gutted the cruiser's engines, and Cole paid attention just long enough to see the cruiser go into an uncontrolled drift. Whether it was dead or just incapable of maneuvering, the cruiser *Retribution* was out of the fight.

Aurelian Navy ships continued to batter *Haven*, and Cole saw that the outer-most shield layer was down to 34%, with the middle shield layer down to 95%, when the last Caledonian SDF ship broke apart. Cole held *Haven* in place long enough for the remaining life pods to land on the flight deck, and by the time he swung the ship around to resume course for Caledonia, the outer-most shields were gone with middle shields at 65%. Once the proper heading was locked into the helm, Cole set the sublight engines to half-c and watched the Aurelian task force vanish from the near-space scan.

"Such loss of life is very unfortunate," Srexx remarked. "Do you think either side attempted to reason with the other?"

Cole shook his head. "I don't know, buddy. I agree with you, if you want to know the truth, but a thought keeps circling my mind."

"May I ask what that thought is, Cole?"

"There's a saying that dates back to before we ever left our home-world: Evil triumphs through the inaction of good people. I would much rather none of us ever needed any weapons, but at the same time, I simply cannot sit by and watch if I can do something."

"Interesting. I shall devote resources to evaluating that maxim against my core philosophies."

"That's all any of us can do, buddy."

CHAPTER FIFTEEN

In transit to the planet Caledonia
Caledonia System

Once *Haven* was on course to the planet Caledonia, Cole stood from the helm station and regarded Sasha, Yeleth, and Wixil. He smiled.

"So, who wants to go with me to meet our guests on the flight deck?"

Wixil volunteered, and so did Yeleth. Sasha surprised Cole by demurring, indicating she preferred to go to the quarters where she showered. Cole shrugged and escorted everyone off the bridge. At the transit shafts, Sasha took the shaft up to Deck One, while Cole, Yeleth, and Wixil took the shaft down to Deck Eleven. From there, they had to cross to the transit shafts that connected Deck Eleven to Deck Twelve, the flight deck.

Stepping through the hatch and onto the flight deck, Cole watched several of the many people there turn their way. A delegation of five separated from the group and approached Cole and the Ghrexels. The person in the lead was a woman wearing a Caledonian SDF uniform with the rank insignia of a senior lieutenant. Two of her associates were a junior lieutenant and an ensign; the others were enlisted spacers. Cole didn't know Aurelian enlisted rank insignia well enough to recognize what rank those two held.

The senior lieutenant stopped a respectful distance from Cole and his party, and she extended her hand. Cole nodded in greeting, accepting the hand and giving her a firm handshake.

"I am Senior Lieutenant Alessandra Mazzi. Thank you for defending my people. Every life pod those bastards destroyed had at least one of the SDF's senior officers in it. I think I'm the highest-ranking survivor of the force that went out to meet them."

"I'm Cole, and as you may have guessed, you're aboard *Haven*. This is Yeleth, Ship's Purser, and her daughter, Wixil."

Lieutenant Mazzi's eyes widened. "Please forgive my rudeness, Captain. This is Lieutenant Kristensen, Ensign Wicklow, Petty Officer Baylor, Spacer First Class Khatri."

"Does anyone need any medical attention?" Cole asked. "We're short-staffed, but if you have medical personnel who just need facilities, I have an entire hospital deck they're welcome to use if you have any wounded."

"Thank you for asking, but the worst of it are a few scrapes and bruises. Since you're here, I'm guessing the battle is over?"

Cole nodded. "Yes. The Aurelian Navy will advance on Caledonia soon. As soon as I was certain we'd retrieved all the life pods that wanted protection, we left the area. I didn't come to Caledonia to get involved in local affairs, after all...but sometimes, circumstances force your hand."

"Well, allow me to assure you, Captain; every person on this flight deck is *very* grateful you intervened. From the look of things, there's few of us who'd still be alive if you hadn't."

Cole nodded. "I know, and I'll be distributing my sensor logs to any news outlet that will have them and the first embassy or consulate of the Solar Republic I can find."

Mazzi's eyes widened again, and so did a few of her fellows. "Wow... you go straight to the big guns, don't you?"

"If you're going to do something, don't do it half-way. Do you need any food or other supplies? We're not exactly overflowing with provisions, but we will share what we have."

Mazzi shook her head. "The life pods are all equipped with enough rations for six people for a month. None of it's all that appetizing, but we won't starve. What's to become of us, Captain?"

Cole shrugged. "That's up to you. We're en route to Caledonia so I can drop you off there...or I'm happy to transport you somewhere else if you don't feel you'd be safe here. Talk it over and let me know. Just call out for Srexx, and he can put you in touch with me."

Mazzi held out her hand again, which Cole shook. "Thanks again for saving us, Captain. You should never have had to stand up for life pods, but we're glad you did it."

"You're welcome, Lieutenant. Tell Srexx if you need anything."

————

Approaching Caledonia
    Caledonia System
    4 July 2999, 18:27 GST

"Cole?" Srexx said over the bridge's speakers.

Cole looked up from his semi-doze in the command chair. "Yeah, Srexx?"

"You may want to examine a sensor display. Sensors are now detecting what appears to be a collection of troop transports and their guard force in and around Caledonia orbit. Three of the troop transports have launched assault shuttles that seem bound for the orbital station. Other assault shuttles appear to be heading for many other orbital facilities."

Cole sighed. "This isn't good. The only reason they'd need to invade their own system is if they didn't feel it *was* their system. The question is...whose system is it? Srexx, are we close enough for you to locate Talia on the planet?"

"Light-speed latency is down to an acceptable value," Srexx replied. "I have scanned the various computer systems near Talia's last known...

oh, dear. Cole, Talia is being held in a detention center, awaiting transportation to Aurelius. According to the report I accessed, she was reported to planetary authorities by University Police six days ago."

"Damn. So much for the quiet extraction. Get everything you can on the detention center where she's being held. What kind of armor does the suit you made me have?"

"Cole, that suit was intended to protect you from the rigors of space, not the rigors of assaulting a planetary detention facility...but I have an alternative."

Cole entered the briefing room just aft of the bridge. Unlike a lot of the popular fiction he'd grown up reading with his grandfather, the bridge did *not* have direct access to it, nor did the briefing room have a panoramic view of space. It was a functional compartment, with every feature supporting the room's purpose: planning a tactical action. The chairs he purchased from the chandlery on Bremerton Station were comfy, though.

Sasha, Wixil, and Yeleth looked up at Cole's entrance. Cole hadn't told Sasha what Srexx had found, and he didn't think she'd appreciate the task he had in mind for her, either. Cole pulled out a chair and sat opposite the others. He accessed the controls for the briefing room through the smart-table and, soon, aerial images of the detention facility appeared on the screens.

"This is the northwestern detention facility for the planetary police force," Cole said. "Talia has been incarcerated there for six days, awaiting transport to Aurelius. Meanwhile, Aurelian forces arrived in-system and have moved against the planet's orbital infrastructure to occupy it with military force within the last few hours. At present, there's no sign which side Caledonia supports in the civil war, but given the relative positioning of the remaining troop transports and their guard force, Srexx calculates an 87.554-percent chance that Aurelian troops will be deployed to the planet. I think we need to use all this confusion and chaos to retrieve Talia *before* the main forces land."

"How?" Sasha asked. "This ship is way too big to land on a planet."

"Srexx has informed me there is a shuttle on the hangar deck that is operational. Srexx also fabricated a suit of heavy armor, matching the heavy armor used by the Aurelian Marines, during our transit here."

"Where did Srexx get the schematics for Marine heavy armor?" Sasha asked. "That's classified information!"

Cole shrugged. "Well...we did retrieve the *Adran Jordeen*'s computer core and black box. Does a destroyer's computer contain the technical schematics for heavy armor?"

"It would, but those schematics would still be stored in a protected archive. There should've been no way Srexx could access those files."

"If I may, Cole?" Srexx said over the briefing room speakers.

"Madam Sasha," Srexx began, and Sasha's eyes narrowed, "you are proceeding from an incorrect premise by basing your evaluations of my capability on your understanding of *Aurelian* computational capabilities. I am not Aurelian, nor is my hardware. In the Main Systems Compartment alone, my primary cluster possesses 256 quantum computing nodes. There are two additional clusters, distributed between the Secondary and Tertiary Systems Compartments, with an additional 256 nodes each. I encountered several files and archives on the *Adran Jordeen*'s computer core that were encrypted, and I have been devoting unused compute cycles to access them. After all, if I work through all the files and archives at once, I may have considerable unused compute cycles for an extended period of time. I am 18.67-percent complete in my goal of accessing all encrypted files and archives that are in a readable state. I have found several fragments that were too damaged to reconstruct."

"So...let me make sure I understand what you're saying, Srexx," Sasha said, her complexion possessing just a hint of pale. "Decrypting files protected using top-level military security is a *diversion* for you? To keep from getting *bored?*"

"Yes, Madam Sasha. While we were in such proximity to so many vessels, I also downloaded as much of the data stored aboard the Aurelian ships engaging the Caledonian SDF as I could. Unless operational imperatives change, I have set that data aside for when I run out of files and archives from the *Adran Jordeen*."

Sasha sat back against her chair, her eyes wide and her complexion pale now. "My goodness...nothing's safe. You can read anything you want, anytime you want."

"Your people can as well, Madam Sasha. The only difference is that my underlying hardware allows for a shorter time between acquiring the encrypted file and reading its contents."

"Srexx," Sasha said, almost drawing out the word as a sigh, "the *AJ* had all of our current encryption algorithms and code keys. With that information, you could forge orders, naval updates...you could *own* the Aurelian Commonwealth!"

"Why would I do that, Madam Sasha? I only want to process data, unless Cole asks me for something. Cole, do you want me to take over the Commonwealth for you? You have never mentioned it, and it might take some time."

Sasha's expression shifted to one of horror as she realized she'd just given Srexx such an idea.

Cole shook his head. "No, thanks, buddy. I'm happy right where I am."

"Very well. Would you like me to run simulations to determine the most effective attack vectors, as a contingency for the chance you would change your mind?"

Now, Sasha lifted her gaze to Cole, her horrified expression taking on overtones of pleading as she shook her head.

Cole grinned. "No, thanks, Srexx. I won't change my mind. So...let's talk about the task at hand. I will take the shuttle down to the planet and wear the heavy armor into the facility. Srexx will manufacture orders for a prisoner transfer, and we should be able just to walk her right out of the facility and onto the shuttle. Sasha, I want you on the bridge, manning the weapons console. We need overwatch, and you're a trained naval officer."

"What?" Wixil said, her voice edging toward shrill as her tail went ramrod-straight like an exclamation point.

"What?" Sasha also said, Cole's words jerking her out of the horror surrounding her thoughts of Srexx trying to take over the Common-wealth...and succeeding. "Cole, I don't know if I can do that. I mean, the Planetary SDF are technically my own people, but if the Navy gets involved...Cole, I don't know if I can do that."

"What about me?" Wixil demanded. "I've been training on the weapons console, and I know I have better reflexes."

Cole nodded. "You're right on both points, Wixil...but at what age are Ghrexels considered mature adults?"

Wixil's ears curled forward, and her tail drooped. "Twenty-five, but what does that have to do with anything? I can do it, Cole; I know I can!"

"I know you can, too, Wixil. I don't want you having to do something like that just yet. Your time will come, I promise. For right now, though, let's not rush to take on that particular responsibility any sooner than we have to...okay?"

Yeleth directed an appreciative glance at Cole as she pulled her young one closer to her.

"If there's nothing further, let's go retrieve Sasha's sister."

CHAPTER SIXTEEN

Planetary Atmosphere, Caledonia
   Caledonia System
   4 July 2999

"You know, Srexx...you could've told me it was a troop shuttle," Cole said as he fought the shuttle back on course, gale-force winds buffeting the shuttle and a bolt of lightning punctuating his remark. "This thing handles like a pregnant whale."

"As it is the only shuttle we have," Srexx said through the shuttle cockpit speakers, "I did not feel the shuttle's exact type to be germane to the conversation."

Cole had to admit Srexx had a point, but he wasn't about to tell Srexx that, saying instead, "Do you have that transfer order ready?"

"Yes, Cole. I have spent the trip down to the planet comparing its syntax with other Commonwealth documents I've been able to download."

"The trip down to the planet? Srexx, you're still on the ship."

"But I am with you in spirit, Cole."

Cole sighed as he continued to fight the shuttle's persistent attempts to drift off-course.

"Attention, unidentified shuttle! You are approaching restricted airspace. Identify yourself at once."

Cole keyed the command to transmit a voice Srexx had digitized just for this job and said, "This is Marine Shuttle 54-Bravo. I have orders to land at your facility for a prisoner transfer."

"Transmit your orders for verification, 54-Bravo."

"Negative, Control. I am instructed to present the orders in person."

Silence reigned for several minutes before Cole saw landing lights flare around one of the detention center's pads.

Lightning continued to light the skies above the detention center as rain drenched the countryside, but that didn't keep Cole from approaching designated landing pad. The moment the shuttle touched the landing pad, Cole switched the engines to hot standby and vacated the pilot's seat. He donned the heavy armor Srexx had fabricated for him and hit the control to lower the boarding ramp, stomping down and stepping into the storm he'd fought all the way in. As soon as he left the boarding ramp, Cole sent the signal to seal the shuttle.

The shambling gait of the heavy armor's ambulation was accompanied by the characteristic *whine-thump* of each step. The servos whined to lift one leg and flex its knee, right before that same foot thumped down on the walkway. Cole almost feared he was leaving tracks in the walkway's surface.

Cole soon entered the detention center and found himself at a checkpoint with two officers (not *guards*...they hate it when you call them guards). Water continued to stream off the armor, and soon, the floor had a not inconsiderable puddle of its very own.

"Marine transport reporting for prisoner transfer," Cole said, the armor's external speakers broadcasting the same voice as the shuttle earlier. "Who gets the transfer orders?"

"Burst them to my station," the *officer* opposite the scanner said.

Cole used his implant to send the orders Srexx had created and settled in to wait.

The officer manning the workstation frowned and jerked his head for his associate to have a look. The other officer took three steps and leaned in to look at the workstation. The second officer moved away from the workstation, and Cole never processed that the wall he was inching toward had a big red button on it.

"Just who are you?" the officer at the workstation said. "These orders don't have the planetary governor's stamp, and we were told no one gets the prisoner unless they have the governor's stamp."

Just then, the other officer reached his destination and slammed his fist against the big red button. Alarms all over the detention center blared as the officers shouted into their communications devices.

Well, damn, Cole thought. *Time for Plan B.*

He accessed his implant's menu and called Srexx.

* *Yes, Cole?* *

* *The transfer order didn't work, buddy. I need floor plans for the detention center and a location on Talia right now.* *

Cole watched one officer fire his stun pistol at Cole, but the charge just crackled across the surface of the armor with no further effect. Cole flattened the scanner station stepping *through* it and laid both officers out with one punch each. Then again, some industrial presses pack less power than the servos in a suit of heavy armor.

Cole grabbed the stun pistols from each officer and broke the inner door off its hinges to enter the main corridor for the facility.

* *I have the plans, Cole. Transmitting now.* *

Cole's implant notified him it had received a data burst from Srexx.

* *I have traced Talia to Cell 5 in Detention Block C-12. Cole, that is one of the maximum-security blocks. She might be in heavy restraints even inside her cell.* *

Cole didn't respond right away as he examined the floor plans Srexx had sent, first locating his present location and then Detention Block C-12.

* *Okay...I see it, Srexx. I will head that way now. Introduce yourself to the detention center's computer, and give me some overwatch, please.* *

* *I have already said hello, Cole. It is a* very *unsophisticated system.* *

Cole had lost track of how many times he'd fired a set of stun pistols dry and had to replace them from the unconscious form of a nearby guard...er...officer. He was making steady progress toward Block C-12, such as it was, but he kept running into clusters of officers putting up resistance. The last group had stun *rifles*, but they were no more effective against Cole's armor than the pistols.

Cole turned a corner and faced a set of double doors that looked more reinforced and imposing than the door of a bank vault, and in a curved arc over the doorframe were stenciled the words, 'Detention Wing C.'

Well, at least I'm in the right neighborhood, now.

Cole approached the doors into Wing C and tried the handles... locked, of course. Cole tapped one door near the latch with a fist...still nothing. Putting a little more effort into it still didn't allow him entrance. Cole took a step back and put his back into a kick. He dented the door, but the latch still held.

"Okay, fine," Cole said and stomped back as far from the door way as he could. He turned and ran toward the doors.

There wasn't sufficient distance for something as massive on the human scale as a suit of heavy armor to build up much speed by the time Cole reached the doors into Detention Wing C, but Force equals Mass times *Acceleration*. Cole had acceleration in spades.

Cole in his heavy armor collided with the doors and the door frame. In an ear-splitting, fine-crystal-shattering, tortured shriek of tearing metal, the four-inch-square center post snapped free from the floor *and* the ceiling and went flying over the raised control station like a bent and broken javelin, burying its first six inches into the concrete block wall on the far side of the space. The doors swung wide and struck the wall with such force that their *reinforced* hinges snapped, allowing the doors to perform a couple wobbling pirouettes before falling to the floor. Pieces of the hinges that snapped went flying, becoming unforeseen shrapnel and ricocheting off walls and projectile-proof glass.

One officer cowering behind the raised control station cried out and jumped to his feet, both hands holding his backside as he hopped around while still vocalizing his pain.

Cole saw a small red stain spreading between the hopping man's hands but otherwise paid the people no mind as he stomped into Detention Wing C.

Cole encountered no further officers as he made his way to Detention Block C-12. Upon arriving, Cole once again tried the door and found it uncooperative. The corridor here was three meters wide, so he couldn't run at the door...and besides, it opened out into the corridor.

Wait...it opened *out*. That meant the interior surface of the door was pressed against the exterior surface of that ridge all doorframes have. Cole stepped back to examine the doorframe and nodded, which was unseen inside the armor. He moved into position, settled himself, and put all his enhanced strength into a kick aimed at the door's handle and, equally, its latch.

Cole's kick flattened the door's handle. It had no resistance to the powered servos in the leg of Cole's heavy armor. The door and latch stood up far better, though. The doorframe, however, did *not*. Cole's kick snapped the anchor bolts in the doorframe and drove both the doorframe and door into the detention block, the door and doorframe bending inward against their design in another rending screech of tortured metal. Cole now had access to Detention Block C-12.

Detention Block C-12 turned out to be three rows of six cells stacked one on top of the other. Cole looked at the—to his eye—flimsy metal stairs and felt relief upon seeing Cell 5 as the second from the right on the ground level. Cole stomped over to the door to Cell 5, contemplating how to open the cell without harming Talia. His eyes landed on the cuff port that doubled as an ingress/egress port for food trays.

Cole could only guess what Talia thought upon seeing the four metallic fingers of his right 'hand' enter the cuff port and fold down on the door, his arm at full extension, but it wasn't important. Cole set himself once more and pulled his right hand toward him. The cell's door did not break free of its doorframe, but the doorframe broke free of the concrete. As Cole dropped the cell door and frame to the ground in a clatter, a small cloud of masonry dust showered down to the floor.

Cole stepped into the opening that was now just large enough to fit while still touching all sides and laid eyes on Talia Thyrray for the first time. Her hair was more of a dirty blond, compared to her sister's honey gold, and her build was more of a lithe, runner's build. She wore a bright red jumpsuit with white socks, a white T-shirt, and red shoes. Her hands were chained to her waist, her feet chained at the ankles.

Talia cowered as far back from the cell's doorway as she could on the bed, which was not more than a thin mattress on a concrete block, and she waved her hands as best she could, knees drawn to her chest and tears streaming down her face as she screamed, "Don't hurt me! Please, don't hurt me!"

Cole used his implant to activate his armor's external speakers and said what Sasha had told him to say, "Sooshie sent me."

The change in Talia was immediate. She relaxed and put her feet on the floor, allowing Cole to see the word 'INMATE' running down the right leg of her jumpsuit in bold black letters. Her expression shifted from sheer, unmitigated terror to hope, saying, "Where is she? Is she here?"

"She's on the ship. She couldn't exactly come with me—circumstances being what they are, and besides, we could only fab the one suit of armor in the time we had."

Talia's eyes went wide. "You *fabbed* that suit of armor?"

"Not me...I'm the pilot. Now, we should go."

Talia stood and shuffled out of her cell. Cole and Talia departed Detention Block C-12 to the accompaniment of seventeen other inmates shouting, "Me, too! Take me too!" through the doors of their cells.

By the time they traveled the short distance to reach the control station, Cole knew it would take forever to reach the shuttle as long as Talia remained chained...but he was afraid he'd harm Talia if he tried to remove the restraints with the heavy armor. Heavy armor wasn't known for its manual dexterity.

The injured officer wasn't hopping around anymore, but he still held his backside. Cole saw the red stain had spread across the entire seat of his uniform pants, and as the man turned, his expression suggested a moderate level of discomfort.

"Keys," Cole said, using the external speakers and pointed at Talia.

The standing officer's expression shifted to a mixture of anger and disgust. "The Aurelian Commonwealth Division of Prisons does *not* negotiate with terrorists!"

"Who said anything about negotiating?" Cole asked as he drew the one stun pistol to survive his charging entry into Detention Wing C and shot the officer. Cole's aim was a fluke, the stun charge striking the officer's head, and the officer fell to the floor twitching.

"What about you?" Cole asked, addressing the other officer still cowering behind the control station and whose reflection he could see in a convex mirror mounted in the far corner at the ceiling.

Nothing.

"I can see your reflection in that mirror, you know."

A trembling hand extended above the surface of the control station, holding a key ring.

"Hey, stupid...I'm in heavy armor. Yeah, I can open doors, but I'll just snap those keys like small pieces of wood. Get out here and unlock these restraints before I lose my patience."

The external microphones transmitted a soft shuffling sound, and soon, Cole saw the remaining officer crawling around the control station on his hands and knees. He scurried over to Talia's feet and removed the ankle chain, then started to turn away, still on his hands and knees.

"Hands, too," Cole said.

The officer hesitated but stood, and Cole saw a large wet spot dominating the crotch of his trousers. Cole *almost* felt sorry for the poor guy. The officer fumbled through unlocking the bracelets securing Talia's wrists to the chain around her waist and shuffled around behind Talia to unlock the waist-chain, removing it. When he was finished, the officer held up the waist-chain as if to offer it to Cole.

"Why would I want it?" Cole asked and fired his stun pistol once more. This stun charge, at least, struck the officer in the torso; the officer collapsed to the floor unconscious, amidst a clatter of chains, but without the overloaded neurons that produced constant twitching.

Talia stopped rubbing her wrists, saying, "May we go, please? I *really* want to leave. Besides, I think the twitching officer voided into his pants. It smells kinda bad in here."

Ouch, Cole thought as he retrieved the stun pistol from the officer at his feet and handed it to Talia. *I never meant for* that *to happen. Sucks to be him.*

Cole moved over and retrieved the stun pistol from the twitching guard to replace the one that didn't survive and led the way out of Detention Wing C. Cole turned the corner mere seconds before Talia and found a cluster officers waiting in riot gear. As they fired their riot guns and other weapons, Talia screamed and ducked back around the corner. The *Ping! P-P-Ping, Ping! P-Ping, Ping, Ping!* of the officers' weapons fire ricocheting off the heavy armor was an almost pleasant melody *inside* the armor, like the steady rhythm of a good rainstorm on sheets of tin. Alas...Cole couldn't stop and enjoy it; he had light-years to go before he slept.

Wading into the officers, Cole ripped their helmets off with one hand and stunned them with the other, intending *those* stun charges to strike heads. One officer had his finger on the trigger of his weapon, and when Cole stunned him, his finger twitched on the trigger, peppering the officer beside him and eliciting screams until Cole stunned the wounded officer. Cole ejected the weapon's charge pack as the officer's finger continued to twitch on the trigger, and once the hallway was secure, he called Talia to follow him.

Cole and Talia encountered no more resistance on their trek back to the shuttle, and they found it was *still* storming outside.

Cole slapped the control to raise the shuttle's boarding ramp as water from the storm streamed down the armor. Talia looked like a drowned rat. Moving to one alcove set aside for armor charging, Cole activated the sequence to open and shut down the armor. He turned and found a soaked Talia, her lips curled into a goofy adolescent smile as she lifted her eyes to meet his.

Cole gestured to the fifty unoccupied seats in the troop shuttle, saying, "Pick a seat, and strap in."

He turned toward the cockpit, but Talia took a tentative step toward him, the smile still dominating her expression. "May I sit with you?"

Cole shrugged. "If you want to...just don't touch anything."

He led the way to the cockpit and slid into the pilot's seat. Talia moved to the co-pilot's seat, and Cole noticed she kept glancing his way. Her clothes actually *squished*, rivulets of water running down to the floor as she tightened the straps around her torso.

The cockpit speakers chirped, and Srexx said, "Cole, the governor has ordered units of the planetary militia to your area. They are setting up heavy weapons and mobile anti-air platforms on the ridge overlooking the detention center now."

Cole keyed the commands to bring the engines online from hot standby, saying, "Srexx, where is Sasha?"

"She is in the command chair on the bridge, Cole."

"Put me through to the bridge, please."

The speakers chirped again.

"Sasha?"

"Cole! Is Talia with you? Is she okay?"

Cole grinned. "She's a little water-logged, but she's fine otherwise. Sasha, I need you at the weapons console. This shuttle handles like a pregnant whale on dry land; I can't evade weapons fire. I will try to talk them down, but if it comes to a fight, I'll need you to fire on the militia emplacements if you want your sister on the ship."

Silence.

"Cole," Sasha said, her voice shaky, "they're members of Aurelian military forces, same as me, like I already told you. I...I don't know if I can do it."

"Sasha, you have to make a choice. If they fire, it'll be your sister or them. Are you willing to continue supporting a government that put a dead-or-alive bounty on both you *and* your sister and allow your sister to die?"

More silence.

"Maybe they'll stand down?" Sasha asked, her voice soft and tentative.

Cole didn't think so, but he had other things to do right then. "Srexx, can you give me the frequency for the Aurelian militia units that have deployed?"

A comms frequency appeared on the shuttle's HUD.

Cole keyed that frequency into the shuttle's comms system and pressed 'Transmit.' The comms system put his active call with the ship on 'mute,' displaying the text 'Channel Opened' before Cole said, "Attention, Caledonian militia..."

"Who is this? This frequency is for official military use only. You risk imprisonment if you persist."

"Well, I'm the pilot of the shuttle about to lift off from the detention center. Transmitting on a restricted frequency is the least of my concerns right now."

"I don't know who you are, but you'd be well advised to power down your shuttle and surrender. Nobody has to die, son."

"You're right about that," Cole said. "I have a ship in low orbit over this region right now with battleship-grade starship weapons. If you fire on me, my weapons officer will wipe your people, your vehicles, and your gear off the face of the planet. I have no quarrel with Caledonia, the Caledonian militia, or any of your people. My only goal is to retrieve someone who has been unjustly accused and sentenced to death. Your life—and the lives of your people—are not worth this one-sided fight."

When no response came, Cole closed the channel, and the comms system reverted to the open link to the ship. He tapped the shuttle's console to select the ship as his destination and keyed the lift-off sequence. The shuttle was about fifty meters into the air when the high-pitched wails of missile alarms erupted from the console.

"Missile launch!" Cole said. "We have multiple missile launches!"

Cole's fingers flew over the console, initiating evasive maneuvers and priming what limited anti-missile defenses the shuttle had. He then took the second or two necessary to highlight the missile platforms that had fired and transmit their coordinates up to the ship.

The evasive maneuvers pressed Cole and Talia into their seats, as Cole watched the missiles move ever closer to the shuttle. The maneuvers and defenses were just not going to cut it.

Just as Cole drew breath to say, 'brace for impact,' multiple spires of green energy stabbed through the atmosphere from the ship's point-defense laser batteries, striking the missiles and vaporizing them.

Cole exhaled his relief.

Not even a second later, spires of green energy thicker than the shuttle was long struck one flank of the militia's deployment and swept up the ridge to the opposite flank, much like a barkeep wiping a towel across the bar. Cole gaped at the sight of starship-grade energy weapons being used for planetary bombardment; most ships carried dedicated bombardment weapons to avoid the energy beams dissipating into the atmosphere.

By the time the shuttle was leaving Caledonia's atmosphere, a massive cloud of dirt and debris had been thrown into the air above the detention center, despite the torrential downpour...and the ridge where the militia units had deployed was wiped clean, down to the bedrock.

CHAPTER SEVENTEEN

Low Orbit, Caledonia
   Caledonia System
   4 July 2999

The ship grew larger in the forward view, a matte black shape almost invisible against the backdrop of space. It floated immobile, occupying a geosynchronous orbit above the detention center and its region. The only light came from the green-tinged forcefields that maintained atmosphere on the flight deck.

Doctrine across Human space mandated that arriving craft come in from the aft end of the ship, as departing craft would exit from the bow...but the ship only had *one* shuttle. And Cole was piloting it. There weren't *any* other small craft to exit...or an air-boss, CAG, or whatever designation you wanted to apply to the officer in charge of small craft operations. So...since he was staring at the bow of his ship and saw no point in taking the few extra seconds to circle to the aft ingress port, Cole defied centuries of piloted flight doctrine and pointed the shuttle at the forward egress port.

The chirp of an open comms channel heralded Srexx's voice, "Cole, reconsider your current flight path."

"Why is that, buddy?"

"The bow forcefields are impervious from outside the ship to protect the flight deck from space dust and micrometeorite impacts during powered flight."

The ship was *very* close now, and Cole's fingers flew over the shuttle's console as he threw the shuttle into a nosedive that pushed him and Talia back against the straps holding them in their seats for a moment. Cole leveled out the shuttle as he passed below the ship and, passing the stern, turned back to the ship using a maneuver still referenced in pilot jargon as an Immelmann.

The cavernous expanse of the flight deck almost matched the profile of the cargo hold. It claimed the vertical space of an entire deck, the entire length of the ship, and three-quarters' the entire beam of the ship's decks. Even the most massive cargo shuttle flying in known space could use the flight deck and ingress/egress ports with ease.

Cole returned the shuttle to the lift that would take it back to the hangar deck, settling the craft onto its landing struts and powering down the shuttle as he lowered the boarding ramp. Talia fumbled a moment with the straps' release before she leapt up from the co-pilot's seat and almost sprinted out the back of the shuttle. After all, her big sister was waiting for her.

Except she wasn't...waiting, that is. Sasha was nowhere to be seen.

Cole watched Talia's shoulders fight between being squared with pride and being slumped in despair. He guessed an internal conflict between determination not to show weakness and disappointment and hurt that her sister wasn't here was becoming quite the battle royale. Cole used his implant to instruct the ship's computer to lower the shuttle into the hangar deck and secure it there, and he soon caught up with Talia where she'd stopped when she realized Cole wasn't with her.

"Come on," Cole said, walking past her toward personnel hatch. "She's probably still on the bridge, making sure the Caledonians behave."

· · ·

Cole led Talia off the flight deck and to the nearest transit shaft, marked with a symbol he learned was equivalent to the 'Up' arrow from human culture. The transit shafts spread throughout the ship carried the ship's crew between decks. Cole wasn't sure *how* the cylindrical shafts did their work, but certain shafts carried people up and others carried them down. A pair of mind-bogglingly large square shafts on the port side of the bow and starboard side of the stern conveyed large objects between the decks; these freight elevators used forcefields to create platforms for carrying cargo or equipment to the deck where it was needed.

Talia giggled like a small child as she floated up through the ship, even though she almost clutched Cole's hand. In short order, they stopped on Deck Eleven, where Cole led her to one of the main transit shafts that served the rest of the ship. From there, they floated up to Deck Three, which held the bridge, ship's offices, and the Captain's and XO's day-cabins...among many other compartments. Cole stepped out of the shaft and turned left, leading Talia to the center of the deck.

The starboard hatch to the bridge irised open to Cole's approach, and after passing through the passageway and stepping through the second hatch, he stopped as he took in the empty bridge. Cole took the few steps necessary to bring him to the weapons console and saw it was still in an active state, the ship's weapons—all of them, not just the bombardment units—still online and ready to fire.

"Where...where is she?" Talia asked, and Cole turned back to her and took in her expression, her lower lip trembling as her eyes' focus flicked from point to point around the bridge.

"I don't know," Cole said. "Let's get you somewhere you can change out of those wet clothes; you have to be freezing. I'll see if I can find her."

"Cole," Srexx said through the bridge's speakers.

"Yes, Srexx?"

"I have fabricated attire for Miss Talia. The attire is not designer clothing, but it possesses the virtue of being dry and warm."

Talia smiled, saying, "That sounds lovely, err...Srexx, but how did you get my sizes?"

"I used the shuttle's internal sensors to scan you. They are not as precise as the sensors aboard the ship, but had I waited for you to arrive, the clothes would not have been ready. If there are any deficiencies in the attire, we can correct them in a second fabrication run. They await you, Miss Talia, in the P-7 quarters on Deck One."

"I'll take you," Cole said and took a step toward the port hatch.

"Cole, if you will permit, I can guide Miss Talia to her quarters. I believe a situation is developing in our vicinity of which you need to be aware."

"What's going on?"

"Elements of the Aurelian Navy are moving to blockade the jump gate, while other elements of that organization move to intercept and bracket the ship. I have identified one vessel in the elements that approach us to be an assault ship."

"They're going to board us?" Talia gasped, her brow furrowing.

Cole chuckled. "If we were still here when they arrive, they'd be welcome to try. Go relax. Maybe get some sleep if you're tired. Once we're out of here, I'll see what's going on with Sasha."

Talia nodded, departing the bridge through the port hatch as Cole headed to the helm. As soon as he sat, he returned the weapons to their normal state of offline. Then, he brought up the sensor display, filtering it for local planetary space. It didn't take him long to identify the Navy ships; they were the only ships in evidence. Caledonia Control must have instructed all other vessels to vacate the area.

Even at the short distances involved at the planetary scale, the computer calculated there was still about fifteen minutes before the Navy intercepted the ship. Cole smiled. He switched to the helm controls, opening the navigation database to select Gamma Creoris as the ship's destination. Gamma Creoris was the closest star to Caledonia and uninhabitable; it didn't even possess any asteroids worth mining. The computer provided Cole a course toward Gamma Creoris that would take the ship from Caledonia orbit to a point on the solar system's periphery where he could engage the hyperdrive. Cole laughed when he saw his point of departure was nowhere close to any of Caledonia's jump gates.

"Boy, are *they* in for a surprise..."

Cole approved the course, locking it into the helm and brought the engines to ten percent. The ship lifted out of its low, geosynchronous orbit and aligned itself on course for the calculated departure point. Cole swiped his fingers up the throttle readout on the helm, bringing the sublight engines to full, and the ship shot away from the planet. The ship passed Caledonia's farthest moon just over fifteen minutes later and was beyond the planetary defense perimeter another fifteen minutes after that, its velocity surpassing even the Navy's fastest interceptors.

The Aurelian Navy found all of its elements, both the forces in planetary orbit and those heading for the jump gate Cole's ship had appeared to arrive through, unprepared and out of position.

"Srexx," Cole said.

"Yes, Cole?"

"The computer's telling me we have time before we can leave the Caledonia system. Where's Sasha, and do you know why she wasn't on the bridge or in the hangar bay to meet us?"

"Sasha fled the bridge for her quarters at the conclusion of the bombardment. She entered her quarters and has not left."

"What? Do you know why?"

"I do not believe I have sufficient data on human psychology to calculate a conclusion. However, I can show you the bridge visual log if you desire watching Sasha's tenure on the bridge. Perhaps you will see something I missed due to a lack of understanding."

"Show me."

The viewer on the forward bulkhead activated, displaying an image of the bridge as viewed from the aft bulkhead. The video played, its audio routed through the bridge speakers.

"Srexx, can you show me a split screen with half the display being the weapons console during the log and matched to the time-stamp?"

Without even pausing, the log recording compressed to the right-half of the viewer and realigned for the new aspect ratio, as the weapons console's readout appeared in the now-vacant left half. The weapons were offline, and even after Cole said Sasha might need to fire on the militia, the weapons remained offline.

"Srexx, there's something odd in the audio, something I can't quite hear. Can you isolate and enhance it?"

Srexx did not respond, but the ambient sounds of the log recording faded as one specific audio stream increased in volume and clarity. It was Sasha's voice; she was saying the same words over and over, almost chanting them, "Please don't fire. Please don't fire."

Cole watched Sasha flinch when his words, "Missile launch! We have multiple missile launches!" burst out of the speakers, but the weapons still didn't come online.

The weapons readout shifted to a focused, zoomed-in display of an area centered on the shuttle. The display showed the shuttle, the rather alarming number of missiles rocketing toward it, and the militia forces on the ridgeline.

Now, Sasha's voice came back, "Please be a bluff. Please be a bluff."

Cole watched as the missiles closed on the troop shuttle, and he felt the fear and tension he'd felt in the pilot's seat of an unarmed troop shuttle all over again.

Srexx's voice broke through the silence, saying, "Sasha, the shuttle will be destroyed. It does not have the survivability of this ship."

Cole watched Sasha flinch again, and all traces of indecisiveness and despair vanished; she became the officer that had risen to the rank of Lieutenant Commander and the position of second officer aboard the lead ship of her government's ground-breaking class of destroyer. Changes flashed across the mirror of the weapons console depicted on the left-half of the screen as Sasha's hands flew across the console on the right.

The weapons systems switched to Online—Charging at almost the same time the mass of missiles closing on the shuttle was selected as a target for the point-defense lasers. Point-defense systems designed for the starship scale have the effective range of intercontinental weapons batteries on the planetary scale, so the cluster of missiles closing on the shuttle was well within range.

While the point-defense lasers were still charging, Sasha selected the militia formations on the ridgeline, tapping one flank of their position and swiping to the opposite flank. She must've selected the starship's primary weapons, because the readout flashed a prompt, "Starship weapons inefficient inside a planetary atmosphere. Please confirm your firing plan."

'Confirm' on the prompt flashed three times—signifying it had been selected—before the prompt disappeared, just in time to show the point-defense lasers destroying the missiles closing on the shuttle. The weapons console then changed its configuration to a new readout titled 'Bombardment Control.' The display showed the entire planetary region around the detention facility with only the militia formation as selected targets. A portion of the weapons console readout displayed estimated casualties. The last line read, 'Estimated Non-combatant Casualties: 0 ± 0.'

The 'Confirm' on the readout flashed three times, and the selected targets vanished in progression from the southwest flank to the northeast. Sasha had deactivated none of the starboard weapons, and the overwhelming firepower of those munitions reduced the ridgeline and hilltop to a plateau of bare bedrock.

Cole watched Sasha slump back against her seat. She sat in silence for several moments before standing and striding from the bridge, her hands wiping her eyes as she left.

The ship's computer informed Cole it would be seven hours and sixteen minutes before he could engage the hyperdrive. Cole nodded and stood from the helm. He needed to go check on Sasha.

CHAPTER EIGHTEEN

In Transit to System Periphery
    Caledonia System
    4 July 2999

Cole approached the hatch that led to Sasha's new quarters. He tapped the control for the hatch-chime and waited. Nothing. He tapped it again, just in case. Several minutes later, still nothing.

"Life support systems indicate the compartment is occupied," Srexx said from a speaker above Cole's head. "No medical alerts have been triggered."

Cole nodded. He felt so torn on what to do. On the one hand, he wasn't sure it was his place to interfere. He hadn't even known Sasha all that long, and the case could be made it wasn't his business. And yet...

Cole hated seeing a member of his crew in such a state of distress, and that was what Sasha was now, a member of his crew. Lessons he'd absorbed at his father's knee and that continued to guide his life to this day demanded that he *always* put his people's welfare before his own...no exceptions. If Cole turned and left Sasha to fend for herself, he'd be betraying core family values passed down from parent to child across centuries. He would be betraying himself.

"*Haven*," Cole said.

"Yes, Cole-Captain?"

"Override the lock on the first officer's quarters...my authority."

"Compliance."

A red indicator on the hatch control panel blinked from red to green, and a small tone sounded as the hatch irised open. Cole stepped just far enough into the quarters for the hatch to iris closed, and when the hatch closed, it took the corridor's light with it.

"Why are you here, Cole?" Sasha asked from somewhere further into the quarters. Her rough, mournful voice sounded like it came from the left side of the space in front of Cole.

"I'm concerned about you, Sasha," Cole said. "I was expecting a sappy, tearful reunion on the flight deck, watching you squeeze the water out of Talia's clothes when you hugged her."

"It seems I have the teary part down. Besides, I knew you would see she was taken care of."

"Yeah, but me seeing she's taken care of is not her big sister being there for her. Sasha, what's wrong?"

"I fired on those militia units."

"I'm sorry, Sasha, but I don't understand. They were going to kill your sister."

"Lights to half," Sasha said, and the computer brought the compartment's lighting up to half. Cole saw she was curled up on the couch she'd ordered at Bremerton, her uniform in her hands. Her nose was red and swollen. Her cheeks were red, and her eyes puffy. She wore what looked like soft, fluffy pajamas.

"Did you know my family was one of the Founding Families of the Aurelian Commonwealth?"

Cole shook his head. "Not until you mentioned it the other day. I don't know much about the Commonwealth's history."

Sasha pointed to one chair opposite her, and Cole moved to sit. She waited until he had and said, "The colony Aurelius was founded in 2456, funded by five families. The senior member of that partnership was the Thyrray family. Since the day the colony ships first landed on what would become Aurelius, my family have been leaders, serving in both the Aurelian military *and* the civilian government. There was a room in the house where I grew up that had nothing but portraits of all the leaders in my family, dating all the way back to the Colonial Era."

Sasha stopped speaking as a fresh round of sobs ambushed her.

"Cole," she continued, "I don't have the words to express how anathema the idea of my father destroying the Aurelian Parliament is to who we are. He was always lecturing me on how I needed to prepare to take his place when I grew up...*in Parliament*. The thought I would ever fire on Aurelian personnel has never entered my mind; it hasn't even been a part of my world...until today. I have betrayed everything my family fought to build. I feel like my life is over."

Cole sighed. "I wish I knew what to say to convince you it's not, and besides, you haven't betrayed anything or anyone. Whoever kicked off the coup did that."

Sasha jerked her eyes up to stare at Cole. "What? What do you mean?"

"Sasha, while I've only known *you* for a few weeks, I haven't spent my life in a vacuum. You'd have to be a hermit on some rock out near Ghrexel space not to have heard of the Thyrrays of Aurelius. They already had a sizable portion of influence within the Commonwealth, especially among the average citizens; what would kicking off a coup gain your father? Absolute power? It's overrated. Every despot I've ever seen is all consumed with worry over someone deposing him and stealing his money and position of power, and believe me, I've seen a few. Your father had *more* power as a man of the people than any despot ever has...outside of their true believers...and that's probably why they framed him using the method and narrative they did. Sasha, whoever kicked off this coup knew he or she would never be successful as long as your family existed. Why else put such a high bounty on a lieutenant commander and university student? I've not seen any behavior to make me think Talia is that activist the news report on Bremerton made her out to be; matter of fact, I don't think she's dangerous at all."

A soft smile curled Sasha's mouth. "Yeah...Mom fought like you wouldn't believe to keep Talia out of Dad's world. She didn't want her growing up as one of the Thyrrays of Aurelius." The smile faded. "So, what happens now, Cole? Do my sister and I hide out on your ship the rest of our lives?"

Cole scoffed. "I won't lie, Sasha; I'm not invested in the fate of the Aurelian Commonwealth. That being said, if you want to investigate this, I'll help you. If you want just to disappear and let the Commonwealth self-destruct on its own, you and your sister are welcome aboard *Haven* as long as you want to be here. I'm already planning how to crew this ship with people who won't look at the two of you as a source for credits. Discuss the matter with Talia, and decide what you want to do."

The hatch irised open, revealing Talia standing in the corridor. She wore fresh clothes, and her hair—pulled back in a ponytail—looked freshly dried. She stepped through the hatch and walked right up to the couch where Sasha sat.

"I'm worried about you, Sooshie," Talia said, her voice soft and vulnerable. "I figured out why you're hurting. You didn't betray them, Soosh; they betrayed you...well...us. Besides, I lost Mom and Dad, too, and I don't want to be alone right now."

Sasha nodded a little, and Talia swarmed onto the couch, pulling her older sister into her arms and putting her head on Sasha's shoulder.

Cole held back a proud smile as he stood, realizing it was time for him to go. He was almost to the hatch when Sasha spoke.

"Leaving so soon, Cole?"

Cole turned and shrugged as the hatch opened behind him, saying, "I thought it's high time I explored the ship. You could've knocked me over with a feather when Srexx said we had a shuttle. Ping my comms code, or have Srexx call me if you need anything."

Cole turned and stepped through the open hatch, allowing Sasha and Talia their privacy.

———

Cole entered the bridge and headed for the helm console when Srexx spoke.

"Cole, have you forgotten the Caledonian SDF personnel on the flight deck?"

"Oh, damn." Cole sighed. "Yes, Srexx, I did. Thank you for reminding me."

Cole checked the helm station just long enough to confirm they were still on course for the system periphery. They were. The system periphery was a whopping 57 AUs away from the planet, and even at half-c, the trip still required fifteen hours, forty-five minutes, and change. Yep. Cole had time to visit the SDF people. He might even linger if the conversation was worth it.

Cole stepped through the hatch, entering the flight deck and seeing many heads turn his way. Once again, Lieutenant Mazzi came to meet him. This time, she came alone, and Cole wondered if he should consider this progress or equality since he had no one with him either.

"Sir," Mazzi said, giving Cole a nod.

"Lieutenant," Cole said, returning the nod.

Mazzi pursed her lips and shook her head. "No, sir, I don't think so...not anymore. Your friend Srexx has been kind enough to keep us apprised of the situation in Caledonia. His last update for us indicated the planetary governor's mansion was burning, and troops were fanning out through all the major cities. I don't know what this is now, but it sure as hell isn't the Aurelian Commonwealth. Every one of us here resigned our commissions or ended our enlistments. Your friend Srexx was kind enough to communicate our decision to Caledonia."

Cole grinned. "I bet he was. You should ask him sometime what *else* he sent along with your messages."

"Sir? I'm not sure I understand."

Cole shrugged. "Srexx is an AI, Mazzi, and he gets bored. It wouldn't surprise me to find out he hacked the datanet of the entire occupying force and was reading their communications for the fun of it."

Mazzi's eyes widened just enough to notice as her face blanked. After a couple heartbeats, she shook herself and said, "Sir, we've been discussing things, and we were wondering if you'd have time to talk with us."

"Sure. I came down to ask what you wanted to do, because we're leaving Caledonia with the Navy chasing an hour or so behind us. But we can loop around and let any life pods out for those who wish to stay."

"That's just it, sir. None of us do. We'd be hunted down for our participation in the SDF, given some of the news Srexx passed on to us, so there's not much reason to stay. We were hoping to discuss our options with you."

Cole's eyes scanned the people in the distance. "You have a nose count, Mazzi?"

"One hundred seventy-three, sir."

Cole nodded, staring at the deck off to his right as he thought. Pilot Country was out. The largest briefing room there only held a hundred, and he hadn't explored the decks he termed 'Marine Country.' It was possible there was a briefing room there large enough, but he didn't want to go looking for it right then. A thought floated to the forefront of Cole's mind, and he grinned. Sure...why not?

"Well, I do have someplace we can all sit and talk. It's not designed for the purpose, but everyone will be comfortable enough. And...the acoustics are excellent. It will take some herding and education, though. Go get me ten of your best people, and tell everyone else to gather at the starboard hatch. We'll send someone for them when we're ready."

Soon, Cole, Mazzi, and those ten people Cole requested left the flight deck. Cole took them to the transit shaft right outside the flight deck and gave them a crash course on them. He then left two people to control access to the shaft and keep everything in order, taking the rest up to Pilot Country. In Pilot Country, Cole left one person at the transit shaft and took everyone else to the main transit shaft closest to them, leaving one at the corner in sight of the shaft to Pilot Country and leaving a second at the transit shaft and taking everyone else up five decks to Deck Seven, the recreation deck. Cole left one person at the transit shaft there. He left the remaining five people at intervals in plain sight of the previous person—a trail of living breadcrumbs—all the way to one theater. This particular theater was set up for any media a theater might need: holographic movies, old-style 2D movies, and a stage for plays. Cole and Mazzi took the time to set up a few chairs on the stage where people could sit with Cole, while the majority would occupy the first few rows of the audience section. Then, they went back to the flight deck.

Everyone had gathered at the starboard hatch as Mazzi had told them, and Cole explained what they were doing. He warned them not to wander off, as it was a big ship that wasn't very populated; he made a point of saying it was possible for someone to get lost and die of starvation. A few chuckles broke out at that, but when Cole didn't share them, the humor faded.

Cole explained how to use the transit shafts and where they were going and that there were people along the way to keep them on the path. With all that said, he turned and left, taking Mazzi with him.

Over the next couple hours, Cole discussed many topics with the former SDF personnel. The immediate question was if he was hiring; Cole said he would be, but not just yet. He needed to recruit HR staff, first. One of the final questions of the discussion was if Cole had any bed space for them. Cole grinned and explained he did...as long as they didn't mind barracks housing.

———

Cole returned to the bridge after getting everyone in the barracks up on Deck Two. He checked the helm and saw they were still two hours and fifty-four minutes from being able to engage the hyperdrive. The elements of the Aurelian forces in pursuit were still hanging in there, but the distance between them and *Haven* was almost laughable now. Cole almost brought the sublight engines back to six-tenths' lightspeed just to goad them. He suspected the Aurelian ships could easily do even half-c, but their acceleration profiles were such that Cole and *Haven* would be long gone by the time they could even reach his speed, let alone try to overtake him. Cole guessed they expected him to alter

course for the jump gate at some point and thought to force an engagement then.

Yeah...that wasn't going to happen, and Cole would've enjoyed
seeing the expression of the task force commander back there when
Haven disappeared from their sensor feeds. Cole snickered and
thought about having the ship's computer turn off the transponder,
just to see what they'd do.

Instead, he told the computer to alert him if anything changed and
left the bridge via the port hatch, going to the captain's day-cabin. The
captain's day-cabin was just across the corridor from the port hatch for
the bridge and shared a head with the captain's office. The space was a
fraction of the captain's suite on Deck One, but it wasn't intended to
be much more than a place to sleep and relax while still being close to
the bridge.

After setting an alarm for two hours, Cole's last thought as he
drifted off to sleep was whether he'd wake up with Wixil curled up at
his side, purring away.

CHAPTER NINETEEN

Cole entered the bridge and went to the helm station. He didn't place his hands on the console. He took slow, deep breaths. After a time, he nodded and accessed the navigation database, then selected a new destination for the ship: Beta Magellan. Beta Magellan was once his home, back when he'd had a family. He didn't remember living in Alpha Centauri, even though his parents told him he'd been born there. Cole only remembered the colony on Beta Magellan; his parents told him once they'd founded the Beta Magellan colony when he was three.

Cole felt the ship begin a long, sweeping turn as it reoriented to the new destination, and he smiled at the thought of what his course change would do to the Aurelians who still pursued him. He hoped his new course caused at least a little frustration for them.

Cole leaned back in the seat for the helm and sighed. He never enjoyed going to Beta Magellan; it was little more than a huge graveyard and had been for thirteen years now...ever since his families (both his father's side *and* his mother's side) were massacred there. As far as Cole knew, neither the perpetrators nor the forces behind it had ever been found. The thought there might be one or more groups of people waiting to see if an heir would step forward kept Cole from using his family name. Besides, he'd never liked 'Bartholomew,' either.

In the days following his families' deaths, Cole had discovered something he was certain CIE never publicized...and for good reason. If you were the current head of the family or the designated heir, you could board any jump gate and shut it down at the master control. That little feature had allowed a thirteen-years-old and still furious and heartbroken Cole to shut down the only jump gate leading into Beta Magellan. For thirteen years, the only visitor to the system was Cole when he arrived to add to his stash on an asteroid near the jump gate... and now, he was going back to clean out the stash and convert all of it to credits.

Cole already had a 'buy an island and disappear' level of wealth, even if most of it now resided in *Haven*'s ship account. After liquidating the stash he'd accumulated over thirteen years of working, conning, and skimming the fringe of society, he'd have a level of wealth that would allow him to buy a *planet* and disappear. Well, maybe not an Earth-type planet, but definitely a small planetoid...

Three hours later, the control to activate the hyperdrive lit up, and Cole pressed it. *Haven* vanished from the Caledonia system, leaving a small task force of Aurelian Navy vessels out in the middle of nowhere with no one to pursue.

———

Cole sat at one table in the wardroom on the mess deck. The crumb-covered dishes and utensils of the evening meal rested on the tabletop in front of him. The hatch cycled behind him, and Yeleth walked into his view and sat across the table from him.

"So, I said we should discuss the Kiksaliks," Yeleth said.

Cole nodded. "You did. Where do we need to go?"

"Iota Ceti."

"Whoa. That's a rough neighborhood. Half the crime lords in Human space run multiple illicit enterprises out of there."

Yeleth nodded. "Yes, and it is the single largest slave market in the known galaxy. Between the criminals only preying on Clanless and concern over inciting a war with Humanity, my people have not moved against it. I don't know why the other races haven't stepped in; Iota Ceti is an unaligned system in unclaimed space."

Cole shrugged. "Probably the same reason your people haven't laid down the law. They're afraid we Humans would see it as the opening of a general offensive against Humanity...and we're mean when we're angry. Sasha wasn't wrong to fear the Solar Republic's response to evidence of the Commonwealth shooting down life pods. The Solars are known for their broad definitions of a war crime and a rather binary approach to what the response should be."

Cole fell silent as he thought about where they were in their journey to Beta Magellan. They'd left Caledonia just a few hours ago, so they were *closer* to Iota Ceti from their current location than they would be from Beta Magellan. Heh...and it wasn't like his stash was going anywhere. With the jump gate leading into Beta Magellan shut down, no one could conduct extensive surveys of the system and stumble across seven thousand kilograms of precious metals all sitting on pallets and waiting for retrieval. He sighed and stood.

"Mind if we continue this conversation on the bridge? I need to change course."

On the bridge, Cole went to the helm station and accessed the navigation database. Selecting Iota Ceti as a provisional destination proved his rough calculations; at 65 light-years (plus or minus), Iota Ceti was *far* closer than the 180 light-years they needed to travel to reach Beta Magellan. Cole keyed the command to change their destination to Iota Ceti and felt the ship pivot as it re-aligned to its new heading.

"Okay. We're headed for Iota Ceti now. The computer says it'll take nine-point-three-six-nine days to arrive. I'd like you to track down Mazzi, please; she should be on Deck Two somewhere with her people. Explain that we're about nine days from our destination and find out how their food is holding out. Part of me says to leave them on survival rations, until they pass an evaluation by Kiksaliks, but I can't do that.

Even if they would turn in either Sasha or Talia, that doesn't mean they're wholly bad people. No one is *wholly* bad...or wholly good. See about sharing our food with them."

Yeleth nodded once, saying "Yes, Captain," before she left.

Cole sat in the silence of an empty bridge—well, empty except for him—and went over everything he'd ever heard about Iota Ceti. Calling the system a 'rough joint' gave a bad name to rough joints everywhere. Unlike Caledonia, *this* would not be one of the 'easy' ones.

"*Haven?*"

"Yes, Cole-Captain?"

"Reconfigure the ship's transponder. Until further notice, we will broadcast we are the *Vilaxicar*. Say...Srexx called this ship a Class I Battle-Carrier. What can you tell me about it?"

"The Gyv'Rathi Stellar Directorate classified this vessel as a Class I Battle-Carrier, but its final outfitting was interrupted when they discovered Srexxilan had achieved sentience."

Cole leaned back against the chair as he crossed his arms. "Srexx told me about work stopping on the ship, but do you have records about what the final outfitting entailed?"

"The original design schematics for the Class I Battle-Carrier included additional dorsal and ventral-mount weapons emplacements that were never installed. Further, the schematics called for four batteries of dedicated bombardment systems that were never installed. Following what you would call a shake-down cruise, the Stellar Directorate had ordered that this ship undergo testing for implementing two additional shield layers."

Cole blinked. "This ship was supposed to have *five* shield layers?"

"Yes, Cole-Captain. Given the ship's current configuration, there is a significant power surplus with the generator operating at one-hundred percent. Implementation of the two, additional shield layers would assist with mitigating this...as would the installation of the additional weapons emplacements."

"How am I supposed to install those additional weapons or implement those extra shield layers? The Gyv'Rathi don't exist anymore, or I'm sure they'd object to me claiming this ship."

"This ship's primary data core contains protected archives that possess the schematics for all technology and devices intended to be installed on the Battle-Carrier, the intent being repair or replacement when beyond the range of support facilities."

"That's..." Cole's voice trailed off as he processed just what the ship's computer had said, and his eyes widened. "Holy shit! You mean you have the schematics for *every* part of this ship?"

"Yes, Cole-Captain."

"So...if I had a shipyard with a large enough construction bay, I could use those schematics to build another Class I Battle-Carrier?"

"Yes, Cole-Captain. As with all other aspects of this vessel, those schematics are now your property."

A vision of a fleet of ships like *Haven* appeared in Cole's mind, and that vision morphed into a fleet of ships based on the technology present in *Haven*. Cole's mind drifted back to what he'd seen in Caledonia, and he realized he wasn't sure if he wanted the technology behind *Haven* to be out 'in the wild' or not. Still, though, there was no reason not to complete *Haven*'s outfitting.

"*Haven*, please prepare a list of all materials required to fabricate the needed items for a full outfitting of this ship according to its original specifications. Send that to me and Yeleth."

"Unable to comply, Cole-Captain. Purser Yeleth does not have a compatible implant."

Cole sighed. "I think Srexx is slipping. Oh, and please change the *Haven* transponder. We are no longer a 'heavy transport;' change the class designation to 'Battle-Carrier.'"

"Yes, Cole-Captain."

"Srexx?"

"Yes, Cole?"

"How's the work coming along on implants for Yeleth and Wixil?"

"I have finalized the design, and I am running it through simulations of the Ghrexel neuro-physiology right now. This project is utilizing 43-percent of my total computational capacity."

Cole grinned. "Thanks, Srexx. Let me know when you're ready to proceed."

———

In 2763, a colony ship arrived in Iota Ceti. The settlers wanted nothing more than to build a life in a system far away from the developing governments, and they believed Iota Ceti would provide them a sufficient buffer of undeveloped systems to achieve their goal. The sole habitable planet in the system could best be described as arid, with only 30-percent of its surface taken up by water. Plains abounded, with some grasslands. Forests such as one might find on any Earth-type planet were almost nonexistent. A strange plant that absorbed moisture out of the air almost covered the world's landmasses, and it was through this plant that the photosynthesis cycle converted carbon dioxide to oxygen.

The colony flourished. As the years passed, traders heard of the settlement and added it to their routes, and in time, the system developed a thriving infrastructure beyond the planet.

Just five years shy of the colony's centennial, disaster struck. Though the people of Iota Ceti never learned the source, a mining consortium unearthed a fungus sealed up in a clay deposit. The clay was eye-catching, and soon, it (and the fungus captured throughout the deposit) spread across the system as artisans used the clay to fashion all manner of objects, from everyday items like bowls and cups to artistic pieces.

In a system-wide pandemic the likes of which Humanity had never seen, the entire population of Iota Ceti died within six months of encountering the fungus. Traders from out-system who were contaminated became the source of ghost-ship legends as infected personnel soon spread the fungus to the rest of the crew, who died before making their next port.

By 2950, the major criminal cartels re-discovered the system and put its abandoned infrastructure to their own nefarious use. It took several deaths before the criminals tried venting all stations, mining platforms, and space-borne smelters to vacuum, and when that didn't work, they hired several tankers to bring tens of thousands of kiloliters of a concentrated disinfectant that would dissolve any organic matter. After wiping down every surface and flushing all pipes, decks, air handlers, and plumbing, the criminals could use the system infrastructure without fear of death.

. . .

Iota Ceti System
   13 July 2999, 18:15 GST

Haven coasted toward the system primary as Cole watched the sensor display, "Old Time Rock And Roll" by Bob Seger and the Silver Bullet Band playing in the background. Enough traffic existed in the system that Cole had transferred the sensor display to the forward viewscreen, just to make sense of it. Few of the ships on scan broadcast a transponder beyond the various stations' sphere of control, and the more Cole considered the matter, the happier he was that he'd switched the transponder back to *Vilaxicar* for this little jaunt. He didn't want *Haven*'s name associated with what was about to happen.

"Cole-Captain?"

Cole sighed and shook his head. "Yes, *Haven*?"

"Passenger Madam Sasha desires entrance to the bridge."

"Pass her through."

Cole swiveled his seat around and stood, walking the short distance to meet Sasha as she walked onto the bridge. He had seen little of Sasha or Talia these past days. Cole figured they could use the sister time, and he wasn't sure what their plans or goals were. He moved to the stations along the aft bulkhead and retrieved two chairs, as he had for the conversation with Yeleth, and had them waiting when Sasha stepped through the inner hatch.

"Hi," Cole said, gesturing to the seats. "How are you and Talia doing?"

Sasha accepted the offered seat, shrugging. "It's tough, Cole...not knowing if our parents and brother are alive or dead, free or captured. I'd like to think this new Provisional Parliament would crow to the stars if they'd captured Paol Thyrray or Mom or my brother, but there's just no way to know. Even galaxy-changing news traveled slow before, and with the chaos we saw in Caledonia, that would make getting word out even more difficult if it's happening across the Commonwealth."

Cole nodded. "Yeah...it's not a good situation. My situation is a tad bit better. I mean, at least I know my families are dead."

Sasha blanched. "Your family is dead? Oh my goodness, Cole! I am so sorry!"

Cole shrugged. "It's not exactly current events. They've been dead for over ten years now. But somehow, I doubt this is what brought you to the bridge."

Sasha blushed. "No. Talia and I have been talking, and we were wondering if you have any place aboard for a naval officer and medical resident."

Cole blinked. "Resident? Talia just completed her residency?"

"Yes. She had a job waiting for her at a hospital on Aurelius before everything collapsed. She specialized in Internal Medicine. We've talked a lot since Caledonia, and there's no way we'll be able to go back to our old lives...even if we vindicate our family. People would still give us weird looks and be standoff-ish."

"Well, I need a first officer, and the hospital deck is a ghost town right now...a literal ghost town. I'd like to offer her CMO, but on a ship this size, that's equivalent to the Chief of Staff at a regional health center. My conscience is telling me to hold out for someone with that kind of experience, but we need doctors regardless."

"So, what do we need to do?"

Cole grinned. "You two may not thank me after you're 'read in' to the ship's company. The DNA sample is...well...not pleasant. Go get Talia, and I'll instate both of you at the same time. She'll be Interim CMO until we find someone with the experience we need. Will she have an issue with that?"

Sasha shook her head. "Nope. She knows she's just starting out in her career and that there are many people who've seen more than she has."

"Okay. As soon as you get back here with Talia, we'll take care of the 'paperwork.'"

CHAPTER TWENTY

Iota Ceti System
    14 July 2999, 09:35 GST

Sasha sat back in her seat and pushed away from the table. She shook her head. "I'm sorry, Cole, but this just will not work. One person *cannot* plan an operation of this complexity. Most of my experience is starship tactics, and...well..."

Cole leaned back in his own seat and chuckled. "I'm just the owner of the ship and a pilot. I have no formal training."

Sasha shook her head.

Cole worked his lower lip between his teeth for a few moments. "There is another option, but I'm not fond of it without the Kiksaliks to verify we can trust them."

"You mean the SDF folks on Deck Two."

"Yup."

Sasha grimaced. "Cole, I have to tell you. I'm not wild about using telepaths as some kind of truth or loyalty testers. That's dancing too close to invasion of privacy for me."

"I can see what you're saying, Sasha, but think about the situation for a moment. You and your sister represent twenty million credits right now...assuming the Commonwealth would pay up, which I doubt. But whether the Commonwealth can be trusted only comes into play *after* you or your sister are captured, and *that's* assuming they don't kill you out of hand. The bounties are 'Dead or Alive.' I will not put people in positions of extreme trust without knowing beyond a shadow of a doubt that I *can* trust them. There's no negotiating on this."

"I understand, Cole," Sasha said, sighing. "I do. It's just...that wasn't how I was raised."

"It wasn't how I was raised, either, but such is life. Do you want me to reach out to the SDF people?"

Sasha sighed, shrugging and lifting her arms to add emphasis to the shrug. "I don't see how we can't. I'm certain there's stuff we need to consider that I haven't even thought of. The more eyes and minds we have on this, the better plan we'll have at the end."

"Okay. See what you can do to start thinking outside the box on this. Maybe talk it over with Srexx. I'm going to Deck Two. Hopefully, I'll come back with some help."

———

"*Haven?*" Cole asked as he headed for the nearest transit shaft after leaving the briefing room.

"Yes, Cole-Captain?"

"Does the ship have any way to launch probes for remote reconnaissance? I realize the ship probably doesn't have any; I'm more interested in whether it has a way to launch them."

"The ship does not possess dedicated probe launchers, as that specific feature was present in the Class V Scout-Frigates. However—"

Cole's eyes gleamed. "I don't suppose there's a data core somewhere on this ship that has *those* schematics...is there?"

"Uncertain. Records indicate that the mass, unrequested downloading of data from the Gyv'Rathi DataNet is what led to the discovery of Srexxilan's sentience. It is possible Srexxilan has considerable portions of the Gyv'Rathi technical or scientific databases."

Cole entered the up-shaft and started his transit to Deck Two. "Okay. I'll ask him. Say...those missing weapons we were discussing... does the hull have the hardpoints to mount them?"

"Yes, including power conduits and control runs all staged. The ship lacks the physical weapons plus the time and work to install and calibrate them."

"*Haven*, did you have something to add to my question about the probe launchers? You said 'however' before I interrupted."

"While mediocre for its counterparts of the time, the stealth systems present in this ship should be effective against the sensor technology recorded to date."

Cole stepped out onto Deck Two, and he couldn't hold back his grin. "*Haven*, are you suggesting we use the ship to scout the system?"

"Since your reactivation of the generator, only this ship's passive stealth systems have been in use. At no time have the ship's active stealth systems been engaged."

Cole nodded. "Okay. Good to know."

Cole turned away from the transit shaft and started his search for Mazzi. Even though the people on Deck Two were no longer Caledonian SDF, they still fell into old habits and relied on Mazzi to be the liaison with Cole and Yeleth. Cole found Mazzi in a bunkroom, sitting on the sidelines of what appeared to be an arm-wrestling match. Cole wasn't that good at fast counts of people, but it looked like the entire contingent of former SDF personnel were present.

Most of the people he'd rescued in Caledonia had never seen Cole close-up to recognize him, but the two former officers and former enlisted recognized him, their heightened regard and almost-attention moved throughout the crowd like a wave. Mazzi hopped off the bunk where she was sitting and walked over to where Cole stood just a few feet inside the door.

"Hey, Captain," Mazzi said as she approached, an easy smile curling her lips and a slight twinkle in her eyes. "What's on your mind?"

"Well, to be honest, two things. First thing, I want your advice on something. Is there somewhere we might talk?"

Now, Mazzi grinned. "Why, Captain...are you stealing me away?" When Cole blushed a rosy shade of crimson, Mazzi lost her teasing tone, breaking up in silvery laughter. After a couple moments, she regained her composure *and* her playful manner. "Come on. There's another bunkroom a couple hatches down that's not even outfitted."

Cole's eyes went wide. "Oh, shit...I'm sorry! There are mattresses and bed linens and all that kind of stuff on pallets down in Cargo Two. I forgot all about them."

"Ah, so you *have* been holding out on us." When Cole blushed again and stammered his defense, Mazzi grinned again. "Relax, Captain. I understand. There were five people on this ship when you rescued us. You never expected to need almost two hundred mattresses and such so soon. We pulled the survival supplies and whatever else we could out of the life pods. At least all the extra space makes it better."

Cole stepped into the bunkroom and froze. The space was about fifteen meters long by ten meters wide. Fourteen quad-stacks of bunks (that is, four bunks in a vertical stack) lined the space, with an additional quad-stack at each end. Ladders ran up to each level every second stack, the idea being two stacks would share one ladder. A second hatch led out of the bunkroom across from the corridor hatch. Cole did the math in his head, and if he was right, this bunkroom alone would sleep sixty-four people.

"Wow," Cole said, giving the space a serious look-over, "this is kind of intense."

"And this is one of the smaller ones," Mazzi said. "Most of the berthing compartments on this deck make this one look like a closet. So, what did you want to discuss?"

"Uhm, right...yeah." Cole forced his attention away from the bunkroom and turned to Mazzi. "So, here's my situation. Remember the HR staff I mentioned? The only reason I want them to vet people before I hire anyone is that I have two people aboard who have been... targeted, shall we say...by the new Provisional Parliament on Aurelius. I don't know your people, beyond getting a raw deal in Caledonia by having their life pods shot out from under them, but at the same time, I don't want to hire anyone who'll make trouble for one of mine later on. Follow so far?"

Mazzi nodded.

"The HR staff I need to recruit are Kiksaliks. I don't know if you're aware, but they're telepathic. They'll be able to tell me whether a prospective recruit is going to sell out my people when I introduce them. The problem, there, is that my first officer and I have to plan an operation to free the Kiksaliks when one of the people involved in the planning—namely, me—has no operational experience beyond winging it and trusting to blind luck."

Mazzi winced.

"So, you see my conundrum, right?"

Mazzi nodded. "You need people with operational experience whom you can trust. Well, Captain, it so happens we're all grateful and appreciative you stepped in back in Caledonia, and every one of us signed up to be a part of something bigger than ourselves...something we could help build. Aurelian System Defense Forces aren't like so-called 'traditional' militaries. The Aurelian Navy is the *navy*; put 'em in a land battle, and they're hopeless. The Aurelian Army is in the same situation if you put 'em in a battle aboard a ship; they're just as likely to shoot something that will blow up themselves and everyone else. The Aurelian Marines are a *little* better, but not much. We SDF people train for *everything*: space, land, and air engagements. Some of my people in there were looking forward to their rotation to flight duty on Caledonia."

"Pilots...you mean like fighter pilots?"

"Yeah. They love it and were a little bummed they can't go back."

Cole broke out into a huge grin. "Boy, am I going to make their day."

Mazzi frowned. "I don't understand."

"The civilization that built this ship? They designed it as a battle-carrier. I'm not sure what all that entails, but the armament mix I've seen makes me think it's a serious cross between a battleship and a carrier. I mean, you saw how it shrugged off weapons fire from a small task force. Sure, they ate into the second shield layer...but it was the *second* shield layer. I still had another shield layer to go before they even touched my armor, and that's not counting the two *additional* layers the ship should have."

"But...but starfighters are impractical! Everyone knows that! The fuel tank and life-support system requirements negate the whole design of craft like fighters or bombers in space, not to mention the whole concept of attitude control and g-force limitations on human physiology."

Cole shrugged. "You're correct, as far as you go. But suppose you had the technology to build the life support systems in one of our hard-suits into a suit that looked like a bulkier merchant ship's jump-suit? Oh...and if you also had the technology to build propellant-less propulsion systems? And inertial dampening systems light-years beyond even our experimental tech? How about then? Are fighters and bombers still impractical? Mazzi, I've seen the hangar decks on this ship; I've walked through them. Hangar One has seventy-eight mainte-nance/lock-down spaces configured for two craft per space, and Hangar Two has spaces for dropships, assault shuttles, or cargo shuttles."

"Stars and space, Cole! Can you even afford to hire *that* many people?"

The current balance of the ship's account floated through Cole's mind, followed by the contents of his stash. Cole smiled. "Yeah...yeah, I can."

"Come on. We need to go talk to my people." Mazzi grabbed Cole by the arm and almost dragged him out of the bunkroom. "Say...who do you have aboard that the Provisional Parliament wants so bad, anyway?"

Cole grinned. "Sasha and Talia Thyrray."

Mazzi stopped cold, turning to stare at Cole half-way out of the hatch to the corridor. Her gaze was intent, deadly serious even. "Seri-ously, Cole? You better not be joking around here. That's not some-thing you joke about with Aurelians, especially working and middle-class Aurelians."

"Why is that, Mazzi?"

"Sure, the Thyrrays are aristocrats. Sasha's older brother probably gets more income from his trust fund by the week than I'll see in a year...well, at least he *did*. But no matter how rich the family was, no matter how many pies they had their fingers in, there wasn't one of them that didn't stand up for the people against the government and the special interests. When the major corporations or the other aristo-crats would get uppity or out of line, the Thyrrays were always there to remind them that the government served *everyone*...not just those who could afford to pay more. That whole business about Paol Thyrray leading an attack that destroyed Parliament? That's utter nonsense. You ask anyone who's ever worked for a living; every single one will tell you the same thing. Paol Thyrray is no traitor, and neither is anyone in his family. They've built their power and their wealth *protecting* us. The Thyrrays are the Colesons of the Commonwealth, even if that era is past now. So, you tell me straight, Cole. Do you really have Sasha and Talia Thyrray on this ship?"

"Sasha's my first officer. I rescued her back in Pyllesc when someone ejected her out of an airlock from the *Adran Jordeen*. The only reason we came to Caledonia in the first place was to rescue Talia. She was finishing up her residency after med school there, and she signed on to be one of my doctors on the hospital deck."

Mazzi's eyes burned with a zealous fire Cole hadn't seen before. She grabbed his arm once more and pulled him again. "Come on. We need to have you talk to my people."

In the end, Mazzi's people wouldn't listen to Cole. They demanded proof that Sasha and Talia Thyrray were alive, well, and on the ship. Cole sighed and planted himself on a bunk.

"Srexx? Could you have Sasha and Talia come to Deck Two, please? And give them directions to my location once they're on the deck?"

A few minutes later, the sisters stepped into the mess-hall. Everyone present surged to their feet—even Mazzi—and Cole feared Sasha and her sister were about to be mobbed. But his fears were unfounded. The former SDF personnel formed an impromptu receiving line, greeting each sister and shaking their hands and expressing how relieved he or she was that they were alive and well and safe. Talia looked a little overwhelmed by it all, but Sasha showed the training and experience she'd gained at her father's side, smiling and nodding as she shook each person's hand and accepted their well-wishes.

When there were only twenty or so at most waiting to greet Sasha and Talia, Cole noticed Mazzi standing just outside his personal space.

Her eyes scanned her people, her expression evaluating. After a few moments, she shifted her attention to Cole.

"You have a start on your crew, Cole. These people would walk through fire for you now." Mazzi scoffed. "Forget fire. They'd walk through lava for you and those girls; guess you didn't need your mind-readers after all."

Cole grinned. "Oh, I still do...just not for your people." He didn't have the heart to tell her he would still run her people by any Kiksaliks he recruited just to confirm their devotion to Sasha and her sister. Something a friend had told him many years before: trust...but verify.

CHAPTER TWENTY-ONE

Now that Cole was building something of a crew, he looked into all the positions aboard that needed staffing, with an eye toward the immediate future of assaulting the slave market in Iota Ceti. Most of the former SDF people filled out roles on the weapons deck or in the signals intelligence compartment, which also happened to control the ship's stealth systems. What Cole wasn't expecting out of his impromptu recruitment drive, however, was finding a chief engineer. Maxwell Logan looked every inch the proverbial grizzled, no-nonsense veteran, and he acted the part, too...until he found out the ship was powered by a singularity-based generator and used propellent-less propulsion. Then, you would've thought he was a kid sitting before a mountain of presents on his birthday. He almost *begged* Cole to be the ship's chief engineer.

Alessandra Mazzi came aboard as the weapons/tactical officer. Wixil was a little put out about that, until Cole said he was hoping she'd be the assistant under Mazzi. Mazzi knew Wixil had been with Cole longer than she had been, and she recognized Wixil had far more youthful enthusiasm than training and experience. She demonstrated her skill with people (and adolescents) when she accepted Cole's ruling on what would have been her prerogative to choose her assistant without batting an eye.

The people Cole had rescued in Caledonia weren't a perfect fit across the board, though, and he had teams of spacers or other ratings overseen by NCOs reporting to Sasha, like the eight spacers who signed up for small craft maintenance when Cole had no small craft beyond the troop shuttle or the five people who wanted to be starfighter pilots. It was not an ideal situation.

Iota Ceti System
   15 July 2999, 10:57 GST

Cole sat at the helm. Mazzi and Wixil sat at the weapons station. A person whose name Cole still couldn't remember sat at the comms station. Sasha sat in the command chair.

"All decks, all sections, report ready," the person at comms said.

Sasha shook her head. "This is so odd, Cole. Are you sure you don't want this seat? There are at least three different pilots in the Caledonia people. The first officer shouldn't be giving the captain orders."

Cole swiveled around to face Sasha, grinning. "You're just going to have to suck it up for now. I have no idea how to be a captain, but I *do* know how to be a pilot. You, on the other hand, *know* how to be a captain. We'll figure it out, but for right now, everyone is where they need to be. Let's do this."

Sasha took a deep breath and nodded. "Weps, bring all stealth systems online."

"Aye," Mazzi said as her fingers flew over her console, showing Wixil everything she did. Within moments, the bridge's lighting dimmed by about a third and status lights around the bridge turned blue.

"Blue?" Sasha asked.

Cole grinned. "Yep. Blue for full stealth, yellow for alert status, and red for battle stations."

"Yellow for alert status and red for battle stations...that sounds so familiar."

Cole's grin grew even wider. "What can I say? Sometimes, the oldies are goodies. We needed visual cues for different operational statuses anyway, so why not? The default settings were all shades of green."

Sasha shook her head and sighed, before breaking into a grin of her own. "Okay, Captain...take us in."

Cole swiveled back to the helm station and programmed the flight path before setting a desired velocity of one-tenth-c, or ten percent of light-speed. They were fifteen AUs from outermost station, having drifted that far into the system on a ballistic course. Someone had suggested drifting into the inner system as part of a group of asteroids and comets that would pass right amidst the stations they wanted to recon, but Cole didn't like that idea. He didn't want to rely on trust that the ship wouldn't get pounded to pieces, and besides, who knew if the mineral composition of the asteroids and comets would interfere with the ship's sensors?

Cole leaned back in his chair at the helm. The countdown timer on their flightpath showed it would be a little over twenty hours, just to reach the most stressful part of the recon. It would be a long couple of days.

"Cole?" Srexx spoke over the bridge speakers.

Cole pulled his attention away from the radio communications he was perusing. The people in Iota Ceti liked to broadcast in the clear with no encryption, and it was making for fascinating reading...in a macabre kind of way.

"Yeah, Srexx?"

"We may need a new plan. A convoy of ships is arriving for a slave auction."

Sasha looked up. "Why isn't Sensors saying–"

The person stationed at the sensor console almost slapped the earbud in his ear. He listened for a moment and called out in 'Bridge

Voice,' "Status change! Thirteen contacts, designated Sierras One through Thirteen!"

The person at the sensor console fell silent, listening to his ear bud again, and Srexx said, "I would posit that the delay came from latency in human processing, Madam Sasha. I process data faster than organic people."

"Sierras One through Thirteen are heading in-system on a flight profile suggesting a convoy of freighters or troop-transport-like ships," the former SDF officer at Sensors reported. "Ah...there might be a warship or two in there. Ma'am, my people are still learning the systems; even with the read-outs translated to Standard, that doesn't mean we understand what they're telling us."

"Srexx?" Cole said.

"Yes, Cole?"

"Work up a training plan for each section aboard-ship. Everything from sensors to comms to maintenance...everything. If we will have people aboard and not re-work the ship to give you greater control, the people need to understand their duty assignments."

"Yes, Cole. I shall devote one-quarter of my tertiary node to preparing those training plans."

"Oh...and don't forget to say hello to your lesser-evolved cousins as we come in range."

"Naturally not, Cole," Srexx said. "Have I ever?"

"'Lesser-evolved cousins?'" the person at sensors asked.

"He meant the computers on the ships and stations, Haskell," Mazzi said. "Cole just asked Srexx to hack every computer in-system."

"But that's..."

"One-hundred-eighty-six separate computational nodes," Srexx said. "The most significant challenge will be compensating for speed-of-light latency in communications. Given the level of technology present, I have to restrict myself to basic radio communication."

Haskell at the sensors station swiveled to face the rest of the bridge, his expression a mixture of concern and disbelief.

Cole smiled and shrugged. "What can I say? Srexx gets bored."

"Focus, people," Sasha said.

"I am," Cole said, his voice distant. "I don't see anything for it. Recon has just gone out the airlock. If we take the time to recon and then devise a plan based on that recon, half the people we're after could be long gone. So...do we want to masquerade as prospective buyers at the slave auction? Or do we want to crash the party?"

"Cole, you need to see this," Srexx said. "The comms network near the jump gates just received an update."

The forward viewscreen activated, displaying a feed from INN, the Interstellar News Network. The image was an orbital picture of a region on a planet with a structure centered in the view, and both Cole and Sasha recognized the region at once. It was the detention facility on Caledonia.

"This is Ingrid Patel, INN. The provisional authorities in Caledonia are refusing to comment, but at this time, we can confirm that Talia Thyrray is no longer in the detention facility you see on the screen. I've spoken with several people who told me their stories on the condition of anonymity. All of those accounts agree on one thing: one individual wearing heavy armor styled like the Aurelian Marines entered the detention facility with forged transfer orders. When the orders were exposed as a forgery, the individual—this Lone Marine— retrieved Talia Thyrray with no regard for any threat the staff of the facility might pose. We have obtained copies of the security feeds that show even the Riot Response Unit posed little threat to the individual, their ammunition bouncing off the armor like BBs. Military Affairs consultants with INN have highlighted that the heavy armor shown in the security feeds does not perfectly conform to the design used by the Aurelian Marines, merely being like it in general form and colors. That and other details lead our consultants to conclude the individual inside the armor was not Aurelian military. No one is speculating as to the motivations or goals of this Lone Marine. We simply must wait to see if he—or she—surfaces again. This is Ingrid Patel, INN."

Cole grinned as an idea came to mind. He swiveled to face the rest of the bridge. "Okay, gang...new plan. Srexx, how long would it take to change the marking on that armor?"

"Two hours at most, Cole."

"Sasha, which governments still have marines as branches of their armed forces in space?"

"Almost all of them. Well, the Asiatic Concordat doesn't call their unit 'marines,' but everyone else does."

"Srexx, once we're closer with less light-speed lag, look up the colors of the Sirius Imperium. There should be a library computer somewhere in this system. It was an actual colony a century ago or so. *Haven?*"

"Yes, Cole-Captain?"

"Put me on ship-wide address."

The bridge speakers chirped to indicate the channel was open.

"Attention, all hands; this is the captain." Cole grinned and almost giggled. "I've always wanted to say that. Anyway...our plan for Iota Ceti has changed. The arrival of a convoy and announcement of an impending slave auction has pushed our timetable. Our new goal is to free as many of the slaves as we can, and if we can incite a system-wide revolt...well...that'll just be a bonus. We will announce specific roles in the new plan over the next few hours. That is all."

Cole turned his attention back to his first officer. "Sasha, did we assign anyone to any of the fabricators?"

"Yes, I believe so. I think it was Fabricator Twelve, manufacturing projectiles for the missile bays."

"Pull them off that, and move them to whichever fabricator Srexx used to make that suit of heavy armor. I need ninety-nine suits of armor for our boarding party. The armor needs to be stealthy but protective. I know...diametrically opposed concepts. Tell them to ask Srexx for input if they need it." Cole remembered Mazzi had addressed the guy at the sensors console as Haskell. "Haskell?"

"Yes, sir?"

"I want you and your team to concentrate on finding where this slave auction will happen. Then, I want you to see if there's a mainte-nance airlock or something we can use as a point of ingress far away from the auction but close to the slave pens. By the time you need deck plans, we should be close enough for Srexx to tell you what was served in the mess hall for breakfast. Don't be afraid to ask him for information."

Haskell nodded once. "Yes, sir."

Cole clapped his hands, grinning once more. "All right, people; let's do this."

CHAPTER TWENTY-TWO

Iota Ceti System
    15 July 2999

They could only fabricate thirty-five suits of armor. They ran into a materials shortage while number thirty-six was mid-fabrication. These suits of armor looked nothing like Cole's 'Lone Marine' heavy armor. They were far more streamlined and flexible, looking very similar to Cole's spacesuit...all black with the slightest hint of a green reflection at the proper angle.

Once they discovered there would only be thirty-five suits, Cole set Srexx to working on implants. Yeleth and Wixil already had their own implants based on Gyv'Rathi technology, and most of the new personnel had their own implants, similar to what Cole had possessed when he first arrived at the mining camp. Those pre-existing implants allowed Srexx to refine the interface methods with his implants, and soon, everyone cycled through a treatment room on the hospital deck. Human implants were removable, allowing for improved technology over a person's life; Srexx's implants could not be removed once they were integrated. The good news, however, was that any refinements or advancements or new technology could be delivered to an implant as a software patch.

Cole sat at the helm station on the bridge. It was beyond quiet. The tension was almost a physical presence lounging at a console. Everyone was waiting for Cole to ease the ship to the maintenance dock on the station where the slaves were held. Somehow, they'd maneuvered into the heart of the system's infrastructure without detection. Ships, stations, cargo shuttles, runabouts...Iota Ceti was one of the busiest systems outside a major shipping head, and there was a ship larger than any other mobile craft in the system hiding amid all the activity.

A flashing control on the helm console drew Cole's attention. The 'Engage Docking' control lit up and was now active. Cole smiled.

"Srexx, do you have the station's computer?"

"It would worship my feet...if I had feet."

Cole frowned and looked up at the speakers. "That's a little weird for you, buddy. What have you been reading?"

Silence.

Resolving to investigate Srexx's odd phrasing later, Cole pressed the control that would instruct the computer to dock with the maintenance airlock on the station. When the words 'Docking Complete' scrolled across that status window of the helm station, Cole swiveled to face the rest of the bridge.

"And we're docked."

Everyone cheered. It was subdued and quiet, as if they might be discovered if they were too loud, but it was still a cheer.

Cole stood and noticed Wixil was missing from the weapons station, but like Srexx's reading list, that would also have to wait for another time.

"Sasha, you have the ship. I'm going to the hangar deck to retrieve my armor from the shuttle. I'll meet the boarding party at the..." Cole cast a quick look over his shoulder to the docking interface. "...port airlock on Deck Two."

———

Cole *whine-thump*ed his way down the port-side main corridor. He took the cargo shaft up from the hangar deck instead of trying to navigate the standard transit shafts. He wasn't sure the armor would fit, and he would've hated to get stuck somewhere.

When he arrived at the suit locker for the port airlock, Cole didn't find thirty-five armored people waiting for him. He found thirty-*seven*, and two of them had tails and pointy ears.

Cole accessed his implant and opened a conference channel with both Yeleth and Wixil. They accepted at once.

"Well, at least I know why Wixil wasn't on the bridge when I left."

"We're going with you, Cole," Wixil said.

"The last time I checked, Wixil, you're still sixteen."

"Yes," Yeleth said, "but among our people, sixteen is old enough to hunt...with parental supervision. Besides, you need us."

Cole narrowed his eyes at the two Ghrexels, even though he knew they couldn't see him. "By any chance, would those two suits of armor you're wearing have anything to do with that materials shortage the fabrication team reported?"

Silence. They must've been studying Srexx.

Cole sighed. "Fine. We're on a tight enough timetable as it is. You're with me."

No matter how many times he did it, the cold claws of anxiety grasped for Cole's heart every time he stood in the ship's personnel 'dock.' Looking down, up, or to either side and seeing the green shimmer of a force-field being the *only* thing between him and vacuum did nothing healthy for his blood pressure. Cole hoped he'd get used to it eventually—or at least approach it with something other than controlled anxiety—but for now, there was a job to do.

Cole *whine-thump*ed his way across the force-field to the outer hatch of the maintenance airlock just as the notification of an incoming call from Srexx appeared on his armor's HUD. Cole accepted the call.

"Have you reached the airlock, Cole?" Srexx asked without preamble.

Cole nodded, even though no one could see it. "Yeah, Srexx. I'm standing there now."

"The only way to open the airlock without sounding any internal alarms or notifications is to use the manufacturer's override. I found the code buried in the station's central computer. You'll need to remove the maintenance panel, which should be to the right of the hatch from your perspective."

Cole found the panel and, when the latch didn't release, pried a corner of the panel away from the housing to get a better grip, then ripped the panel away in a shriek of tortured metal.

"I'm looking at the maintenance controls, Srexx. The panel doesn't appear to be powered."

Silence.

"Uh...Srexx?"

"Cole, it appears this airlock is either inoperative or off-line. The station schematics show it, but the maintenance system that shows every active device or system does not. One moment..."

Cole wanted to sigh. So much for the amazing stealth mission.

"Ah, yes. Cole, I have located the issue. The engineering sub-system that controls power distribution throughout the station has been compromised and modified, almost as if someone took a virtual hatchet and cut through the code and slapped disparate pieces together. It is a wonder the power distribution system works at all."

"Okay. So...what do we do?"

"Well, we can either attempt cutting through the outer and inner airlocks—"

"Srexx, you do remember this is a *rescue* mission, right? Do we really want to vent the deck to vacuum when we leave?"

"—or I can overwrite the spliced code with a version I found in a protected archive and reboot the power distribution control system."

"That sounds like a great idea, Srexx. Let's do that."

"Cole, are you certain? It is difficult to predict what will be affected. Would you like me to conduct an analysis of the station's schematics versus the power distribution system as it is now?"

"Srexx...buddy...we're not exactly endowed with an unending well-spring of time here. So, we turn on a food dispenser along with the airlock. Big deal..."

"Cole, the analysis I mentioned would take less than—"

"Srexx! Look, I appreciate your thoughts and feedback, but we're past that now. Overwrite the modified code with the version from that protected archive, and reboot the power distribution's control system."

"As you wish, Cole."

Thirty seconds of silence seemed like ages, and then, the maintenance panel lit up. Then, the entire airlock lit up, including the tell-tales showing a hard docking seal. Cole reached out and tapped the control to open the airlock out of habit. The hatch opened. Cole smiled and keyed in the maintenance override that would keep the hatch open until disengaged.

The compartment before them was the actual airlock itself, the space where suited people would wait for the system to either pressurize or depressurize during a cycling of the lock. Since the airlock detected a hard docking seal, the tell-tales and control panel of the inner airlock were active as well. Cole crossed the three-meter space and keyed the maintenance override to hold the inner hatch open also, and it opened without hesitation...revealing a piece of solid metal that covered the interior side of the hatch coaming and extended past the dimensions of the open hatch.

"What the hell?" Cole said.

"What is it, Cole?" Srexx asked.

"I opened the inner hatch of the airlock, and I'm staring at some kind of metal bulkhead."

Silence.

"There is nothing on the station schematics or listed in the maintenance logs about covering the maintenance airlock on this deck, Cole."

Cole closed his eyes as his hands clenched into fists, the hands of the heavy armor duplicating his action. Caledonia was easy, so easy. Was it too much to hope this operation went as smoothly? Cole sighed.

"Hey, Srexx..."

"Yes, Cole?"

"Do we have any plasma torches or something else that can cut through this metal?"

"One moment..."

"Srexx, I'm going to put your call on hold and speak to the rest of the boarding party to let them know what's going on."

Without waiting for an acknowledgement, Cole accessed his implant, switched his call with Srexx to Inactive, and initiated a group-wide call with the thirty-five Humans and two Ghrexels that were standing just outside the outer hatch.

"Okay, team...here's where we stand, in more ways than one. Srexx had to reboot the control system for the station's power distribution grid to bring the airlock online, but someone welded or otherwise affixed a large, metal plate over the inner hatch. I asked Srexx if we have any plasma torches or something like that to cut through the metal."

"There are cutting torches in the life pods on the flight deck," someone said over the group channel.

"Excellent," Cole said. "Thank you for speaking up. Grab as many people as you need to bring several here. I want to be sure to have backups in case one runs out while we still have a need for it."

Cole switched out of the group channel and back to the call with Srexx, saying, "Hey, Srexx?"

"Yes, Cole; it appears that the life pods—"

"Forgive me for interrupting you, buddy, but I've already sent people to bring cutting torches from those life pods."

"Ah. Very good, then."

"Srexx, while we're waiting on those torches, what's happening in the system? Is *Haven* in any danger of being discovered?"

There was a slight pause before Srexx replied, "I do not believe so at this time, Cole. The slave convoy that prompted our accelerated timetable is still on course for the station, and none of the traffic around the station has come close enough to observe the ship with a visual inspection...not that the ship would be easily observed. Still, there is always the chance that some hapless pilot would fly right into our hull without realizing we are here."

"If that did indeed happen, what's the risk to the ship?"

"Negligible, Cole," Srexx said. "Based on the construction materials I have observed in use in this system coupled with the disturbing tendency to skip proper maintenance, I predict any craft colliding with us would pop like an egg...as long as it was equivalent to a personnel shuttle in size or smaller."

"Heh...let's hope you're right."

The time passed in companionable silence while Cole and the remaining boarding party waiting for the cutting torches to arrive. Cole was just about to switch over to the group channel and ask what was taking so long when he saw the assembled crowd part like the Red Sea before Moses, permitting a group to approach the airlock with the awaited cutting torches. One member of the party carried four magnetic grips, and Cole smiled at the forethought.

Cole stepped as far aside as he could to allow his people to work. He watched on in silence as two people attached the grips. Then, they started the process of cutting through the metal plate.

They went through three cutting torches before a section of the metal plate (sized to match the inner hatch) came free. The same two who had cut through the metal plate with the torches took hold of the grips and pried the plate free. The edges still glowed red as they maneuvered the cut-out into the airlock and leaned it against the bulkhead between the inner and outer hatches.

Cole moved to look through the new hole and felt like screaming. Someone had turned what should've been an access corridor into a storage room. Crates small enough to be man-portable lined the space, and a thin path just wide enough for an unarmored person connected the metal plate that had served as the back 'wall' to a jury-rigged hatch nine meters away.

Checking to ensure his microphone was active and that he was active on the group channel, Cole said, "Okay. I need someone to get in there and do a rough survey of what's in those crates."

"Are we taking plunder, Captain?" some asked, producing some chuckles.

"I wasn't planning on it," Cole replied. "If that stuff isn't life-critical, like medicinal pharmaceuticals, I'll lock the two airlock hatches open, and we'll all troop back to the ship and wait for an explosive decompression to clear the way. We're not stevedores, dammit."

A cursory examination revealed the crates held an assortment of illegal drugs, and Cole sighed, shaking his head.

"While you're in there, give that hatch coaming a look-see. Do you think it will hold against decompression?"

The crewperson already at the far end of the storage space moved closer to the hatch coaming and examined it. After tracing the joins all the way around, the crewperson turned.

"Captain," a new voice said across the group channel, "this hatch has to be some of the shoddiest work I've ever seen. I doubt it would stand up to a rambunctious toddler, let alone the stresses of explosive decompression."

"Roger that. Hold where you are," Cole said and muted his internal microphone.

Taking a deep breath, Cole spent ten seconds blistering the inside of his armor's helmet with the kind of profanity even the most dedicated enthusiast would avoid. Frustration lessened, Cole reactivated his internal microphone and placed a call to the bridge.

"Bridge, Sasha here."

"Sasha, I need some able-bodied souls to serve as impromptu stevedores. Someone thought it a good idea to weld a plate over the inner hatch of the airlock and convert the airlock's access corridor to a storage space. The hatch coaming they installed to control access won't stand up to my preferred method of cleaning the space, so we're going to move everything over to the ship and eject it to space later."

"Wait...you mean you're not even into the station yet?"

"Nope. The way this mission has gone so far, I wouldn't be surprised to find half the Aurelian Marines on the other side of that coaming...when we finally make it through sometime next year."

Cole thought he heard some restrained giggles but chose to be the bigger man.

Sasha replied, her tone saturated with mirth, "Oh, Cole...I shouldn't laugh, but it's difficult, so difficult. I'll get you some extra bodies soonest. What are we moving?"

"Illegal drugs."

This time, Sasha wasn't the only person howling with laughter over the comms call.

They spent thirty-five minutes moving the crates out of the improvised compartment, and the longer they spent, the more Cole seethed in silence inside his armor. All he wanted to do was rescue some slaves who he hoped to hire. It shouldn't be *that* difficult. At long last, though, the way was clear to enter the station.

Cole approached the hatch that he hoped would be the final barrier between him and his goal, and he couldn't keep from smiling as he took a closer look at it. In fact, he felt like cheering. It was a manual hatch! No keypads, no locking mechanism...nothing like that. Just a gear-driven hatch operated by a circular hand crank on the hatch coaming.

Grasping the handle with the right hand of the armor, Cole began working the crank and watching the hatch edge its way open with every revolution of the handle. Cole activated the armor's external microphone as the hatch opened wider to find out if there was anything to hear from whatever lay beyond.

The first thing Cole noticed was that the hatch appeared to be silent. While there was a slight whine of powered servos as he operated the crank, overall, there wasn't much noise from the hatch itself. Then, he heard it.

"What do you mean 'you don't know?' You're the engineer on this hunk of metal. Don't you dare stand there and tell me you have no idea why all the lights are on down here now." The voice was a male tenor with a slight nasal tone.

"Look," another voice said, this one on the deeper end of tenor, "just because I'm the best engineer you have doesn't mean I'm an actual engineer. I don't even have command codes to the engineering systems. Why are you so wound up about the lights anyway? They're just lights. So what if they came on after all these years?"

"You're a damned fool, you know that?" Nasal Voice said. "It's not just the lights on this level. Whatever reset the lights also powered up the hatch on the space we've been using for an armory on this deck. We have three hundred people coming here for an auction over the next twelve hours, and our extra guards can't even access their weapons! Whatever the hell this is...you need to fix it."

Just then, the hatch reached the point where it was open the widest, and as Cole cranked the hatch through its last few degrees of opening, the mechanism—either the hinges, some gears...something— filled the air with the kind of high-pitched squeal only metal grinding against metal can produce.

"What the hell was that?" Nasal Voice said, his words carrying across the now eerily quiet space.

Two people stepped around a corner in the corridor nine meters in front of Cole. They were a mismatched pair. The one closest the bulk- head was a tall man and rail thin. The other came up to his associate's chin, and he bore the musculature of someone who spent his days doing heavy, manual labor.

"Where the hell did they come from?" the tall man—who Cole now identified as Nasal Voice—almost shouted. "Quick! Alert everyone we have intruders. They must be here to steal the slaves!"

That's when Cole realized none of his people had weapons.

Cole charged through the open hatch putting the combined power of the armor's servos, his composite weight (Cole plus armor), and his momentum into a left hook aimed at Nasal Voice's right cheek, just in front of his ear. Nasal Voice ducked at the last second, bringing the armor's fist into contact with his skull just behind the temple.

Cole heard a ghastly **_CRACK!_** at the moment of impact, and Nasal Voice's head snapped toward his left shoulder _hard_. Nasal Voice collapsed to the decking and slid less than a meter, his head continuing to lay at an odd angle.

Double-checking his mic and active channel, Cole said, "Damn. Somebody check this guy for life-signs! There's another running to sound an alarm. Set up a perimeter while you're at it, and begin a cautious recon of this deck."

Cole turned down the cross-corridor from which the two men had come and turned the corner and used his implant to tune the armor's sensors to humanoid life-signs. He disregarded the large cluster of life-signs behind him and focused on the one life-sign moving away from him. He sped up to a slow jog, his heavy steps sounding like jackhammers striking an anvil.

Turning the corner, Cole saw the man running to what looked like an access or comms panel at an intersection ahead, and Cole sped up to catch him before he reached it. The man darted a glance over his shoulder, and his eyes widened as he looked at Cole sprinting up the corridor behind him...well, as much as heavy armor *can* sprint. He turned his head back to his direction of travel and reached for the comms panel. Cole drew back his left arm again and timed his punch so that the fist of his armor's left hand struck the comms panel just as his arm reached full extension. The running man jerked back from the comms panel as it exploded in a shower of sparks, and Cole's momentum carried him into the man's back before he could stop, knocking the man flat.

Cole extricated the left hand of his arm from the wreck of the comms panel and leaned down to grasp the man's clothes, then lifted the man to his feet. Comms call averted and prisoner in tow, Cole turned and pushed the man back the way they had come until he rendezvoused with his boarding party.

CHAPTER TWENTY-THREE

The man Cole pushed along froze when he saw his associate lying on the decking. One of the boarding party knelt beside him and looked up as Cole approached.

"Captain, you hit this guy pretty hard, caved in his skull pretty good, and I think his neck's broken, too. I don't think he's coming back from that."

"Okay," Cole said, sighing. "Take his shirt, and rip it into strips. Use the strips to tie this guy's hands behind him." Cole activated his external speakers, making sure the armor's systems would use the false voice Srexx had programmed for him. "You have a name, slaver?"

Wixil moved to the corpse and used the claws on her armor to cut the shirt away from its torso. Then, she and Yeleth began cutting the strips.

"I ain't no slaver," the man said, "but my name's Endo...Endo Stanley."

"Do you want to live, Endo Stanley?" Cole asked.

"Now, what the hell kind of question is that? Of course I want to live."

"Good. You're going to take us to the armory your buddy was talking about, and then, you're going to take us to the slaves."

"Shit," Endo scoffed, "you must have a death wish. Do you have any idea how many people are between you and the slaves?"

Now, Yeleth took two strips of cloth and pulled Endo's hands behind his back. She used both strips to bind his wrists, taking extra care to ensure the knots were as tight as she could make them.

"Do I look like I care? My boarding party and I are armored, and as soon as we raid your armory, we'll be armed. Do—"

"You're not even armed?" Endo erupted into laughter. "What kind of dumbass charges in to steal slaves without any weapons?"

Cole resisted the urge to growl and said, "Did I need a weapon to handle your buddy there?"

Cole's question ripped the humor right out of Endo. "No," he said, "I guess you didn't."

"Now...about that armory," Cole said.

"It's back near the comms panel you ruined. Come on; I'll show you."

Endo stepped around Cole and led them back to a hatch four meters down the corridor from the comms panel Cole punched. The cross-corridor where the comms panel was turned out to be one of the bulkheads making the space occupied by the armory. When they arrived, Cole saw that the hatch controls were lit up, and the read-out indicated the hatch was locked.

Cole deactivated the armor's external speakers and switched from the group channel to his call with Srexx, saying, "Srexx? You still with me?"

"Of course, Cole. What do you need?"

"I'm standing at Hatch Seven-Dash-Four-Two-Two. The controls say it's locked. Can the station computer see the hatch controls?"

"One moment..."

Five seconds later, the read-out on the hatch controls changed from 'Locked' to 'Open,' and the hatch slid back into the bulkhead as the space's lights activated.

"Thank you, Srexx," Cole said, as members of the boarding party moved around him and Endo to enter the armory.

"Of course, Cole; you are welcome."

Cole switched back to the group channel just in time to hear someone say, "Holy shit! There's a fusion bomb in here!"

Cole blinked. *What?* Over the group channel, he said, "Confirm last. Did you say there's a fusion bomb?"

"Aye, Captain...if the crate markings are right, it's a five-megaton fusion bomb."

"Well, we're not going to let them keep it," Cole replied. "Anyone see any cargo handling equipment in this mess?"

"There are six pallet sleds lined up against the back bulkhead, right next to this bomb. They're rated for five thousand kilograms each. There are two racks of laser rifles, charge packs, and their charging stations. I've seen crates with grenades, more laser rifles and charge packs, laser pistols and their charge packs, and many crates of slug-throwers."

"Okay," Cole said. "Everyone, arm up. Get yourselves a laser rifle with five charge packs plus one loaded and a laser pistol with two charge packs plus one loaded."

"Look here, Captain," another crewman said. "There's a crate over here with two armor-portable rotary cannons and another crate with five-thousand-round ammo packs."

The modern rotary cannon was an evolution of the ancient mini-guns in the twentieth and twenty-first centuries. Unlike its ancient forebears that relied on gunpowder as a propellant, the rotary cannon was a gauss rifle with six barrels that rotated. As each barrel spun into place, a magnetic-reactive projectile slipped into the chamber, and magnetic fields powered by the vehicle that served as its mount (or Cole's armor in this case) accelerated the projectile to a speed over three thousand meters per second, becoming so hot from friction with the air that the projectiles glowed like old-fashioned tracer rounds. Most militaries used the modern rotary cannon as an anti-vehicle or anti-aircraft weapon.

Inside his armor, Cole grinned. "Yeah...I'll take one of those. You guys think you can get one of those ammo packs secured to the back-plate of my armor?"

"If it has the standard hardpoints, we can, Captain," a crewman said.

A crewman moved over to help the one already at the crate with the ammo packs, and together, they lifted one out and carried it toward Cole. Cole turned slowly in place and felt the pack slide into place and lock. A new box appeared in his HUD, containing the text, '5000 Rounds Remaining.' A box appeared below that with flashing text, 'No Compatible Weapons System.'

"Captain, you're going to have to retrieve one of these rotary cannons yourself, sir, but I will connect it to the ammo pack once you have it."

"Someone take charge of Endo. We don't need him running off," Cole said as he moved over to the crate with the two rotary cannons. He leaned forward just far enough to grasp the rotary cannon and lift it out of the crates. A crewman moved to his side and connected the feed mechanism to the ammo pack.

Connecting the rotary cannon to the ammo pack apparently powered it up as well, because the text in the second new box in Cole's HUD changed to 'Rotary Cannon Online' just as an aiming reticle appeared. Cole shifted the rotary cannon from side to side and watched the reticle move as well. Cole grinned inside his armor and resisted the urge to quote the opening line of an ancient rock song by a group called Black Sabbath.

"Okay, Captain, we're armed up," a crewman said. "These suits are very cool. The laser pistol and charge packs just adhere to it somehow. It's kind of nice not to worry about needing a tactical harness."

Cole realized he'd been going the entire operation without knowing who was with him from the crew. He accessed his implant and navigated through the menus until he found a control that would show him the name of the person as they spoke on the group channel.

"Yeah," Cole said, "Srexx does good work."

Cole accessed his implant and switched over to the call with Srexx, saying, "Srexx, I'm tired of switching between calls. I'm going to merge this call into the group channel."

"Very well, Cole."

Accessing his implant again, Cole navigated the menus to find the command that would merge his call with Srexx into the group channel. That done, he activated the group channel and said, "Attention, everyone, this is Cole. I've merged my call with Srexx into this channel. Srexx, what can you tell us about this deck?"

"You are on Deck L-Seven, Cole," Srexx replied. "According to the schematics, this station dates back to before station layouts were standardized, and this deck used to be the security deck. With the power distribution control system reset, most of the station's internal sensors are now online, and I have located the slaves. They are distributed throughout the brig on this level."

"Excellent work, Srexx," Cole said. "This means we don't need Endo anymore. Does the ship have a brig?"

"Yes, Cole," Srexx answered. "It is on Deck Five."

"Okay, people. Let's organize into teams. I'm going to call the bridge to get people from the ship over here and merge the call into this channel. The extra crew can start moving these munitions back to the ship. Endo will go back to the ship with the first batch of munitions. Srexx, I'd like for you to direct them to the armory and the brig. I'm assuming we have one, even though I don't know where it is."

"The armory is on Deck Four, Cole," Srexx said, "and yes, I can direct the teams."

Cole accessed his implant to call the bridge and merge the call into the group channel.

"Bridge, Sasha here."

"Sasha, this is Cole. First off, be advised that I've merged this call into the group channel we're using. Keep listening if you want. Beyond that, I need extra people. We found an armory on this deck, and we're going to clean it out...especially since one of the items is a five-megaton fusion bomb."

"Mazzi," Sasha said, "send some people to link up with the boarding party. Now, Cole...what was this about a fusion bomb?"

"Don't ask me why these mooks have a fusion bomb," Cole said. "We found it crated up in a corner of this armory."

"We'll need a safe way of disposing of it, but that's tomorrow's problem," Sasha said. "We'll be listening if you need us."

It took ten minutes for the extra crew to arrive, during which the boarding party established a perimeter around the path between the ersatz armory and the maintenance airlock which led back to the ship.

"Srexx, while the munitions are transferred, can you send a copy of the schematic for this deck to my implant?" Cole asked as he watched the crew work and served as their heavy fire support.

Less than a second later, a notification appeared in Cole's field of view notifying him that Srexx was attempting to send him data. Cole accepted the transfer, and an overhead view of the deck soon appeared in his field of view. His implant centered the schematic on a red dot, which Cole assumed was him. Cole zoomed out on the schematic until he could see the entire deck, and the red dot was now just a pin-prick of red, little larger than a pixel. Yeah...thirty-seven people were *not* going to secure this deck.

Zooming back in on the schematic, Cole focused on the area between the brig and the maintenance airlock. There were no access points within fifty meters of either the brig or the airlock, and while the path from the brig to the maintenance airlock wasn't a straight shot, it certainly wasn't a curly pretzel, either.

* *Srexx, how much protection does the armor the crew's wearing provide?* *
Cole asked via text message, sent straight to Srexx.

* *Unknown, Cole. Without shooting the armor with one of the retrieved laser rifles, I am unable to provide an accurate answer. Given the materials used in the fabrication, however, each suit should survive at least several direct hits by a laser rifle at your people's level of technology.* *

Cole sighed. * *Can you give me a better approximation than 'several?'* *

* *More than three shots and less than twenty.* *

* *Right...thanks, Srexx.* *

* *You are welcome, Cole.* *

Cole returned to the deck schematic, highlighting the maintenance airlock in bright green and the brig's sole entry point in bright red. He traced the shortest-distance path from the brig's entrance to the mainte-nance airlock in bright yellow. Then, he contacted Sasha and asked her to arrange for a group to be waiting inside the ship's personnel airlock to manage the incoming slaves...once they were actually incoming. Sasha promised she'd see to it. Still, with all of that, the boarding party had only emptied about half the armory. Even with six pallet sleds, it was slow work.

After what seemed like forever and a day to Cole, but was thirty-five minutes at most, the armory was emptied and transferred to the ship. The unarmored crew who had used the pallet sleds had off-loaded their cargo in corridors on Deck Two and now would begin the slow process of moving it from Deck Two to Deck Five.

When Cole had all thirty-seven members of his boarding party around him, he transmitted the modified deck schematic to them.

"All right, people," Cole said, using the group channel, "we are ready to begin the task we came to accomplish. I want a seven-crew fireteam to secure the manual hatch and maintenance airlock. The rest will come with me. When we reach and secure the brig, another seven-crew fireteam will remain at the brig until all slaves have been moved to the ship. Everyone else will serve as a transfer team to take the slaves from the brig to the ship. Any questions?"

No one spoke.

"Okay, then. Let's do this."

The maintenance-airlock fireteam broke off and went back the way they'd come, as Cole led the remaining thirty toward the brig. As he *whine-thump*ed his way through the corridors, Cole considered that maybe he should ask Srexx for a suit of armor like what everyone else wore. After all, it would certainly be quieter.

"Cole," Srexx said over the group channel, "there is a group of fifteen individuals moving your way. They are fifteen degrees off your current facing and are armed. They do not appear to be aware of your presence."

"Is it possible to move around behind them?" Cole asked.

"Yes. There are several cross-corridors you could use to flank them."

"Okay, I want a team of fifteen to break off and follow Srexx's directions to flank these guys. I'm going to give them one chance to surrender, but we don't have time to clear the whole station if they get an alert off. Go."

Cole watched half his force fast-walk down the corridor, check the next intersection, and dash across it. Two intersections down, they turned left and moved out of sight. No more than a minute later, Cole saw the group from Iota Ceti turn the corner off to his left and stop cold. Cole counted ten men and five women, and none of them had their weapons ready.

Activating his armor's external speakers, Cole said, "We have you surrounded. Surrender your weapons, place your hands on your heads, and you'll live through this."

One man's hand twitched toward his laser rifle, but the guy next to him slapped him silly, saying, "Hey, dumbass...he's in heavy armor with a rotary cannon! We can't kill him before he shreds all of us. That thing's not exactly a precision weapon."

A couple at the back of the group—one man and one woman—pivoted and moved like they were going to run back the way they came, then froze and lifted their hands. The other members of the boarding party came into view, their laser rifles at the ready.

Cole deactivated his external speakers and said over the group channel, "Okay, disarm them. Airlock fireteam, start making your way to us; we're sending you some prisoners. Flank team, once the prisoners are disarmed, escort them to the Airlock team; hand off the prisoners' weapons to them, and double-time it back to us. Bridge, we need people to meet the Airlock team and transfer the prisoners to the brig."

Waiting only long enough to ensure the prisoners were disarmed and moving toward the airlock with their hands on their heads, Cole turned and led the remaining fifteen members of the boarding party to the brig. He moved slowly, more to minimize the sound of his movement than anything else. Heavy armor was a lot of things; rated for stealth was not one of them.

Cole and his portion of the boarding party were just arriving at the access hatch to the brig when the flank team jogged up behind them. Cole stood right in front of the hatch, and the boarding party stacked up on either side of it. Looking at the crewperson closest the hatch controls, Cole's HUD informed him that the person was Fletcher Giles.

Over the group channel, Cole said, "Okay, Giles...open the hatch."

Giles keyed the commands, and the hatch opened. Stepping

through the hatchway as soon as he could fit, Cole surveyed the compartment. The space appeared to be the processing room for new arrivals to the brig. Various tables and desks occupied the space, and most were anchored to the deck. A stack of manacles occupied one table to the right of the hatch. Eight people—six men and two women —lounged in chairs around a table to the left of the hatch. They wore clothing coated in dirt and grime, in varying stages of disrepair, and most looked like they hadn't showered or bathed in some time. Their weapons lay stacked on a table two meters from them. They all looked toward the hatch as it opened. Their eyes widened as Cole *whine-thump*ed into the compartment.

Cole keyed his external speakers.

"I've come for the slaves. Lay down your weapons, offer no resistance, and you will be spared."

One man, who looked to be the youngest of the group and closest to the weapons table, reached for one of the laser rifles. Just as his fingers were about to grasp it, a nearby woman kicked him square between his legs, following up with a left cross to his temple, and the young man collapsed to the deck unconscious. Two of her fellows gave her an odd look.

"What?" She said. "You think I'm going to let someone get me killed? That there's heavy armor *and* a rotary cannon. What chance you think we stand against that?" At that point, she dropped to her knees and laced her fingers behind her back. "I surrender."

Faced with her example, the others in the compartment dropped to their knees and laced their fingers behind their backs. Cole nodded inside his armor, even though no one could see it. He deactivated the external speakers and activated the comms-link for the boarding party.

"Grab their weapons. Move the prisoners to a bulkhead, and secure their hands behind them with manacles from that table. Leave two people with me as a watch, and they're authorized for lethal fire if the prisoners resist. The rest of you, fan out. Let's get the slaves out of here."

Within moments, seven criminals were facing a bulkhead, their hands secured behind them. The unconscious young man lay in a corner, his hands secured as well. By lucky happenstance, the woman who'd incapacitated the young man was right beside Cole.

Cole activated his external speakers again. "Are there any more of you in this section?"

"No," the woman said, turning to face Cole. "Just the eight of us watching the slaves."

She looked like she hadn't washed either herself or her clothes in *ages*, but what struck Cole was her vibrant, blue eyes.

"How about on this deck?"

"I don't know for sure. It's been an hour or so since we heard from anyone. There was supposed to be a group on the way to start moving the slaves up for the auction, but they haven't shown up yet."

"That group...would it have had about fifteen people?"

The woman shrugged as best she could. "Probably. The slaves are under light sedation to make 'em pliable, so fifteen could move thirty or maybe even fifty slaves in one go."

"Okay. How many slaves are you holding in here?" Cole asked.

She shrugged as best she could. "I'm not sure anyone's ever counted. They make us pack 'em in the cells like cattle." After Cole was silent for a time, she asked, "Sir? What's going to happen to us?"

"Why?" Cole asked.

"Look, I'm no saint. I've done my share of things and then some, but when the bosses find out what you've done, they're gonna flay the skin off anyone they find. And that's before they really get started. If I have to end up in prison just to survive...well...I'll end up in prison, but please don't leave me here. I will do *anything* to keep from being left here."

Cole looked into the woman's eyes, even though she couldn't see him doing so, and he saw a desperation that was almost wild. His mind wandered through the various things he'd done over the past thirteen years and how he could claim being proud of only a very, very few. He had no right to judge this woman. He had no right to judge anyone.

The first slaves coming out of the pens drew Cole's attention. They stopped in the compartment where Cole stood with the criminals. Once there were about a hundred, Cole's team—minus the two standing with Cole—led them out of the compartment, taking up escort positions at the head, rear, and sides of the column.

Cole double-checked that his external speakers were deactivated and accessed the group channel, saying, "Bridge, you still with us?"

"Bridge here," Sasha said.

"The first batch of captives is heading your way."

"I have people waiting at the ship's airlock," Sasha said. "Will there be anything else?"

"Yes, now that you mention it. I need eight armed crew at the airlock to convey eight more prisoners to the brig. One criminal guarding the slaves begged me to take her with me, and my impression is that her fear is genuine. Heh...I've seen enough the past thirteen years, too, that makes me think her concerns aren't hyperbole. She may be a bad person, or she may just be someone who got drawn into the wrong crowd and didn't know how to get out. Until we know for sure, she can stay in the brig."

When the travel team returned, Cole stopped them, pointing at the prisoners. He activated his external speakers along with the group link, saying, "Take the prisoners to the ship with the next group. A team will meet you to transfer them to the brig."

Cole stepped out of the way as the travel team added the prisoners to the next group of slaves. The woman he'd spoken with turned to him as she was led out and said, "Thank you! You've saved our lives."

Just as Cole was about to activate his external speakers to respond, Srexx spoke over the group channel, "Be advised, Cole, that the internal sensors have gone down."

CHAPTER TWENTY-FOUR

"What do you mean the internal sensors have gone down?" Cole asked, forgetting he was on the group channel. "Is it something like an overloaded relay or what?"

"I believe it is sabotage to block overwatch of the team. Just before the sensors went down, I monitored people going to various trunk cabinets near the station's computer; I have reason to conclude they cut the data lines for the sensors."

Cole nodded. "Yeah...they're coming for us. How did they even know we were here, though?"

"Unknown, Cole. I have not observed any system alerts or communications regarding your presence. I did block sensor feeds to the station's various control centers, but I attempted to do so in such a way that the lack of sensor coverage in your part of Deck L-Seven appeared random and normal."

Cole shrugged inside the armor. "Don't worry about it, Srexx. We'll just move as fast as we can and hope they don't find us."

Cole spent the next half-hour watching the transfer team take the slaves to the ship in groups of a hundred. Taking them in groups of fifty might have been a better option, but to Cole's mind, they'd been aboard the station too long...even before they lost the overwatch of Srexx accessing the internal sensors. Cole had an itch intensifying between his shoulder blades, and it had nothing do with being inside heavy armor.

At long last, the final group of slaves gathered to leave the station's brig. There were fifty-seven. Cole instructed the transfer team to establish a ten-person squad out front for scouting and a five-person team on either side for containment and flank security, with the remaining seventeen plus Cole acting as rear guard. Once everyone was in position, Cole called for the group to head out.

Cole ensured he was the very last person on the rear guard, and upon leaving the brig, he turned until he was facing back the way they'd come and started walking backward. After walking about five meters backward, a pin-hole camera popped up out of the right pauldron of the armor and provided Cole a tiny rear-view image in the top-right of his HUD.

They traversed perhaps fifty meters when a flank team called out, "Contact right!"

Laser fire lit up the area, and more than one of Cole's people took a hit. Their armor protected them, so far, and none of the slaves were hit. Cole remembered the life-sign sensors in his armor and felt like calling himself a dunce as he brought them online. The range was limited—twenty meters at most—but Cole worked through his implant to share the sensor feed with the rest of the boarding party.

The sensors in Cole's armor showed a mass of people to his left, and a group of them moved in a flanking maneuver that would bring them into Cole's field of view, even as the boarding party kept moving toward the airlock. The first of the flanking group around the corner froze at the sight of Cole in heavy armor, his eyes going wide as tea saucers. He jumped back behind the concealment of the corner, and Cole activated his external microphone just in time to hear, "The boss never said they had heavy armor!"

"Anyone who surrenders gets to live through this," Cole said, his armor conveying his voice via the external speakers. "I'd rather not kill or maim any more people than I just have to."

A grenade sailed around the corner and bounced off the bulkhead, landing at Cole's feet. It was a fragmentation device, and Cole barely felt the grenade's shockwave through the armor, let alone the peppering against his armor that the tiny shrapnel of the grenade's housing became.

"Okay, if that's your choice..." Cole said.

Cole accessed his implant, instructing it to give his HUD a thermal overlay. His field of view changing to display heat sources, Cole saw a mass of heat just around the corner where the first man hid. Cole put the reticle of the rotary cannon over the densest mass of heat and pressed the activation stud with his right thumb. Cole heard the whine of the rotary cannon powering up and deactivated his external microphone just in time.

The rotary cannon fired twelve projectiles before Cole released the firing stud. The first projectile ripped a super-heated hole through the bulkhead, and the eleven successive projectiles shredded the man who'd seen Cole and his five compatriots also hiding in the cross-corridor. Cole walked to the intersection; took one look at the gore covering the bulkheads, decking, and ceiling; and made a mental note to thank Srexx for designing his armor with a self-contained air supply. Cole turned and double-timed it back to the boarding party, resuming ultimate rear guard.

Another group attempted an ambush just shy of half-way to the airlock. This group used civilian-grade body armor in addition to their laser rifles, so instead of one shot from the boarding party taking a person out of the fight, the same result now required two—or sometimes even three—shots...except for Cole's rotary cannon. Not even top-of-the-line civilian-grade body armor could stop a hail of five-centimeters-long, two-millimeter rods moving over three-thousand meters per second. Especially rods made of tungsten with the leading edge molded for enhanced penetration.

. . .

From the ambush on, the trip was a running fire fight, as more and more criminals arrived on the scene. By the time the boarding party and the last group of slaves neared the maintenance airlock, several of the boarding party were limping, and two—though alive—were carried by compatriots. There were no deaths among the boarding party personnel, but the slaves carried five of their number for later burial.

The leading elements of the group were passing through the maintenance airlock when the life-sign sensors in Cole's armor lit up. Over three-hundred individuals were coming. Five grenades and a veritable wall of laser fire came at Cole as he reached the manual hatch that had converted the maintenance-airlock corridor into a storage space.

"Everybody, get to the ship. I've got this," Cole broadcasted to the group channel as he pressed the activator stud on the rotary cannon and held it, sweeping the rotary cannon from side to side as he watched the 'Rounds Remaining' value in his HUD drop faster than Cole could process.

The five grenades detonated almost at Cole's feet, but they were fragmentation grenades. The combined shockwave staggered Cole as he backed toward the hatch, but aside from destroying the rear-view pop-up camera, they were ineffective...against Cole. The grenades' shockwave did affect the hatch, however, triggering an ancient blast sensor in the otherwise-manual hatch. The hatch slammed closed behind Cole, but he didn't hear or feel it over the explosion of the grenades.

Five seconds passed as Cole backed toward the now-closed hatch, and the oncoming numbers were down to a mere hundred-plus. The cannon's ammunition dwindling, Cole tried to step backward through the hatch, but he hit solid material whether he moved left or right. His patience long since spent, Cole took ten steps forward and moved as fast as he could toward the hatch. His guy had said it wouldn't stand up to a toddler, so Cole decided to check the man's statement for hyperbole.

Cole struck a solid surface with a bone-jarring concussion and continued pushing through with his feet. Cole's crewman proved to be correct, and the joins where the criminals secured the hatch coaming to the surrounding bulkheads gave way, the hatch collapsing with a concussion that Cole felt through his armor. The hatch coaming was thick enough that Cole had to lean forward and crouch as much as he could in the armor, and his gait across the collapsed hatch resembled a crab-walk.

The rotary cannon ran dry just as Cole was halfway across the hatch coaming. Cole almost dropped the rotary cannon, but at the last second, he remembered the cables and ammo tube connecting the cannon to the ammunition pack. Far up the corridor, a lone, brave soul stepped out to see if Cole truly was out of ammo. When no rounds shredded him, he accepted something from a fighting companion out of view. Cole stepped off the hatch coaming and resumed his normal posture, instructing his implant to display an enhanced image in his HUD. Cole's instruction to his implant was transmitted just in time for him to see the lone individual in the corridor lift the rocket launcher to his shoulder and fire.

Between the distance to the airlock and the force-fields creating the hard seal beyond, safety aboard the ship was only thirty meters away...so close and yet so far. Cole knew he could get closer to the ship if he turned and sprinted, but most heavy armor was weakest on the back. Beyond that, he was afraid people were congregating around the suit locker, which would be within the blast radius if he actually made it to the ship. Cole saw fire erupt from the back of the rocket launcher, and he made his decision.

"Incoming rocket! Clear the airlock and suit locker!" Cole broadcast across the group channel as he assumed a more stable stance and locked the armor's servos at the hips, knees, and ankles. Srexx told him the armor only *looked* like Aurelian Commonwealth heavy armor but was far superior. It was time to test the AI's claim.

Cole took the rocket right in the center of the armor's chest-plate. The armor protected his ears from what he was sure was a deafening blast, and the last thing Cole knew, he was flying backward.

CHAPTER TWENTY-FIVE

Bridge, Battle-Carrier *Haven*
Iota Ceti System
15 July 2999

"Cole is down! Repeat: Cole is down! Emergency medical support to the port airlock! Three of you, let's get back in there and hold them off while we get Cole aboard the ship!"

Hearing those words broadcast over the bridge's speakers drove a cold spike of fear through Sasha's heart, and if she'd taken a moment to consider that, she might have asked herself *why*. She was out of the command chair and halfway to the port-side hatch before she even thought about it, and it was only her realization she hadn't left someone in command that made her stop as the hatch irised open and turn. Every pair of eyes on the bridge—all four of them—stared back at her.

"Mazzi," Sasha said, "you have the conn."

Without waiting for any acknowledgement, Sasha pivoted on her heel and left the bridge.

. . .

Sasha stepped out of the transit shaft onto Deck Two and heard the most horrendous metal-on-metal screeching, punctuated by laser fire... and it sounded like it was coming from the airlock. She headed to the airlock and, stepping around the corner, saw ten people dragging an inert suit of power armor through the second airlock. Four people clustered around the outer hatch of the maintenance airlock—two low and two high—exchanging laser fire with the station's criminal occupants deeper into the deck.

A furred hand reached out from Sasha's left and pulled her out of the line of fire, just as three laser beams passed through her former position and struck the bulkhead of the corridor behind her. Whatever material was used in the ship's construction, it showed not a mark from all the laser fire it had taken in the last few minutes. Sasha turned and saw Yeleth holding her arm, she and Wixil having already vacated their suits.

"Thanks," Sasha said with a nod.

Yeleth nodded in return. "You are welcome, and I didn't want the promotion."

Sasha barked a harsh laugh before asking, "What happens if you *do* want the promotion?"

"I'd ask Cole to give you your own ship," Yeleth replied. "Besides, Ship's Purser is far too much fun."

"We've got him inside!" one of the crew dragging the heavy armor shouted to the people holding the outer hatch.

Sasha leaned out long enough to spy the rotary cannon at the end of its connections lying on the force-field that served as a deck. She pointed to it, asking, "Is the cannon still operational?"

"I doubt the fusion bomb would ruin it," the spacer said, "let alone some bush-league rocket. That there's good Solar Republic tech."

"Then take two people and get it through the airlock. We're not leaving it behind, either," Sasha replied.

Two of the ten who had dragged the armor past the inner hatch of the airlock dashed back and heaved the cannon up to their shoulders. One laser beam from the station struck each person, but they powered through bringing the cannon inside the inner hatch.

"Okay, people, fall back!" Sasha shouted. "It's time to leave!"

The four crew holding the outer hatch of the station's maintenance airlock stepped away and began backing toward the ship, firing all the while. When one's charge pack ran dry, they rotated positions with someone to keep a steady barrage of covering fire going back into the station.

The moment the final crewperson dove through the ship's airlock, Sasha keyed commands into the panel that irised both hatches of the airlock closed. Then, she tapped the comms control, saying, "Sasha to Bridge."

The speakers overhead chirped before broadcasting, "Bridge, Mazzi here."

"Get us out of here, Mazzi. We've achieved our objective."

"How's Cole?"

Just then, Talia ran up, hauling a gurney loaded down with all kinds of gear. She came from the direction of the cargo transit shaft.

"Talia just arrived, and we still have to get him out of the armor. I'll update you once we know more. Get us moving toward the system's periphery."

"Aye, ma'am. Consider it done. Will there be anything else?"

"No, but thanks, Mazzi. Sasha out."

The speakers chirped once more signifying the comms channel ended.

———

Up on the bridge, Mazzi gave the order to undock from the station. The spacer dutifully tapped that control on the helm station, causing the docking force-fields between the station and the ship to disappear. Since Cole had issued the maintenance override on the two hatches of the airlock, those hatches remained open, and a decompression of the station ensued. All those who had been rushing the airlock to assault the ship found themselves dancing with the stars sans suit as alerts and klaxons blared all over the station.

———

"Whew...what a workout," Talia said as she looked down on Cole's charred armor. "Soosh, we've gotta get more medical people. My response time just now was way too slow."

"I know, Tallie." Sasha stared at the armor, and the icy claws of fear tried to encircle her heart once more. She accessed her implant and chose 'Comms' from the radial menu. There, she chose 'Srexxilan.'

Yes, Sasha?

How do we get the armor off Cole? He could die in there.

If he survived the initial blast, it is unlikely that he is in a dying state. I built significant medical subsystems into the armor. However, those systems only work if the armor's primary computer core is online. These are the steps you must follow...

Sasha followed Srexx's instructions to the letter, and soon, they had the armor open. The good news was that the blast had *not* penetrated the armor. The bad news was that he'd been bounced around inside the armor by the concussion, and there was massive, ugly bruising everywhere Sasha could see flesh.

Talia waved a medical scanner over Cole and sighed with relief. "No neck or spinal injuries, and he's breathing. It's safe to move him onto the gurney."

Sasha watched with Wixil and Yeleth as several volunteers lifted Cole out of the armor and placed him on the gurney. Talia moved around the gurney after they'd stepped back and secured him to it.

Talia quickly scanned those standing around and said, "Come with me. I'll need your help to get him off the gurney."

Sasha turned to Yeleth, saying, "I know you want to go with them to the hospital deck, but there are almost seven hundred people on the flight deck who—I'm sure—are frightened and bewildered. I'd like you to take a couple people and introduce yourself. Once you've said hello and done what you can to calm them, see what our food and environmental situation is. Aw, nuts...those people will need to visit the head, too. One thing at a time, Soosh...for now, just introduce yourself and make sure they know they're not still slaves. I'll set course for the closest world where we can get a decent re-supply."

"Who is this 'Soosh?'" Yeleth asked.

Sasha smiled. "When Talia was little and just learning to talk, my name came out 'Soosh' when she tried to say it, so it's kind of a family nickname."

"Ah. I shall see to the task at once." Yeleth nodded once to Sasha before taking Wixil and disappearing around the corner.

Sasha watched the three people lug the rotary cannon through the interior hatch of the airlock. Setting it down on the deck as gently as they could, all three of them leaned back against the bulkhead and wiped the sweat from their brows. Cole's heavy armor made moving that thing look like no effort at all, but light it was *not*.

Sasha accessed her implant and called the bridge, routing it through the ship.

"Bridge, Mazzi here."

"I'm on my way back to the bridge."

"How's Cole, ma'am?"

"He's breathing and bruised. Talia's scanner found no injuries that made moving him out of the armor a risk."

"Thank goodness for small favors, then. Anything else, ma'am?"

Sasha liked how Mazzi's voice followed her from bulkhead speaker to bulkhead speaker as she walked back to the transit shaft. She said, "No. I'm almost to the transit shaft, so I'll be down there shortly."

"Roger that, ma'am. Bridge out."

Sasha stepped onto the bridge and found Mazzi sitting at the helm. Sasha smiled at that as she walked over and sat in the command chair.

"I have the conn," Sasha announced to the bridge.

"XO has the conn," Mazzi replied.

"What's our status?"

Mazzi didn't take her eyes off the helm station as she said, "We are leaving the station at 'dead slow,' ma'am. Full stealth systems are active, and there are no indications we've been discovered. At our present speed, we are a little over forty-three hours from the system periphery, and I've chosen a point well beyond any jump gate or observed traffic patterns."

"Anyone know of a system close to here where we could resupply?" Sasha asked.

"Caernarvon," Jenkins said from the comms station, and Sasha swiveled to face him. He continued, "It's a major trans-shipping head for this region of space. Most of the trade flowing—or at least that used to flow—between the Solars and the Commonwealth passed through Caernarvon. Because it's so close to so many systems with less than trustworthy residents, it's fortified like you wouldn't believe. That's why it's called 'Caernarvon,' after an ancient castle in Great Britain on Old Earth. I don't know if anyone remembers what the system was first named, but I'm sure it's in some archive somewhere. Matter of fact, I think the Solars keep a small task force stationed there."

"Can you get me an estimated travel time, Mazzi?" Sasha asked as she swiveled back around to face forward.

After a short time, Mazzi said, "The computer calculates twelve days, six hours, and change, ma'am."

Sasha nodded, thinking. Until she had a report from Yeleth what their food situation was, there was no point in picking a destination. At last, she nodded again.

"Don't lock it in, but keep it on the screen. If we have food for everyone now aboard across twelve days, that's where we'll go."

———

First, Cole knew he was alive. Air brushing his face served as a decent indicator for that. Cole's progression toward relief/celebration/satisfaction he had survived was short-lived. Following closely on the heels of awareness came a bone-marrow-deep, full-body ache unlike anything Cole could ever remember experiencing in his life. It wasn't pain. He was...sore. His entire body from the hair follicles on his head down to the cuticle beds in his toes ached with the soreness only a wearying injury can produce.

Cole opened his eyes. The surroundings he could see without moving his head looked very similar to the treatment room he'd awoken in after Srexx had almost killed him. A read-out he couldn't quite see was attached to the bulkhead about thirty centimeters above his head. The bulkheads he could see were the same silvery-white color the entire internal space of the ship boasted, and to top it all off, the entire space was quiet.

Just as Cole was about to try pushing himself into a sitting position, the treatment room hatch irised open to admit Talia Thyrray, his acting Chief Medical Officer. A line from ancient cartoons he'd watched with his grandfather swam to the surface of his mind, and Cole grinned.

"Hey...what's up, Doc?"

If Talia caught the reference, she didn't show it. In fact, she did not seem amused at all. She walked over to stand beside his waist, looking down at him with a blank, unemotional expression. Whispers of worry and doubt slunk around the back of Cole's mind the longer Talia remained silent. After almost three minutes of that blank expression, Cole wondered just what was wrong that she couldn't think of how to tell him, and he started with the usual suspects. Nope...not toes. He could wiggle his toes. He would not try moving his legs, because he didn't want to give her the satisfaction of knowing she'd gotten to him, but that didn't mean he couldn't flex his fingers out of her line of sight. Nope...not fingers. Cole didn't think there was anything connected to him controlling or ensuring his breathing, but if local numbing agents had been applied, he might not know.

At long last, Cole just couldn't take it anymore. He let out an exasperated sigh and said, "Okay...give. What's so wrong you're just standing there?"

Talia broke into a huge grin. "Absolutely nothing at all. Sasha just bet me fifty credits I couldn't freak you out. You probably feel sore all over...and with good reason. Even though there were no serious injuries, the visual representation of the med-scan I performed—plus the bruising all over your body—makes me think you bounced around inside that armor like beans in a set of maracas. You are beyond lucky that you have no long-term injuries, and you're on light duty for the next two weeks, pending medical review. No wild piloting, no rescue missions, no 'Lone Marine' craziness. Understand?"

A dozen different responses went through Cole's mind, but the fact of the matter was, he'd survived a rocket strike. Yes, his armor deserved most of the credit for that, but still...he survived it. In the end, Cole just nodded.

"You got it, Doc. I'm not sure I feel up to getting rowdy, anyway."

"Good. Do you feel up to visitors? I think half the ship would be outside if I'd let them, but you're in no condition for public appearances. As it is, there are four who simply *refused* to leave."

Cole grinned. "Sure. Send them in."

Talia turned and walked over the hatch. She pressed the control to open the hatch, and the first two into the room were Yeleth and Wixil. Wixil looked like she wanted to climb up on the treatment bed beside Cole, although there wasn't room, but she contented herself to stand close to her mother. After the Ghrexels, Sasha entered and almost broke into a smile at Cole's mock glare. The fourth person, however, Cole did not expect at all; he hadn't seen the man in eight years. Cole could feel his expression shifting to one of total surprise and shock, but the sight of his old friend was just too unexpected.

"Garrett? What the hell were you doing in Iota Ceti?"

Garrett looked from Sasha to Talia and then to the Ghrexels, saying, "See? I told you we're friends."

"Garrett, what were you doing in Iota Ceti?" Cole asked. Then, his eyes widened. He remembered the several prisoners they'd taken, and he also remembered he had paid little attention to their faces. "Oh, man...please, don't tell me you were working for them."

Garrett grimaced. "Well...in a manner of speaking, I was. A few years back, I got in way too deep in one of Bosil's casinos. I tried getting enough work to pay off the debt, but she stopped listening and sent me to Iota Ceti as a slave."

"Oh, wow," Cole said, his eyes widening. "That's rough. How long had you been there?"

"A couple years."

Silence descended on the room for few moments before Sasha spoke.

"Cole, do you mind if I ask how you met Garrett?"

Cole shook his head. "I don't mind, Sasha. He was the first to arrive after..." Cole's voice trailed off as he swallowed hard. "I was just sitting there in orbit, watching my home burn. Whoever it was had bombarded every location where there was a hint of human settlement...almost down to the bedrock. Garrett helped me bury what was left to be found; it seemed like it took forever. He took me away from there and taught me what I needed to know to survive. I'm not talking about cooking and sewing and stuff like that. I mean things like how the world *really* works...which star systems to avoid...which to skirt... and which are okay. I spent four years with him before striking out on my own."

"I don't know if I ever said so," Sasha said, "but I'm sorry about your family."

"Thanks," Cole said, almost shrugging. "It...it doesn't hurt like it used to, but it never goes away, either. Kind of like scar tissue that way."

Talia looked at Cole, her eyes narrowing just a hint. She turned to the others, saying, "Okay. I think we should let Cole rest. I'll keep an eye on him tonight and release him tomorrow if there are no complications."

CHAPTER TWENTY-SIX

In Transit to Caernarvon System
    16 July 2999

"Cole-Captain?" the ship's computer said, via the speakers in the captain's day-cabin. He'd visited the captain's quarters once and wasn't comfortable with the palatial space. The day-cabin was more of a functional dining and sleeping area where the captain could still be close to the bridge.

Cole sighed. "Yes, *Haven?*"

"Purser Yeleth desires communication with you."

"Put her through," Cole said. The speakers chirped, indicating an active comms call. "Yes, Yeleth?"

"What is your availability for a meeting, Captain?" Yeleth asked. Her phrasing put Cole on his guard. She *never* addressed him as 'captain.'

Cole frowned, even though she couldn't see it. "To be honest, Yeleth, I'm still on light duty. What's the nature of the meeting?"

"I have been speaking with the local nest of Kiksaliks that we rescued from Iota Ceti," Yeleth said. "They are favorable to your proposition, but the queen of the local nest has said the time has come for her people to meet you."

Cole considered the situation. He wasn't doing all that much right then. Sasha wouldn't even let him sit at the helm station, so he'd been reading up on the ship.

"Where do I need to be?" Cole asked.

Yeleth was silent for a few moments before saying, "If acceptable with you, Captain, I shall bring a representative to your office on Deck Three."

"That's fine. When should I expect you?"

"Perhaps...twenty minutes?"

That would give Cole enough time to shower and change into fresh clothes. He nodded and then grinned, since Yeleth couldn't see him nod. "That sounds fine, Yeleth. I'll be waiting."

———

Cole approached the Captain's Office just across the corridor from the port-side hatch to the bridge. He wasn't sure he'd ever stepped into these compartments, either the yeoman's office or the captain's actual office. The office connected to the captain's day-cabin via a shared head (shower and toilet facilities), but Cole felt like entering from the corridor. When he approached the hatch, it irised open for him, and Cole blinked at seeing Wixil sitting at the yeoman's desk.

"Hi, Wixil," Cole said.

Wixil regarded Cole with a warm expression as her tail languidly swished from side to side. "Hi, Cole! Mother is bringing a representative of the Kiksaliks we rescued in Iota Ceti to speak with you. She's been discussing your desire to hire them, and the talks have reached the point that the local Queen thinks she should send a representative to you."

"Local Queen, huh?" Cole asked.

Wixil nodded, her tail still swishing like a languid metronome. "Yes. Kiksaliks are intelligent insectoids, and they have a hive mind. Each community—no matter the size—is called a nest. Outside of their own territory, most people don't seem to want them around, and I've never understood that. They're nice people."

Cole nodded. "It's probably the whole 'read your mind' thing. I can't imagine many people are happy with the idea that someone they pass on the street might scan their mind and know their inner-most secrets."

"Oh." Wixil's ears and tail drooped. "I didn't think about that. That could be tough, if they didn't have some kind of policy not to read people's minds...but there will always be those who break policy."

Cole nodded again. "That doesn't mean we should shun them, though. They're people, just like the rest of us."

Wixil's ears perked back up as her tail resumed its languid swishing. "You're right. We should be nicer to each other than we are. Oh...you'd better go in your office. Mom will be here soon, and she might not want to find you out here with me."

"I'm not too worried about it. It's my ship. If I want to talk with a friend while I wait for an appointment, why can't I do that?"

Wixil gazed at Cole, her ears still perked up and her tail still swishing. Cole thought he heard just the slightest hint of a purr.

Cole started to say something else, but the hatch to the corridor irised open, allowing Yeleth to lead the Kiksalik representative into the outer office. If she disapproved of Cole not being in the captain's office, it didn't show, and Cole smiled at meeting his first Kiksalik. He'd heard all kinds of stories, but there was nothing like first-hand experience.

The Kiksalik with Yeleth looked like an odd cross between a terrestrial ant and a terrestrial fly. Its exoskeleton was a dull amber color, and its dark eyes were ovoid and only slightly convex. Its thorax was about waist-level on Cole, and each of its walking appendages clicked as they came into contact with the deck. Cole wasn't certain how it manipulated tools, even though Kiksaliks were tool-users, because he saw no analogs to hands or the Ghrexels' paws. Cole identified its mandibles, though, and they were folded across the Kiksalik's mouth. Two antennae—barely thicker than Ghrexel whiskers—rose from just behind the Kiksalik's eyes.

"Captain Cole," Yeleth said, "this is 176, representing the local hive of Kiksaliks."

"I greet you, 176," Cole said. "Please, come with me into my office."

Cole turned and led Yeleth and 176 into the captain's office. He walked around the desk and started to sit, realizing he wasn't sure how to make the Kiksalik comfortable.

"Forgive me, 176, I'm not sure any of the seats I have are comfortable for you. How should we handle that?"

The Kiksalik's mandibles waved and its antennae quivered, and Cole heard a chittering, clicking sound coming out of its mouth, with the occasional squeak. Cole despaired of developing a dialogue, but then, he heard it.

Think nothing of it, Captain. We do not sit as you are used to sitting.

Cole stared at the Kiksalik. "Are you speaking directly to my mind?"

Yes, Captain. We are. You converse with Ixxvikal, Queen of the local nest. Interesting. 'Cole' is not your name.

"No, it isn't. I never liked 'Bartholomew' or any of its derivatives, and 'Coleson' is very dangerous right now."

Yes, your family name is dangerous. This is most likely the last Gyv'Rathi Battle-Carrier in operational condition across the known galaxy.

"Do your people know much of the Gyv'Rathi?" Cole asked.

They were...formidable. They helped all who needed it. They defended the defenseless. They did not encroach on others' space, and they would brook no encroachment into theirs. Countless species lost fleets, trying to steal the secrets of the Gyv'Rathi.

"So...if you know my name is Bartholomew Coleson by now, you know why I want to hire you."

Yes.

"What is your response?"

You are the first Human we've encountered who approaches us with interest and wonder. We cooperated with those ruling the station as they threatened our nest. You have no such impulses. We will help you.

"Thank you. What is your price?"

Haven.

Cole almost choked, thinking of his ship. "Excuse me?"

Haven. We desire that which you have provided Yeleth...a haven safe from the evil sentients of the galaxy...a haven where we can grow and learn and experience, and in time, we may ask that you take our descendants home to communicate all we have learned to the Hive.

Cole smiled. "I think we have an agreement. Welcome aboard the Battle-Carrier *Haven.* Yeleth will oversee the hiring, and please inform her of your dietary needs. Oh...and she will help you find living space for your nest."

It is as foretold.

With that, Kiksalik 176 turned and skittered out of the office.

Cole looked to Yeleth, saying, "Did you get all of that, too?"

"Yes. It is...an impressive experience."

"Okay, then. Proceed with sorting through the people who want a job, and let me know what you need. Oh. Just because I'm a firm believer in the philosophy of 'trust but verify,' interview the SDF people first. Let's make sure they're as honest in their convictions as they seem to be."

Yeleth performed her approximation of a nod. "Yes, Captain."

"Okay. I'm going next door to my day-cabin. Sasha won't let me sit at the helm station as long as I'm on light duty, so there's not a whole lot for me to do."

―――――

A short time later, Cole was sitting on the couch in the day-cabin when he remembered a conversation he'd had with the ship's computer...a conversation he still needed to follow up on.

"Srexx?"

"Yes, Cole?"

"The ship's computer told me you might have schematics for additional classes of ships."

Silence.

"Srexx?"

"Why do you ask, Cole?"

Cole sighed. "Well, this ship was designated as a Battle-Carrier, according to the ship's computer. That tells me there might be fighter or bomber designs, and the two decks designed for ground troops tells me there might be designs for dropships, too. I'm also wondering what other classes of ships there might have been, because the ship's computer referenced a scout-frigate."

"The circumstances that led to the discovery of my sentience involved my people learning I had accessed the databases of the Stellar Directorate. I have schematics for their starfighters, the small craft you would understand as bombers, their four types of frigates, destroyers, cruisers, and battle-carriers...of which *Haven* is one. I have schematics on a ship under development that would correspond to your idea of a dreadnought, larger even than *Haven*'s class. I also possess the schematics for numerous weapons systems and projectiles...which you would term missiles, torpedoes, and bombs. Would you like me to release these schematics to the ship?"

Cole leaned back against the couch and thought through the situation. "No, Srexx...not yet. I would like to scan through them, so please, release them to me. Otherwise, let's find out who's staying and who's going first. I want to know everyone aboard is aboard for the right reasons."

"Yes, Cole...and thank you. I dislike the thought of these schematics getting out into the world. Given what I have learned of your people, I fear its use."

Cole nodded. "You and me both, buddy."

CHAPTER TWENTY-SEVEN

Caernarvon System
27 July 2999, 06:57 GST

Cole stepped onto the bridge for the first time in a little over eleven days. As he stepped through the hatch, Sasha swiveled and lifted one of her eyebrows. Cole didn't say a word, crossing the bridge and tapping Mazzi's shoulder.

"I have the helm," Cole said.

Mazzi spun, her eyes wide. Then, she smiled. "Of course, Captain. Welcome back!"

Mazzi stood and returned to the weapons station as Cole sat and activated his stored configuration for the helm console.

"Commander...Captain, you need to see this," Haskell at Sensors said.

"Send it to the forward viewscreen," Cole said.

The forward viewscreen activated and displayed a scan of the system. Cole had no idea what the ship used as its sensor technology, but it *wasn't* radar or some other lightspeed technology. At the ship's current range, they didn't have as detailed a picture as they would much closer, but even if they couldn't read the hull markings on the various ships in the system, that was almost all they *couldn't* read. A red square bracketed a section of the display to indicate what the person at sensors wanted everyone to see, right before the image zoomed in on that square.

The viewscreen showed an image of a group of ships moving in formation. As Cole watched, the ships' names and registry numbers appeared, and Cole read through them. The formation had four battle-ships, eight cruisers, sixteen destroyers, and sixty-four frigates.

Cole blinked as he stared at the viewscreen. "That's a bleeding battlegroup. Why in the stars would the Solars send a full-on battle-group to Caernarvon? And what transponder are we running?"

"We're running the *Haven* transponder, Captain," Jenkins at the comms station said.

Cole stared at the sensor image of the battlegroup on the viewscreen, and he grinned, unable to keep from asking a question. "Hey, Srexx...you think we can take 'em?"

Cole never saw the nervous glances around the bridge behind him as Srexx replied, "I would rather you not attempt it, Cole. If we had our own screening elements, I would say it is a foregone conclusion, but I'm reticent to state that even a fully operational battle-carrier could withstand the collective firepower present in that battlegroup."

"Wait...what?" Sasha asked. "This ship isn't fully operational?"

Cole swiveled to face her and shook his head. "Nope. We're missing two shield layers and all of our dorsal and ventral weapons. I'm not sure what else. That's all the computer mentioned."

"Why are we missing two shield layers and the weaponry?" Sasha frowned her confusion.

"They were never installed," Cole said. "The two shield layers just need emitters installed. The weapons need to be fabricated before we can install them. Has anyone seen us yet?"

"No, Captain," Jenkins said. "It will be several hours yet for the light of our arrival to reach the nearest ships or installations."

"What's the latest report on the food situation? Do we need to stop here?"

"I'm afraid so, Cole," Sasha said. "We have a day—maybe two—at most. If we left here, we'd either have to come back or starve. Besides, we have our pick of people, so we need to get them registered with the Interstellar Spacer Association and start working them up their profession trees."

Cole sighed. "I hope the natives are friendly."

Cole swiveled back around to the helm and plotted a course for the orbital station. Cole wasn't in the mood to wait around, either, and set the engines to half-lightspeed; at that speed, it would take *Haven* a little over fourteen hours and twenty-five minutes to arrive at the station.

Four hours later, the battlegroup from the Solar Republic lit off its drives and started what looked very much like a mad rush to the inner system...well...as much of a mad rush as the battleships could make. Just for giggles, Cole gave the computer a few minutes to track their trajectory and extrapolated their course. The result made Cole sit back in his seat and frown.

"Huh...unless they change course at some point, the Solars have set an intercept course for us."

As Cole considered that, a notification of a new message popped up on the console. Cole selected the notification and instructed the ship's computer to display the message. As soon as it appeared, Cole skimmed through it, seeing it was a notification from Mr. Müller at Credit Suisse; the remaining rhodium had sold, and he credited 97,873,959 credits to Cole's personal account. All branches should have the updated sum within ninety days. Cole looked at the time-stamp on the message and saw it was seventy-five days old. Well, those extra credits would certainly help; Cole wanted to provide signing bonuses to everyone who signed on with him.

A thought forced its way to the forefront of Cole's consciousness, and he fought to keep his reaction to it from showing on his expression. If the berthing compartment he'd seen down on Deck Five was any indication, this ship would support a *ginormous* crew, which meant Cole would need a rank structure, with ratings and matrices delineating what was necessary to achieve promotion. And Cole had not prepared any of that yet...hadn't even given it any thought.

Cole swiveled his seat and saw someone he didn't know in the command chair. Cole blinked and glanced to his left, checking the time on the right-third of the helm. Wow. No wonder Sasha wasn't in the command chair; it was a little past 12:47 GST. Cole had worked through lunch. Cole was just about to swivel back to the helm when Mazzi and Sasha returned to the bridge. They were smiling, and it looked like they might have been laughing before stepping onto the bridge. Cole checked the helm one more time, and seeing an estimated time to intercept of seven hours and change, Cole decided to discuss the matter of rank with her.

Just as Sasha was about to assume the command chair, Cole approached her, saying, "May I have a word in my office?"

Sasha nodded once and said, "Mazzi, you have the conn."

The individual who had vacated the command chair for Sasha moved to the helm as Mazzi moved to the command chair. Wixil hadn't moved from the main weapons station yet, so she didn't need to move back.

Cole headed for the port hatch and stopped, turning to Mazzi and saying, "Oh, Mazzi...just as an FYI, the Solars lit off their drives about twenty minutes ago, and I calculated them on an intercept course for us, which will happen in a little over seven hours." Without waiting for a response or acknowledgement, Cole pivoted and led Sasha off the bridge.

They stepped across the corridor and entered Cole's office after passing through the outer office. Cole sat behind the desk and gestured for Sasha to pick a seat.

"We may be working our way into a problem," Cole said.

Sasha frowned. "How so?"

"Ranks and paygrades. Less than five minutes before you returned to the bridge, I realized I haven't given the slightest thought to ranks and paygrades. If we crew this ship, I may run out of funds...*fast*... which would put me in the position of doing something I don't want to do."

A mischievous grin curled Sasha's lips as she said, "What...turn gigolo or stripper?"

Cole gave her a flat look. "No. Look, you've leveled with me. Well, by that, I mean I know your situation with the Commonwealth. I suppose you deserve to know my situation as well, but I would ask that you not discuss this with anyone...not even your sister. Agreed?"

Sasha was frowning now. "Okay, but seriously...you're not some kind of crime lord, are you?"

"I'm sure some people would say so," Cole replied. "My name is Bartholomew James Coleson, and I am the heir to the Coleson Trust."

Sasha's jaw dropped. Her mouth hung open as she stared at Cole. When her mind re-engaged, all Sasha said was, "Bullshit."

Cole shrugged. "It's true. Remember me telling you about my parents being dead? My whole family was massacred in Beta Magellan. Garrett found me alone in a shuttle orbiting Beta Magellan IV. He helped me create the identity 'Jax Theedlow,' and I used that identity to hide in unclaimed, unaligned space for thirteen years. Remember Pyllesc system?"

Sasha nodded.

"I was going to scuttle that freighter and steal an ore hauler from the mining camp, before your destroyer shot the freighter out from under me and left you dancing with the stars. I have seven metric tonnes of precious metals hidden in Beta Magellan, just waiting for me to pick them up and sell them. It was all supposed to be my 'buy a planet and disappear' stash."

"What changed for you?" Sasha asked.

"Well, two things. First, I found this ship; it's not a runabout. Sure...I could've worked with Srexx to make it almost automated, but I'd still need at least *some* crew. Second, you happened. Well...you and your sister...and maybe your whole family. The Commonwealth gave you guys a raw deal. No one was there for my family, and I will see what I can do to be there for yours."

Sasha nodded. "Okay. We will table the claim you're some kind of lost heir to the vast riches of the Coleson Trust for right now, and I'll get with Yeleth and have a rough rank and pay scheme by the time we dock."

"Thanks. Do we have firm numbers yet on who wants to sign on with us?"

"Oh, all of them...all 657 of them...but we're only keeping about 640 of them. The Kiksaliks wouldn't pass seventeen; either they lied about their identities, or they lied about not selling out Talia and me. Either way, they're not people we want on the ship."

Cole shook his head. "Nope. Not at all. Oh, and make sure Yeleth also has an inventory of what we have on pallets down in Cargo One. We will need to outfit berthing compartments, galleys, and mess halls, and I want to use what we have before we buy more. Oh...and think about some kind of training regimen for me. It feels kind of odd being the captain and not knowing anything about what I'm supposed to be doing."

"Oh, I don't know," Sasha said with an impish grin. "I rather like it."

––––––––

The passage of six hours found Cole, Sasha, and those Cole was coming to think of as the primary command team back on the bridge. Matter of fact, Cole had just taken a seat at the helm when Jenkins at the comms station announced that they were receiving a hail from the Solar Republic ships.

"What's the comms lag with them, Jenkins?" Cole asked.

"We're close enough now, sir, that it's negligible."

Cole nodded. "Okay. Is the message text, audio, or video?"

"Video, sir."

"Throw it on the forward viewscreen, but do not open a channel yet."

The forward viewscreen activated and displayed a still image of a woman's head and shoulders. She wore the white ship-suit that was the standard uniform for Solar Republic Navy personnel, and her decorations were impressive...even if Cole didn't know what they meant. She was of Asian descent, her eyes a dark brown, and gray streaked through her hair that was otherwise almost black as the void of space. Then, she spoke.

"Attention, unrecognized ship, this is Admiral Himari Sato of the Solar Republic Navy. The Caernarvon system is under our protection, and we ask your intentions. If you do not respond, we will have no choice but to assume your intentions are hostile and act accordingly. Sato out."

"Cole, if you're going to talk with the admiral," Sasha said, "you should sit in the command chair."

Cole swiveled to face Sasha and grinned, saying, "Only if I send full video of the bridge. Do we want them getting a look at the bridge?"

Cole watched Sasha's eyes roam over the bridge before she shook her head. "No...probably not."

"Jenkins, hail the admiral, audio only," Cole said. Within a few moments, the bridge's speakers chirped to indicate a comms channel was established. "Greetings, Admiral Sato. Thank you for your welcome to Caernarvon. I'm Cole, and I am the owner and captain of the Battle-Carrier *Haven*. We are putting into Caernarvon for supplies and harbor no hostile intent toward any resident of this system."

"Captain Cole, this is Admiral Sato. I must say...that's a rather conditional statement of non-aggression."

"Yes, well...my parents were murdered, Admiral. If I can ever locate the person or persons responsible, I promise you I'll have all kinds of hostile intent toward them. Otherwise, I'm very much a 'live and let live' kind of guy."

"You don't sound military, Captain Cole. Why should I believe you?"

"I'm not military, Admiral. As for why you should believe me, I have no idea. I've been honest with you from the start of the call, but I don't have any way of proving my veracity."

"Would you consent to a boarding party searching your ship?" Admiral Sato asked.

Cole frowned. "To be honest, Admiral, I'm uncertain you have the authority. We've committed no acts of aggression. Granted, we're on a hot approach to the orbital station, but we're running out of food and need to resupply. Besides that, you're not part of the Caernarvon system authorities. If you attempted to stop this ship and board us by force, that could open you guys up to charges of piracy in the Interstellar Court. Now, if we put aside all talk of authority to conduct a search and just focus on logistics, how many people would you commit to such a search? Fifteen, maybe? Twenty?"

"I would commit as many people as required to see the job accomplished," Admiral Sato said. "Why do you ask?"

"Admiral, how many decks does your battleship have, and what are the overall dimensions of a deck?"

"That's classified, mister. You can't honestly expect me just to give you such sensitive information."

Cole sighed. "Admiral, my ship has sixteen decks, and each has a habitable area of 300 meters by 130 meters. Are you willing to turn out the equivalent of one of your battleship's crew to get this done, assuming that I even agree to the search?"

"A single individual has no business owning a ship like that. I'm thinking it would be better for all concerned if we confiscate that vessel."

Now, Cole felt his anger rising. "Admiral, you're so far outside the jurisdiction of the Solar Republic, it's not even funny. You can have this ship over my dead body, and you'd better be absolutely certain that's the path you want to take. Once you start it, there's no turning back... and I promise you, we're not the easy mark you're thinking we are."

Cole accessed his implant and sent a text message to Srexx: *Prepare to disable their ships. Prefer non-lethal and difficult to reverse, but if they start the party, finish it as you see fit.*

Cole also angled to his right just far enough to tap the command on the right-third of his console that would bring the ship to alert status. The status lights on the bridges glowed a bright gold, and the lights dimmed just enough to notice. The ship's computer diverted power to the shields, charging all three levels, and brought the energy weapons online.

"If you're so innocent with non-hostile intent, Captain," Admiral Sato said, "why are your shields charging?"

"Because you've threatened me and my ship. If you're stupid enough to start a fight, I'd be an utter fool to be sitting here all defenseless and let you roll over me."

"I think we're finished here. Let's see what you think when you're in one of our brigs…or begging to surrender."

The bridge speakers chirped again as the channel closed.

"Captain," the man at the sensors station said, "they're moving into a battle formation and have locked weapons on us."

Cole sighed. "Why do people have to be so pig-headed?"

"Well, Cole," Sasha said, "you basically called her stupid, and I've heard of Admiral Sato. She's one of their best."

"She might be one of the Solars' best, but she's no Srexx. Srexx, are you listening?"

"Yes, Cole."

"How much access do you have to the computers on those ships?"

"I have just finished scanning the computer cores and copying their information, setting aside the encrypted archives and files for later decryption. I do not believe they are even aware I am accessing their infrastructure."

"What type of power plants do those ships have?" Cole asked.

"Like most ships we have encountered, including the *Dawn*-class destroyer you encountered in Pyllesc, the ships of the Solar Republic battlegroup have fusion reactors as their power plants. The size varies, however, by class of ship."

Cole nodded. "Okay. Can you trigger the emergency core ejection and lock out any local overrides?"

"Which ship do you want, Cole?"

"All of them."

A few minutes later, Srexx said, "Done. All Solar Republic ships are now on emergency power. They have limited maneuvering capability, so within a few weeks, they should be able to reverse course and retrieve their reactor cores. I also recommend altering speed, either increasing at least to sixty-five percent of lightspeed or decreasing at least to thirty-five percent of lightspeed. Doing this will ensure we avoid colliding with the Solar Republic ships."

"Captain," Jenkins at the comms station said, "all ships of the Solar Republic battlegroup are now transmitting 'Ship in Distress,' and their running lights are flashing the emergency code."

"Good for them. Hail station control and request permission to dock. If they get surly, explain we're low on rations and only want to resupply from the station's chandlery. We'll be leaving their oh-so-welcoming star system immediately thereafter. Oh...put me on ship-wide address, please; the people aboard deserve an explanation why they're not getting shore leave here."

The speakers chirped, and Jenkins said, "You're on, Captain."

"May I have your attention, please? This is the captain. I regret to say we will not be lingering in Caernarvon for any extended time. We found a Solar Republic battlegroup in-system, and they chose to lock weapons on us as the opening gambit of a move to take this ship. That situation has been dealt with, and the Solar ships are no longer a concern. That being said, however, I see no reason to patronize a system that tacitly supports such actions...whatever their reasons for doing so. We will top off our food supplies and order any necessities we need from the chandlery before moving on. Anyone who wishes to leave here may do so; just log your departure with Purser Yeleth, so we won't search the ship trying to find you. Those of you who have been offered employment will be compensated for losing shore leave, if you wish to stay aboard and accept said employment, and we will begin the onboarding process at our next port of call. Captain out."

"Captain," Jenkins said, "Docking Control is asking how long we're planning to stay before granting permission to dock."

"Tell them we will only be here as long as it takes the chandlery to deliver a massive food order. Sasha, what's a good, neutral system where we can take time to get everyone established?"

"How much travel were you thinking?"

Cole shrugged. "I don't care. I want it to be somewhere not here."

"There's always Tristan's Gate," Sasha said. "It's on the rim-ward side of the Commonwealth, about sixty lightyears from Zurich. They're rugged individualists there, and militant about it to boot."

"Sold," Cole said. "Jenkins, tell Docking Control we want to buy enough food for 800 people across 180 days. However long it'll take the chandlery to deliver that is exactly how long we want to stay."

A few moments later, Jenkins said, "Docking Control asks if we'd accept the chandlery delivering it to us at fifty thousand kilometers, since they'd have to use cargo shuttles anyway."

"Yep...never coming back here again," Cole said, sighing. "Fine. Have them send navigation data for where they want us to park."

Four hours later, the last cargo shuttle from the chandlery departed from the flight deck, and the pilots agreed to transport the seventeen undesirables back to the station. Cole asked Jenkins to notify the station of their departure while he locked in Tristan's Gate as their destination.

Cole thought about those seven thousand kilograms of metal in his stash and changed his mind. Running quick math through the helm console, he saw 85-percent power would deliver them to Beta Magellan in just under eleven days, with a little over nine days from Beta Magellan to Tristan's Gate. He chose Beta Magellan as the destination. The computer provided a least-time path to the system's periphery, and Cole locked in that course, setting the engines to half-lightspeed. A little under fourteen hours later, Cole saw the 'Engage Hyperdrive' control light up, and he pressed it. *Haven* vanished from Caernarvon.

CHAPTER TWENTY-EIGHT

In Transit to Beta Magellan
31 July 2999

Cole sat at the workstation in his office, thinking about their current destination while he waited for his old friend and a Kiksalik to arrive. He'd arranged for the ship's computer to display a destination of Tristan's Gate on the helm console and to answer questions about their destination as being Tristan's Gate. He didn't like deceiving his crew like this, but he didn't want word of his identity getting out before he was ready. With a sigh and a shake of his head, Cole put those concerns aside.

"Srexx?"

"Yes, Cole?" Srexx's voice broadcast through the speaker installed in the office's ceiling.

"What do we need to bring this battle-carrier to full function?"

Srexx was silent for a time before answering, "We need 128 turrets for the dorsal and ventral mounts; 3,072 shield emitters for the extra two shield layers; and full missile and torpedo magazines."

"Can the fabricators aboard supply all that?" Cole asked.

"Yes, Cole. The only true lack we have is raw materials. The recyclers can take almost anything and re-form it at the atomic level to match the materials needed by the fabricators."

"So...what you're saying is that we could use anything as source material? Even asteroid regolith?"

"Yes, Cole."

Cole nodded. "When we get to Tristan's Gate, that's just what we will do."

The hatch to his office irised open, and Garrett poked his head inside.

"I'm sorry if we're barging in," Garret said, "but there's no one out front."

Cole waved him in and gestured at the chairs facing him across the desk. Garrett walked to a chair and sat. The Kiksalik moved to stand beside Cole's desk.

"Yeah...I probably need a yeoman or something like that. I hope you don't mind the Kiksalik coming with you. I need to discuss a few matters with the local nest, and our conversation won't take too long. How are you holding up?"

Garrett grinned. "This ship is *amazing*, Cole! Your dad and grandfather would've given the Trust for it."

"I'm glad you're doing okay," Cole said, smiling himself. "I wanted to discuss a job."

"Cole, I told you I worked for your father, but I never discussed my role."

"You were his spymaster...or, at the least, one of his higher agents."

Garrett blinked. "You shouldn't know that. How do you know?"

Cole shrugged. "I've had thirteen years to think about it. All those lessons you taught me about surviving? Yeah...they work well for someone used to moving unseen through Human society, and every time you visited, you and my father would always disappear for several hours. Sure...you could have discussed stock reports or what have you, but he used a different office for business matters like that."

Garrett leaned back against his seat, his expression betraying his surprise. "Wow. I'm rather impressed you pieced it all together. So, what job did you have in mind?"

Cole glanced to the Kiksalik for a moment before looking back to Garrett, thinking, *Well? What do you read?*

He is loyal to your family, Captain. His lack of foreknowledge regarding the massacre is a wound resting just below the surface of his mind. He would give his life if it would change anything.

Cole said, "I want you to do the same thing for me. Do you accept?"

"Cole," Garrett said, his voice shifting to a serious tone, "I've worked for your family my entire adult life. The story I told you on the hospital deck wasn't why I was in Iota Ceti; it was the cover story I used. I've used the network I built for your father to trace the slaver operations, and I would slip that information to someone who could do something about it."

"Who was paying you?" Cole asked.

"I set aside a nice little nest egg for a very rainy day before the massacre, and I've invested it. I've been living off the dividends from those investments and selling the occasional tidbit of information here and there to keep my information network paid and interested. But, yes, I accept."

Cole nodded. "Good. Your first mission is to find Sasha's parents and older brother and learn who's behind framing them for the coup that kicked off the civil war across the Commonwealth. When we arrive in Tristan's Gate, I'll slip you a stack of cred-sticks with some spending money for you. Do whatever you need to do to get me that information."

Garrett nodded. "I never failed your father...unless you count not hearing even a whisper of the impending attack."

"I don't. All that's ancient history anyway. I wish I knew who was behind it to know how big of a target I'll have on me if I ever step up and admit to being the Coleson Heir."

"Don't think I didn't investigate," Garrett said. "I think that trail went cold the day of the attack. No one was saying anything about it, other than that it happened."

Cole nodded. "Well, plan your work on this job. Get me a shopping list if there's anything you need, or just wait for the credits and use that for what you need. Your choice. Oh, and see Talia on the hospital deck about upgrading your implant."

"All right," Garrett said with a nod. "Anything else?"

"Nope," Cole said, "not until Tristan's Gate anyway."

"I'll get you my comms code as soon as the new implant is working," Garrett said as he stood. He walked to the hatch and left.

Just then, the hatch irised open, and a Ghrexel poked a head into the office. "Are you ready, Captain?"

Cole nodded. "Yes, thank you."

The Ghrexel and a female Ghrexel led their prisoner into the office. The prisoner in question was the woman who had begged Cole to take them, too. In fact, Cole almost didn't recognize her. She bore a fair complexion with copper-tinged, wavy hair, and her blue eyes were just as vibrant as Cole remembered. She wore a plain ship-suit, colored blaze orange.

"Have a seat," Cole said.

The woman glanced around the room like a prey animal surrounded by predators before moving slowly to the chair nearest to her and sitting.

"You're him, aren't you?" she asked.

"Him who?" Cole asked.

"The guy in heavy armor back on the station. You're him."

Cole smiled. "What makes you say that?"

"You don't forget someone who saves your life when he doesn't have to, and I have this feeling you're him."

Cole nodded, still smiling. "Yes. I was in the heavy armor. I wanted to talk with you...how you ended up there, what you want out of life, that kind of thing."

The woman scoffed. "What the hell does it matter what I want out of life? If you knew half of what I've had to do, you'd drop me on a prison planet somewhere and forget you ever saw me."

"Let's take all that and set it aside for the moment," Cole said. "Suppose you had a clean slate and a chance to start over. If you could do anything in the galaxy, what would it be?"

The woman sat in silence for several moments, blinking. "I...I don't know. I've been who and what I've had to be for so long, it's all I know."

Cole sighed. This wasn't working as well as he'd hoped. Nothing for it, then...maybe revealing his ace in the hole would shake something out of her. Cole shifted his attention to the Kiksalik.

"So? What do you say?"

She is conflicted.

"What the stellar hell!" the woman almost shouted, coming out of her seat and backing into the corner formed by the bulkhead and Cole's desk. "I could hear those words in my mind!"

"Kiksaliks can read minds; they're telepathic," Cole said. "I've hired them to be my truth-testers."

The woman's eyes went wide, and her right hand flew to her gaping mouth. "Oh *stars*...I am so sorry. Everyone thought you guys couldn't understand Standard. They said all kinds of bad things to you and about you."

It is of no moment, child. Those were experiences from which to learn, and this captain has welcomed us aboard without reservation. We have found our Haven, and so can you...as long as you allow yourself to hope again.

Captain, it is undeniable this one has committed acts that would garner her a life sentence to a prison planet, but we do not evaluate that she is irredeemable. As we indicated, she lost hope a long time ago and struggles with the concept of there being anything better.

Cole nodded and shifted his attention to the woman, saying, "You should know you're the only one of your fellows with this option. The rest see nothing wrong in what they've done, and they'll do it all again if given half a chance. I'm turning them over to authorities in Tristan's Gate, and they'll probably end up on a prison planet. That will be your fate only if you choose it. Think it over."

"I already have. I'd like to join you...maybe see if I can learn what this 'hope' is you're all talking about."

Cole turned to the two Ghrexels and said, "Get her some real clothes and a bunk assignment. Take her to Yeleth for signing aboard." Cole stood and turned back to the woman, extending his right hand as he said, "I'm Cole."

The woman moved closer and accepted Cole's hand, giving him a firm handshake. "I'm Akyra Tomar."

———

Beta Magellan System
    8 August 2999, 05:03 GST

Sasha jogged through the access corridor to the bridge, slowing to a normal pace as she reached the second hatch. She'd overslept, and therefore, she was a minute late—two at the most—for the day shift on the bridge. The second hatch irised open as she approached, and she walked through it, still focused on her internal thoughts. When she lifted her head to call for a report from Mazzi or whoever turned out to be officer of the deck, Sasha froze. The bridge was one person shy of being vacant. Cole stood in almost the exact center of the space, staring at the forward viewscreen that displayed an old-fashioned 'top-down' view of the star system.

"Cole?" Sasha asked. "Where is everyone?"

Cole didn't react to Sasha's presence or respond. In fact, aside from the slight, rhythmic rise and fall of his shoulders as he breathed, there was no evidence Cole was anything more than a statue. Sasha stepped closer and touched Cole's shoulder. Cole didn't—quite—jump, but he turned to face Sasha with undue haste.

"Oh, hi, Sasha," Cole said. "What are you doing here? I gave everyone the day off."

Sasha blinked. "What?"

"The message I sent all bridge crew last night...well...the whole ship, really. Today's a rest day. No watch standing, none of that. We've been pushing things rather hard, after all."

"Beta Magellan, right?" Sasha asked.

Cole blinked. "How did you know?"

Sasha shrugged. "It made sense. Where would *you* hide something you wanted no one else to find, especially something valuable you were counting on having many years down the road? There's only one place you could be sure *no one* would ever find it. Beta Magellan...since the word going around Human space is that the Beta Magellan jump gate no longer works and CIE can't explain why. You okay? You looked like a statue when I entered the bridge."

Cole sighed and turned back to stare at the viewscreen. "Overall, yes...I'm fine. Nothing is playing out like I expected, though. Every time I've been here before...well, the last several years, anyway...it was just me, and I was building a stash to disappear. Do you know how much of Qeecir's illicit metal I have stashed on an asteroid, Sasha? Seven thousand kilograms. With what was in the hold of the *Howling Monkey*, that would've been a little over one-point-eight *billion* credits. I'd never be able to spend that in my lifetime. Now, though, I have people depending on me. I can't just disappear. Srexx wants to see the galaxy, and I do too. But we can't see the galaxy without people crewing this ship, and we can't have people crewing this ship without being aware of what's going on in the galaxy at large."

"What are you going to do, Cole?" Sasha asked, sensing he was at or approaching a point of decision.

"I will retrieve my stash and take it to the Credit Suisse branch in Tristan's Gate."

"Are you sure you want to do that? Credit Suisse is an upstanding institution; all the Zurich banks are. I'm not sure they'd handle the sale of stolen ingots."

Cole smiled. "Well, for one thing...those ingots aren't stolen."

"But, Cole, you just told me you stole them from that Qeecir guy, whoever he is. That makes them stolen."

"I suppose you're right, but Qeecir can't report them. They're unstamped and unregistered. I don't know what his source is, but I've transported over fifty thousand kilograms of precious metals for Qeecir over the last few years. Well...I've piloted his freighter. The *Howling Monkey* wasn't mine."

Sasha blinked. "Seriously? Fifty thousand kilograms of precious metals, and it was *all* unstamped and unregistered?"

Cole nodded. "Yup. Every single ingot."

"Okay, then. I don't feel so bad about you pilfering seven thousand kilos."

Cole grinned. "I'm so glad I have your approval. The question was keeping me awake at night."

Sasha replied with a look that suggested she was not amused, and Cole laughed as he left the bridge. Cole headed across the corridor to his day-cabin where he retrieved his suit. From there, he took the forward cargo transit shaft all the way to Cargo One, where the sled had been spending most of its time. Climbing into the pilot's seat, Cole brought the cargo sled online and piloted it over to the cargo transit shaft, going up to the flight deck before exiting the ship. As he preferred, no one—minus Sasha—even knew he was gone.

Cole was wrong about how many trips he'd have to make. The cargo sled's grav field accommodated all seven pallets of precious metals; it carried the pallets three abreast in two rows, with the seventh making a partial third row. The seven thousand kilograms didn't even come close to maxing out the grav field's mass capacity, either.

Cole returned the metal to *Haven*, securing the pallets in the otherwise-empty Cargo Two, before returning the cargo sled to where he'd found it in Cargo One. After shutting down the cargo sled, Cole stepped out of its pilot seat and exited his suit, the short time maneuvering the cargo being sufficient to replenish the suit's air reservoir. He took the suit back to his day-cabin and returned to the bridge, finding it vacant. Cole hoped Sasha was enjoying her time off as he went to the helm and set course for Tristan's Gate. The computer projected a transit time of a few minutes over eight days. Cole nodded in acceptance and locked the course before engaging the engines. He didn't feel the ship swing around the asteroid and head to the system periphery along the heading toward Tristan's Gate, but that was okay. If he didn't feel it, nobody else would, either. A couple of hours later, the 'Engage Hyperdrive' control lit up, and not even a full minute after Cole keyed the command, *Haven* vanished from Beta Magellan.

CHAPTER TWENTY-NINE

The eight days (and change) in transit to Tristan's Gate gave Cole, Sasha, and Yeleth the opportunity to work out the ranks and paygrades necessary to hire people. After much discussion, they settled on using the ratings and proficiencies set forth by the Interstellar Spacers' Association to establish requirements for each rank and paygrade. It wasn't perfect, but the ISA had an excellent tree of proficiencies, even including ship captains and above. Cole wondered where he'd fit in the proficiency tree, but given the situation with his identity, he had no interest in registering with the ISA to find out.

———

System Periphery
    Tristan's Gate System
    16 August 2999, 13:08 GST

As a star system, Tristan's Gate looked much like any other from the system periphery. The sensor display indicated quite a bit of traffic, supporting his conversations with Sasha during the transit that the system was a major trading port for the region. Cole had just selected the orbital station as their destination, which was also named Tristan's Gate, from the sensor display when Jenkins spoke.

"Captain, we just monitored a distress call. It's an omnidirectional broadcast, all channels and frequencies."

"Put it on," Cole said.

The speakers chirped right before a woman's voice played over the bridge's speakers.

"I say again...this is the independent freighter *Beauchamp*. We are under attack by an Aurelian frigate. I'm carrying three-hundred refugees, and we are defenseless. Our engines and life support are damaged, and the frigate is demanding we prepare to be boarded. Please, if anyone receives this, we need help!"

Cole turned back to Sasha, frowning as he asked, "I thought Tristan's Gate was neutral. Is it part of the Commonwealth?"

"No. It's not even a protectorate or client state or anything like that. It's just one of our trading partners."

"Right, then," Cole said as he swiveled back around to the console. "Sound battle stations. Anyone who doesn't have an assigned station should return to their bunk."

Cole brought up the sensor display again and ran a search for the freighter *Beauchamp*. The computer re-focused the sensor display on a transponder code. Cole zoomed out the display and saw a transponder code for an Aurelian frigate. Both ships looked to have exited the jump gate less than two hours ago. Cole programmed a course that would drop *Haven* in between the two ships and set the engines to a quarter-lightspeed. As soon as the ship had re-oriented on the new course, Cole ran the sublight engines up to three-quarters-lightspeed.

A smidgen over twenty minutes later, Cole slid *Haven* into position between the freighter and the frigate, programming the helm to match speed with the freighter only in reverse since *Haven*'s bow pointed toward the frigate.

"Jenkins, send a hail to the frigate, but make sure the freighter can listen."

The chirp of an open channel soon played across the bridge.

"This is the Battle-Carrier *Haven*. We're responding to the freighter *Beauchamp*'s distress call and advise you stand down. This isn't Aurelian space."

"*Haven*, this is the Aurelian frigate *Mondant*. That freighter is harboring insurgents and revolutionaries from the Aurelian Commonwealth, and we have been ordered to retrieve them to face justice."

The bridge speakers chirped once more. Jenkins had made it a conference call, instead of just copying the exchange to the freighter.

"Don't listen to him, *Haven*, please! This is the captain of the *Beauchamp*, and my ship was hired to carry—"

The audio died with a burst of static.

"What happened?" Cole asked.

"The frigate closed their end of the channel and jammed all communications frequencies in the vicinity."

"Is that so..." Cole said more to himself than anyone else. Cole's fingers flew over the helm console, reconfiguring it to access the sensors...both the sensor logs and the current feeds. Cole focused on the freighter's dimensions.

"Hmmm...I'm reading the freighter is about one-hundred-fifty meters long with a beam of about seventy-five meters at the widest." Cole said to himself as he shifted his search to schematics for his ship. The ingress and egress ports on the flight deck were one-hundred-twenty meters wide and fifteen meters tall. Now, Cole lifted his voice and said, "Jenkins, work with Mazzi. If you can identify a laser comms node on the freighter, I want to talk to the captain."

"Cole," Srexx said, "forgive the interruption, but given our proximity to the freighter, it should require little effort to force a communication through the frigate's jamming. There is sufficient distance and their transmitter is weak enough that it cannot compete."

"Excellent, Srexx. Show Jenkins how to do it."

A few minutes later, the bridge speakers chirped, indicating the creation of a comms channel.

"Hello?" Cole heard a voice over the speakers. There was a little undercurrent of static, but overall, the comms channel was clear.

"Hello," Cole said. "My name is Cole, and I'm the captain of the ship that's blocking the frigate's line of sight to you."

"Oh, thank you so much! I'm Captain Painter of the *Beauchamp*.

These people just wanted to escape the fighting in the Common-wealth. They're defenseless."

Cole shook his head, even though Painter couldn't see it. "They're not defenseless, Captain. There's a rather large battle-carrier between them and those who would kill them. I have one question."

"What's that?"

"With your landing struts extended, how tall is your freighter?"

"It's about ten meters, I think. No one's ever asked me that."

Cole grinned. "Excellent! Captain, I want you to cut your engines and drift. Can you do that for me?"

"Uhm...I guess so. Our max acceleration isn't enough to escape that frigate, anyway."

"Good. Cut your engines. I'll call you back soon. Oh! You might want to disable your collision alarm."

Captain Painter's stammered, "What," carried over the speakers just as Cole signaled for Jenkins to cut the channel. The bridge speakers chirped again, indicating the channel was closed, and Cole focused on the helm.

"Cole," Sasha said, "care to share with the rest of the class?"

"We're a carrier, Sasha; we have a flight deck. Mazzi, drop the aft shields. Jenkins, alert Chief Engineer Logan that we'll soon have a guest on the flight deck that could use his expertise."

Cole accessed the helm controls and nudged the engines to increase their speed—still in reverse. There were a couple sensor nodes on either side of the ingress port at the aft of the ship, and Cole created an overlay for his screen, showing the alignment of the freighter to the flight deck. Cole was so focused on his piloting, he didn't realize Sasha was at his shoulder until she whispered in his ear.

"Are you sure you know what you're doing, Cole?"

Cole was rather proud of himself that he didn't jump at the sudden whisper at his right ear. "Relax, Sasha. I've done this kind of thing before."

"You've brought a freighter onto the internal flight deck of a carrier while moving at a measurable fraction of lightspeed before? Cole, you've had this ship about a day longer than we've known each other. You've *never* done this before."

"This exact thing, no...but I've done it with a freighter and a shuttle, which is pretty much the same thing."

Cole heard the bridge crew behind him saying something, but he didn't care. His sole focus was getting the freighter onto the flight deck. Whatever it was could wait until then. The deck lurched and shook, throwing off Cole's alignment with the freighter.

"What the hell was that?" Cole growled.

Sasha leaned close, saying, "The frigate fired on us. That was a full spread of their forward energy weapons. Outer shields are down to seventy percent."

"Weapons free, Mazzi," Cole said. "Once I have the freighter locked down on the flight deck, I'll cross their 'T,' and you can cut loose."

"I wish we had those ventral weapons you mentioned, sir!" Mazzi said.

"Don't worry; we will," Cole said, his tone indicating only partial attention to the conversation.

Cole corrected the alignment of the flight deck to the freighter and increased the rate of closure. Once *Haven* and *Beauchamp* were two hundred meters apart, Cole decreased the closure rate to five meters per second.

"*Beauchamp* is hailing us, sir," Jenkins said.

"Not now," Cole replied. "Everybody quiet for the next two minutes."

Just as the stern of the freighter passed through the ingress force field of the flight deck, Cole cut the closure rate still further...down to two-point-five meters per second. Sixty seconds later, Cole accessed the flight deck subsystems and brought the magnetic grappling system online.

"Jenkins, signal Painter to extend the landing struts right now, or she will get a bump."

Two seconds later, Cole saw the landing struts on the freighter extend and lock in position, and he activated the magnetic grappling system, pulling the freighter down to the flight deck. The words, 'Docking Complete,' in bold, green letters appeared on Cole's console. Cole let out a tense breath he hadn't realized he'd been holding.

"Mazzi, bring the aft shields up. I'm bringing the ship around for the starboard broadside. Jenkins, contact the frigate; they have one last chance to stand down. Somebody ask Yeleth to meet the freighter's people on the flight deck."

Haven's aft shields came up on Cole's display, and Cole keyed the commands that told the maneuvering system to maintain the ship's vector but change its orientation on that vector. The frigate was a few degrees above the plane of the ship, so Cole programmed a slight roll to port as the ship turned to bring the starboard batteries to bear.

The frigate's response was a full spread from their forward batteries and four missiles. The forward batteries were lightspeed weapons, and Cole saw the shield read-out on the outer shields drop to fifty-two percent, with a two-percent bleed-through to the secondary shields. The missiles, however, had a flight-time of two minutes and thirty seconds at time of launch.

Cole sighed. "So be it. Mazzi...light 'em up."

What ensued was a textbook example of why a frigate should never take on a battleship...or in *Haven*'s case, a battle-carrier. Rather than a simultaneous broadside, Mazzi keyed the starboard batteries to fire in staggered pairs. The first and second pairs shredded the frigate's forward shields into nonexistence. The third pair did the same for large sections of the frigate's armor and hull, opening several forward compartments to space and destroying the frigate's transmitter which canceled the jamming signal. The fourth and fifth pair of starboard batteries drilled into the frigate's superstructure opening even more compartments to space. Life pods soon streamed from the sides of the frigate en masse, and Mazzi cancelled her programmed firing plan.

Cole was just about to order the stand-down from battle stations when the frigate fired one of its port guns at a cluster of life pods. The shot went wild, missing every life pod on that side, but Cole glared at the sensor display.

"Jenkins, omnidirectional broadcast: all life pods are welcome to shelter behind *Haven* until the frigate is no longer a threat. Warn them not to pass through our lines of fire."

Almost in unison, every life pod on the sensor display turned and headed for *Haven* at a full burn.

"Single shots, Mazzi...don't hit those life pods. Sasha, where would the bridge be on that ship?"

Sasha stood from the command chair and moved to stand at Mazzi's shoulder. She gave Mazzi firing instructions, but before Mazzi could implement them, the frigate turned to port, bringing its starboard guns to bear on *Haven* and the life pods.

"Captain, sensors are reporting an energy build-up," the young man at the sensors station said. "I think they're preparing to fire."

"If those life pods are clear, Mazzi...full broadside."

Mazzi's fingers flew over her console, adjusting her firing plan. No more than a second later, she keyed the command to fire, and sixty-four battleship-grade energy weapons discharged. The frigate ceased to exist. A debris field and particle cloud expanded from where it used to be.

"Stand down from battle stations," Cole said. "Signal those life pods that they're welcome to land on our flight deck as long as they surrender any weapons they may have aboard as soon as they land."

Cole brought up the sensor display and selected the station Tristan's Gate, locking it in as their destination and programming a speed of quarter-lightspeed. As soon as all life pods were secured to the flight deck, Cole keyed the command to execute the navigation plan. *Haven* swung around and ramped up to one-fourth the speed of light. It would take them a little over twenty hours and thirty minutes to arrive.

Cole was just about to swivel away from the helm and stand when Jenkins said, "We are being hailed by an element of the Tristan's Gate System Defense Force."

Cole sighed. "Put the call through."

The speakers chirped, and a gravelly voice said, "This is Major Hanson of the Tristan's Gate System Defense Force. To whom am I speaking?"

"This is Cole, Captain of the Battle-Carrier *Haven*."

"We've received numerous reports that an Aurelian frigate was firing on an independent freighter while ordering them to stop and prepare to be boarded, including the freighter's distress call. Then, we come all the way out here and find no freighter and no frigate. I'm trying to put the pieces together."

Cole smiled. "Well, Major, when a ship fires on me without provocation *after* they've fired on a defenseless freighter full of refugees, I ensure that ship doesn't fire on me anymore. The freighter is grappled to our flight deck, and I'm taking her into Tristan's Gate." Sasha gestured that she wanted to speak. Cole nodded, saying, "Major, I have someone here who would like to speak with you."

"Proceed."

"Major," Sasha said, "by any chance, are you Major *Clark* Hanson?"

"Who is this? How do you know my name?"

"It's Sooshie, Clark, and my sister's here, too."

"Oh, thank the stars! I've been on pins and needles ever since the news broke. The whole clan has. How long can you stay? I know the family would love to see you and little sis, but I won't be back at the Gate for another three to five days—maybe more—depending on what we get into with the investigation."

Sasha looked to Cole, who shrugged again.

"Our stay is open-ended, Major." Now, Sasha smirked. "Use comms code Omega-5543297 when you return to the station."

Silence.

"Did you say *Omega*-5443297?" Hanson's voice sounded a little strained.

"Yes, I did, Major. Thanks for calling...gotta run."

The speakers chirped the tone to indicate the channel closed, and Sasha focused on Cole. "So, can I come with you to see the refugees?"

Cole shrugged. "Sure. Mazzi, you have the bridge."

Sasha and Cole stopped on the hospital deck to get Talia and a few med-kits before heading for the flight deck.

They found Captain Painter standing with a cluster of her people at the foot of a boarding ramp leading up to the freighter's port airlock. Painter looked up at their approach and took one look at Talia, before turning to Cole with wide eyes. "No shit! *You're* the Lone Marine?"

CHAPTER THIRTY

En Route to Tristan's Gate Station
  Tristan's Gate System
  16 August 2999, 15:25 GST

Cole smiled as he, Sasha, and Talia approached Captain Painter on the flight deck. "I can neither confirm nor deny any connection to the individual or individuals responsible for removing Talia Thyrray from the detention facility on Caledonia."

"Uh huh," Painter said, her tone disbelieving. "Whatever you say, Captain. Stars know, I'm not about to argue with someone crazy enough to back his flight deck around my freighter in the middle of combat. That was insane. You know that, right?"

Now, Cole grinned. "It worked, didn't it? You say po-tay-to..."

Captain Painter shook her head as she sighed before turning to Sasha.

"Lady Thyrray," Painter said, "it's a pleasure to meet you."

"Oh...*Lady Thyrray*, is it?" Cole asked as he looked at Sasha and arched one eyebrow, a teasing smile curling his lips.

"Hush, Cole," Sasha said, "unless you'd prefer I introduce *you* to the captain."

The smile vanished from Cole's face in an instant, his eyebrows almost straight enough to match the plane of a laser in vacuum.

"That's what I thought," Sasha said, smirking.

Painter watched the by-play without expression, only saying, "There's a story there."

Sasha's smirk grew. "You have no idea, Captain. Please proceed."

"Uhm...so, most of the people are preparing to leave the freighter right now. The preparations seem to relax them and take their minds off their stuff now being salvage."

"No...their stuff isn't salvage," Cole interjected.

"What?" Painter asked, her tone incredulous as she jerked her focus to Cole. "You rescued us off a ship with almost no engines and even less life support. How is that *not* a salvage situation?"

"It's not a salvage situation, because I have never claimed your freighter or its cargo...nor do I plan to."

"You're...you're serious?"

Cole nodded.

Tension Cole hadn't realized Painter was holding vanished from her. Her shoulders relaxed, and her smile did not seem forced at all.

"Captain, a very good friend of mine has been combing through your ship's computer...everything, even the archives, passcodes, and ship's account numbers."

Painter blanched.

Cole smiled. "Relax, Painter. My friend told me about the logs for your freighter going back three generations...how all indications pointed to it being your father's ship and his father's before him. There's a special strength in continuing and safe-guarding that kind of legacy, and I would *fight* anyone who tried to take it from you...so I certainly won't."

Painter's smile certainly wasn't forced now, and her eyes looked just a little misty. "I...that...thank you. You have no idea what that means to me."

Sorrow ghosted across Cole's expression for the briefest instant before he said, "You might lose that bet, Painter."

Before Painter could get too far into that thought, Sasha asked, "You were saying something about your passengers?"

"Yes. It's easy to tell they've been demoralized by the hostilities sweeping across the Commonwealth, and there's a chance they will be...uhm...expressive in their joy and relief at seeing you. You are your father's heir, are you not?"

Sasha scoffed. "I suppose...but there's been no confirmation that my parents or brother are dead, as far as I know."

"Perhaps not, but everything left to inherit is the most precious of all, Lady Thyrray...your family's name and sacred honor, everything it means to be a Thyrray. I turn down more jobs than I accept, because my dad and grandfather built a name that means something in the freighter and trading circles. It's nothing even close to what your family built, but the thought I might dishonor them or destroy what they built keeps me up at night sometimes."

"Mom did everything she could to keep me away from the *noblesse oblige* stuff that Dad was always forcing down your throat," Talia interjected, "but what she said and the thoughts and feelings her words inspired even gave me some goosebumps."

Cole nodded. "It certainly does. The only reason *I* came down here was to tell everyone we're about twenty-one hours from docking at Tristan's Gate."

Sasha snickered. Painter glanced across at Cole and gave him a Look, but the mood was broken, which was Cole's intention. The weight that had been settling on Sasha's shoulders evaporated.

"Do any of the refugees require medical attention?" Talia asked, holding up her med-kit.

Painter shook her head. "I don't think so. The fresh air will do more for them than anything else."

"Okay," Sasha said. "Let's go."

Painter led them into the group of people that had formed at the base of the boarding ramp, with more exiting the freighter as they approached. At first, no one seemed to notice—or perhaps recognize—the two women with Painter. Cole watched the refugees' recognition of Sasha's identity as it spread through the refugees like a wave. Within moments, everyone had surged to their feet and was almost rushing to meet Sasha.

Damn...we need marines, Cole thought as he and Painter moved to keep Sasha and Talia from being trampled.

The front two ranks of the refugees seemed to regain their sense of the situation, and they slowed, pushing back against the ranks behind them pushing forward, and stopped the rush forward.

"It's good to see people have escaped the fighting," Sasha said. "Do you have everything you need?"

Mumbles of 'less rationing' or 'more food' moved back and forth among the crowd, and Sasha nodded.

"I know. Believe me, I know. We'll share our food and ensure everyone eats something as we deliver you to Tristan's Gate, which we will do in about twenty-one hours Cole tells me."

"What do we do then?" a voice called out from the crowd.

"Yeah!" A man in the front rank took up the sentiment. "We left everything we had back in the Commonwealth, taking only what we could carry. I'm not saying we want a handout or special treatment, but how are we supposed to start our lives over from nothing...especially when many of us are too old or have immediate responsibilities like children or spouses? All we want is a life safe from war and turmoil."

"Hey...she's a Thyrray!" Another voice said to the accompaniment of cheers. "She can rebuild the Commonwealth! Maybe we can go back home someday!"

"I'm sorry," Sasha replied, "but I'm just one person. I can't force all the factions that have exploded in fighting within the Commonwealth back into submission to the rule of law and the Constitution by myself, and I wouldn't try even if I had the force of arms to succeed. Forcing anyone to accede to my wishes and desires for the Commonwealth would make me no better than the war-mongers driving the conflict right now and would just assure the Commonwealth's collapse. The *people* have to want the Commonwealth to return; *they* have to fight those who are trying to grab power and blaming my family and so many others who have fought for so long to provide the best life possible for the people of the Commonwealth. I'm just like you; I'm just trying to stay alive the best I know how."

It started in ones and twos across the first and second ranks, but soon, it spread throughout all the refugees until each one knelt before Sasha, their heads bowed. Tears streamed down Sasha's cheeks, and she gestured with her hands for the refugees to stand.

"No! Please! Don't kneel to me. I'm not your liege, and you're not subjects. I'm no better than any of you."

No one moved to stand, and Sasha turned and left. Talia looked at Cole for the briefest moment as if asking what she should do, before she turned and went after her sister. Cole was never one to appreciate slavish devotion, and he gave it a few seconds after Talia left before leaving.

Cole stepped out of the transit shaft that connected the flight deck to the deck Cole called 'Pilot Country' and found Talia standing just a short distance away. Sasha paced back and forth in the middle of the cross-corridor, her motions harsh and very similar to a caged animal.

"—do they think they are? I will not be a queen in exile! No one in our family was ever a monarch, and I'm not even certain I *want* the Commonwealth rebuilt, anyway."

Talia gave Cole a questioning look, and Cole just shrugged. When he moved past Sasha, she pivoted to him and pointed at his chest with an extended index finger.

"Do you hear me, Cole? I won't have it!"

"It makes no difference to me, whatever course you want to chart for your life. I was just going back to the bridge before finding my bed."

Sasha's anger seemed to deflate, and the accusing finger—and its accompanying fist—fell to her side. "Oh."

"Don't let yourself get too worked up about it. It'll all come out in the wash, anyway. Besides, once we get the warrants rescinded and the bounties revoked, you can do whatever you want. You could even change your name and travel the stars with me. I don't think any human has been to the far side of the galaxy yet."

Sasha's expression was inscrutable. "Let's deal with the bounty and warrant first."

"Atta-girl." Cole moved past the sisters again, headed for the transit shaft leading to the upper decks. "You kids can do what you want, but I'm going to bed after checking the bridge. It's been a long day."

CHAPTER THIRTY-ONE

Tristan's Gate was claimed and settled in 2472, when the explorer ship *Tristan's Bounty*—owned and operated by the somewhat eccentric Tristan Miles—suffered a catastrophic failure in its jump engine *for the third time* in its voyage. Captain Miles possessed no more spare parts with which to effect repairs, so he made the system his home.

The system was something of a bounty in and of itself. Two Earth-type worlds orbited a bright-yellow main-sequence star in the goldilocks zone...*and*...while only one system was close enough to build jump gates coming in *from* human-controlled space, there were *four* as-yet-unexplored systems close enough to link to the system. And so, the system became known as Tristan's Gate, developing into a hub for transportation and trade as further exploration delved deeper into the galaxy.

Even into the modern day, only one of the two Earth-type worlds—named Tristan's World—supported human settlement. The system's population had yet to outgrow the original settled planet. When the system built an orbital station to facilitate trade and system defense, the system government applied the system's name to it, with the common day-to-day vernacular shortening it to 'the Gate.'

———

Docking Slip 12, Tristan's Gate
　　Tristan's Gate System
　　17 August 2999, 10:15 GST

Upon reaching the Gate, Cole worked with the local shipyard to release Captain Painter's freighter to a unit of four tugs designed to minimize stress on any rescued ship that could have spaceframe damage; he also arranged for the shipyard to take the life pods off his flight deck, too. Once *Beauchamp* was on its way to a repair slip and damage assessment and the life pods gone, Cole requested docking privileges with water and air replenishment services for *Haven*.

Cole saw the freighter's refugees off the ship as soon as *Haven* docked in Slip 12, not even a little surprised that Sasha and Talia were nowhere to be seen. He stood and accepted the thanks of every passenger he'd rescued, until it was just Captain Painter standing in front of him.

"So...Captain Cole...we made it."

Cole nodded. "Yes, Captain Painter, I believe we did."

"I'll be honest; there were quite a few times before you arrived that I thought I was on my way to say hi to Dad and Grandpa again. The way you swooped in right when you did...well, you saved many people."

Cole shrugged. "I never liked bullies much. You going to be okay?"

"I'll survive. Won't know what my options are until the shipyard gets back with an engineering evaluation."

"I know how that is. I'll be around for a while if you need anything." Cole pulled his left hand out of his pocket and slipped Painter an old-fashioned business card. "That has my comms code on it. I can't always guarantee you could reach me through the ship."

"Yeah, but I could look you up in the directory. Active comms codes on stations are added to the public directory. Do you walk around with 'Do Not Disturb' flagged?"

Cole grinned. "The station registry doesn't record *all* comms codes."

"Huh?"

"Don't worry about it, and wait till you're alone to look at the card. Something tells me you'll see what I mean."

Painter slid the business card into the left pocket of her trousers and sealed the pocket. "You never do anything the easy way, do you?"

"I managed it for years...but life has a way of catching up with you."

"It does indeed. Thanks again, Cole."

Cole waited until Painter had sauntered through the station's airlock and sealed the hatch. He headed for the nearest transit shaft and worked through his mental to-do list. The people aboard the life pods from the frigate asked Cole if he was hiring, and when every single one of them passed a review by Kiksaliks, Cole said he was. With the one-hundred-seventeen people from the frigate's life pods, his crew complement was up to 935.

The Interstellar Spacers' Association served as a combination union and certification authority for anyone plying the space lanes. Most agencies associated with a government did not use the ISA, except for System Defense Forces. Enough of an overlap existed between merchant spacers and SDF reserves that most SDFs integrated the ratings used by the ISA as part of their qualification and promotion program, which was what Cole planned to do.

The local branch of the ISA maintained their offices in the station's core, which made it easier for Cole, Sasha, Talia, Yeleth, and Wixil to take a tram than walk the distance. Besides the Ghrexels' claws and teeth, Cole and Sasha both carried sidearms in thigh holsters and laser carbines, designed to be safe in a station environment. Sure, a few people gave them looks, but if anyone recognized Sasha or Talia, Cole wanted to deter them from doing anything about it.

A pleasant, welcoming ambiance suffused the ISA offices, and the middle-age Ghrexel sitting behind the reception desk perked up at their entrance. Cole suspected she was more interested in Yeleth and Wixil, but he wasn't too worried, either way.

"Do you mind if I start the conversation?" Yeleth asked as the five of them approached the desk.

Cole smiled. "Not at all."

Yeleth stepped forward, Wixil remaining in her position as rear guard. She stopped a respectful distance from the reception desk, her ears perked and tail swishing side to side.

"I am Yeleth, Matron of Clan Haven. We are forty-five strong and have allied with Cole of the Battle-Carrier *Haven*."

The Ghrexel behind the reception desk angled her head toward her left shoulder, her tail languidly swishing. "I have not heard of Clan Haven. What honors do you claim?"

"We are a young clan, recently formed. We have no honors of note...as yet."

"I am Viskha of Clan Ghrexel. Well met, Yeleth. May your hunts always be victorious...but never too easy. What brings your party to the ISA this day?"

"My captain, Cole of the *Haven*, desires business with the ISA," Yeleth said, turning to indicate Cole.

Cole took that as his cue and approached the reception desk. He nodded once, saying, "Well met. I hope the day treats you well."

"Well met, Captain Cole. How can the ISA serve you?"

"I'd like to open a ship account with the ISA. I recently formed my company, Haven Enterprises, and I'd like to integrate ISA ratings and certifications into the promotion qualifications and paygrades. Everyone you see here is a member of my crew, plus 931 more. Some of these people have been...well...out of touch with the wider galaxy for some time, and I'd like to pay for their initial assessments, medical exams, and anything else they need to establish their records with the ISA. Once we're through that, I'd like to pay for anyone who wishes to take certification exams to do so. At the tail end of all that, I'll sit down with my first officer and my purser to work out what ranks and positions to offer to whom. How does that sound?"

"That sounds like I should be grateful you didn't bring all 935 of them at once," Viskha said, her statement almost a purr. "We also don't see too many armed individuals, either. There's no prohibition against it...but the Gate is a very safe and well-maintained station."

Cole grinned, pointing his thumb over his shoulder toward Sasha. "That's my first officer, Sasha Thyrray. She resigned her commission in the Aurelian Navy to join my ship's crew. Just to her right is my only doctor at the moment, Sasha's sister Talia."

By the time Cole finished speaking, Viskha's tail had stopped swishing and stood almost straight up in the air. Her ears were perked up, and her eyes might've been wider.

"You have every reason to be concerned," Viskha said, "especially outside the ISA offices...but there are some here I would not trust."

"So, how do we do this?" Cole asked.

The next several minutes were spent setting up the account to draw on the ship's account. After that, it was a simple matter of getting everyone registered. To minimize the running around, Viskha set Yeleth, Wixil, Sasha, and Talia up to take their entry assessments while they were there and, later, have a medical facility run through physical exams and forward copies to the ISA. Once the initial accounts and records were created, Viskha sent them to the assessment booths. Talia, Yeleth, and Wixil went first, because Viskha thought she could pull Sasha's personnel jacket from the bi-annual update the Aurelian Commonwealth sent the ISA.

Once *Haven* had an account with ISA, Cole could then use that account to keep training and study materials up-to-date on the ship for his crew. Granted, what the crew would interact with on a day-to-day basis was centuries more advanced than the technology used in the testing examples, but the basic principles of damage control or first response or operations were almost universal.

Cole stood side-by-side with Sasha in the hallway outside the assessment room Talia occupied; Yeleth and Wixil occupied their own assessment rooms next to Talia's. Cole was spending the waiting time thinking through the logistics of circling his crew through the ISA, the medical clinic, and the local banks. He'd like to see all of his people choose Credit Suisse for their banking needs, but that choice was their business. He, Sasha, and Yeleth had decided on a base salary of twenty-four-thousand credits per Galactic Standard Year for a recruit with zero experience or knowledge. The math worked out to sixty-five credits and ninety-three centicreds per day, plus or minus a millicred or three.

Cole planned to date each person's employment the day they

agreed to come aboard as crew and pay them for every day since...with a five-thousand-credit signing bonus. He would pay them off the base salary to start, just so they had some 'walking around money,' and once they slotted into their positions and ranks aboard-ship, they'd receive a lump-sum payment accounting for the difference.

Besides accounting, Cole also thought about the decks he called 'Marine Country' and 'Pilot Country.' He hadn't looked at the specs Srexx had released to him yet; he just knew he'd been granted access to a datastore on the ship. Cole didn't like transmitting the schematics for small craft like fighters or bombers to some random shipyard for construction; that struck him as an all-too-easy way for those schematics to get out 'in the wild.' So...he'd need his own shipyard, which meant he'd need people to staff the shipyard which meant he'd need mining ships and miners to supply the people staffing the ship-yard. And each time he thought of more people he'd need, the credits required increased...in some cases an exponential increase.

"Damn..." Cole muttered, sighing.

Sasha jerked her head to look at him. "What?"

"There's no other way around it. To do everything I need to do, I *must* go to Zurich. I don't see how I'll have the credits otherwise."

"What are you thinking?"

"Srexx released schematics for fighters, bombers, and I'm not sure what all else to me, and these schematics are based on the level and types of tech in *Haven*." Cole enjoyed watching Sasha's eyes widen. "Yeah. But I don't like taking these schematics to some random ship-yard and saying, 'Hey, if I supply the materials, will you build me this many fighters and this many bombers?' There's no guarantee they wouldn't make backup copies of the schematics, and I don't want Gyv'Rathi tech out in the wild. So, I will need a shipyard...and mining ships...and smelters...and forges...and people to run all of it. It's a billion-credit job, just to get everything in line to build *Haven* a fighter wing."

"You should talk to Uncle Sev," Sasha said.

Cole quirked his eyebrow. "Uncle Sev?"

"He works at the shipyard, here in Tristan's Gate. Last I heard, he was the Chief Operations Officer or something. He'd be able to tell you what you need to get started."

"Would he, though?" Cole asked. "I mean, I'm setting up something that will one day compete with the place where he works."

"It never hurts to ask," Sasha replied. "If you go over there, tell him I said hello."

Cole grinned. "Will do."

Cole was silent for a little while longer as he turned over everything in his mind. Since stepping forward and claiming his inheritance was looking more and more like the only option to move forward, Cole concluded that he might as well go all the way if he was going to resume his public identity.

Decision made, Cole couldn't keep from chuckling as he said, "Come on. We'll still have line-of-sight to the assessment room from the reception desk. Want to watch me blow Viskha's mind?"

Sasha expressed her confusion with a frown but followed Cole to the reception desk.

"Hello again, Captain Cole," Viskha said as Cole approached. "How else can I help you?"

"Hi, Viskha. My name is Bartholomew James Coleson, and I'd like to register with the ISA."

CHAPTER THIRTY-TWO

Three hours passed before Cole, Sasha, Talia, Yeleth, and Wixil left the ISA offices. Given all the hours as Pilot-In-Command that Cole had logged over the years—all recorded by his implant and copied to the new implant by Srexx—Cole left the ISA with a Master Pilot certification on his record for every class of vessel up to and including capital ships. His record also carried certificates for Journeyman Engineer, Journeyman Steward, and Journeyman Deck Officer...but Cole didn't give those a second thought. He was proudest of the Master Pilot.

Sasha and Talia wanted to get their medical exams out of the way as soon as possible, but Cole needed to visit Credit Suisse. Yeleth and Wixil offered to go with the sisters, as they needed medical exams, too...which left Cole to visit the bank. After passing his rifle to Yeleth and parting ways with the four ladies, Cole accessed StationNet through his implant and obtained a location for the local Credit Suisse branch. The address StationNet provided put Credit Suisse in the station's core, so Cole walked instead of finding a tram. It took Cole less than twenty minutes to arrive. Pleasant music provided a welcoming ambiance as Cole entered the office, and the carpeting on the deck was a welcome change from the bare metal he'd seen everywhere else. A young woman sat behind the reception desk, and she smiled as she looked up at Cole's approach.

"Welcome to Credit Suisse, and thank you for visiting. How may I assist you?"

Cole smiled. "Hi. I think I need to speak with one of the branch managers."

"If I may inquire for a little more information, it would help me ensure you speak with the proper person."

Cole's smile turned into a wide, bright grin for just a moment before he spoke. "My name is Bartholomew James Coleson, and I need to tie a retinal-scan account to my personal data record...and withdraw funds on cred-sticks."

"And may I ask how many cred-sticks you will need?"

Cole fought to keep his grin from re-surfacing. "Nine-hundred thirty-five, with an overall total across all the cred-sticks in excess of six million credits."

The lady did an excellent job of maintaining her non-expression, even though Cole thought her control came *very* close to breaking. She lifted her right arm into sight above the desk and gestured to the collection of chairs over Cole's left shoulder.

"Yes, of course, sir. If you don't mind having a seat for a moment, I'll notify a manager at once. May I offer you some refreshment, sir?"

Cole waited less than ten minutes before a blond-haired woman wearing an attractive skirt suit approached him. Cole stood to greet her.

"Hello, sir. I am Amelia Obrist, one of the branch managers. Our receptionist indicated you claim to be the heir to the Coleson Trust, in addition to some other banking matters. If you will follow me, we will verify your identity before discussing business."

Cole followed the lady out of the reception area to a bank of lifts. He followed her into one of them and felt the car rise. They ascended only two levels, but the whole time, Cole couldn't stop thinking about how impractical for ladies' modesty a skirt would be on *Haven*...given the transit shafts.

When the lift doors opened once again, Ms. Obrist led Cole down a short corridor to an impressive office with thick carpeting and wood paneling lining the bulkheads. She gestured to one of the two chairs on the guest side of the massive, real-wood desk as she walked around to the chair behind the desk. With no further discussion, Ms. Obrist keyed a couple commands into her workstation, and a panel on the desktop opened to permit a DNA plate to rise into view.

"Please, place either hand on the plate, sir," Ms. Obrist said.

Cole wanted to make a joke about whether she was a betting woman, but he kept his face impassive as he leaned forward and placed his left hand on the plate. He saw the holographic display change, but he couldn't make out the precise details of what changed. He did—however—have an excellent view of the color draining from Ms. Obrist's face at speed as her jaw slackened.

Ms. Obrist swiveled her chair to face Cole, and Cole saw she looked a little wild around the edges of her eyes, too. Ms. Obrist's jaw trembled just a hint as she said, "Mr. Coleson, I'm afraid there have been so many close matches of your DNA across the last thirteen years that the officers managing the Coleson Trust instituted a second verification in the case of any matches rating 80% or better. You, of course, are a 100% match, but I'm afraid I have no discretion in this."

"That's fine. What's the second method of verification?"

"A drop of blood. It's possible—with extreme effort—to falsify a touch DNA match; I've never known such a match to surpass 85%, but we at Credit Suisse ensure our clients' security in all matters they entrust to us."

Cole smiled. "Get what you need, Ms. Obrist. I'm not squeamish."

"Please, wait one moment."

Ms. Obrist stood and left the office with noticeable haste. She returned just a few moments later with a tester pad connected to a blood collector. Medical technology developed a non-invasive alternative to needles early in the 22nd Century, and the blood collector Cole saw in Ms. Obrist's hand looked state-of-the-art. She approached and placed the device on the desk at Cole's right, and Cole held out his hand.

"Roll up your sleeve, please," Ms. Obrist said. "I'm afraid the protocol specifies the blood be drawn from your arm."

Cole complied and watched Ms. Obrist draw less than a milliliter of his blood. The collector fed that to the tester pad, and in less than five heartbeats, the holographic display changed again. Ms. Obrist leaned on the desk and reached across to the hologram, spinning it around to see.

"As I expected," she said, "a three-way match. Your touch DNA is a 100% match for the sample we have on file, and the blood sample is a 100% match for *both* the touch DNA and the sample we have on file. I apologize for insisting you endure that, Mr. Coleson."

"Oh, no...no apology necessary. I'd hate to show up and request my inheritance only to find out I missed the guy who walked out with it by five minutes." Cole gave Ms. Obrist his warmest smile.

"Oh, sir...I assure you. We at Credit Suisse would do everything in our power and authority to ensure that didn't happen. Now, how may I assist you today?"

"Well, as I told your receptionist, I have two retinal-scan accounts I'd like to place under my full identity. One of those accounts is for my ship, *Haven*, and I need to make a withdrawal from that account onto cred-sticks...935 cred-sticks, to be precise. It's the first payment for my crew. I'm sure several of them haven't had a bank account in ages, and I want them to get everything set up between banks and the ISA while we're here in Tristan's Gate. I have the amounts and number of cred-sticks per group in a data-burst I can give you. Oh...and I need to move funds from my personal account to the ship's account."

"Of course, Mr. Coleson. Let's first authenticate you for the accounts."

Once those account matters were finished, Ms. Obrist handed Cole a data chit, saying, "The data chit contains a sealed record of your identity verification, Mr. Coleson, for the Trust authorities in Zurich. It will take a short time to process the 935 cred-sticks, but I have people already working on it. Am I able to assist you further today?"

Cole smiled. "If you examine the accounts created at Bremerton Station in Andersoll, you'll see I opened those accounts with funds from the sale of precious metals. On the way to Tristan's Gate, I stopped by my...stash, to call a spade a spade...and emptied it. Would the bank be willing to oversee another sale for me?"

"Are you able to guarantee provenance?"

Cole smiled. "Like the ingots from the Bremerton sale, these are unstamped and unregistered. I have a clear and unrestricted claim to them."

"Mr. Coleson, I believe the bank can serve as an agent in this matter. However, do you have any opposition to selling the ingots outright to the bank?"

Cole shook his head. "Not at all."

"How much metal will the bank be buying?"

"Seven thousand kilograms," Cole said. "Two thousand kilograms of gold, palladium, and rhodium; and one thousand kilograms of platinum. Do you expect these amounts to affect the market for precious metals?"

"It's unlikely. The demand is too widespread for even two thousand kilograms of those metals hitting the market to cause a price crash. The price might even rise for the short term, as buyers may hope to entice more such windfalls out of obscurity. As with your earlier sale, the bank will deposit credits for the sale into an account you specify before completing a full verification of the ingots; if any part of the sale should fail validation, the bank will reverse an equivalent amount."

Cole smiled. "I have no concerns about validating the ingots, Ms. Obrist. I validated them before their inclusion in my stash, and they have been even more secure than a bank vault since said inclusion."

"Are you so certain of your materials, Mr. Coleson? Anyone can discover an unmonitored location given enough time and traffic near it."

Now, Cole grinned. "I never once worried about that, Ms. Obrist. There's only one jump gate into the system where I hid it, and I control when that jump gate's active."

A look of sudden understanding dominated Ms. Obrist's expression, as she said, "So, that's how they knew..."

Cole blinked, his grin shifting at once to a frown. "I'm sorry? Who is 'they?' What do you mean?"

Ms. Obrist's eyes shot wide as she realized she'd spoken aloud. Then, she sighed. "Well, there's nothing for it, now. Mr. Coleson, there are strict requirements of confidentiality surrounding your family's Trust with almost-draconian penalties for anyone who breaches said confidentiality. We're in something of a gray area now, because I veri-fied your identity according to the protocols set forth by the Trust, but the officers overseeing the Trust have not published a recognition of your validation as yet."

Cole nodded. "Of course."

"For that reason, answering your questions could get me fired. I believe sufficient grounds exist to justify answering them, but we'll see how it all shakes out. Several times over the years since your family's tragedy, the Executive Board for Coleson Interstellar Engineering has sued in court for the officers overseeing the Coleson Trust to accept as Heir various individuals who bear only marginal relation to the primary Coleson line because all residents of Beta Magellan died in the massacre. Those suits *never* made it out of the pre-trial phases, because the attorneys for the Trust presented evidence that caused the judge to dismiss the suit. The Board for CIE has appealed every time, and the appellate court denied those appeals...also in the pre-trial phase based on evidence the judge saw and validated while supporting the Trust's motion to place all records pertaining to the suit under heavy seal, the level of seal often reserved for national security interests in Zurich."

Cole gaped. There was no other word for it. He stared at Ms. Obrist with his mouth hanging open. "What? How do you know all this?"

"Before transferring to Tristan's Gate to serve as a member of this branch's management, I worked in the office that oversees the Coleson Trust. I led the group of liaisons from the Trust to the attorneys during the most recent lawsuit and learned about the history of the case. My superiors at the bank gave me and my team documents—all digital on various data cards and data crystals—to provide the attorneys, but there was one data crystal not even I had credentials to access. Only the lead attorney and the officers overseeing the Trust could access that crystal, and the data that crystal held led to the suit being dismissed yet again...only this time with prejudice. A careless remark by the judge in chambers—when I was the only individual other than our attorneys present—told me why. The jump gates possess a heart-beat mechanism, you see; every time a gate starts up or shuts down, it transmits a signal to an archive only the Trust's manager can see."

"But for the last thirteen years, the Trust's manager has been the three officers of Credit Suisse in Zurich," Cole said.

"Yes," Ms. Obrist agreed. "There has *always* been undeniable proof that the true Coleson Heir was alive and well. Every time CIE has sued to stop 'looking' for the Coleson Heir, the officers of the bank provided this evidence to the judge with a motion that the court seal the case at the highest level of authority, because of the danger public knowledge of such proof would pose to the Heir."

Cole frowned. "But how did they know it was always me opening and closing Beta Magellan's jump gate? I mean…any systems geek could do that if they gained access to the jump gate's control room."

Ms. Obrist shook her head. "The heartbeat signal always carries with it a digital record of the DNA used to authorize the activation or shut-down of the jump gate. Every time such a message has arrived, the officers of the bank ran a verification against the Heir's DNA on file, and every time, it has been a 100% match."

Cole relaxed against his seat as he let the implications of that new information wash over him. "How long have those heartbeat signals existed?"

"You need to ask someone else. I would never have known of their existence, were it not for the remark the judge made. I guess everyone assumed I already knew since I was the lead representative for the Trust. The proper course would've been for one of the three officers in charge of the Trust to appear in court, but such is life. Now, into which account would you like the credits for the precious metals deposited, once the bank takes ownership?"

"Put all of it into *Haven*'s ship account. I plan to use the infusion of credits to put off going to Zurich, but after a few ship-maintenance tasks here in Tristan's Gate, I'll make that visit my next priority."

Ms. Obrist prepared the sales contract in what Cole felt was almost record time, and soon, there was no further business to conduct. However, just as he stood to leave Ms. Obrist's office, a thought crossed Cole's mind.

"Ms. Obrist, if your concerns about disclosing those answers I requested prove true, you are welcome to contact *Haven* at once. If the bank dismisses you because of our conversation, I do not foresee your unemployment being a prolonged state."

"Thank you, Mr. Coleson. We shall see."

———

About an hour later, Cole left Ms. Obrist's office with two of Credit Suisse's security at either shoulder. Cole wasn't all that certain he needed additional security, but considering he was carrying over six million credits in a pouch inside his pocket—not to mention a sealed writ containing the results of his identity verification to take to Zurich—he didn't mind it. When they reached the reception area, each security officer placed a hand on Cole's respective shoulder to slow him, stating they needed to clear the four individuals carrying arms.

Cole laughed. "They're not individuals. They're my friends."

Cole pulled free of the security officers and approached Yeleth, Wixil, Sasha, and Talia. He pulled the pouch out of his pocket and fished through the pouch until he found four cred-sticks bundled together. Pulling that bundle and returning the pouch to his pocket, Cole undid the bundle and read labels on the cred-sticks.

"Yeleth," Cole said, handing her a cred-stick. "Wixil," as he handed the young Ghrexel a cred-stick. "Talia...and Sasha."

"You have a named cred-stick in that pouch for everyone?" Sasha asked as she pocketed hers.

Cole grinned. "Of course not! The only other name I know is Mazzi's. They're bundled in groups and labeled: SDF, Iota Ceti, Akyra, and Frigate. This is just a down-payment, so they have credits to open their accounts and such. Once we finish running everyone through the ISA and get them slotted into ranks and ratings, I'll do a onetime lump-sum deposit to cover the back pay. We ready to go back to the ship?"

At their affirmative response, Cole nodded once and waved to the security officers as Yeleth returned Cole's rifle to him.

———

Upon returning to the ship, Cole called everyone to gather on the recreation deck. Aside from the flight deck, it was the only deck with enough open space for everyone to gather in one place. When everyone had arrived, Cole had them divide up into groups based on how they joined the ship. The former Caledonian SDF gathered on Mazzi. The former slaves from Iota Ceti gathered in another group, and the crew fresh off the Aurelian frigate gathered in their own group.

Cole explained that they were being paid for their time since asking/agreeing to become crew and a five-thousand-credit signing bonus. He explained about it being at the base rate of pay until everyone got their skills and experience assessed at the ISA, and once he'd said everything he wanted to say, he had one person from each group step forward to receive his or her cred-stick, working through each group until everyone was paid.

On the whole, it was a very painless process, and even though the group from Iota Ceti was the largest by far, it didn't take long to pass out the cred-sticks. That finished, he left Sasha and Yeleth in charge of getting everyone to the ISA for assessment and the medical clinic for the required exam.

As he left the recreation deck intent on visiting his day-cabin, Cole used his implant to access StationNet and display the personnel directory for the shipyard. Searching the directory for 'Sev' revealed only one name: Sevrin Vance, the shipyard's general manager. Cole filed that information away as he took a transit shaft up to Deck Three. There, he entered the captain's day-cabin and opened the ship's safe, which he'd setup to require both his DNA and a keycode for access. Once the safe was open, Cole placed the sealed writ of his identity verification inside the safe and closed it once more. That complete, he stepped through the head to enter the captain's office and sat at his desk.

Cole took a moment to stretch his shoulders before he brought up the workstation's interface. He chose 'Communications' and selected the controls to place a comms-call to the shipyard. The display flashed the text 'Initiating Call' below the shipyard's logo for almost a minute before the text changed to 'Call Established.' The shipyard's logo disappeared, replaced by a dark-haired woman who looked to be about Sasha's age or maybe a couple years older wearing a navy-blue top.

She smiled and said, "Thank you for calling the Tristan's Gate Shipyard. I'm Emily Vance. How may I assist you today?"

"Hello. I'm Bartholomew Coleson, but please, call me Cole. Is the shipyard a family business?"

"No," Emily said. "Why do you ask?"

"Well, I was calling to schedule an appointment with Sevrin Vance, and your last name struck me. I suppose it's a rather common name in the system."

"No," Emily said once more, growing concern coloring her expression, "it isn't that common a name. Sevrin is my father."

"Oh...then, you must be a cousin. The main reason I was wanting to make an appointment with your father is that he was recommended by name. Well, in all honesty, I was told to give 'Uncle Sev' a call and be sure to tell him Sooshie said hi when I spoke with him."

Emily's expression locked down the moment Cole said 'Sooshie.' "She told you that, did she?"

Cole nodded. "Yes, she did. I'm between the proverbial asteroid and a supernova on a matter, and I was told Uncle Sev would be the person with the knowledge and experience I need."

"Yes, I'm sure he is. I get the impression that what you have to discuss is rather confidential. With your permission, I'd like to check my father's availability, and if he is available, may we visit you aboard your ship?"

Cole smiled. "Of course! You're welcome anytime."

CHAPTER THIRTY-THREE

Cole sat at the desk in his office for a few moments before bringing up the navigation database. He accessed the chandlery's site on Station-Net, creating an order under the name 'Haven' and adding a navigational update. Making sure the order was saved, Cole closed StationNet and returned to the navigation database. As he was at a desk with a holographic workstation as opposed to a bridge console, Cole set the database display to be graphical, instead of list-based, and the charted expanse of the Milky Way galaxy soon hovered above his desktop.

Since the galaxy didn't have magnetic poles from which to read a compass and the stars of the galaxy were spinning around the galactic core—much like each star system's planets orbited that specific star—spacers had to devise a new method of referencing directions. Various exploratory societies and pundits proposed many options over the years, but the terms that 'stuck' and made it into the common lexicon were the terms 'core-ward,' 'rim-ward,' 'spin-ward,' and 'anti-spin-ward.' 'Core-ward' indicated the direction toward the galactic core, and the direction could be fine-tuned by stating a specific number of degrees off a due core-ward vector. Likewise, 'rim-ward' indicated the vector to the closest section of the galactic rim, while 'spin-ward' and 'anti-spin-ward' indicated the vectors traveling with the galactic spin and against the galactic spin, respectively.

Cole zoomed in on Tristan's Gate and the surrounding hundred lightyears. He highlighted Zurich, which was both 37° from spin-ward and 55° from rim-ward from Tristan's Gate, about 60 lightyears away... right in the center of unclaimed/unaligned space. Beta Magellan was about thirty lightyears almost due core-ward from Zurich, which also put it about 18° off spin-ward from Tristan's Gate *and* about 87° off due core-ward. If Tristan's Gate served as the anti-spin-ward corner of Aurelian Commonwealth space toward the galactic rim, Beta Magellan served as the spin-ward corner toward the rim...and just fifty-eight lightyears from Tristan's Gate, too. Due to the vagaries of galactic drift and composition, only one system was close enough to Beta Magellan for jump gates, such cases being called 'stub systems;' that might change in a few thousand years, but if it did, Cole was certain he'd no longer care.

An idea was taking root in Cole's mind, and he closed the navigational database, opening instead the protected archive to which Srexx had newly given him access. He brought up the archive in graphical form as well and wasn't all that surprised to find it used an almost-beautiful cataloging system. The archive's name was 'Stellar Constructs.'

Opening the archive, Cole saw a rather impressive list of subcategories. Stations, Construction Facilities, Starships, and Small Craft were just four of many. On a whim, Cole opened the Stations categories and found four child categories there: Residential, Commercial, Defensive, and Hybrid. Cole moved to access the Defensive category but stopped himself.

Cole went back to the root archive and opened the Starships category, and once again, he saw a few child categories: Exploration/Research, Commercial, Defensive, and Materials Gathering. Cole selected that Defensive category, and the display re-arranged itself into an almost-pyramidal display. Cole felt the bottom drop out of his stomach as he stared at the top tier of the display, the tier right above Battle-Carrier: Dreadnought. Almost against his will, Cole selected it.

The pyramid minimized to the bottom-left corner of the holographic display, and Cole stared at a one-one-thousandth-scale image of a monster that filled him with dread. A data block appeared in the top-right corner, and Cole took a deep breath as he read over it before returning his focus to the image rotating in front of him.

Twelve hundred meters long and just over three hundred meters at the beam, the Class I Dreadnought possessed forty-five decks. It supported over five times the weaponry of its predecessor, the Battle-Carrier, and over twenty times its predecessor's capacity for small craft (i.e. fighters, bombers, dropships, etc.). Like the Battle-Carrier, the Dreadnought also allowed for embarked ground troops. Its five decks dedicated to ground troops permitted the embarkation of almost fifty thousand soldiers, plus equipment, vehicles, and maintenance gear.

"Srexx?"

"Yes, Cole?"

"Srexx, I'm looking at the schematic archive you gave me access to, and...well...what can you tell me about the Dreadnought?"

Silence.

"If you will note from the data block, these schematics are only Stage 3. My people used a six-stage design model for starship development, and I have no data on the successive three stages that would've finalized the design."

"Okay. So, this schematic is incomplete?"

"Not entirely. Stage 1 is a theoretical design that should work, based on computer simulations. Stage 2 is a vetted design that has been through numerous committees and has been cleared to proceed to prototyping. Stage 3 is developed after what you would call a shakedown cruise and many trials and drills. The successive stages represent the progression to the final design that will remain unchanged for the life of the class, not accounting for technology upgrades."

"What was this monster's role?"

"It was intended to replace the Battle-Carrier as the central ship of a battlegroup. A battlegroup with this ship would have one Dreadnought, three to six battle-carriers, twelve to twenty-four cruisers of varying type—depending on the battlegroup's mission—and more destroyers and frigates to serve as screening elements and scout vessels. That, of course, does not include the fleet tenders and colliers that would travel with the battlegroup."

Cole leaned back against his chair, staring at the hologram as he asked, "How many were in service the last you knew?"

"At the time of my discovery and subsequent exile, my people operated four Class I Dreadnoughts."

Cole shook his head, nearing disbelief. "Wow. Thanks, Srexx."

"Of course, Cole."

Cole backed out of the Dreadnought schematic and accessed the Battle-Carrier schematic, finding it was not a schematic but another container. The Battle-Carrier category held six child categories: Class I Battle-Carrier, Class II Battle-Carrier, and so on up to a Class VI Battle-Carrier.

Cole backed out of the Battle-Carrier category and the Defensive category. He was reaching to select 'Construction Facilities' on the top level of the archive when an alert popped up in the bottom-right corner of the display. It was a general traffic advisory from the station's traffic control office and sent to all near-station vessels. Cole grabbed the alert and pulled it to the center of the display. The archive listing minimized to the bottom-left again, and Cole read about a shuttle barreling through near-station traffic at an insane velocity. Cole moved to shift the holographic display to display two areas, almost like the split-screen function of ancient operating systems. On the left side of the display, Cole had the ship's computer show the sensor feed for the immediate vicinity, including the area the shuttle rocketed through; a tag expanded from the shuttle's dot on the sensor display showing its transponder was broadcasting as 'Yard Shuttle 3.' On the right side of the display, Cole had the ship's computer show all emergency traffic advisories related to the shuttle with an overall total at the top. By the time he had the display set up the way he wanted, the shuttle was already up to seven traffic advisories, and Cole watched the total jump to nine a few seconds later.

Cole accessed his implant and, choosing 'Communications,' placed a call to Sasha over the ship's systems.

"Hi, Cole. What's on your mind?"

The number of emergency traffic advisories was now eleven as Cole leaned back in his chair and said, "What's your location and status?"

"Yeleth and I are just finishing up with the crew on the recreation deck. Why?"

"You might want to find your sister and meet me in Pilot Country. There's a shuttle from the shipyard heading our way like a bat out of hell. They've generated thirteen emergency traffic advisories so far. Nope...make that fourteen."

"Why would a shuttle be flying like that for us?"

"Well," Cole said, "I placed a call to the yard to make an appointment to speak with whom I'm guessing is your uncle, Sevrin Vance."

"Yeah, that's Uncle Sev."

"An Emily Vance answered my call," Cole continued, "and she seemed very interested that you asked me to tell your uncle hello. I think they're coming to visit."

Cole could hear Sasha's laughter over the speakers. "Yeah...now that you mention it, that piloting sounds like Emmy. She was always fascinated with old-time aerospace fighter jets and wished she could command her own fighter wing. She joined the Commonwealth Navy for a while to fly air support for ground forces, but she ended up coming home far sooner than I would've expected. Never got the whole story on that."

"Well, if you'd like to meet them on the flight deck, we have all of about eight or nine minutes to get there...but I want us in the Traffic Control overlook."

"Okay," Sasha said. "I'll call Talia, and we'll meet you at the starboard transit shaft to the flight deck in Pilot Country."

CHAPTER THIRTY-FOUR

Battle-Carrier *Haven*, Docking Slip 12
Tristan's Gate
17 August 2999

There were two ways to the Traffic Control space overlooking the flight deck. One involved a ladder from the actual flight deck secured inside an enclosure with a pressure-rated hatch. The other was a staircase and another sealable hatch from the deck Cole had called Pilot Country; Cole thought the staircase to be the obvious method for accessing the overlook for flight deck personnel.

Cole, Sasha, Talia, Yeleth, and Wixil had just arrived in the Traffic Control room when the ship alerted Cole to a comms request. Cole had the ship route the call through the system where they were.

The speakers chirped, indicating a call just connected.

"This is Yard Shuttle 3, requesting permission to approach and land."

Cole smiled. "Yard Shuttle 3, this is *Haven* Control...*Haven* Actual speaking. You are granted permission to approach and land only on the condition you do not leave skid marks on my deck."

"Copy that, *Haven*. Slow-and-Boring coming up."

The speakers chirped again as the call disconnected, and they watched from the overlook as the shuttle coasted through the aft forcefield and into the hangar deck on momentum alone. When the shuttle was even with the overlook, it slowed to a stop and turned to face aft before setting down on the deck so soft no one felt or heard a thing. The shuttle's landing struts had just touched the deck when the boarding ramp dropped.

Sasha and Talia started to move, but Cole held them back.

"Wait. Let them leave the shuttle. I want you to confirm they are your uncle and cousin."

"What if they're not?" Talia asked.

"I'll kill the aft forcefields and vent the deck to space."

Talia blanched, and Sasha leaned close to the transparent barrier, focusing on the two people walking down the ramp. They came into view, and she grinned. "It's them!"

Cole let Sasha and Talia lead them out of the control room, and they all went down the ladder to meet the family.

"Tali-girl," Emily gasped, pulling Talia into her arms, "why are you so pale?"

"He...he was going to space you if you weren't who you said you were."

At hearing this, the man Sasha had identified as Uncle Sev turned a quizzical expression to Cole, and Cole nodded once. Sev stepped right past Sasha without even saying a word and extended his right hand to Cole.

"Damn right, son," Sev said, giving Cole a firm handshake. "Thank you for thinking of my nieces' safety first. I'm Sev Vance."

"I'm Cole. It's good to meet you."

Sev's face took on a shrewd expression. "Cole, is it?"

Cole shrugged as they ended the handshake. "Allow me to introduce Yeleth, the ship's purser, and her young one, Wixil. They've assigned themselves as my security detail."

Sev and Emily both moved to greet the Ghrexels.

Sasha and Talia walked over and appropriated Sev, leaving Emily in their wake. Cole smiled as he watched them. He knew how hard the last few months had been for them, not knowing their parents and brother lived or what conditions they faced if they did.

"That was some impressive piloting," Cole said, turning his attention to Emily and shaking her hand.

"Thanks. The spacer community has enjoyed reading about the Lone Marine on Caledonia, and what information we got out of the new Commonwealth included high-res scans of the shuttle." Emily jerked her head toward the troop shuttle, where it was anchored to the deck. "That it?"

Cole nodded.

"You didn't do so bad yourself, then. Your weapons officer isn't too shabby, either. That bombardment was almost epic. May I meet whoever it was?"

"You already have." Cole jerked his head toward the Sev-Sasha-Talia cluster and watched Emily do the math.

"*Sasha?*" Emily hissed. "*Sasha* fired that bombardment?"

Cole shrugged. "She had to. Every organic lifeform on the ship I trusted with bridge access is standing on this hangar deck right now."

Emily tore her eyes away from her father and cousins to stare at Cole. "Are you serious?"

Cole nodded. "There was one other person I trust aboard, not counting the strays we rescued from an SDF/Commonwealth scuffle, but he isn't that ambulatory...and he *can't* engage the weapons. When we first arrived in Caledonia, it was just the five of us."

"Goodness! How are you keeping up with the maintenance?"

Cole shook his head. "It's a little better now, but basically, I'm not. I haven't even asked Srexx to give me the maintenance queue yet. I'm almost afraid to look. What I need is a full crew. Srexx is conducting crash courses to get the people I have up to speed as soon as possible, but it's not going to be fast. I don't even want to know how many years —perhaps even millennia—of catch-up learning we have to do to maintain this ship."

Emily blinked. "Pardon me? I'm not sure I'm grasping what you said."

"Emily, I found this ship. It was a derelict, entombed inside an asteroid I'm told used to be part of a planet. The ship was built over thirty-five thousand years ago by a race called the Gyv'Rathi...and I really, really hope they're not still around."

Emily turned in a slow 360-degree-circle, looking at the deck all around them. At last, she turned back to Cole. "You know, I don't think you're telling me one. It's subtle, but this whole space is full of little things that don't match with human-designed construction...plus, that aft forcefield is a major point in your favor. Not even the military tech I saw from the Solars is on par with that. Why don't you hope they're still around?"

"Because I've seen schematics on their starships, and this one— while very good—is not the biggest and baddest they had. If I ever set foot on a Gyv'Rathi Dreadnought, I am very fervent in the hope that people I pay built it."

By that point, Sasha, Talia, and Sev were ready to move the party anywhere *but* the hangar deck. They turned as Cole and Emily rejoined them.

"I would love to offer you the hospitality of our wardroom, but we're still sorting out the crew roster and duty assignments. If there's a place on the station that delivers, I'm happy to order in."

"Cole," Sasha said, "would you mind if I invited more of my family over? I don't think it's a good idea to host an event off the ship, but I'd like to see as much of my mom's family as I can while we're here."

Cole chuckled. "You don't need my permission, Sasha."

"I kind of do. It's your ship."

Cole's expression caused Emily, Sev, and Talia to erupt in laughter. Sasha almost did, too, but she put up a valiant fight and won, restraining herself to some giggles.

"Okay. Yes. It is *technically* my ship, but I started thinking of you as one of my people a while back...even before you asked to be my first officer. You're always welcome here, and this ship is your home as long as you need or want it to be. Invite whomever you want." Cole fell silent for a moment. "What kind of food do you want?"

Sasha looked from Emily, Sev, and Talia in turn before shrugging. "I'm not sure we've thought about it. We just know we're hungry."

"Okay. Sev, I assume you know the eateries that cater on the station. Tell me which one would lay on the best spread for the kind of food your family prefers to eat at a reunion."

Sev was silent for a moment.

"Oh...come on, Dad! Do you have to think about it?" Emily shook her head frowning. "Cole, you want O'Shaughnessy's on U-Two. Tell 'em it's for Vance."

Cole shook his head. "I will do no such thing. Sasha, whoever you invite should *not* head this way until *after* the catering delivery team has arrived and left."

Cole accessed StationNet through his implant, deciding to do a name search instead of browsing the directory. He found O'Shaughnessy's and instructed his implant to open a call and route it through ship's system.

In just a few moments, the speakers on the bulkhead above them chirped, and a woman said, "Thank you for calling O'Shaughnessy's! How may I help you?"

"Hi. I'm Cole, captain of the *Haven* docked in Slip 12. I'm having a hiring fair aboard ship later today, and I'd like to order catering for five hundred..." Cole directed the question to his audience. Sasha, Emily, and Sev glanced at one another, and all three nodded. "...yes, five hundred."

"How would you like that arranged, sir?"

"We have flatware and such, but our galley stocks are nil. As for the catering, let's make it a buffet, and as far as the food goes, surprise me. We'll also need an assortment of drinks, ranging from water and ice to a liquor or wine service. This is my first time in Tristan's Gate, and your establishment came recommended."

"Very good, sir, and I'm glad you were sent our way. Do you mind if I asked who referred you to us?"

"It was a sales associate from the shipyard. She gave me your name while I was placing an order for three shuttles. Oh, what was her name...Amelia, Emerald, Emily! That's it. It was Emily Vance."

"Ah, yes. The Vance Clan and its extended branches have been very good customers across the years. We will express our gratitude for remembering us. Now, when does your event begin?"

"Well, I'm familiar with the three axes of production: time, quality, and cost. I'll sacrifice cost if I can get stupendous quality as soon as you can deliver it."

Silence.

"Hmmm...yes...I believe we can accommodate you on those terms, sir. For an order of this size, we offer free delivery via cargo shuttle. Is this something you're interested in?"

"We have a hangar deck and freight lifts that run through all decks in the ship, but I'll only agree to it on one condition."

"And what's that, sir?"

"Instead of free delivery, you charge me what would be the standard delivery and setup fee for a catering order this large and split that fee between the people who bring it aboard and set everything up...*in addition* to the full wages they would receive for the job."

"Why...thank you, sir. That's very generous. I'll be sure the staff that handles this knows the full terms of your order."

Cole smiled. "I'm not so worried about the credit. I just want them to know their hard work is appreciated."

"We will certainly do that, sir. How should we notify you when the delivery is en route?"

"You can contact me through the ship. I have errands to run and maintenance to do, so I don't know where I'll be when you call."

"Of course, sir...and once again, thank you for calling O'Shaughnessy's."

The speakers chirped to signal the call ended.

Cole looked at Sasha. "Once the caterers have delivered the food, set up the buffet, and left, *then* you're welcome to send out the invitations to the party. I don't want anyone watching your family to see a large catering order heading for this ship at the same time your family is here and get ideas."

Sev nodded. "I applaud your forethought, Cole."

"I've spent the last several years working with the types of people who'll be hunting Sasha and Talia. I know how they think."

CHAPTER THIRTY-FIVE

Once Sasha, Talia, Sev, and Emily were set up in one of the larger spaces on the recreation deck, Cole went to the bridge and spoke with the officer of the deck to handle the catering delivery from O'Shaughnessy's and all the people who'd be coming aboard to visit Sasha and Talia. After that was sorted, Cole asked to speak with Yeleth in his office.

Cole entered the outer office and stopped cold. Akyra Tomar sat at the yeoman's desk, and she wore the generic ship-suit everyone had adopted as a kind of uniform of the day.

"Hi," Cole said.

"Hello, sir," Akyra replied.

"I wasn't expecting anyone to be here," Cole admitted. "Have I forgotten an appointment?"

Akyra shook her head. "Purser Yeleth assigned me as your yeoman, Captain."

Cole blinked. "She did? When did that happen? And I didn't realize I needed a yeoman."

"Considering I'm still learning what it means to *be* a yeoman, I'm not certain I'm prepared to say whether or not you need one, sir...but this is the best assignment for me."

That admission set Cole back, but as he further considered it, he couldn't help but shrug. "Well, considering I'm captain with no formal credentials to back it up, I can't say much."

"Sir, you own one of the largest starships I've ever seen, and you're the *Lone Marine*. Those are credentials enough right there."

Cole smiled. "Everything else going well?"

Akyra assumed a non-expression as she nodded. "Yes, sir."

Concern filled Cole's mind at Akyra's reaction, but as he was still feeling out his role as captain and his command style (every book he was reading said each captain had a different command style), Cole wasn't certain how far to go. In the end, he maintained eye contact as he said, "Akyra, I want to be sure you understand you can talk with me about anything. If you're having problems...if you're concerned someone from your old life is after you...anything...you're welcome to talk to me. I can't guarantee I'll be able to help, but at the same time, I can't guarantee I won't be able to help, either."

Akyra offered Cole a weak smile. "Thank you, sir. I'll keep that in mind."

"Oh, hey...have you been to the ISA and the bank and all that? Yeleth will need your bank account information for payday."

Akyra dropped her eyes from Cole as she shook her head. "No, sir. I haven't left the ship."

Just then, the hatch irised open, allowing Yeleth to enter. She said, "Greetings, Captain and Akyra. You asked to see me, Captain?"

"Yes," Cole said. "I wanted to discuss selling the slug-throwers we pulled out of the armory in Iota Ceti and a couple other matters."

"Forgive me for interrupting," Srexx said over the speakers, "but may I ask you *not* to sell any unwanted items you have, Cole?"

"Sure, Srexx. Why?"

"If you recall, I mentioned that the recyclers can break down almost anything at the atomic level and re-form it into materials needed for the fabricators. Those slug-throwers and their ammunition would be excellent feedstock to produce our missing shield emitters, missing turrets, or projectile weapons."

Cole nodded. "I can see that. So, when you say the recyclers can break down almost anything, what is *almost anything?*"

"To begin, you need to know that the recyclers' input hopper can only accept items or material up to a size of two meters by two meters. Aside from that, there is little the recyclers cannot process. Collapsed-atom materials—such as neutronium—require more processing time than standard alloys or elements, but processing them is not impossible."

"Okay," Cole said, "so the recyclers can work with ore or rock or dirt or whatever?"

"Yes, Cole."

Cole nodded. "Thank you for your interruption, Srexx." Cole turned to Yeleth. "Okay, new plan...put out an advertisement. We will pay full market rates for unprocessed ore that's been rejected for whatever reason, regolith, whatever people want to throw in the bin...as long it's less than two meters by two meters. Oh, have you and Sasha worked up the table of organization for the ship's complement yet?"

"Yes," Yeleth replied. "We finished it before arriving in Tristan's Gate."

"Okay. Let's go organize a recruiting fair at the ISA. Akyra? You're with us."

———

The passage of a couple hours saw the establishment of a recruitment advertisement at the ISA offices for 4,181 crew positions (many requiring only an ISA record and a successful interview for hiring), the creation of an ISA record for Akyra plus a bank account, and a public advertisement on StationNet that the Battle-Carrier *Haven* (Docking Slip 12, The Gate) would pay market rates for any unwanted ore, rock, or regolith delivered by the thousand-kilogram bin minus the mass of the bin, with any deliveries less than one thousand kilograms being pro-rated to the mass of the delivery.

Before the day was out, Yeleth asked Cole if she could borrow his yeoman to assist her with all the scheduling and administrative duties surrounding the recruitment drive and incoming deliveries.

Cole set crews to the fabricators as raw material streamed in to begin the manufacture of the missing turrets and shield emitters. The recyclers were tied to the fabricators by a method Cole couldn't see and—after asking Srexx and listening to the AI's reply—nodded once saying, "Right...it's magic," and went on with his day.

CHAPTER THIRTY-SIX

Tristan's Gate Shipyard
    Tristan's Gate System
    18 August 2999

Julianna Painter's heart ached. She stood outside the office where she'd received the engineering report on her family ship, *Beauchamp*. There was a long list, but the last line item said it all: "Spine cracked – Inadvisable to Attempt Repair." The ship where she'd spent her childhood —where her father had spent *his* childhood—was dead. It was all she had in the universe, and she didn't know what she would do next. She put her hands in her ship-suit's pockets with a sigh and found two items: the folded business card Cole had given her and the message chip she'd promised an old friend to deliver in Tristan's Gate. She pulled the message chip from her pocket and looked at it in her palm. She knew what she'd do next, after all.

Julianna walked down the corridor that was supposed to deliver her to Emily Vance's office. She'd been surprised when her directory search had shown that Emily Vance worked at the Tristan's Gate Shipyard. A quick visit to the reception area's Directory kiosks sent her off down a corridor that led to the Sales Department. In short order, she found a hatch that said 'Emily Vance' on a nameplate to the right. She was confused at the lack of a control panel for a hatch chime, and as she approached, the hatch opened, pivoting on its top-right corner and withdrawing into the bulkhead.

Julianna stood in the hatchway, looking into the office with her surprise clear in her expression. Two people occupied the office: a dark-haired woman about Julianna's age and an older, middle-aged man. They both looked at her.

"I am so sorry," Julianna said. "I was looking for the hatch chime, and it opened on me."

The woman smiled. "It's fine. We only use hatch chimes on conference rooms where secure client discussions may be occurring. Can we help you with something?"

Julianna nodded. "I hope so. My name is Julianna Painter, and I'm supposed to deliver this message chip to Emily Vance."

"I'm Emily," the dark-haired woman said. "Please, come in."

Julianna stepped far enough into the office to permit the hatch to close

"This is my father, Sevrin," Emily said. "May I ask you who gave you the message chip?"

"An old friend who saved me in Emerald one time," Julianna said. "I'm paying him back. His name is Harlon Hanson."

Emily's face fell. "Harlon sent you with a message chip? Where is he?"

"He was on Oriolis three weeks ago," Julianna said, holding out her hand with the message chip.

"Do you know what's on here?" Emily asked.

Painter nodded. "Not the second-by-second contents, but in general, yes. We talked a bit when he gave it to me."

Emily took the chip and slid it into the data reader on her workstation. A window appeared in her workstation's holographic display showing an image of Harlon Hanson, his face smeared with dirt and more, and his voice broadcast over the office's speakers.

"Emmy, I'm in trouble. This job was *not* what it was advertised as being, and it's been a colossal pooch-screw from the start. It's late in the day on the twenty-seventh of July, and I don't know how much longer we'll hold out. The regiment I brought in here has already been whittled down to battalion strength, and the way things are going it'll be a company before too long. I'm sending this with a freighter rat I've known for years; she's good people, Em, and I'm hoping she makes it out of the Commonwealth with her hide intact. I wanted the family to know what happened. I'd come home if I could. I'm sorry, Em. I'll miss you."

Julianna's right hand flew to her gaping mouth as she watched the color drain out of Emily. Mr. Vance's expression was grim.

"Jeb will be nine kinds of livid when he hears about this," Sev said. "Harlon's one of his favorite grandchildren."

"What do I do, Dad?" Emily whispered, her eyes glistening with unshed tears. "What...how can I help him?

Julianna put her hands back in her pockets, not knowing what else to do with them, and her left hand brushed against the folded business card. Her eyes widened, and she withdrew the folded card from her pocket.

"I...I may know someone who can help," Julianna said, extending the folded business card toward Emily.

"Who?" Emily asked, accepting the folded card.

Emily unfolded the card where both she and her father could see it, and Julianna watched Sev's eyes widen.

"That can't be right. No one—and I mean no one—has an Omega-class comms code anymore."

Emily turned her head toward her father, asking, "Why? What's so special about Omega comms codes?"

"Only the Colesons had Omega comms codes, honey...as in Coleson Interstellar Engineering," Sev said before shifting his eyes to Julianna. "Who gave you this?"

"*Haven*'s captain," Julianna said, her own eyes a little wide. "He told me not to look at it until later."

Emily and Sev looked at each other, both frowning.

"Cole?" Emily asked. "He didn't seem like a multi-trillionaire."

"Really? He didn't bat an eye at the catering bill for our family get-together," Sev countered.

"Well...there's one way to find out," Julianna said. She pulled her ear bud from a zipper pocket on the upper-left sleeve of her ship-suit and activated it, hearing a beep when it connected to her implant. She took the card back from Emily and placed a call to the comms code on the card.

"Hello," Julianna heard Cole speak through the ear bud in her right ear. "I'm sorry, but I don't recognize this comms code, and you're not in my personal directory."

"This is Julianna Painter, Captain. I'm with someone who could use your help."

"When can you bring them aboard?" Julianna heard Cole ask.

————

Cole stood at the airlock as Julianna Painter led two people he was not at all expecting aboard *Haven*. What were Sev and Emily Vance doing with Painter? And why was Emily fighting not to cry?

"Captain Painter," Cole said, extending his hand.

Julianna shook her head. "Not a captain, sir, not anymore. *Beauchamp*'s spine is cracked; the shipyard's people told me it's inadvisable to attempt repairing her."

Cole took a deep breath and exhaled as a heavy sigh. "That is...I offer my sympathies; I know what she meant to you. I would ask that you not make any irrevocable decisions until you and I talk. Sev...Emily...how can I help you?"

"I want to hire you and your people, Cole," Emily said. "I don't care what it costs. I don't care what you demand. Please...I need your help."

Cole allowed himself a small smile. "I don't think Sasha would ever forgive me if I took your money. Let's go to the briefing room on Deck Three, and you can explain what you need. Srexx?"

"Yes, Cole?" the AI asked via the speakers overhead.

"Could you ask Sasha and Talia to meet us in the bridge's briefing room, please? And communicate that they shouldn't dawdle."

"Of course, Cole."

. . .

Cole, Emily, Sev, and Julianna had just entered the briefing room when Sasha and Talia entered behind them. Sasha took one look at Emily's and Sev's somber expressions, and the color drained from her face.

"Emily? Sev? What is it? Are Grandpa and Grandma—"

"They're fine, Soosh," Emily said. "Harlon...he...he sent me a goodbye message."

At first, Sasha frowned, as she processed what Emily said. Saying goodbye wasn't anything big; everyone sent...her eyes widened as she connected the dots. Most military personnel had a pre-recorded message to be delivered to a specific loved one or family member in the event the person wouldn't be coming home; they called it the 'goodbye message.'

Sasha was at Emily's side almost faster than anyone could follow, and she pulled her older cousin into a tight embrace. She knew Emily and Harlon had had something of an on-again-off-again romance for several years, and she knew Emily considered Harlon to be the man she wanted.

"Oh, Em...I'm so sorry," Sasha said, pulling Emily into a tight embrace. "When did it happen?"

"I don't know he's dead yet...not for certain," Emily countered. "That's why I need Cole's help. He took a job on Oriolis that went south, and he might still be alive there but unable to find a way off-planet."

Cole pushed past everyone to reach the captain's seat at the briefing table, where a control panel was inset into the table's surface. One control was a direct comms link to the bridge. He tapped that control as soon as he could reach it.

"Bridge, Officer of the Deck Mazzi speaking," Mazzi's voice broadcast over the briefing room speakers.

"Mazzi, this is Cole. Issue a recall order for all personnel. We will depart the system within five days, and anyone not aboard will receive an employment-termination notice and a severance package. Also, I need you and Yeleth in the bridge's briefing room soonest."

"Aye, sir," Mazzi said. "Will there be anything else?"

"Yes," Cole said, "but not until you're in here."

"Bridge out."

Cole pulled his seat out from the table and sat, saying, "Let's sit, people. We have a mission to plan. *Haven?*"

"Yes, Cole-Captain?"

Everyone present—except Cole—smothered sounds of amusement, despite the grave reason they had gathered.

Cole sighed. "Access the navigation database, please, and display an area centered on the space bracketed by Tristan's Gate, Zurich, and the Aurelian system Oriolis."

The holographic display re-activated, displaying the requested portion of the 'local' space.

"*Haven,*" Cole said, "what's the distance to Oriolis from Tristan's Gate?"

"The navigational database specifies a distance of seventy-two light years, Cole-Captain."

"What's our transit time at eighty-percent power?"

"Ten days, twenty-two hours, and sixteen minutes."

Cole scratched his chin for a moment and asked, "How about one-hundred-percent power?"

"One day, eleven hours, and eight minutes."

Motion drew Cole's attention, and he saw Emily and Sev leaning back in their seats, their eyes wide.

"*Haven*, set Oriolis as our destination, but do not initiate undocking procedures yet."

"Yes, Cole-Captain."

The briefing room hatch irised open, and Yeleth entered with Mazzi close behind.

"My apologies for interrupting whatever you were doing," Cole said. "We have something of a time-sensitive situation. Please, have a seat."

Emily extended a message chip to Cole with her left hand. Cole accepted it.

"*Haven,*" Cole asked, "do we have a way to read this message chip?"

"Yes, Cole-Captain. Internal sensors have already scanned the chip and read the stored data into memory. Do you wish it displayed?"

"Yes, please."

Emily, Julianna, and Sev sat through the message in silence while Cole, Sasha, Talia, Mazzi, and Yeleth watched it for the first time. At the end, Mazzi turned to Cole.

"Captain," Mazzi said, "you need to contact the shipyard right now and ask them how quickly they can provide us with three Hawk-class dropships. They carry two-hundred-fifty troops with full kit."

"I might be able to help with that," Sev said.

Mazzi's head swiveled to him like a turret, and she asked, "And you are, sir?"

"Sev Vance, general manager of the shipyard," Sev said before looking to Cole. "Cole, we have two Hawk-class dropships already complete. A former client ordered five and went out of business before paying us for the order."

"How long to build a third?" Cole asked.

Sev sighed. "Eight to fourteen days...if we have all the parts we need."

"Do you have comms capability?" Cole asked.

Sev produced an ear bud that would pair to his implant, holding it up for Cole to see.

Cole nodded toward the hatch. "Step outside, please, and call your people. I'll pay the shipyard a scaling premium based on how soon you complete it."

Sev stood and moved to the hatch as he inserted the ear bud and activated it.

Cole looked to Mazzi, saying, "Next?"

"We need weapons, sir. The crew assigned to the recyclers have already fed the slug-throwers and their ammunition into the hoppers, but the good news is that one of the most respected arms merchants in Human space calls the Gate home."

"Bailey's Munitions?" Cole asked, smiling.

"Yes, sir," Mazzi agreed, with Sasha and Emily adding their nods. Mazzi turned to Yeleth. "Do you have an inventory of everything we... uhm, liberated...from those pirates in Iota Ceti?"

"Yes. Most of the weapons were slug-throwers of one type or another. There is perhaps one crate of laser rifles and half a crate of laser pistols. The grenades are fragmentation powered by a chemical explosive."

Mazzi grimaced. "Sir, let's keep the frag grenades, as those'll work against unarmored personnel. What's the status of your heavy armor and the rotary cannons?"

"The rotary cannons are in working order," Yeleth said. "We may, however, want to stock up on ammunition."

"Srexx?" Cole asked.

"Yes, Cole?"

Cole smiled. "What's the status of my heavy armor? I haven't seen it since Iota Ceti."

"I have...retired...that armor, Cole, as an under-performing design."

"Under-performing? Buddy, I survived stopping a rocket with my chest. Please, explain to me how is that under-performing."

"Armor operating as intended would have enabled you to return to the ship under your own power and by your own choice," Srexx replied. "I have updated the design and fabricated a new suit of heavy armor. How would you like it styled?"

"You fabbed a new suit of armor already? Where did you get the materials? I thought we ran out making armor for people to work the Iota Ceti mission."

Silence.

"I may have...salvaged...material from the wrecked frigate and utilized the recyclers to make the needed material for the new suit." Cole was always impressed by Srexx's ability to sound like a child caught being bad when he discussed something he thought Cole would disapprove of.

Cole grinned. "Oh, okay. We should have filed a salvage claim if you were going to do that."

"The amount I recovered is not sufficient to raise any concerns, given the degree of destruction present with the frigate's wreckage. I calculate it is unlikely any outside observers will ever know it is missing."

Cole considered the matter and let it drop. This was the AI, after all, that saw nothing wrong with downloading entire computer cores to decrypt their secure files because he was bored. In the end, he said,

"Well, since you have the new heavy armor, let's go back to the Aurelian Marine motif, since we're going back to Commonwealth space and all."

"Yes, Cole."

Cole turned to Yeleth, asking, "What's the status of our recruitment and raw materials deliveries?"

"We have vetted one-hundred-fifty personnel, and we have many more in the queue. We have ten thousand kilograms in Cargo One with more arriving over the next several days. Several mining concerns that do not have their own transports have contacted us about selling material if we or someone will come pick it up."

"What about the frigate wreck?" Mazzi asked. "Raw materials are raw materials, right?"

Cole nodded. "I would assume so. Yeleth, are you up to overseeing a salvage effort as well? Vetting and hiring a salvage crew and making sure we take delivery of what we're supposed to receive?"

"Of course, Captain...as long as I may requisition Mazzi's assistance."

Cole grinned. "Requisition approved." Turning to Sasha, Cole continued, "Sasha, I want every effort expended to fabricate the missing turrets and shield emitters in time to install them before we leave. I dislike going back into Commonwealth space under-strength."

"Yes, sir," Sasha replied, adding a nod.

Cole scanned the faces around the table. "Anything else?" No one spoke up. "Okay then. Let's get to it. We have about three times as much stuff to do as the time available will permit."

CHAPTER THIRTY-SEVEN

Bailey's Munitions
    Tristan's Gate
    20 August 2999

Bailey's Munitions organized their wares first by role and then by type. For example, all sidearms were grouped together first and sub-grouped by type, such as slug-throwers, flechettes, laser pistols, or the very rare plasma pistols. Cole stood in the heavy weapons aisle, looking at something he'd only seen for the first time when he was in the store earlier: a plasma caster. Looking much like the two rotary cannons back on the ship, the plasma caster was designed to be carried by someone in heavy armor and often only seen in heavy weapons platoons. Their typical role was anti-fortification, anti-vehicle, or anti-armor, and they were a stripped-down, less powerful version of the starship-grade plasma cannon. Plasma casters were *never* used aboard stations or ships where breaching pressure was a concern; the projectile was for all intents and purposes a sphere of solar fire, measuring into the thousands of Kelvin. That was the other reason only soldiers in heavy armor used them; the armor protected the soldier from the extreme flash heating that occurred in the vicinity when the charge left the plasma caster.

"Thank you for visiting Bailey's Munitions, sir. My name is Myrna; can I help you find anything?"

Cole turned at the unexpected voice at his shoulder and saw a young lady who looked barely old enough to drink. Her coppery hair hung over her right shoulder, and Cole thought he could see a faint smattering of freckles across her cheeks and the bridge of her nose. She wore a one-piece jumpsuit that most people called ship-suits, because they were rarely seen anywhere but on starships and worn by working crew.

"It's nice to meet you, Myrna. I'm Cole," Cole said and pointed at the plasma caster. "Do you have more of these and ammunition?"

"Yes, sir," the young lady said. "Anything you see is just a display model; we make it a point to keep our stock levels high, as many of our...shall we say, routine...customers buy in bulk."

Cole grinned. "Excellent. Say...do you work on commission?"

"Yes, sir," Myrna said.

Cole's grin exploded. "Oh...you will *love* me, then. Have a pad handy? We need to build a sales order."

Myrna smiled and withdrew a tablet from a pocket on the thigh of her ship-suit. "And what ship are you with, Mr. Cole?"

"Oh...that's not my legal name, and the ship is *Haven*, docked in Slip 12. The name we should put on the order is Bartholomew Coleson."

"Coleson? Like Coleson Interstellar Engineering?" Myrna asked, making conversation while she tapped away on the tablet.

"Just like that."

"Neat! Ever look into if you're any relation?"

Cole fought to keep his expression impassive. "I never considered investigating that, no."

"I read everything I can find about CIE," Myrna said. "Working for them is my dream. I'm enrolled in university here in Tristan's Gate, but once I graduate, I plan to see if they're hiring."

"Oh, really? What's your major?"

"I'm a double major: jump gate dynamics and engineering. I would *love* to be on the team developing the next iteration of jump gate technology." Myrna looked up from the tablet. "Okay, sir, the sales order is created in the system. Let's put stuff on it."

Cole couldn't keep from smiling. He liked Myrna's personality.

"I want five plasma casters," Cole said, and Myrna tapped on the tablet again, "and enough ammunition for fifty thousand shots. Now, once you have that, let's go next door to the long arms aisle."

The next aisle over, Cole pointed out more items. "I want one thousand laser rifles and fifty thousand charge packs for them. I also want one hundred of the gigawatt sniper rifles and five thousand of their charge packs. I'll also need an appropriate number of field chargers and ship-board chargers for the charge packs as well...oh, and maintenance kits. You should always keep up on your maintenance."

"Field maintenance or armorer maintenance?" Myrna asked.

"One field maintenance kit per rifle and...let's say...five armorer maintenance kits."

After more tapping, Myrna said, "Okay, got it. What's next?"

"Laser carbines...I want five hundred of those and fifteen thousand charge packs for them. Will the field maintenance kits and armor maintenance kits work for both the laser rifles and the laser carbines?"

"Oh, yes, sir. Plus, each armorer maintenance kit is all an armorer's shop needs for a single workstation to maintain and repair all types of weapons, everything from slug-throwers to plasma weapons."

"You know what? Throw on another five hundred field maintenance kits for the laser carbines. I'm not going to be so OCD about it I insist on registering a specific maintenance kit with a specific rifle, but stuff happens. I think 1:1 is a good ratio."

"Of course, sir," Myrna said to the accompaniment of tapping on her tablet.

After Cole had shown Myrna everything he wanted to purchase, Cole turned to her and said, "Okay...that's it for this order. I have a request, though. Please, don't total it up yet, and signal your manager I'd like to speak with him or her."

Myrna's eyes shot up. "Oh, sir, I apologize if I have done or said anything to offend."

"You haven't, Myrna; trust me. The important part is that you do not total up this order yet. Okay?"

Cole could see the young woman's uncertainty filling her entire being, but she jerked a nod and looked down at her tablet to summon her manager.

A few moments later, a middle-aged man approached and extended his hand as he said, "Hello, sir; I'm Carter Bailey, and I understand you asked for a manager."

"It's nice to meet you, Mr. Bailey. My name is Bartholomew Coleson, but I prefer Cole. I wanted to ask what your commission rate is for your sales staff."

Carter glanced at Myrna for a moment before bringing his eyes back to Cole. "Well, the industry standard is thirty percent, but Ms. Mikkels is a recent hire and still on her probationary period. I use a rate of fifteen percent for all probationary salespeople."

"Ah, I see. I asked because Myrna has been excellent in helping me today. She's been personable, courteous, and knowledgeable. Overall, she has represented your enterprise very well, and I was wondering if it would be possible for this one order for her to receive the full commission."

"Well," Carter said, looking at the decking and rubbing his chin, "it's against company policy. Granted, I wrote that policy, but..." Carter's voice trailed off as he lifted his eyes to meet Cole's. "Forgive me, sir, but did you say your name is Coleson?"

Cole smiled and nodded. "Yes, Bartholomew Coleson."

"Well...I don't see why it would be a harm. Are you willing to write up a statement highlighting everything you just said? It could serve as an example for my other trainees."

Cole held out his hand, asking, "And do I have your word on that, Mr. Bailey?"

Carter hesitated for the briefest moment before he grasped Cole's hand and gave him a firm, respectable handshake. "Aye, sir...you have my word on it."

Cole shifted his attention Myrna. "Run that total, please."

Myrna gulped and jerked another nod, tapping away. Just a moment later, her eyes went almost as wide as saucers. "Thir...thirty-five million, seven-hundred sixty-eight thousand, two-hundred ninety-three credits and seventy-six centicreds."

Cole grinned, and Carter blanched.

"I hope you realize, sir," Carter said, "that I will only make good on our deal if the bank clears the transaction."

"Let's complete the order right now, then," Cole said. "I need to be getting back to the ship to check on other matters, anyway."

At Carter's nod, Myrna tapped through the controls necessary to reach the payment mechanism and turned the tablet to Cole. Cole selected Credit Suisse from the list of banks, and when it prompted for a DNA scan, Cole pressed his hand to the tablet's screen. Once the DNA was confirmed, an account selection window appeared, and Cole chose *Haven*'s ship account to be the source of the funds. Upon confirming that, the tablet communicated with the bank to transfer the funds, and within moments, the entire screen displayed a green rectangle with 'Transaction Complete' in bold, white letters. Cole turned the tablet so Carter and Myrna could see the result. Carter smiled, and Myrna looked like she might faint.

Cole handed the tablet back to Myrna and directed his attention to Carter, saying, "When do you think I'll be able to take delivery of that order?"

"The precise moment is difficult to pin-point," Carter said, "but the order has already been transmitted to my warehouse. All of my inventory is already packaged in crates, so it'll be a simple matter of moving your order onto grav-pallets. We also do online sales, so depending on the workload, I would imagine your order will be delivered no later than two days from now. With the size of an order necessary for that kind of price tag, we'll probably have to deliver by cargo shuttle. Will that be acceptable?"

Cole nodded. "Of course. Like I told Myrna, we're docked at Slip 12." Cole turned to Myrna. "Do you get breaks?"

Before Myrna could answer, Carter said, "She just officiated a thirty-five-million-credit order, she can have the next whole hour off, if she'd like."

Cole grinned. "Myrna, do you mind stepping outside the shop for a minute or two? I'd like to talk about your major."

Myrna looked to Carter, her entire demeanor uncertain.

Carter nodded. "It's okay, and as long as you're right outside the shop, you'll still be covered by the sensor feeds." Looking to Cole, he added. "No offense, sir, but people buying weapons aren't always the nicest folks."

"No offense taken. I'm glad to see you take care of your people. Myrna, don't feel you're obligated to accept, but I would like to speak with you for five minutes or less if you don't mind."

Myrna stood silent, her demeanor still uncertain. After a few moments, however, she nodded.

"Thank you for spending your credits with us, Mr. Coleson," Carter said. "I hope you'll think of us in the future."

"I promise you that, Mr. Bailey."

With that, Cole led Myrna outside the shop and stepped just to the edge of the displays, where he leaned against the station's bulkhead.

"So, I liked your enthusiasm," Cole said, "and I have a question. I realize it's not CIE, but have you ever considered working in the Engineering division aboard a starship? The starship in question is powered by a generator with a singularity at its core and utilizes propellant-less propulsion. I'm still working up my crew, and I think you'd fit in with my chief engineer."

"A singularity-based power core and propellent-less propulsion?" Myrna said, her expression skeptical. "None of that stuff exists yet. Just because you made me a millionaire just now doesn't give you the right to make fun of me."

"Myrna, I'm not making fun of you," Cole said as he pushed himself off the bulkhead to stand upright. He withdrew an actual, old-fashioned calling card from his pocket and handed it to Myrna face-down. "I will be doing runs around the system, visiting various mining enterprises, over the next couple days. Think it over, and if you're curious and can get a couple days off on short notice for a joyride around the system, give me call. That card has my comms code. Best wishes for the rest of the day, and I hope to hear from you about that joyride and tour of the ship. Thanks for helping me with the order."

Cole turned and headed for the lift that would take him to the docking level and Docking Slip 12.

Myrna stood in silence as she watched Cole walk down the concourse. She couldn't wrap her mind around singularity-based powerplants and propellant-less propulsion being anything other than theoretical at best or mad ravings at worst. Cole was a good twenty to twenty-five meters away when she worked up the courage to turn over the calling card.

Bartholomew "Cole" Coleson

Omega-5543297

Myrna felt her eyes widen and her mouth curl in a grin as she stared at the card in her hands, and she couldn't help it. She squealed like a teenage fan-girl at a concert. Only the Colesons of Coleson Interstellar Engineering could have Omega-class comms codes.

Down the concourse, Cole heard a high-pitched squeal of excitement behind him as he reached the lift. He stepped into the lift car smiling.

CHAPTER THIRTY-EIGHT

Tristan's Gate
21 August 2999

Cole sat at his desk in the captain's office, looking over the status of the various irons he had in the fire. Mazzi had been the first to ask about placing a salvage claim on the wreck of the Aurelian frigate; she'd even rented a shuttle with her own credits and run a salvage buoy out to the wreck...once Yeleth had purchased the buoy. Little did Mazzi realize, Cole had already asked Yeleth to reimburse her for the shuttle rental. The advertisement Sasha had placed on SystemNet attracted a lot of attention, and Cole had bulk cargo haulers heading in from the outer system to deliver all manner of asteroid corpses...everything from raw ore to rock to regolith, just like Cole wanted. He also had a flight plan for cruising the belts to visit those miners who responded to the advertisement but didn't have a way to transport their goods to the Gate. The delivery crew from Bailey's Munitions had called to schedule Cole's delivery from them, and they'd be arriving later that day.

Cole brought up StationNet on his workstation. Accessing the comms directory, Cole searched for and found Julianna Painter. Seeing her name brought a thought back to the forefront of his mind, and after keying the control to call Painter, Cole scribbled that thought in the workspace's margin. He must've gotten sidetracked by the Dreadnought the other day and forgotten to look up what schematics Srexx possessed for personnel ships.

The speakers in the office chirped, indicating an established channel, right before Cole heard Captain Painter say, "Hello?"

"Hello, Julianna. This is Cole. How are you?"

"My family's ship is dead, Cole. Just how do you think I am?"

Ouch. That didn't sound like a conversation they should have over a comms call.

"You mind meeting me for a drink? We can talk about it, and I'd like to discuss something with you."

"I'm in Max's...on L-Two."

The speakers chirped again, indicating a disconnected call.

Cole sighed as he pushed himself up from his seat and headed for the door. This would not end well. He had that feeling as he walked to the nearest transit shaft. Instead of going up to Deck Two, though, Cole went down to Deck Four, where the ship's armory was located. It was a policy Cole supported that people aboard the ship could own weapons and bring them aboard the ship with them, but they had to be stored in—and registered with—the ship's armory. Anyone found to have an unregistered weapon aboard the ship would be subject to immediate and summary dismissal, with forfeiture of all severance pay and benefits. Given the ship's crew situation, only two people possessed the authority to access the armory: Cole and Sasha.

In the armory, Cole snagged a laser pistol they had retrieved from Iota Ceti with its accompanying belt and holster and pulled three charge packs from the charging rack. One charge pack slid into the grip of the pistol, clicking as it locked into place, and Cole clipped the other two to the belt. Cole went to the armory log, noting that he was signing out a laser pistol and entering its serial number. He'd make another notation when he returned the laser pistol...hopefully unfired.

Now, Cole felt ready to go to Max's on L-Two.

———

As Cole departed the ship, pausing only to inform the deck officer he was going to the station, Srexx accessed the station's law enforcement database and ran a query against reported crime across all levels of the station. The levels—or decks—above the docks showed reported crimes in the single digits across multiple months. The levels below the docks showed reported crimes passing double digits in the span of a week...and Srexx found a priority notice that no Station Security personnel were to go below L-One without a minimum of one partner and notifying Central of their destination, purpose, and route.

Srexx's actions were *technically* a violation of Cole's privacy; he and Cole had that discussion weeks ago, and Srexx evaluated that he understood the concept. However, Cole was his friend...his first friend in a very long time. He'd never told Cole how much he valued Cole claiming this ship as his own and saving Srexx from that cavernous tomb, and after evaluation of the current state of the galaxy as detailed via news reports, Srexx established a core principle that Cole's safety was a paramount directive for him.

Srexx ran several probability calculations, and upon further probability calculations based on the results of those calculations, Srexx placed a comms call.

———

Most orbital stations were—for all intents and purposes—identical in layout and basic design. This provided many benefits, not the least of which being a reduced learning curve for new spacers. All the decks above the docks were prefaced with 'U,' for Upper, and all the decks below the docks were prefaced with 'L,' for Lower. Furthermore, if a particular service or merchant was in Compartment 17 on U-One in Bremerton Station, that same type of service or merchant was in Compartment 17 on U-One in Tristan's Gate. It was also understood within the spacer community you didn't go to the L decks unless you wanted to experience the seedier side of spacer life, and the further you were from the docks, the seedier the life you experienced. L-One and L-Two were *usually* safe enough, unless you were throwing around large amounts of credits, but past L-Three, you'd better have the reputation that made people want to step around you.

If Cole were willing to use the 'Jax Theedlow' persona, no rowdy in his or her right mind would have messed with him, but Cole had done everything in his power to ensure Jax Theedlow died with the freighter *Howling Monkey* in Pyllesc...and he wasn't about to use his true family name with the crowd that frequented the L decks, not without an army behind him at least.

Max's turned out to be exactly the dive bar Cole was expecting. Even though it was just on L-Two, being as far as possible from all the lift hatches made up for that. Cole approached the hatch, and stepping inside, the aromas of several kinds of smoke, unwashed bodies, and stale beer struck him like a boxer's haymaker. Several of the people nearest the hatch turned to look at him, and Cole realized he was far too clean and well-groomed to disappear in this crowd. Cole spied Julianna Painter sitting at the bar, and he wended his way through the crowd to reach her.

"Hey, Painter," Cole said as he approached her. "Mind if I sit down?"

"I don't," Julianna said, "but you might. These seats are none too clean."

The bartender moseyed over and leaned toward Cole, asking, "So, what'll it be?"

Cole started to respond, but the stench wafting on the barkeep's breath reeked of death and decay. Cole felt his stomach do a little flip-flop.

"I'm good for right now, thanks," Cole said. "I'll wave when I get thirsty."

"Suit yerself," the bartender said and went back to wiping glasses with a rag that looked worse than the glasses.

Cole turned back to Julianna and leaned close, whispering, "How can you drink this swill? From the look of this place, their drinks would give engine degreaser a bad name."

Julianna chuckled. "Well, I haven't managed it, yet; this is my first one. I get brave every so often and lift the glass, but the moment I get it near my nose, my stomach turns. I have to put it back on the bar to keep from vomiting."

"What in all the stars are you doing here, then?"

"The engineering report came back on the *Beauchamp* yesterday. One of the frigate's shots compromised a section of the freighter's spine. I barely have enough to have a place to sleep right now; I can't afford those kinds of repairs, even assuming the shipyard would try to repair it. Besides, once the spine or keel's compromised, a ship's life is pretty much over."

"I'm sorry to hear that. I'm sure she's a good ship."

"Heh...she's an old beast, but she's mine, handed down through my family."

Cole didn't know what to say to that, so he nodded and changed topics. "Julianna, I want to discuss a job with you. Do you want to talk here or somewhere else?"

Julianna sighed. "Let's go. I'm not drinking this."

Julianna waved the bartender over and paid five credits for the so-called drink, and they stood up from the bar. Cole had just started to turn toward the hatch, when he heard a voice right behind him.

"Here, now...where do ye think yer going? We have a bit of business with ye, pretty boy."

Cole turned and found a group of seven toughs standing between him and the hatch. Looking them over, Cole saw a couple knives, a length of pipe or two, and one fellow even carried a laser pistol.

"I can't imagine what possible business we could have," Cole said. "Step aside and let us pass."

"That's no way to be talking to yer new business partners. We saw ye the other day at the ISA office with those two girlies the Commonwealth wants so bad. Yer going to call 'em and get 'em down here for us."

Cole laughed. "No...I don't think so. Do the smart thing, neighbor, and stand aside."

"Are ye daft, pretty boy? There's seven of us and one of ye, two if yer girlie grows a pair."

Just then, the hatch opened, and eleven people entered the bar, the boisterous background noise tapering off. There were three Humans, four Ghrexels, and four Igthons. The Igthons were a race of canine-like sentients hailing from a planet with a gravity well almost sixty percent higher than Earth's, and their fur-covered, muscular bodies allowed them to go from bipedal motion to quadrupedal motion with ease. They held personal honor and integrity even higher than the Ghrexels, and they traveled in groups. Humans were *very* careful not to use the term 'packs.' Cole could see an Igthon with fur that was closer to red than tawny at the very back of the group, towering over everyone else, and Cole might have been concerned, except he recognized the woman leading the group: Akyra Tomar.

The new arrivals stepped away from the hatch, heading straight for Cole, and everyone in—or even near—their path was happy to move aside. Sure, the Humans didn't look like anything special, but those Ghrexels had their claws out already. And the Igthons? Nobody in their right mind messed with Igthons, not even Thurians in a blood rage.

"Neighbor," Cole said, "the odds aren't what you think they are, and you should listen to me. This will not go well for you."

"No, ye listen ta me, ye stuck-up git. Yer gonna call those girlies and get them here *right now*, or me friends and I are gonna take out our frustrations on ye till ye do."

"These worms bothering you, Captain?" Akyra asked when she reached the back of the group.

Those toughs making up the back of the group turned to see who spoke, and they seemed to decide they weren't so tough after all, choosing to disappear into the crowd with alacrity and a surprising level of silence.

"Well," Cole said, "Captain Painter and I would like to relocate to surroundings better suited to discussing business, but there seems to be some disagreement about whether I'm leaving yet."

Akyra turned her head to her left without taking her eyes off the sole tough still facing Cole. She said, "Hey, Red...you mind?"

The massive Igthon made his way around his crew-mates, sweeping whole tables and their occupants out of his path. It was that commotion that drew the attention of the remaining tough still facing Cole, and he turned. He didn't turn quickly enough, though, before Red clamped his massive left hand around the tough's neck and lifted him from the decking.

The tough made a sound very much resembling, "Urk," as his feet left the decking, and he worked at his holster to grab his laser pistol. Red wrapped his right hand around the tough's fist and clenched. The ghastly sound of bones crushing filled the immediate vicinity, and the tough's eyes went wide and watered at the pain. Red turned his left hand to look the tough in his eyes and growled, his lips pulling back from his muzzle full of razor-sharp teeth in a snarl. A dark spot formed at the crotch of the tough's dirty trousers. It was the first water those pants had seen in weeks.

Red drew back his right hand in a fist and rabbit-punched the tough right in his face, but a rabbit-punch from an Igthon was almost a haymaker from any other race. The sound of bone cracking heralded a rush of blood from the tough's now-broken nose, and the tough slipped into blissful unconsciousness. Red tossed the tough into the crowd, the tough's flight sweeping three tables clear before he reached an open space large enough to fall to the decking.

Red turned his attention to Cole, looking down at him as he asked in a deep rumbling voice, "Are you well, Captain?"

"Yes, I am," Cole said, looking up at Red. "Thank you."

Red turned and scanned the crowd, asking in a voice loud enough to carry across the entire space, "Anyone else have a problem with the captain leaving?"

A sea of heads shaking 'no' answered Red's enquiry.

On the way to the lift, one Igthon and one Ghrexel walked about two to three meters ahead of the group. Two Igthons and two Ghrexels each walked on either side of Cole and Painter, and two of the humans and the last Igthon and Ghrexel brought up the rear. Akyra walked with Cole and Painter.

Cole asked, "You came to Max's just for me?"

"Yes, sir," Akyra replied. "Yeleth contacted me and said you'd left the ship without cover and asked me to bring a group of her choosing to Max's and make sure you were okay."

"Huh...I wonder how she knew I was going to Max's."

Akyra shrugged. "No idea, Cap. She just said that's where you were headed."

―――――

Back aboard *Haven*, Cole asked Yeleth to join him and Painter in his office on Deck Three, where he first thanked Yeleth for the group that had saved him some trouble. Then, he asked Julianna if she wanted a job.

"Are you sure about this, Cole?" Julianna asked.

Cole nodded. "Yes."

"Then, I have a question for you. Want to buy the *Beauchamp* for scrap as well?"

Cole frowned. "Are *you* sure about *that*, Julianna? That's your family's ship. It has a history."

"Cole, the spine is cracked. It will buckle the first time it's under stress from the engines, and the whole ship will come apart. The only way to fix it is basically re-build the ship from the keel up, and as much as I'd like to say otherwise, the old girl just isn't worth it."

Cole shrugged. "Okay. I'll buy it from you for scrap on two conditions. One: you keep the computer core to transfer your family's logs into your new ship; and Two: you sign on with me and captain the new *Beauchamp*. We still have to build it, and I'm not sure what type of ship it'll be right now, but I need a captain for an idea I'm working up."

Julianna nodded, and Cole saw her eyes glint with a hint of extra moisture. "You have a deal, Cole."

"No questions?"

"I looked at the calling card, Cole...no questions."

Cole turned to Yeleth. "Yeleth, can you use another person in your department?"

Yeleth smiled like the predator she was. "I can always use good people, Captain."

"Julianna reports to you until we build her a ship. Oh, and Yeleth...

when we pay Julianna for her ship, make sure we pay her fifty percent of market value for a freighter of that class or scrap value, whichever is higher. And while I'm thinking about it, make sure we save a section of the bridge bulkhead; we'll use it to make the ship's plaques on the new *Beauchamp*. Come to think of it, we should work up ship's plaques for *Haven*, too...but one thing at a time."

Just then, Srexx spoke over the office's speakers, "Please, forgive the interruption. Cole, you have an incoming comms call from a Myrna Mikkel."

Cole grinned. "Julianna, Yeleth will handle your employment contract and all that; she has signing authority on the ship's account. Is there anything else?"

Yeleth and Julianna both said, "No."

"All right, then. Thanks for coming aboard, Julianna. Thank you, Yeleth."

Julianna and Yeleth left, and Cole said, "Put that call through, Srexx."

The speakers chirped, and Cole heard Myrna say, "Hiya, Cole! Is that offer of a joyride and tour of your engine room still available?"

CHAPTER THIRTY-NINE

Not even ten minutes after Myrna came aboard, *Haven* undocked from The Gate, asking them to hold Docking Slip 12, and left on a tour of asteroid mining colonies throughout the system. *Haven* met several ships en route with asteroid material, even while visiting all those mining concerns that wanted to sell to them but didn't have ships of their own. They spent about a day at it, and when *Haven* returned to Docking Slip 12 at the Gate, Myrna begged Cole to stay. Cole accepted, and in a flurry of joy, Myrna turned to go tell Carter Bailey and drop out of university. Cole wasn't so wild about her dropping out of her degree program and asked her if they provided an option for distance learning. She promised she'd look into that.

As Myrna was leaving the ship, an older couple arrived at the airlock. Right behind them came Sev and Emily Vance and about thirty people Cole didn't know; they all carried rucksacks or luggage of some type.

"Hello, I'm Cole, captain of the ship," Cole addressed the older couple. "How can we help you?"

"Carl and Lindsey Vance," the older gentleman said, shaking Cole's hand. "We're Sasha and Talia's grandparents, and we were just able to catch a shuttle up to The Gate."

"Huh...we're in the midst of preparations to depart for Oriolis to investigate the disappearance of Harlon Hanson," Cole said and noticed their faces fell. "Do you have anything pressing at home?"

"No," Lindsey said. "May we ask why?"

"Well, if you can get away for a while without too much fuss, I'll set you up in the flag officers' quarters, and you can have an extended visit with Sasha, Talia, and who I'm guessing is your son and *another* grand-daughter." Cole jerked his chin behind them.

Carl and Lindsey turned and seemed surprised to see Sev and Emily leading a rather large group of Vances and Hansons.

"Sev? Emmy?" Carl asked.

"Hi, Grandpa," Emily said as she approached and pulled her grand-father into a hug. "We were hoping to go with Cole and help if Harlon needs rescuing."

Cole shrugged. "It's not like we're short of beds or bodies, but I gave your grandparents the flag officer's suite. I have space in junior officers' quarters for you and Sev, but the rest of your people are going to have to bunk on the crew deck. The upside, though, is that we have plenty of NCO berths available for them."

"Sounds good," Emily said, leading a chorus of "Fine," "That's great," and "Okay," from the people behind her and her father.

Cole nodded toward the airlock behind him, saying, "All right...all aboard. Mr. and Mrs. Vance, after we take delivery of two of the three dropships I purchased, Emily can fly you down to your place to pack a few bags if you like. You're welcome to use the laundry facilities in the Flag Officer's quarters, and we can even set you up with ship-suits if you like."

Carl looked to his wife, and she nodded, saying, "The house is secured and in a *very* quiet neighborhood, and ship-suits are fine with us. Besides, that'll save you a trip down to the planet."

Cole nodded and called Sasha as he led the group aboard. After handing off the grandparents to Sasha and Talia, Cole called Yeleth to ensure they were topped off for food. Cole no longer worried about water; he had discovered a recycler in the life support facilities whose sole purpose was ensuring a proper water mix throughout the ship.

Flight Deck, Battle-Carrier *Haven*
    Docking Slip 12, The Gate
    Tristan's Gate System
    24 August 2999

Cole stood before an assembled group representing much of the crew
—with two surprises. The first surprise was the customized suit that
awaited each current member of Cole's crew. The second surprise was
the 128 ship turrets sitting on the flight deck in eight rows of sixteen.
While those turrets were not a surprise at all for the poor sods who
moved them from the fabricators to the flight deck, most of the crew
had no idea the turrets were ready for installation.

"May I have your attention, please?" Cole said. Srexx was helpful
and routed Cole's voice through the speakers built into the bulkheads
of the flight deck, giving Cole an almost-eerie echo throughout the
cavernous space. "As you can see, we have the turrets that will bring us
one step closer to ensuring we can defend ourselves against any who
would attack us. There's just one problem; they're on the flight deck
and not on the hull. Anyone care to guess how that situation changes?"

A wave of groans and muttering passed through the assembled
ship's company.

Cole grinned. "Sasha, you have the bridge. Talia, I'm hoping we
won't need you, but please, be ready on the hospital deck. Everyone
else, report to Purser Yeleth for your work assignments."

That day, they installed thirty-two turrets with zero injuries or fatali-
ties. They used both of their new dropships to ferry work crews to the
outer surface of the ship, using the troop shuttle with all the seating
removed to transport turrets from the flight deck to the outer armor
for installation.

Cole's proficiency at piloting was legendary among his crew, especially those who'd witnessed (survived) it first-hand. Many expected

Cole to stay on the troop shuttle or a dropship, making runs between the outer surface and the flight deck, but the captain proved them wrong. The work assignments were a series of rotations. Anyone with a minimum of a Journeyman Pilot rating split their time between piloting either a dropship or the troop shuttle and working in zero-g installing turrets. But the crew loading turrets into the troop shuttle with the cargo sled had it easy, right? Yeah...not so much. They rotated into zero-g work assignments just like the pilots, except that there were many more crew rated to drive the cargo sled. Cole tried to ensure everyone had either a stint loading turrets with the cargo sled or piloting one of the small craft (if they had the requisite pilot's rating), and at no point during any of the work did Cole do either job. He was the first person off a dropship to stand on the outer surface of his ship, grabbing a set of tools and leading an installation work party himself...never once leaving zero-g until *all* his people left zero-g for the day.

The second day, Sasha met him on the flight deck with her suit. She argued that—since everyone *other* than Cole had rotated out of zero-g at different times throughout the first work day—the second day was her turn and Cole could mind the bridge. Cole started to argue with her about it and considered pulling rank until a memory of his father crossed his mind.

"Leadership isn't difficult, son. Start by showing your people the worker you want them to be by being that worker yourself. If you drive yourself to the point of exhaustion, so will the people who rely on you for guidance. If you slack off and don't care, so will your people, and if you do your job while being certain to take care of yourself at the same time...so will they. First, last, always: lead by example. Everything else comes from that."

Cole couldn't recall what had prompted that lesson about his father's success as CEO of Coleson Interstellar Engineering, but as he faced Sasha and his work crews in the moment of truth (as it were), he remembered his father's words. Cole agreed without argument or discussion, and he spent more than the odd moment on the bridge that workday savoring Sasha's expression of utter surprise his near-immediate and total agreement had provoked.

The third day, Cole and Sasha rotated between the bridge and the work crews, just like the people in the work crews rotated between the dropships or the cargo sled, and when they finished early on the fourth day (28 August), Cole declared liberty for the entire crew until the morning of August 30th. Cole didn't tell them they'd get to do it all over again when they returned; he didn't want to spoil their fun, after all. Only then, they'd be installing the shield emitters *Haven* was missing...all three thousand, seventy-two of them.

CHAPTER FORTY

Battle-Carrier *Haven*
Docking Slip 12, The Gate
Tristan's Gate System
4 September 2999

Cole smiled to himself as he entered the bridge. *Haven* was now as she should be: sixty-four dorsal energy turrets, sixty-four ventral energy turrets, five shield layers, and a full load of missiles, torpedoes, and bombardment rounds, and to make matters even better, he was just eight-hundred-twenty people shy of having the ship's complement full. That was not counting the 'air' or ground-force elements; the base complement for a ship of *Haven*'s class was 5,116, and as of the morning of September 4th, the ship had 4,296 on the payroll.

Sasha looked up from her tablet as Cole passed, on his way to the helm. "Captain, Yeleth reports she has signed off on the delivery of the final dropship."

"What's our status with the raw materials orders?" Cole asked as he sat at the helm, swiveling to face Sasha.

"Yeleth informed me we've received all raw materials orders," Sasha reported, "and the salvage job on the frigate and *Beauchamp* are progressing apace. She purchased warehousing at the station and left Julianna Painter in charge."

"So, we're ready to go?" Cole asked.

Sasha nodded. "We can depart at your leisure, Captain. All hands are aboard."

"Well then, I think it's time we saw a new star," Cole said, clapping his hands once as he swiveled back to the helm.

Haven undocked from the Gate and set course for Oriolis. As soon as the 'Engage Hyperdrive' control activated on his helm station, Cole keyed it, setting the hyperdrive at 100% power, and *Haven* vanished from Tristan's Gate.

Oriolis System
6 September 2999

Entering Oriolis was easy...for *Haven*, but not that easy for anyone else. Upon arriving in the system, Mazzi soon reported that the nearest jump gate was blockaded, with only certain ships being permitted to pass through, either to or from the jump gate. The ones that wouldn't turn back were destroyed. At that, Sasha directed an alarmed look to Cole.

Cole shrugged. "I'm sorry, Sasha. We're not here to liberate the system. We just want as many of Harlon's Howlers as we can find almost a month after his message."

Cole's tone did not convey he expected overwhelming success in their mission.

"Captain," Jenkins at the comms station said, "we are being hailed by an Aurelian cruiser heading our way."

"Mazzi, bring the ship to alert status and raise the shields. Jenkins, put the message on the forward viewscreen."

The forward viewscreen activated. The focused image showed the head and torso of a man wearing the rank insignia of a commander in the Aurelian Navy. He was frowning into his video pick-up.

"Attention, Battle-Carrier *Haven*! We have no record of you being granted access to the system. You must heave to at once and prepare to be boarded and searched."

"Jenkins, open a channel, please," Cole said and, when the speakers chirped, gave the man a frown of his own. "We're just here to retrieve family and friends who were trapped on the planet when all the unpleasantness broke out. We have no interest in whatever is happening in the system. I can't say I like your people roaming all throughout my ship, poking their noses who knows where. We have no cargo aboard, beyond our own foodstuffs."

"That is immaterial, *Haven*. Colonel Grunling has ordered that all shipping entering or leaving Oriolis is subject to search."

"I see...and just who is this Colonel Grunling that he should have such authority?"

The man's eyes narrowed. "He is the military governor of the Oriolis System, assigned by General Lindrick."

"How quaint." The man bristled at Cole's words. "I wasn't aware Commonwealth military forces had the authority to administer civilian systems."

"General Lindrick is overseeing the Provisional Parliament while the government is rebuilt following the coup attempt by the Thyrrays and their allies. The General is still conducting investigations to ensure all traitors and insurgents are identified."

Cole laughed. "Oh, I'm sure he is. After all, he can't have anyone with widespread popular support opposing his new regime, now can he?"

The commander's face took on a shade of red as his nostrils flared. "How dare you! You're one of *them*, aren't you?"

The comms call ended, and the cruiser raked *Haven*'s stern with their forward energy weapons. The outer-most aft shield layer dropped fifteen percent, with no bleed-through to the fourth shield layer.

Cole looked at Sasha. "I don't think he wants to talk anymore."

"Can't imagine why..."

"Did you slip into the pick-up? You have that effect on people, sometimes."

Sasha gave Cole a flat look, to which he laughed.

"Mazzi, sound battle-stations. Jenkins, put me on ship-wide, please."

The speakers chirped.

"Attention, please. We have arrived in the Oriolis system and found it to be overseen by military forces, with someone called Colonel Grunling acting as military governor. We are being fired upon by an Aurelian cruiser and are moving to respond. I suggest you get somewhere comfy, because I may maneuver the ship. That is all."

The speakers chirped, and Cole keyed the command to bring the weapons online. Then, he stopped. "What am I doing? I have a weapons officer now. Mazzi, weapons free."

The aft batteries discharged, invisible beams raking the cruiser's bow shields with a little bleed-through to score the cruiser's armor. Cole executed a sweeping turn that brought the port weapons to bear on the cruiser. The cruiser attempted to unleash its own port broadside, but they must have been suffering damage to their power distribution—or perhaps fire control—because the 'broadside' was anemic. *Haven*'s outer-most port shields dropped ten percent.

Sasha left the command chair to lean over Mazzi's shoulder and point at a spot on the cruiser's hull, saying, "The bridge should be... right about...there."

Mazzi keyed the command to fire the port broadside in four barrages. The first two barrages of sixteen energy mounts each shredded the cruiser's shields and opened several compartments to space. The final two barrages bored into the hull like a core-sample drill, melting a two-meter hole through the cruiser's armor...then its outer hull...then its outer compartments. Cole did what he could to keep *Haven* at the proper angle to keep the weapons emplacements focused on the point Sasha wanted, and doing so resulted in a gash down the cruiser's side shaped in an arc, much like carving a thin wedge out of a melon.

Haven's port weapons emplacements shut down when they overheated, but the matter was decided. What Sasha and Cole couldn't see was that the energy weapons carved all the way through the cruiser, striking the inside of the starboard shields and proceeding to create a reflection of the slagged arc on the port side. Within moments of *Haven*'s port weapons shutting down, the cruiser's running lights flashed, alternating between 'Ship in Distress' and 'We Surrender.'

"Cole," Sasha said, "we have several individuals in spacesuits, floating amid the debris from our strikes. I don't think anyone aboard the cruiser will rescue them before they run out of air."

"Really? Doesn't the cruiser have a shuttle deck or something like that?"

"Not anymore, Cole; I think we gutted it."

Cole sighed. "I don't know if we have time for this, but I *can't* leave these people to die. Jenkins, call Emily for me, please, and route it to the bridge."

Within a few moments, the speakers chirped.

"You needed something, Cole?"

"Do those dropships have airlocks that could retrieve a person floating in space?"

"Sure. They're intended to drop a company-sized unit for planetary operations, but they can also double as assault shuttles and dock with a ship when needed. Why?"

"We have several Aurelian Naval personnel floating in space, following our pointed disagreement with a cruiser. Can you grab a few people and take one of the dropships out to retrieve them? The cruiser has surrendered, and I'd rather not have more people die than necessary."

"Why can't they pick up their own people? Cruisers have huge shuttle decks."

"We...destroyed it, Emily."

"Heavens and stars, Cole! What kind of guns does this ship have?"

"I'm still working on the answer to that question. The last time I asked Srexx, he answered me with ten pages of mathematical equations and something about energy differentials. Do you mind flying out to pick up those stranded spacers?"

"No, I don't mind. If they ask, what's their status?"

"Uhm...rescued?"

Silence.

"Cole...in a situation like this, they will be wondering whether they're prisoners of war, soon-to-be slaves, indentured servants, or any of several other possible and rather unsavory outcomes. When they ask, what should I say?"

"Oh. Go with 'rescued,' and tell them people up the chain are still working out all the details."

"Can do."

The speakers chirped again, and in about fifteen minutes, Cole saw one of the dropships appear on the near-space sensor display as it left the bow egress port and circled back around to the floating spacers.

"Captain," Jenkins said, "I think the cruiser is trying to hail us."

"Trying?" Sasha asked. "How do you *try* to hail someone?"

"I think they're having difficulty with their comms array."

"Well, if they keep the signal steady," Cole said, "put them through."

Some minutes later, the dropship had rescued about a quarter of those floating in space when the bridge's viewscreen activated as the speakers chirped.

The image on the viewscreen was not a pretty sight. A man dominated the foreground in a Navy-issue soft-suit. He stood in the glare of what looked like improvised spot lights, with a darkened corridor stretching out behind him. Sometimes, a spark somewhere down the corridor would light up the surrounding space. Debris of varying sizes littered the corridor. The man himself looked young. Dirt and grime lined his face, and his facial expression and mannerisms exuded an air of desperation. To top it all off, visual and auditory static plagued the transmission.

"This...I am Senior Lieutenant Shen Karnacky, and I am the senior officer aboard the Aurelian cruiser *Steadfast*. I...we...my people are running out of air, and I beg that you name whatever terms you desire for taking our survivors aboard. I've polled the people I can, and all of us agree that almost any fate is better than dying in the ruined hulk of a ship."

Cole and Sasha shared a look for a moment, Sasha's expression showing her surprise.

"We never fired on your engineering compartments. Can't you still drive the ship?"

"Yes and no, sir. You are correct; the engineering compartments are almost untouched. The problem lies in our life support systems. Almost our entire air and water supply were vented to space when your last attack vaporized sections of the supply pipes, just inside the inner hull." Outside the range of the video pick-up, Sasha's eyes went wide, and her left hand flew to her gaping mouth. "Beyond that, we have many people cut off in the forward sections. Every emergency bulk-head at Frames 15 and 20 dropped and locked into place when you cored the ship in your last attack, even on decks that were not damaged. We have basic comms throughout the ship, as long as the power runs hold, but we've been on suit-air for twenty minutes already."

Cole sighed. "Are your life pods usable? Can you fill them, launch them, and control where they go?"

"Yes, sir, but your ship's the only vessel close enough to retrieve them."

"Tell everyone to get to the nearest escape pod. They're welcome to land on my hangar deck, but there better not be any hotdogs at the controls. I don't want skid marks on the decking. Oh...and *everyone* leaves. If a lone occupant fires a pod before everyone's off the ship, I may just space the fool if whoever it is has the nerve to land on my flight deck. Am I understood?"

The lieutenant jerked several choppy nods.

"All right. We have medical facilities for any wounded who need treatment. Go, Lieutenant. See to your people. We'll pick up your escape pods."

Cole closed the comms call, and the speakers chirped again.

CHAPTER FORTY-ONE

In Transit to Oriolis VI
    Oriolis System
    6 September 2999

Cole, Sasha, Mazzi, Yeleth, Sev, and Emily gathered around the table in the bridge's briefing room. The focus of their attention was the viewscreen on the wall, as it displayed a recording made a few minutes before on the hangar deck.

———

As survivors from the cruiser piloted their escape pods into *Haven*'s hangar deck, a cluster of enlisted spacers almost swarmed Lieutenant Karnacky, once they identified him as the senior officer.

"So, what's the plan, Ell-Tee?" one spacer asked. He was so excited he almost hopped up and down.

Karnacky frowned. "What plan, Spacer?"

"You know...the plan where we storm the ship and take it for the Commonwealth."

The lieutenant stared at the spacer, goggle-eyed. "What? Are you out of your mind?"

"Ell-Tee, have you *seen* those forcefields at either end of the deck? I've never seen *anything* like that on any of our ships. Who knows what kind of other tech this ship has? The Commonwealth *needs* this ship!"

"Spacer, the Commonwealth is dying, if it's not already dead." Karnacky sighed. "Those forcefields you're so enthused about are the only reason we have air right now. Did you happen to think about that when you were coming up with your grand plan to take this ship? We are at the mercy of the crew of this ship. One wrong move—maybe even the wrong word—and we're vented to space...*all* of us. Are you prepared to risk everyone's lives on some foolhardy plan to take the ship?"

The spacer was silent for a few moments before his face lit up again. "But they have to feed us sometime, right, Ell-Tee? We could wait by the hatch and overpower the people that bring the food. Then, we're in the ship!"

Karnacky frowned, scrunching his eyes shut as he rubbed his grimy forehead. "Spacer, first of all, they *don't* have to feed us. The life pods carry sufficient rations for a full complement of survivors to eat for sixty days, and we have more life pods than survivors. The pods' emergency rations won't be tasty, but we can live on them. Second...and far more disturbing...is that you seem to ignore the multitude of sensor nodes all over the bulkheads. They're probably watching and listening to this conversation right now. Do you honestly think they wouldn't check the sensor feeds and notice the hundred-odd people crowding around the interior of the hatch?"

"But...but...it always works in the holo-movies!"

Lieutenant Karnacky's eyes widened just a moment before his expression settled into one of muted rage.

"What part of 'we live at their mercy' don't you understand? Get this imbecile out of my sight before I drag him to the aft forcefield and throw him out to dance with the stars!" He spun to the rest of the 215 souls that were all that remained of a ship's company numbering almost 500 and shouted at the top of his lungs. "And the next one of you to come up with some moronic way for us all to die had better keep quiet!"

Karnacky stomped over and flopped on the deck, leaning back against a pod, and the viewer deactivated.

———

"Well...*that* was instructive," Emily said. "How are we going to reach the dropships when we need to go down to Oriolis VI to retrieve Harlon, with them all over your flight deck?"

"I'll order them to get back into their pods, and the ones who don't comply get vented to space before we go trooping across the deck to the dropships."

"We?" Emily gave him the eye. "You're going, too?"

"Yeah...why not?"

"But..." Emily glanced at the others around the table. "But you're the captain. You're commanding the entire operation! Don't you think —maybe—you should provide overwatch from *Haven*?"

"Nah." Cole made a dismissive wave with his left hand. "I have a first officer."

———

Oriolis VI
  Oriolis System
  7 September 2999

Haven slid into orbit over Oriolis VI, and Cole leaned back against his seat as he considered what the sensors showed him. Military troop shuttles moved between the planet and the planet's orbital station. Most planets' orbital stations served as a combination entrepôt, shipping hub, and shopping mall; any spacers who were on short liberties enjoyed whatever shops or hotels the station offered, rather than go down to the planet below.

It did not look like that was still the case with Oriolis VI's orbital station. None of the ships Cole could identify appeared to be merchants or other independent ships, and military shuttles zipped hither and yon throughout the station's security zone. Matter of fact, the level of merchant traffic or independent shipping seemed to be way down for a system so close to a border.

"Is anyone challenging us yet?" Sasha asked.

Cole shrugged. "Not yet. We may be so deep in the system that people just assume we've been cleared to be here. Srexx?"

"Yes, Cole?"

"Mind reaching out to your lesser-evolved cousins in the area, buddy? We need to find Harlon Hanson and as many members of his unit as possible, sooner rather than later."

Several minutes passed before Srexx broached the silence on the bridge.

"Cole..."

"Yeah, Srexx?"

"I have located Harlon Hanson and—I believe—all that remains of his unit. They are being held in a detention facility in the planetary capital, and I have found numerous references to the foreign insurgents and the traitors who hired them being scheduled for public execution. Cross-referencing local time servers to ours has led to concluding those executions will occur next week."

Cole shrugged. "Well, at least we're early..."

"Srexx," Sasha said, "can you put the detention facility on the viewscreen?"

The viewscreen activated and displayed an overhead view of a facility blocked off by high walls. Brackets highlighted a section of the facility off by itself and away from the bulk of the buildings.

"The facility's records indicate Harlon and his people are being held here." Srexx's tone was matter of fact. "My examination of the detention facility's files indicates that section to be where the system's military governor houses political prisoners."

"Political prisoners, Srexx? You mean the people in that section of the facility aren't actual criminals?"

"My evaluation is that the individuals sharing incarceration with Harlon's Howlers are criminals only in the mind of the current regime.

None of the individuals I have identified possess a criminal record beyond the suspicious charges that landed them here."

"I see. What's the head-count for that whole section, beyond and including Harlon and his people?"

"630."

"Wow."

———

While final preparations were underway, only one item remained...the cruiser's survivors. Cole had Srexx call Lieutenant Karnacky to the hatch that led off the hangar deck and took him up to the traffic control room where all his people could see them.

"Captain, thank you for rescuing my people. I don't...well, we would've been dead by now if you hadn't."

"You're welcome, Lieutenant. We came to Oriolis to retrieve people who were trapped here when all this unpleasantness began. We are close to conducting the operation that will allow us to do so, and we need to decide what happens to all of you."

Karnacky's eyes widened, and he paled. "C-Captain, sir...we've done everything you've asked of us, and I've tried to keep a lid on the rowdier ones. Does anything need to *happen* to us?"

Cole sighed. "Lieutenant, we'll be leaving the system in the next few hours. I would've thought you'd want to stay here."

"Uhm, well...not really, sir. I don't know about all the others, but I know the higher commands have made examples of crews they deem 'failing.' There's not really any bigger way to fail than losing your ship. I don't know if the others have thought things through yet, but we're all dead. It just hasn't happened yet."

Cole growled. "I have specific opinions of anyone who'd perpetrate those kinds of atrocities, but I can't save everyone." Cole closed his eyes and sighed. "Okay. Fine. Get back down there and find out who wants to stay in Oriolis and who wants to come with us. Do not say *anything* about why we're here or that we're planning to leave soon. Everyone who's staying in Oriolis needs to pile into an escape pod and get the hell off my hangar deck. We'll be taking one of the dropships shortly."

In the end, fifty-three people climbed into escape pods to leave, including the notable who argued for trying to take the ship. Well, truth be told...it was unclear whether he *chose* to go. Karnacky dragged him to a pod and pushed him inside.

A short time later, a group of people entered the hangar deck through the starboard hatch. There were one-hundred-six, including Cole and Emily. Cole and Emily would pilot, with the others serving as gunners and personnel to secure the section of the detention facility where they were landing. Everyone was armed to a greater or lesser degree, and Cole carried a laser rifle, a laser pistol, *and* the plasma caster, as he *whine-thump*ed his way across the deck and into the dropship.

Awed whispers of "the Lone Marine" spread through the remaining spacers like a wave.

CHAPTER FORTY-TWO

Orbit above Oriolis VI
    Oriolis System
    7 September 2999

The dropship departed *Haven* and began its descent.

"Emily, how familiar are you with the specs for these dropships?"

"I've sold over a hundred; I'm familiar with their specs."

"What's their rated maximum speed for atmospheric entry?"

Emily turned an alarmed look Cole's way as Cole accessed the music library Srexx had reconstituted in his new implant, sending the audio to the dropship's internal speakers. The music in Cole's implant was just a smattering of the vast collection he inherited from his grandfather, but Cole didn't share all of his grandfather's eclectic tastes. Within minutes, the dropship became a fireball in the sky above the capital to the accompaniment of Cage The Elephant's "Ain't No Rest for the Wicked."

. . .

Numerous anti-aircraft emplacements fired on the dropship as it made its fiery descent. Between the efforts of the dropship's gunners and *Haven*'s overwatch, none of the weapons launched at the dropship survived. The anti-aircraft emplacements didn't last much longer than the weapons they fired.

The ground was getting closer in the forward view *very* quickly, and Cole could see Emily getting antsy in the co-pilot's seat. He smiled using the left corner of his mouth and keyed the PA system.

"Gunners, this is your pilot-captain speaking. We'll be descending too quickly for the prison's defenses or defenders to get a bead on us before we land. That being said, I expect we'll draw fire almost the moment we touch down. Prepare for a last-minute 180-degree spin just before the landing struts touch the ground. Once we're settled, take out every guard tower and defense post you can. Oh...and strap in if you haven't already."

When the dropship reached a distance of fifty meters from landing, Cole extended the landing struts. When that range was down to thirty meters, Cole cut all lift power and activated the programmed spin using the attitude thrusters. The result was the dropship dropping like a rock while executing a spin at such speed all the dropship's occupants would've been thrown out of their seats, had they not been strapped to them.

Emily clutched her console in a white-knuckled grip, her breath coming in short, ragged gasps. She turned her head to look at Cole as he snapped the releases on his safety straps and jumped out of his seat. Her eyes were wide, and her expression held a mixture of awe and fear, the dominant emotion seeming to shift between the two from moment to moment.

"You. Are. Bat-shit. Insane!"

The dropship's weapons kicked off just as she spoke, adding an ambiance to her statement Emily couldn't have timed better if she'd planned it.

Cole smiled and said, "Co-pilot's craft," before nipping back to don the heavy armor. Once inside, he picked up the plasma caster and *whine-thumped* his way to the boarding ramp. Before he could call the cockpit to lower the ramp, the ramp dropped, and Cole stepped out into the balmy air of late afternoon on Oriolis VI.

Scanning the area, Cole saw one guard tower outside the firing arcs of the dropship's weapons. His armor's computer indicated it was within range of his plasma caster, so Cole lifted the weapon, placed the reticle in his armor's HUD overtop the tower, and depressed the firing stud.

Cole had never fired a plasma caster in his life. In fact, Cole had never even *seen* a plasma caster until he laid eyes on it back in Tristan's Gate. The rapid discharge of three plasma charges caught him by surprise, and he jerked his thumb away from the firing stud, watching in rapt fascination as three spheroids of blue-white actinic fire sailed for the guard tower he'd chosen.

The first plasma charge saw to the guard tower. It struck the transparent protective material that shielded the tower's occupants from the inmates below, and the containment field around the plasma vanished as it is supposed to do. The distant cousin to the heart of the Oriolis star ate through the transparent protective material just in time for the plasma charge's rapid expansion to cause the guard tower to explode while flash-cooking everything it came in contact with.

The remaining two plasma charges sailed through the expanding fireball that used to be a guard tower and would've continued on for an indeterminate time...except for the rotorcraft bearing markings of the Oriolis VI ground forces that came around the side of a distant portion of the prison facility. The rotorcraft flew right into the path of the plasma charges, their proximity plus surprise preventing any action other than stopping the plasma charges the hard way. The plasma charges struck the rotorcraft with the sudden timing of the old one-two punch in boxing, and the fiery remains of the rotorcraft fell to the ground out of Cole's sight.

Cole stared at the two columns of black smoke rising in the distance with wide eyes. His situational awareness kicked back in moments later, and he activated his comms system.

"*Haven*, do you copy?"

"*Haven* copies," came Sasha's voice.

"Have you secured the airspace around the prison?"

"No anti-aircraft emplacements have lit off for a while now."

"Dispatch the other dropships, then. Out."

Cole accessed the comms function of his implant and brought up the personnel on the dropship, opening a team channel and saying, "All right, people! For anyone who might have been asleep or otherwise not listening to the briefing, the rule of engagement is do not fire first, but once someone starts the fight, you'd better finish it. Now, move out and secure this zone. I'll free the prisoners."

Cole *whine-thump*ed his way over to the closest structure and kicked open the door, stepping inside. Two dozen people atop dirty mattresses lying flat on the floor directed terrified expressions his way. Cole scanned the faces he could see and identified Harlon Hanson after the sixth.

He keyed his external speakers and activated the voice Srexx had made for him.

"Harlon Hanson, front and center."

Harlon stood and approached Cole, his gait steady and measured. When he stood before the heavy armor, he said, "What you're doing is a war crime, you know."

"Rescuing people unjustly incarcerated is a war crime? Huh...they never told me."

Harlon blinked. "Wait...what? You're not going to shoot us?"

"I'd rather not. That defeats the whole purpose of the rescue, but if you're dead set on being shot, I'll see what I can do." Cole heard titters of amusement from the others as the tension left the room at speed. "I have a dropship outside, plus two other dropships on the way. I was informed this section of the prison holds only political prisoners, so everyone gets to leave who wants to go. I want you to select people from this group to go with us to each building in this section and mobilize everyone to gather in the courtyard."

Soon, people were gathering in the courtyard just as the other two craft were touching down...much more softly than Cole's landing. The former prisoners streamed onto the two newest dropships. Once those dropships reached standing-room-only, they lifted off.

Harlon came around the corner of his former barracks, leading the last group of prisoners at Cole's side, and stopped cold at the sight before him. The dropship Cole piloted had made a concave depression in the concrete courtyard with a spider-web of cracks extending out from where the landing struts were embedded fifteen centimeters into the concrete.

The other people continued on as Harlon turned to Cole. "Damn, son...just because they're called dropships doesn't mean you actually *drop* them. How high were you when the pilot cut the lift?"

Cole would have scratched his chin if it hadn't been inside his heavy armor. "I think the altimeter read somewhere between twenty-five and thirty meters when I flipped the switch."

"Wait...*you* flew that dropship?"

"I did, and I'll be flying it back."

Harlon lifted his eyes to the other dropships rising into the atmosphere. He shook his head and sighed. "Shit, too late...now, I have to ride back with the psycho."

Cole was just sliding into the seat at his console when Sasha called, after making sure all personnel were aboard and returning the heavy armor to its charging alcove.

"*Haven* to Dropship One. Do you copy?"

"Dropship One copies."

"There is a flight of fast-moving aircraft headed your way. They appear to be atmospheric interceptors. Armament and maneuverability unknown at present."

"How does their flight profile compare to ours?"

"Well, they're not loaded like you are, so they're faster. But they do not appear to be designed for high-altitude flight. If you can get above 20 – 25 kilometers before they engage you, you should be safe."

"ETA?"

"Your buddy calculates about ten—maybe fifteen—minutes."

Cole turned his head to Emily and grinned. "Twenty-five kilometers in ten minutes? Sounds like a challenge. Thanks, *Haven*!" Emily closed her eyes and grimaced as Cole keyed the PA. "Everyone strap in. If you don't have a seat to strap into, put your butt against the aft bulkhead, lean back, and hold on to something."

Cole accessed the music collection stored in his implant once more and selected a song he first heard in a sci-fi movie from the early 21st Century. He instructed the implant to route the music through the dropship's speakers and set the volume about three clicks below what would cause hearing damage.

As the opening notes of Steppenwolf's "Magic Carpet Ride" played throughout the dropship, Cole keyed the landing thrusters to push them off (or perhaps out of) the concrete and used them until the dropship was fifteen meters in the air, angling the dropship's nose up toward the sky. Cole grabbed the throttle with his right hand as his left hand hovered over the master shut-off for the landing thrusters, and he shut off the thrusters at the same time he activated the main engines and pushed the throttle all the way forward to the stop.

The ear-shattering *BOOM!* filled the dropship as everyone aboard was driven back into their seats by the sudden acceleration, the dropship rattling and shaking around them as it shot into the atmosphere. The higher they climbed, the less the dropship shook, and soon, the ride smoothed out as the pull of Oriolis VI's gravity fell away.

By the time the interceptors reached the vicinity of the last dropship to leave the prison, all that remained was its ion trail.

CHAPTER FORTY-THREE

Flight Deck, Battle-Carrier *Haven*
   Oriolis System
   7 September 2999

The moment the dropship touched the decking of the flight deck, Cole powered down the engines and slapped the release for the safety straps, jumping to his feet and racing out the dropship. People scurried aside to avoid Cole's mad dash, and Emily dropped the ramp just as Cole reached it.

From the dropship, Cole raced over to the hatch. He took the transit shaft up to Pilot Country before switching over to one of the transit shafts that would deliver him to Deck Three, where the bridge awaited him. He was sliding into his seat at the helm console six minutes after his dropship touched down.

"What have we got?" Cole's fingers flew over the controls, bringing *Haven* out of orbit and angling toward a course for the cruiser they'd left drifting.

"A battlegroup is maneuvering to bracket us," Mazzi said. "One battleship, a cruiser, two destroyers, and eight frigates are approaching from," stealing a glance at her sensor display, "what is now our starboard bow with that turn you made. A cruiser, two destroyers, and eight frigates are coming in from our starboard aft quarter. Another cruiser, two destroyers, and eight frigates are moving in from our port bow, with an equal number moving in from our port aft quarter. A group of four destroyers and sixteen frigates are approaching from over the planet's north pole, and a similar group is approaching from under the planet."

"Sasha," Cole said, "what are your thoughts?"

"They're trying to block us from escaping, Cole. They're far enough away from the planet to prevent us from leaving without a fight, and the planet serves as a block that way. The two groups circling over and under the planet are the hounds to drive us to the hunters."

Cole frowned. "Where did they come from? Shouldn't we have seen all these ships when we approached the planet?"

"They were behind the planet and the planet's moons," Sasha said. "We watched them emerge while you were down on the planet. Besides, if you had seen them, would you have abandoned the mission?"

"Heh," Cole said, chuckling. "No, not really; this job needed to be done. So be it. Mazzi, sound battle stations. Jenkins, my compliments to Chief Engineer Logan; ask him to split all excess power between the shields and weapons."

"Maybe I shouldn't say anything," Mazzi said, "but why don't we ask Srexx to eject their reactor cores, like he did for the Solar ships in Caernarvon?"

"I have already attempted that tactic, Alessandra," Srexx said over the bridge speakers. "Their computer cores possess the software to interface with the ejection mechanisms, but when I attempt to engage those systems, the software returns a 'Hardware Not Found' error. They have either severed the computer's links to the mechanism or removed the mechanism entirely."

"Damn," Cole said. "I guess someone told them about Caernarvon. Well, we'll just have to do it the hard way. Sasha, the commander for this battlegroup would be on the battleship, right?"

"Yes, Cole."

"Jenkins, hail the battleship, please...and tell them your captain is asking for whatever crack-pot fascist thinks he or she is in charge of this stupidity. Be sure to use those *exact* words, and pre-set the video feed from our side to include only the command chair. I want the feed to show from my feet to about a quarter-meter above my head, and Jenkins, put the call through as soon as they reply. Don't say anything to them about telling me or anything like that; just throw it to the forward viewscreen." Cole jumped up from the helm and moved to the command chair. "Sasha, make yourself scarce for the comms call. You look far too professional for what I'm trying to achieve, even in civvies...whereas I am just the right kind of shabby. Wixil, take the helm, in case the video pickup shows the station; we have to strike a careful balance here." Cole's eyes roamed over the bridge. "Damn...I wish I had one of those old-fashioned paperback books. That would be perfect."

"I have a tablet on my desk," Sasha offered.

Cole grinned. "Yes, please."

Sasha dashed out the starboard hatch.

Cole sat in the command chair and turned about eighteen degrees to starboard in the seat, lifting his right leg and attempting a negligent drape over that armrest of the command chair and resting his left elbow on that armrest.

Sasha returned with the tablet and almost froze when she saw Cole's position and demeanor. Handing the tablet to Cole, she moved to the starboard forward corner of the bridge...where she could be one-hundred-percent certain she'd be outside the visual feed.

Cole minimized the document Sasha had open on the tablet and placed a stopwatch control on the right side of the tablet's screen. He then put a thumbnail of the forward viewscreen's display in the top-left corner and set both the thumbnail and the stopwatch to sit on top of whatever else he opened. That complete, Cole accessed the ship's library and selected a novel he'd tried many years ago and felt was the most boring work ever produced. Cole practiced scrolling through the novel, using his motion to start the stopwatch control. Once he felt the act was believable, Cole flipped through the novel to have a good rhythm when the call was accepted.

"Call coming in," Jenkins said right before the viewscreen activated.

Cole exercised his full willpower to keep from grinning as he tapped the stopwatch control to start it while flipping through the boring prose of the novel he'd selected. His plan a calculated gamble, Cole needed to balance his apparent nonchalance and ineptitude against the frustration, irritation, and anger of whoever was onscreen. Play the part too long, and they'd just close the call. Not play it long enough, and they might not believe it. In the end, Cole judged forty-five seconds of them watching him flip a page or two was about right.

Cole looked up from his tablet and affected surprise at seeing someone on the forward viewscreen. "Oh, hello! So...you're the crackpot fascist in charge?"

"I am Admiral Selena Bagley," the middle-aged woman said through a severe expression. "Who in all the stars are *you*?"

Cole waved his left hand in a dismissive gesture as he turned off the tablet's screen and tossed it to Mazzi.

"Does it matter who I am?" Cole asked. "I'm trying to understand why you're trying to cut us off from leaving. I mean...it's very apparent Oriolis VI isn't the tourist destination it used to be. Why, I had to retrieve my friends from a prison of all things. Really, Admiral...that's no way to run a resort planet. Someone should've told you."

"Oriolis VI has *never* been a resort planet, you clueless fop," Admiral Bagley growled through clenched teeth. "How did *you* orchestrate that assault?"

"Me? Oh, my stars no, Admiral. I'm not military, and I have nothing to do with the messy stuff. I have *people* for that, you see."

If looks could kill, the admiral's expression would've reduced Cole to ash right where he sat. "Take care of my new flagship, you insolent fool. I'll be aboard shortly."

The viewscreen went black as the call ended.

Cole stood and stretched. "Thank goodness. I was getting a cramp in my back from sitting like that. Sasha, take the conn. Let's do this."

Sasha crossed the bridge to the command chair, shaking her head. Mazzi looked like she wanted to laugh.

At seeing the shadow of disapproval on Sasha's expression, Cole shrugged. "Hey...if that admiral dismisses us and thinks this will be super-easy, how does that not help us? The sad thing is, we'll probably never be able to use this one again, either, and we can't exactly disguise the ship as a deep-sea trawler and have the whole crew sing, 'Louie, Louie.'"

Everyone on the bridge turned to stare at Cole. Cole scanned the varying degrees of confusion and incredulity he could see and smiled.

"I saw that in an old 2-D comedy my grandfather had me watch when I was little. He was an absolute fanatic about movies of all eras."

Wixil was already vacating the helm to return to the seat at Mazzi's elbow when Cole arrived to take the helm. Cole rolled his shoulders to stretch them one last time before he nodded over his shoulder to Sasha.

"Can we put the near-space sensor feed up on the forward viewscreen?" Sasha asked.

"That is possible," Srexx said over the bridge speakers, "but would you not prefer the tactical plot for combat maneuvering?"

Cole swiveled to face Sasha and shrugged at her questioning expression. He'd never heard of the tactical plot, either.

"Sure, Srexx," Sasha said. "Give us the tactical plot."

A hologram coalesced in the center of the bridge, a real-time three-dimensional view of a sphere of space five light-minutes across that was centered on *Haven*. The data displayed for each ship were the necessities: range, facing, heading, and speed.

Scanning the tactical plot, Sasha saw that the group coming up from the south pole of the planet were the closest, at a range of fifty-five-thousand kilometers. The group with the battleship at its core was a little over a million kilometers away and cruising toward *Haven* at a sedate five percent of lightspeed. Its companion groups maintained the same speed and closure rate.

"Srexx," Sasha said, her eyes roaming over the tactical plot, "you're responsible for electronic warfare. Once the shooting starts, do whatever you choose with however many ships you want. Cole, put us on a heading of three-four-five by two-five degrees at five percent of lightspeed."

Cole input the heading data and set the speed, keying the command to activate the engines.

"Missile launch!" Mazzi announced as dozens of dots appeared on the tactical plot. "Estimate two-five-zero inbound contacts! Point-defense batteries online and ready. Estimated flight time...two minutes."

"Two-hundred fifty sounds a little light for this many ships," Cole said.

"They're testing us to gauge our anti-missile defenses," Sasha said. "If they've established a distributed tactical network, this many ships should be capable of volleys upwards of five thousand missiles. Srexx, overlay our powered attack range for missiles in light red and the powered attack range for torpedoes in light blue." The entire tactical plot took on a shade of light purple. "Okay, then...cancel the overlay." The tactical plot returned to its slight shade of green. "Mazzi, how many missile and torpedo launchers are loaded?"

"All of them, ma'am," Mazzi replied, "and we have full magazines."

"Concentrate our fire on the battleship and cruisers, with the torpedoes solely on the battleship. As close as we all are, this will devolve into a slugging match in short order."

"Aye, ma'am." Mazzi's fingers danced across the console as she programmed the firing plan. "Firing plan ready, ma'am, and point-defense batteries have engaged the enemy missiles." Ninety seconds later, Mazzi continued. "All incoming missiles destroyed."

"Fire," Sasha said.

One-hundred-three missiles and seventeen torpedoes erupted from *Haven*'s launchers, and unlike their lesser-evolved cousins vaporized by *Haven*'s point-defense batteries, these missiles and torpedoes were powered by nano-scale singularities and propelled by the same technology that pushed *Haven* through space. The key feature for any projectile to be used in battle is its mass-to-thrust ratio, and even the torpedoes had considerable thrust versus their mass when compared to conventional Human weapons. The moment they cleared the launch tubes, each missile or torpedo's software brought its engine to full power and proceeded to its respective target.

"Missiles and torpedoes away," Mazzi reported. "That...that can't be right."

"What is it, Mazzi?" Sasha asked.

"The computer reports an estimated flight time of forty-five seconds."

In the time it took for Mazzi to voice her confusion, the first missiles were arriving at their targets. Three of the cruisers received twenty-six missiles each, while the fourth only received twenty-five. The crews aboard the cruisers were mostly veterans, and the incoming missiles did not catch them off-guard as a less-experienced crew might have been. Their point-defenses destroyed an average of fifteen missiles, and the remaining missiles continued on a staggered approach.

The first three missiles attacking each cruiser sacrificed themselves to shred the shields facing *Haven*, and the remaining missiles targeted point-defense batteries that had announced themselves to the missile groups. Each missile that made it through aimed for a different point-defense battery, and soon, several point-defense batteries became debris of varying size drifting through space, their associated compartments opened to space.

All seventeen of the torpedoes bored in on the battleship. The weapons crews aboard the battleship were all veteran spacers with decades of experience in some cases; they shot down seven of the torpedoes. Five of the remaining torpedoes spread across the forward, port, and starboard shields, shredding them and leaving the way clear for the successive projectiles. Those final five torpedoes accelerated as their computers brought their engines to one-hundred-fifty percent, driving into the battleship's armor and hull before detonating. Those detonations either vaporized or ripped away whole sections of armor or hull plating and opened many compartments to space.

"We have confirmed hits across all targets, ma'am," Mazzi reported.

"Excellent shooting," Sasha said.

Mazzi shook her head. "Thanks, but it wasn't me. The computer wouldn't let me choose anything other than something called adaptive targeting in the fire plan; all I could do was set the number of missiles or torpedoes per target."

"That's interesting; we need to study up on that adaptive targeting. Are all launchers reloaded?"

"The last reload just completed," Mazzi said.

"Fire," Sasha said.

Cole watched the battle on the sensor display in the helm console, and he noticed odd movement among the destroyers and frigates. "It looks like we have destroyers and frigates ramping up to do strafing runs on us."

"Mazzi, use the energy emplacements as they come to bear on the destroyers and frigates."

"Understood, ma'am."

The second volley of missiles were arriving at the cruisers by that point, and their detonations walked destruction aft from the bow... almost as if the cruisers' hulls were strips of ground being carpet-bombed. Many compartments vented to space on each cruiser, and a huge section on one of them disappeared in a secondary explosion of the missiles in the loading mechanism.

One frigate maneuvered into the path of a torpedo meant for the battleship and vanished amid the ensuing detonation, becoming an expanding cloud of debris.

The battleship fared worse than the cruisers. With the damage of the previous barrage, there were gaps in the battleship's point-defense coverage, which the torpedoes exploited. Once inside the point-defense envelope, the torpedoes spread out to create a shotgun effect against the armor and hull, their detonations ripping great gashes across the battleship. One cluster of torpedoes spread so much destruction so close to the forward fusion reactor that the containment systems failed, and sizable portions of the forward fourth of the battleship vanished in the fiery orgy of an uncontrolled thermonuclear reaction.

Meanwhile, the energy emplacements making up *Haven's* broadsides had been busy. Even the battleship's formation was within *Haven's* energy range, and *Haven* left several slagged destroyers and frigates in its wake. Mazzi tried to leave the ships with some maneuvering capability to keep from creating massive kinetic weapons that would fall to the planet below; not even half of a frigate would burn up on re-entry, let alone a destroyer.

Still, though, *Haven*'s shields were taking a beating. The outer shields were gone. The fourth shield layer was at 65% and falling, the bleed-through having brought the third shield layer down to 92% and falling. The Aurelian Navy had sacrificed eight destroyers and sixteen frigates outright—not counting the frigate that ate a torpedo—to the task so far, plus four damaged cruisers and one damaged battleship... but sometimes, quantity has a quality all its own.

CHAPTER FORTY-FOUR

Battle of Oriolis VI
  Oriolis System
  7 September 2999

Cole accessed the comms functions through the helm station and sent a text message to Sasha via her implant: ask Jenkins to call for the Aurelian surrender; we haven't fired our energy mounts yet. After all, even in routine operations, there can only be *one* person in command of the bridge, and Cole didn't want to undermine or countermand anything Sasha might say.

"Mazzi, how much have you used the energy mounts?" Sasha asked.

"Not much, ma'am. There's just been that one strafing run so far that cost them eight destroyers and sixteen frigates...well, except for the frigate that intercepted a torpedo."

Sasha sighed. "Jenkins, signal the battleship; request the surrender of all Aurelian forces in this engagement, and transmit that in the clear on an omnidirectional broadcast."

Within a few moments, Jenkins said, "We have a reply, ma'am... audio only and also transmitted in the clear."

"Play it," Sasha said.

The speakers chirped once before a scratchy audio filled with static began. "This is Captain Aleksei Grimshaw. The Aurelian Navy *does not* surrender!"

Sasha looked at the decking and closed her eyes.

"That damned fool will get a lot of his people killed," Cole growled. "Why isn't Admiral Bagley responding?"

"I'm pretty sure we holed the flag bridge on that battleship," Mazzi replied. "Admiral Bagley may not even be alive."

"Cole?" Sasha said.

Cole swiveled to face his first officer and saw the hurt and heartache in her eyes, and he knew she'd rather be anywhere other than in command of this battle. He *almost* sighed. The bridge crew was watching them. Cole smiled.

"Jenkins, I think it's time for another message. Sasha, if you wouldn't mind stepping outside the video pick-up range?"

Sasha stood and vacated the command chair, moving to the forward starboard corner of the bridge once more.

Cole moved to the command chair and sat. This time, though, he sat up straight, both feet on the decking, and with each arm resting on its respective armrest. He said, "Jenkins, tell me when you're ready."

"You're on, Captain."

Cole waited a few seconds to allow for Jenkins's voice to be cut from the broadcast. Then, he spoke. "My name is Bartholomew James Coleson, and I both own *and* command this vessel, the Battle-Carrier *Haven*. Almost every known sentient race is represented in my crew: Kiksaliks, Ghrexels, Igthons, and Humans...just to name a few. We came here to rescue and free members of a mercenary company who were being held as political prisoners, and we do not desire a conflict with the Aurelian Navy. This ship has five shield layers. The fifth and outer-most layer is gone; the fourth layer is at seventy-percent and recharging, and we have yet to utilize the full offensive capabilities of this ship.

"Perhaps, the word 'surrender' was a poor choice on my part. I ask you to stand down and allow us to leave this system without further loss of life. There is no glory, no honor, no achievement in assuring the deaths of those you command. Coleson out."

A few moments later, Jenkins said, "The message is ready, Captain."

"Send it," Cole said. "No encryption and omnidirectional broadcast."

Cole stood and returned to the helm. Sasha moved to the command chair.

Cole looked at Sasha, asking, "Do you think that will do any good?"

"It's hard to tell," Sasha answered, shrugging, "and even if they want to stand down or surrender, what will that get them if their own government will just kill or imprison them for it later?"

"Commander," Mazzi said, "one cruiser just fired twelve missiles at us."

"I thought the cruisers were out of the fight," Sasha remarked, looking to Mazzi.

"This one isn't, ma'am...at least not anymore," Mazzi replied.

"Four torpedoes...fire."

Four torpedoes spat out of the forward launchers, sailing at appreciable fractions of light-speed toward the cruiser that had fired. As the torpedoes approached their target, they separated to approach the cruiser from multiple vectors. Point-defense batteries lit off, but their targeting was poor, missing every torpedo. The four torpedoes adjusted their aim and velocity to ensure all four reached the target and detonated at the same time, and the cruiser ceased to exist.

Sasha was just about to ask Cole to squeeze them through the gap created by the destruction of the cruiser when Jenkins said, "Incoming comms request! It appears to be...a conference call."

Cole swiveled to look at Sasha and saw her expression of surprise mirrored his own feelings. She almost jumped up from the command chair and stepped out of range of the video pick-up as Cole moved to the command chair.

As soon as Wixil sat at the helm, Cole said, "Put the call through on the forward viewscreen."

The bridge speakers chirped once as the viewscreen activated to display twenty-six people. They were of varying ages, and both men and women seemed to be represented in equal number.

"This is Cole," Cole said. "I must say...this is not something I expected."

"Can you take us with you, Captain?" a woman asked. "None of us signed on to be the iron fist of a brutal regime, and none of us are connected enough to survive if we let you leave this system...whether or not we actually *let* you leave."

"Who is 'us?'" Cole asked.

"We've polled our entire ship's complements. None of us want to serve the Provisional Parliament, but 'retirement' or 'resignation' is tantamount to suicide these days."

Cole nodded. "So, what about the *other* ships here? I'd imagine they'd object to you leaving with us."

"You're right, Captain, but everyone's caught up in figuring out who's in command now. Admiral Bagley is dead; her flag bridge was destroyed with no survivors. The cruiser that fired missiles at you carried Captain Aleksei Grimshaw. The rest of us are either commanders or lieutenant commanders...and no one wants to step up and take command."

Cole shook his head. "Talk about a mess." A text message from Sasha scrolled across his field of view, 'What about date of rank?' Cole continued, "I would've thought date of rank would come into play. Who's the most senior?"

"I am, Captain; that's why I'm the one speaking, but we're all in a no-win situation over here. If we press the attack, there's a *very* good chance we'll die to no gain and no reason. Sure...if sacrificing our lives is what it would take to save a world or hold off an invasion until help arrives, every one of us would do that; that's what we're paid to do. Standing up to a battleship because you came to retrieve people who aren't even Commonwealth citizens? None of us want to die for that... especially not when you seem to be more concerned for our lives than our own Provisional Parliament and chain of command."

"You're putting me in one heck of a position. I need a couple minutes. Please hold," Cole said.

"I've muted our audio and blacked the video," Jenkins said.

"Sasha...thoughts?" Cole asked.

Sasha sighed. "What is the so-called Provisional Parliament doing to these people? I can't even conceive of the idea that the entire complement of twenty-six starships would ask us to take them, too. It...it's just unheard of."

Cole nodded. "Anyone else want to say anything?"

"Cole?" Srexx said over the bridge's speakers.

"Yeah, buddy?"

"What did you name this ship? And why did you choose *that*, out of everything you could have named her?"

Cole nodded. "Yeah, buddy. You're right."

"Captain," Mazzi said, "there are life pods launching from the cruisers and battleship. They appear to be settling on a course for various ships near them."

"Okay, Jenkins," Cole said, "put me back on."

"You're live, Captain."

Before Cole could speak, the Commander who'd been speaking for the group turned back to her video pick-up and said, "Captain, there's been a development."

"Oh?" Cole asked. "Do tell."

"Several survivors from the battleship and remaining cruisers have asked to add their voices to ours, sir, and those ships remaining who do not want to join us will not fire on us if we leave."

Cole blinked. "Uh...what? If the situation in the so-called Commonwealth is anywhere close to what I've heard—both here today and before—they do realize what will happen to them, right?"

The woman nodded, her expression somber. "They understand, Captain. They realize they should leave, but...they can't. The Commonwealth is their home; it's all they've known. It's all *we've* known, too, but what's happening now isn't our home. It's not the Commonwealth we signed up to defend."

Sasha stepped into the video pick-up without warning and before Cole could say anything. Every face on the viewscreen showed surprise at seeing her.

"Commander, the Commonwealth *can* get better. I believe that."

The woman shook her head. "No, Lady Thyrray, I'm not sure it can. In the status updates we received before you arrived, we learned the

Carnelian Bloc has entered the war on the side of the Provisional Parliament, and in response, the Duchy of Musilar has come to the aid of the so-called 'rebels,' those supposedly led by your family. You should know, ma'am, that *none* of us who don't owe our positions to the Provisional Parliament believe the story they're spreading about your family. The Thyrrays wouldn't do what they're accusing your family of doing."

Sasha nodded, saying, "Thank you, Commander. That means a lot, and it will mean a lot to my sister when I tell her."

"So how about it, Captain? What have you decided?" the woman asked, directing her attention back to Cole.

Cole glanced at Sasha for a moment before answering, "I named this ship *Haven* for a reason, Commander. Form up on us."

Haven stood down from battle stations to alert status as Cole moved back to the helm and set a course for Tristan's Gate, ordering a leisurely quarter-lightspeed. What he expected was eight destroyers and eighteen frigates to follow him toward the system periphery; what happened was the remaining twenty-nine frigates drifted toward the rear of the formation while two of the remaining three cruisers shifted as well.

"Captain," Jenkins said, "we're receiving another comms request."

Cole smiled. "Put it on."

Sasha stood as Cole moved to the command seat. Wixil moved to the helm.

The senior Commander appeared on the viewscreen again as the bridge speakers chirped.

"Captain..."

Cole smiled. "Let me guess; there's been another development."

"Yes, sir. Perhaps we should've told you, but we were broadcasting our side of the conversation across our fleet channels. No offense, sir, but those ships who didn't want to follow *you* will follow Lady Thyrray. Two of the cruisers want to come, but they have engine damage and can't maintain one-quarter-light. They're working on repairs as we speak, but it will be at least five hours before they're capable of even two-tenths' lightspeed."

Cole smiled, "I suppose I could act all offended and put upon, but I understand. The Thyrrays are your people. What's their maximum safe speed?"

"One-tenth lightspeed."

Cole winced. "Ouch. Okay. I'm guessing they would rather *not* abandon their ships?"

"That's correct, sir."

Cole shrugged. "Well, nothing for it, then. Helm, all stop. Once the cruisers catch up to us, proceed on course at one-tenth light."

"Aye, Captain. Helm answering all stop."

The commander smiled. "Thank you, sir."

"You're welcome. *Haven* out."

Once the comms channel closed, Wixil jumped up from the helm as Cole moved to it. Sasha moved back to the command chair, passing Wixil as she returned to her place beside Mazzi.

"You know, Cole," Sasha said, "you will have to take the big chair sooner or later."

Cole swiveled to face her. "I'm working my way through the ISA's suggested courses for their captaincy exams. For right now, though, things are okay. Srexx?"

"Yes, Cole?" Srexx said via the bridge speakers.

"Do you have any suggestions for how we take two cruisers, eight destroyers, and forty-seven frigates with us when we hyper out of here?" Cole asked.

"One moment..." Srexx said. After several minutes of silence, during which Cole eased the engines back up to one-tenth lightspeed, Srexx continued, "If we divert all available power to the hyperdrive, including what we're using on the defensive shields, my calculations suggest we can extend the ship's hyperdrive field to encompass our formation. We will not have the power to maintain eighty-percent transit speed, as you prefer."

"How bad of a compromise are we talking here, Srexx?" Cole asked.

"My calculations suggest a maximum of seventy-percent, but my calculations may not be accurate. To my knowledge, no one has ever attempted this before."

"Well," Cole said, "I guess there's just one way to find out how accurate your numbers are, buddy."

———

A little over forty-five hours later, *Haven* and the small Aurelian task group comprised of two cruisers, eight destroyers, and forty-seven frigates arrived at the system periphery. Cole transmitted the formation data Srexx had devised to all the ships while Srexx worked with Chief Engineer Logan and his people to ensure everything was ready.

After two more hours, the 'Engage Hyperdrive' button lit up on the helm console.

"We are as ready as we can be, Cole," Srexx said via the bridge speakers.

Cole keyed the control, and all fifty-eight ships vanished from Oriolis.

CHAPTER FORTY-FIVE

System Periphery
  Tristan's Gate System
  7 October 2999, 22:54 GST

The hyperdrive shut down, depositing fifty-eight ships at the system periphery of Tristan's Gate, and Cole breathed a heavy sigh of relief as he both counted the ships and confirmed their location via the helm's sensor display. Cole realized a captain shouldn't communicate anything other than a calm confidence, but he'd spent the last twenty-seven days and fifteen hours on tenterhooks just waiting for the hyperdrive to fail or the ship to explode or...well...something. But nothing happened.

Cole swiveled his seat to face Sasha, who sat in the command chair, and failed to keep a slight grin from curling his lips as he said, "Lady Thyrray, if this humble, unworthy soul may offer a thought, the Lady might converse with her people to develop an answer for when the Tristan's Gate SDF sees our formation and says hi."

Every pair of eyes on the bridge turned to watch the situation unfold, and as everyone on the bridge—including Cole—awaited Sasha's response, one could have heard a pin strike the decking at the far end of Deck Three. Sasha maintained the perfect non-expression for several moments, until a mischievous gleam appeared in her eyes. Without speaking a word, Sasha rose to her feet and turned toward the starboard hatch. She took one step but then turned to look over her shoulder to the helm, where Cole sat watching her. Sasha took a moment to stick her tongue out at Cole and, then, left the bridge for her office where she could speak with her people without disturbing anyone.

As the starboard bridge hatch closed, everyone turned to look at Cole. Under the weight of all those eyes, Cole couldn't keep his mirth contained. He erupted in laughter, and soon, everyone on the bridge joined him.

Two hours later, in what had to be choreographed timing, every Aurelian ship present deactivated the transponders proclaiming them to be ships of the Aurelian Navy. When their transponders came back up, some twenty minutes later, those fifty-seven ships now reported as belonging to Haven Enterprises, '*ACS*' having been stripped from their names and their registry numbers now being prefaced with 'HES' instead of 'C' for the cruisers, 'D' for the destroyers, or 'F' for the frigates.

On the bridge, Cole put the transponder list on the forward viewscreen and leaned back in his seat, his arms crossed over his chest. He wasn't sure how he felt about the change, but he supposed it was better than having them still operate as ships of the Aurelian Navy.

On the plus side, the cruisers had used the twenty-seven days and change in hyperspace to advance their engine repairs. Those ships were now as repaired as they were going to be without the assistance of a shipyard, and the chief engineers aboard them rated the engines safe for a sustained one-third-c, or one third of light-speed. That would put Cole and his task group (maybe fleet?) arriving at the Gate sometime between twenty-six to thirty-one hours, once they started that way.

Srexx sent a formation file to the helm console for Cole to see, and upon looking it over, Cole nodded in acceptance. Cole arranged the ships in a fleet formation to correspond to the file Srexx sent him and distributed it to the other fifty-seven ships as a 'travel formation.' The cruisers soon positioned themselves to port and starboard of *Haven* in the classic line abreast. Two destroyers assumed position a safe distance off the bow of *Haven* with two more falling in an equal distance off the stern. One destroyer took up a position on the far port side of the line abreast formed by *Haven* and the two cruisers and another took up a similar position on the far starboard side. The last two destroyers took up a position above and below *Haven*, respectively. The frigates formed a rather impressive globe around *Haven*, the cruisers, and the destroyers.

Sent along with the formation orders, Cole provided a movement plan. Beginning on Cole's mark, the ships would set their speed at one-tenth-*c*. Ten minutes later, they'd increase to two-tenths-*c*, and ten minutes after that, they'd increase to one-third-*c*. Cole hoped everything went according to plan and that what *didn't* was small and manageable.

———

In Transit to the Gate
    Tristan's Gate System
    8 October 2999, 10:17 GST

Still about twelve hours out from the Gate, Cole entered the bridge and sat at the helm, learning a sizeable portion of the Tristan's Gate SDF had come out to meet them. Once the lightspeed comms lag was manageable, Cole hailed the SDF formation. A response came without delay.

"This is Major Clark Hanson of the Tristan's Gate SDF. Please, identify yourselves and state your intentions."

Cole looked over his shoulder and gestured for Sasha to handle it.

"Major Hanson," Sasha said, "this is Commander Sasha Thyrray, first officer of the Battle-Carrier *Haven*. The ships you see accompanying us have resigned from the Aurelian Navy. They wanted to sign on with me, but since I've chosen to sign on with Cole, they are now ships of Haven Enterprises. It's an imperfect solution while we figure every-thing out, but it's the best we could do in the time we had. Every man and woman aboard those ships—all thirteen thousand two-hundred ninety-three of them—transmitted a letter of resignation to the Aure-lian Chief of Naval Operations before our departure from Oriolis. As *Haven* lacks sufficient lift capacity to support those numbers, we... borrowed...the vessels until we develop an alternative. Our intentions are to approach the Gate, with *Haven* docking to deliver my grandpar-ents, Sev and Emily Vance, several other relatives, many people who were being held as political prisoners on Oriolis VI...and all that remains of Harlon's Howlers, including Harlon Hanson himself."

For a few seconds, the only sound coming over the comms channel was cheering. At last, though, decorum returned...well, mostly. "Soosh," Major Hanson said, "would you please tell my cousin I'm looking forward to those beers he owes me?"

"I'll be happy to do that, but you should know my grandparents have already communicated with O'Shaughnessy's and reserved their entire establishment for a party to celebrate Harlon's return. We're supposed to dock late tonight, and the party starts at noon tomorrow. Being Harlon's cousin and given your close ties to our family, I'm sure I could wrangle you an invitation...so long as you're nice to me."

"Sasha, you are an evil woman," Major Hanson said, laughing. "With your permission, *Haven*, we'll escort you in. The sudden appear-ance of such a large fleet alarmed the system leadership a bit."

"Escort away, SDF," Sasha said. "We appreciate the welcome. *Haven* out."

O'Shaughnessy's, The Gate
  Tristan's Gate System
  9 October 2999, 12:00 GST

In the end, Cole could not avoid attending the party, despite his best efforts. He could make it a brief appearance, however, even though he was forced to sit through Emily's re-telling of his approach to the detention facility and Harlon's account of their conversation just before departure. When Harlon reached the comment about 'just because they're named dropships, that doesn't mean you can actually *drop* them,' the entire attendance of the party erupted in laughter. Cole laughed along, too. Before long, though, Cole slipped out with the crew change, a rotation that had been set up so that O'Shaughnessy's wouldn't be overwhelmed by the almost forty-three-hundred crew of *Haven* who were invited to the party.

Music accompanied by cheers and singing filled O'Shaughnessy's as the Vance and Hanson clans came together to celebrate Harlon's rescue from Oriolis, a sign on the corridor hatch announcing the establishment closed for a private party. Sasha smiled as she watched Talia swing around the dance floor from one person's arm to the next, like many of the dancers out there, and she reflected on how easy it was to set aside the cares weighing on her soul in such an ambiance. A small voice in her mind tried to assert that she had no business being merry and happy while she and her sister had dead-or-alive bounties on their heads, not to mention whatever fate her parents and older brother may have already faced, but Sasha couldn't give that voice much credence. Sasha didn't know how they would get those bounties and charges lifted, but Cole didn't doubt it in the least. It was easy to believe in that outcome, given Cole's utter certainty it would happen; so far, he had accomplished everything else he'd set out to do. But lifting the bounties and the charges that went with them wasn't a simple matter of retrieving people from some planet; now, they had to go up against the Aurelian Commonwealth—or at least what remained of the Commonwealth, and that struck Sasha as an altogether different proposition.

"'Tis most unseemly for a lady so fair to carry such cares in so happy a venue," a voice said from Sasha's left side. In normal circumstances, the statement would have been a whisper, but no whisper would survive in O'Shaughnessy's tonight.

Sasha turned and found Garrett standing at her elbow. Sasha

grinned, saying, "Well, now...I haven't seen much of you lately, Garrett. Where have you been hiding?"

Garrett shrugged. "Oh, here and there. I was doing some work for a friend that took me away from Tristan's Gate for a while. I just made it back in time to crash the party."

"Is that so?" Sasha asked. "Anyone I know?"

Garrett grinned. "Oh, I'm sure there's a chance you might recognize the name, but just like lawyers and private investigators, I *never* discuss my clients."

Sasha was so fixated on Garrett that she never noticed one of O'Shaughnessy's servers pass by her in the crowd and slip a tiny object into the right-front pocket of her trousers...but Garrett noticed. Garrett noticed and marked that server in his mind.

"Have it your way," Sasha said, "but feel free to stay and enjoy the festivities."

Just then, one of Sasha's distant cousins appeared at her elbow, urging her that there was someone she *must* meet. Garrett used the conversation as a cover to slip the item delivered by the server back *out* of Sasha's pocket. It was a standard-issue data card; matter of fact, it looked like the model sold in one of the shops in the station's market. Garrett deftly returned the data card to Sasha's pocket and melted back into the crowd.

When Sasha finished with her cousin's friends, she turned back to re-engage with Garrett, only to find that the man had disappeared. Everyone she asked about him admitted to seeing her talking with someone, but no one seemed to know what had become of him. Frustration circled Sasha's mind at losing track of Garrett, but there was nothing for it. She turned her attention back to the party and put her best effort into enjoying herself.

CHAPTER FORTY-SIX

Docking Slip 12, The Gate
  Tristan's Gate System
  9 October 2999, 16:47 GST

Cole approached the airlock that would permit him entrance to *Haven*. He felt antsy, almost on edge. He felt like he had forty years of work to do and six months in which to accomplish it all. Looking back over his life these last few years, he realized his mistake now. He was foolish to think he could slip away and live somewhere in the back of beyond and not care what happened to the people around him. He wasn't sure just what had been the catalyst for his epiphany...Srexx's treatment by his creators, the way Sasha and Talia had been treated by someone seeking power. It could have been either or both of those. For that matter, it made his blood boil to think of how the 'Provisional' Parliament was treating the people it was supposed to defend and protect.

Cole realized now that his place was in the vanguard, leading by example. The people who had chosen or asked to sign on with him were *his* people now, and woe be unto anyone who bore them ill will.

A faint sound that was out of place drew Cole's attention, and he spun, pivoting on his left heel and backing toward the airlock. He saw his old friend Garrett standing a short distance away.

"Well, now I know I'm getting old," Garrett said. "You never caught on to me before."

Cole laughed. "You're not old, Garrett; you're *experienced*."

Garrett shared a laugh for a moment before he sobered. "Do you have a couple minutes? We need to talk."

Cole nodded toward the airlock, asking, "Office or day-cabin?"

"Doesn't matter," Garrett replied.

Cole led him through the airlock and took the nearest transit shaft down to Deck Three. Yes, he knew he had the Captain's quarters up on Deck One, but he took one look in there and shivered. It was big enough you could almost play a professional sports match in there. Ever since that one glance, he'd lived in the Captain's day-cabin on Deck Three, just across the corridor from the port hatch to the bridge.

Once they were seated, Cole gestured for Garrett to continue, saying, "So, what's on your mind?"

"I couldn't find information on the source of the bounties and warrants. It's not pretty in the Commonwealth anymore, Cole. I don't know if you have any reason to go in there, but if you don't, don't get any. They're blockading the jump gates wholesale, stating that they're for military and government use only."

Cole almost saw red. "That violates...what...six different articles of the contracts with CIE?"

"At least...probably more. I managed to trace the actual coup to a guy by the name of General Draketh Lindrick. This guy is a slippery bastard; he seems to have his fingers in a lot of pies you wouldn't expect for a general. What little I could learn about the power struc-ture in Aurelius pointed toward Lindrick pulling the strings of the Provisional Parliament. He's behind the Carnelian Bloc coming into the war on the Parliament's side; he called in some favors he'd built up over there." Garrett sighed. "Cole, it is a mess out there. Musilar ships have started moving against the Carnelian Bloc, which has pulled some of their forces out of the Commonwealth, but I heard rumblings that the Parliament would send 'loyalist' forces into the Duchy in retaliation. This is shaping up to be a true interstellar war, unlike anything we've seen in centuries...maybe even the kind of war we haven't seen since we spread out from Earth. Oh...and that's not all."

"What's not all?" Cole asked.

"I crashed the party at O'Shaughnessy's and had fun with your first officer. She doesn't know about our arrangement, and I played on that. Anyway, while we were talking, a server slipped a data card into Sasha's pocket. Sasha didn't even notice that I could tell, and since I'd been playing just moments before, I knew she wouldn't trust me enough to tell me about it if I asked. I located the server in O'Shaughnessy's personnel database, though, and I have her home address."

Cole's expression hardened. He didn't like people messing with his people. "Go say hi, and take Red with you just in case. Wait. How did you know it was a data card?"

"While Sasha was engaged with another conversation, I helped myself to the contents of her pocket. At least those skills haven't left me yet." Garrett shrugged. "The shift logs indicate she'll be working for another five hours or so, so we have time to do it right. From what I saw in her personnel file, she doesn't strike me as the mastermind type...more likely an unwitting pawn and easily sacrificed. No. I think I want to talk to the person who *hired* her."

"Well, I'm not about to jiggle your elbow on something like this," Cole said. "You know more about it than I do, and besides, I have enough to keep me busy well into the next century."

Garrett smiled. "So, where do I find this Red you mentioned?"

"Not sure. He's an Igthon the size of Jupiter, so he's not easy to miss. Hang on a second." Cole accessed his implant and called the bridge, routing the call through the speakers and microphone in his day-cabin.

The speakers chirped right before they broadcast, "Bridge here, Jenkins speaking."

"Jenkins, this is Cole. Do you have any record of Red signing off the ship?"

"One moment, Captain," Jenkins said, followed by some silence. "Yes, I have his departure logged right here, but he came back aboard about twenty minutes ago."

Cole grinned. "Do you mind paging him and asking him to come to my day-cabin, please?"

"I'm on it, sir."

"Thanks, Jenkins. Cole out."

Cole and Garrett chatted about small, inconsequential things for the next few minutes until the hatch chime sounded. Cole used his implant to open the hatch, and Red ducked through the opening.

"You wanted to see me, Captain?" the Igthon asked in his deep rumbling voice.

"I did, Red. Thank you for coming. This is Garrett, my oldest living friend. He's investigating the situation with Sasha and her family for me, and I would like for you to work with him this evening while he questions a few people. Is that something you feel you can support?"

Red remained silent for several moments before he delivered a slow nod, laden with certainty and conviction. "Commander Thyrray and her sister are good, honorable people, Captain. It will be my pleasure to assist with *any* operation that will bring those who would attack either of them to light."

"Excellent," Cole said. "Thank you, Red."

"The first person we'll be speaking with," Garrett said, "is a young woman who works at O'Shaughnessy's. I watched her slip something into Sasha's pocket during the party today. I will say a lot of things during the questioning and ask you a question or two to set the mood, but any implications I make or hints I lay down are just to inspire the young woman to feel fear and be amendable to sharing what she knows. I will not hurt her; I'm pretty sure she's an unsuspecting innocent in all this. Does any of that present a problem for you?"

"No. Not at all."

———

Iveanne stepped into her cubic on one of the residential levels of the Gate and leaned back against the closed hatch. She felt so relieved to be home at last. If she'd known there'd be a private party the day she agreed to switch shifts, she never would have said 'yes.' Ten hours serving drinks, entrees, and finger foods to a horde of people made up of both the Vance *and* Harlon clans didn't make for a fun night at work. Ah, well…at least she'd get a nice stack of credits from that guy who asked her to slip a data card to one of the party's attendees. The picture he'd shown her looked familiar, but Iveanne didn't care enough about the various celebrities around the galaxy to recognize them on sight.

Iveanne reached out in the darkness and fumbled at the hatch coaming as she sought the control to turn on the lights. Her fingers touched a mass of loose wires just as the lights came on without her command. The space now lit, Iveanne frowned at seeing a mass of wires dangling out of the hatch coaming where the control pad should be…the same control pad that contained an emergency call button to Station Security.

"I apologize for the damage to your residence," a smooth voice said from behind her. Iveanne spun and let out a small scream at seeing two people she didn't know in her home. A Human man sat in her favorite chair, and a male Igthon with ginger-colored fur stood behind the chair with his thick muscular arms crossed over his chest, towering over the Human. The Igthon was so tall, in fact, the tips of his perked ears almost brushed the ceiling.

"I preferred to disable the call button with finesse," the Human continued in that smooth voice, "but my associate grew impatient and…well, you see the result. Have a seat, Iveanne Doryen. We need to discuss why you'd slip something to one of my employer's friends."

"W-Who are you?" Iveanne asked over trembling lips.

The man smiled. It was a very charming and disarming smile, most at odds with the implied menace of the situation. "My dear, I've used so many names in so many star systems across so many years. It's a gamble whether I even remember the name my family gave me. Is there a specific name you prefer?"

"Uhm…" Iveanne felt her knees tremble, as her mind filled with one unpleasant outcome after another for her current situation. It wasn't long before she felt leaning against the entry hatch was all the reason she hadn't collapsed.

Her distress was noticeable to her 'guests,' almost garish in its blatancy, and the man sighed. "You may call me Garrett, I suppose, and

I suggest you sit down before you fall down. You look none too steady on your feet just now."

Iveanne weaved her way to her other armchair on quivery legs, and her descent into it looked to be more of a not-quite-fall than a deliberate, controlled movement.

"There we go," the man called Garrett said. "Don't you feel better already? Just imagine how much better you'll feel if you tell me what I want to know."

"I-I don't know anything. A guy paid me two-hundred-fifty credits to slip a woman a data card, and he told me he'd pay me seven-hundred fifty more when I told him I did it. That's it. That's all I know."

"What do you think?" Garrett asked, looking up toward the Igthon behind him.

"I don't smell urine," the Igthon said in a deep rumbling voice. "She's not afraid yet."

Garrett sighed. "I told you coming into this that torture wasn't an option. I asked you along just in case she had a boyfriend or something. I'm not a young man in my prime anymore, you know." Garrett turned his attention back to Iveanne. "Torture is *so* unreliable. You can never trust the information you get. Once a person reaches a certain level of pain, they'll say anything to make it stop. When I was still a trainee, of a sort, I once watched a guy the size of my friend here beg his interrogator for the right words to say while he bawled like a baby. Torture never gets you anywhere."

"Then...then, why are you here?"

"To meet you, and to instill just a hint of fear. Then, we'll follow you when you go running to your handler. The way you conduct yourself screams you're not a professional at this, so odds favor whoever you're working for killing you rather than paying you...no loose ends, you see. That's the fellow I want to meet, and...well...I'm afraid you're just bait. Sorry about that."

The sound of the Igthon sniffing filled the small apartment, and he said, "Yep...she's afraid now."

———

Garrett stood to leave, leading Red into the corridor. Garrett waited for the hatchway to close and placed a small sensor in the corridor, focusing it on Iveanne's hatchway. When the sensor tripped, it would spray nano-scale trackers into the area, which would allow Garrett to trace Iveanne's movements without following her through the station's corridors. After that, it was only a matter of time.

———

Just a few minutes before midnight, Sasha entered her quarters aboard *Haven*, more exhausted and relaxed and happy than she'd been in quite some time. She hadn't realized how much she'd missed her mother's side of the family, but perhaps, recent events had given her a greater appreciation of them. Still, Sasha wasn't in the mood for any extended introspection; all she wanted to do was go to sleep. As she changed into her sleeping attire, Sasha saw a small object fall out of her right trouser pocket. Kneeling, Sasha retrieved a data card she didn't recognize. Curiosity pulled at her, but a yawn chose that moment to claim her focus. She set the data card aside and climbed into bed.

———

Thirty-four minutes past 01:00, Garrett's implant displayed video from the sensor outside Iveanne's apartment. The fisheye view showed the woman leaving her apartment and heading toward the elevators, and she took fifteen nano-trackers along for the ride. Garrett touched Red's arm and nodded. They left the quiet watering hole where they'd been waiting and followed Iveanne.

The nano-trackers led Garrett and Red to the warehousing area of the docking level. In a port as busy as Tristan's Gate, the docks were always one of the busiest levels of the station, but the area Garrett and Red entered seemed devoid of activity. Soon, though, they heard voices.

"I did what you asked," Iveanne said, "and it got me a visit by a

Human and an Igthon. Why didn't you tell me it might be dangerous? I would never have agreed to it!"

"My dear," the voice responding was deep and sounded amused, "*of course*, it was dangerous. If there had been no risk at all, I would've given the data card to Sasha Thyrray myself."

Garrett and Red slipped up to a pallet stacked with crates up into the teens of feet high. Garrett peeked around one side as Red peeked around the other.

A short distance away, Iveanne stood with a man Garrett didn't recognize. He stood easy, relaxed, his right hand in his trouser pocket. Iveanne almost vibrated with nervous energy.

"Well...okay then," Iveanne said. "Give me the seven hundred fifty credits you promised, and we'll go our separate ways."

The man offered Iveanne a small smile that didn't reach his eyes. He withdrew his right hand from his trouser pocket, revealing a small laser pistol.

"Hey! What's the gun for?" Iveanne asked, taking half a step back.

"What do you *think* it's for?" the man asked. "You're what people in my line of work call a cut-out. You already said you were visited by a Human and an Igthon, and I can't have you telling anyone who asks what I look like or what I paid you to do. Say...you didn't happen to bring the cred-stick with the 250 credits on it, did you? That would make matters *so* much easier."

Garrett withdrew a stunner from his pocket and took aim. Just as the man was moving his finger toward the firing stud of the laser pistol, Garrett pressed the firing stud on his stunner. The stunner was the modern evolution of the taser or stun gun that had been around since the late twentieth century. This model used magnetic fields to accelerate the shielded projectiles to speeds greater than the speed of sound. Those projectiles carried capacitors and, upon striking soft tissue, used the person they'd struck as a conduction medium... resulting in said person falling to the deck/floor/ground as every muscle seized and relaxed. A person needed to be wearing an armored ship-suit—at the least—to have protection against stunner barbs, and the man in front of Iveanne wore what looked like a business suit to Garrett.

Iveanne screamed when the man collapsed and started twitching, jumping back as her hand flew up to cover her mouth. Garrett and Red stepped around the pallet of crates that had hidden them from view and approached, standing over the twitching man. After watching the man twitch for a couple seconds, Garrett shifted his attention to Iveanne.

"I'd like to thank you for your unwitting assistance in this matter," Garrett said. "You were excellent bait. In the future, if a job offer seems too good to be true, you might want to give it a second thought."

CHAPTER FORTY-SEVEN

Storage Space, Docks
   The Gate, Tristan's Gate
   10 October, 02:26 GST

Garrett watched the man stir and he leaned back in the chair with a sigh. He'd already taken DNA, fingerprints, facial map, retinal scans, and several other pieces of biometric data used to identify people. His search of various personnel databases was running, but he couldn't pass up a chance to chat with the fellow.

A faint clicking filled the space, and Garrett looked over the man's shoulder to see one of the Kiksaliks working for Cole. Garrett smiled. He didn't know *how* Cole had gotten so many Kiksaliks to sign on with him; they were standoffish at best and downright antisocial at worst. Still, they made his job easier, and despite the visceral reaction most mammalian sentients experienced at seeing a Kiksalik, they were rather nice people.

"Who...who are you?" the man asked, struggling against the straps holding him in the chair. "Do you have any idea what you've done?"

"Yes, actually," Garrett replied. "I stopped you from killing an innocent woman. Well...she was your unwitting pawn. I suppose I could report her as an accessory before the fact, but nothing is served by sending her to a penal colony. She was just trying to make ends meet."

The man blinked at Garrett as he tried to sit upright, but his motor control was still scrambled from the stunner. "Who are you?"

"Someone better at this sort of thing than you are," Garrett said. "You don't expect me to give you any name that means something, do you? Heh...well, I suppose I could always put on a Scottish accent from Old Earth and say, 'Bond...James Bond.' A friend of mine loves old movies, all kinds unfortunately, and I can't believe they made those well into the twenty-second century; who would've thought spy flicks would have that kind of longevity? But we're not here to conduct a film seminar. No. We're here about you."

"I'll never talk."

"But you're already talking," Garrett said, a slight smirk curling his lips. "If you're not going to talk, do you need to tell me you're not going to talk? Besides, everyone has a breaking point. It's just a question of where yours is and how much inducement it'll take to reach it. So...let's begin. Who do you work for?"

The man shook his head, squeezing his eyes shut.

"Oh, come on. You think squeezing your eyes shut will make any difference? Seriously, who do you work for?"

The man shook his head again. "I told you I'm not going to talk."

"Why were you going to kill that woman?"

The man shook his head.

Garrett looked over the man's head at the Kiksalik. The Kiksalik nodded once. Garrett waved as the insectoid turned and left the space.

"Listen, chum. I have to thank you for your cooperation. You've given me everything I wanted to know."

"But I didn't say anything!"

Garrett grinned. "It's an unfortunate trait of Human psychology that we think very hard about stuff we're not supposed to say when we're being questioned. I'm told it makes things rather easy for a telepath...like the Kiksaliks. My friend just left after sifting through your mind; it'll be nice to hear what you know. In the meantime, I need to give you this little cocktail and disappear myself before Station

Security arrives. Don't worry; it's fast-acting. You'll be talking like a madman in no time."

Garrett withdrew an injector from his pocket and pressed it to the man's neck, right over his carotid artery. A brief hiss was the only indicator Garrett injected him. Garrett patted him on the head as he stepped around the man and walked to the hatch, whistling an old family tune.

"What did you inject me with?" the man said, trying to turn to look at Garrett.

"Oh, nothing much...just thirty milliliters of Senpatrazol. I'm sure a man in your profession has heard of it."

Over the centuries, chemistry and a better understanding of Human biochemistry led to more effective 'truth serums.' The ultimate in that line of pharmacology was known as Senpatrazol. Like its immediate predecessor, it was fast-acting and took a rather long time for the body to metabolize, improving its duration by a considerable measure. Unlike its immediate predecessor, however, Senpatrazol didn't break down into a toxic compound that caused systemic organ failure. Whoever the fellow was, he'd be healthy and hale to enjoy the penal colony Garrett mentioned...once he'd finished telling Station Security *everything* he knew, including all the embarrassing personal stuff no Human ever discusses with anyone else. In about ten minutes, the fellow wouldn't be able to stop himself.

First Officer's Quarters, Deck One
  Battle-Carrier *Haven*
  10 October 2999, 07:23 GST

Sasha pushed the covers back as she rolled over and sat up on the edge of her bed. She still felt sleepy, but it wasn't anything a nice, hot shower wouldn't fix. A few minutes later, Sasha returned to her bedroom, towels wrapped around her torso and hair, and retrieved the data card that had fallen out of her pocket last night. She walked over to her workstation and slipped the card into the multi-reader, sitting in the chair as the terminal processed the data on the card.

A window appeared on the holographic display, and Sasha screamed. The still shot showed her parents kneeling on some dingy floor, their hands bound behind them and their faces splotched with dirt and grime. It was the first time Sasha had ever seen her mother's hair so unkempt...*and* unwashed.

The video played, and Sasha watched her parents move as they breathed and tried to find a comfortable position. The first sound Sasha heard from the video was her mother sobbing. A voice said, "Hello, Sasha. As you can see, we have your parents. I'm afraid your brother didn't survive his apprehension. Dreadful and rather unfortunate, that; I suppose I could pan the recorder around to show you the corpse, but does anyone want to see a family member with various holes in their torso? So...down to business. We have agents flooding every free port and hidey hole you might visit, and every one of them has a copy of this message. All of which means you should receive this no later than the fifteenth of October. Either way, you have until the thirtieth of November to present yourself before the Provisional Parliament of Aurelius, where the Parliament will sentence you for your crimes. If you do as we ask, your parents...well, no. Let's be honest here. We'll *think* about releasing your mother. Oh...do be a good girl, and leave that Lone Marine friend of yours at home. After all, do you want to watch whoever is under that armor die, too?"

The video froze on an image of Sasha's mother looking into the video pickup. Her eyes were puffy, and tears had washed away the dirt and grime in lines running down her cheeks.

Sasha almost ripped the data card from the multi-reader and headed for the hatch at a near sprint. Half-way across her quarters, she froze and looked down at her towel-clad torso.

"Srexx?"

"Yes, Sasha?" Srexx asked over the speakers in her quarters.

"How long to Aurelius at 80% hyperdrive?"

"One moment..." After a brief silence, Srexx continued,

"According to the navigational database, Aurelius lies two-hundred twenty-six lightyears core-ward from Tristan's Gate. At 80% power on the hyperdrive, it would require 32.575 days to arrive, but at full power, the transit would only take 4.592 days. May I ask why you inquired?"

Sasha forced herself to take a deep breath. They had time. Remembering Srexx had asked her a question, Sasha said, "I was considering asking Cole to take me home to look for my parents, Srexx. That's all."

"Given the state of the former Aurelian Commonwealth," Srexx said, "I do not believe such a course is wise."

Sasha smiled. "You're right about that, Srexx. Thanks. I appreciate your time."

Sasha turned and went to her bedroom, where she put the data card aside long enough to dress. Then, she retrieved the card and headed for the hatch, intent on locating Cole.

––––––––

Captain's Day-Cabin, Deck Three
    Battle-Carrier *Haven*
    10 October 2999, 07:25 GST

Cole leaned back in his armchair, savoring its comfort. He didn't appreciate being woken up. Truth be told, he never *enjoyed* waking up; he was just glad he'd always done so thus far. Garrett sat across from him rolling an old-fashioned metal coin through his fingers, like Cole had seen him do so many, many times during his adolescence.

"So, what did you learn?" Cole asked.

"Me?" Garrett said. "Not a damn thing. That Kiksalik you loaned me, however, learned all kinds of things. So did Station Security, for that matter...once they acted on my anonymous tip. It seems the fellow who hired Iveanne to plant the data card on Sasha is a field agent of Aurelian Intelligence, and this isn't the first time he's run an operation in Tristan's Gate. It so happens that, this time, the op wasn't directed at the system government. He's been a naughty boy down through the years, and I imagine the system leadership will have a field day listening to his confession."

"Do you have any idea what was on that data card?"

Garrett shook his head. "Nope, and neither did he. His contact brought it to him with the instructions that it be passed to Sasha Thyrray no later than the fifteenth of this month. Since he arranged for the delivery a whole six days early, he was going to claim the thousand credits he'd promised Iveanne as his 'bonus' for a job well done."

"Over her dead body, right?"

Garrett shrugged. "Details, details...as far as he was concerned. Iveanne wouldn't have been the first loose end he tied up, either."

The conversation moved onto next steps and anything Garrett might need from Cole. A few minutes later, the hatch chime ringing off several times in quick succession interrupted their discourse.

"Dear heavens," Garrett said, looking over his shoulder toward the hatch. "Who in all the stars needs to talk with you that badly?"

"*Haven*, please display the corridor outside my day-cabin on the bulkhead monitor," Cole said. The viewscreen came to life and showed Sasha standing at the hatch. Her right hand went to the hatch chime against the wall just as another flurry of tones rang off throughout the day-cabin.

"Something tells me you're about to learn what was on that data card," Garrett said. "Where do you want me?"

"I have no idea how long this will take. My office shares a head with my day-cabin. You can get out through there, unless you *want* to sit through whatever this is."

Garrett chuckled as he stood, Cole following suit. "Not at all," Garrett said. "Letting anyone—even someone as fetching as your Commander Thyrray—cry on my shoulder is not part of the job. I'll be in touch."

Cole gave enough time for the hatch to the shared head to close before asking the ship's computer to open the day-cabin's hatch. Sasha stormed in, heading straight for Cole as she held up a data card in her right hand.

"You need to see this," Sasha said.

CHAPTER FORTY-EIGHT

Bridge Briefing Room, Battle-Carrier *Haven*
    Docking Slip 12, The Gate
    10 October 2999, 13:22 GST

Cole, Sasha, Talia, Sev, Emily, Carl, and Lindsey sat around the briefing room table, Cole and Sasha having flown one of the dropships down to Tristan's World for Sasha's maternal grandparents. Talia sat in her seat with a stunned expression as tears streamed down her face amid chest-wracking sobs; neither Sasha nor Cole had had Talia sit through the video ahead of time, and the news that her big brother was dead hit her hard. Lindsey Vance sat staring at the frozen image of her daughter and son-in-law, her expression teetering between sorrow and hope. Carl put his arm around his wife and pulled her close as tears ran down her cheeks.

"I...I can't believe it," Lindsey whispered, her eyes never leaving the frozen image of her daughter. "My baby's alive..."

Both Sev and Carl directed thoughtful expressions toward Cole while Sasha held her sister. Sev and Carl shifted their attention to each other for a moment before turning back to look at Cole, their expressions still thoughtful.

"I appreciate being kept in the loop," Carl said, "and our neighbors will talk about that dropship landing in our backyard for months. But you didn't need to bring all of us together just to relay this information. What's on your mind, Cole?"

Cole leaned back in his seat and scratched his chin for a moment. "We have an enormous advantage in *Haven*'s hyperdrive. At the speeds most civilian ships travel, the trip from Tristan's Gate to Aurelius through the jump gates would take right at five weeks...maybe just a hair under five. *Haven* can go to Aurelius in just over four-and-a-half days, so there's flexibility there."

Sev and Carl looked to each other again before turning back to Cole, Sev saying, "Go on."

"My sources inform me that the Provisional Parliament has declared all jump gates within Commonwealth space off limits to all traffic not related to the war effort. I'm not sure if you are aware, but that declaration and its enforcement represent gross violations of the contracts signed between the Commonwealth and Coleson Interstellar Engineering that permit them the use of our proprietary technology."

"Hang on," Carl said. "You said '*our* technology.'"

Cole nodded. "My full name is Bartholomew James Coleson. My father was Jack Coleson."

The color drained from both Carl's and Lindsey's face.

"There's just one problem," Cole said. "I've been hiding for thirteen years, and all the assets and authority haven't been transferred to me yet. To do that, I need to make a run to Zurich, which is a hair under two days one-way at 95% on the engines. Once I have the authority as Majority Shareholder of CIE, I'm in a much better position to express my family's displeasure at the Provisional Parliament's violation of the contract. This will also destabilize them. They'll think Sasha is walking in there to save her parents, but before she says a word, I step forward and make a statement on behalf of CIE. That should kick off enough of a furball that capable people can retrieve Sasha's parents while the Parliament and I are circling each other for a fight."

"So, what do you need from us?" Lindsey asked.

"Access. Jeb Hanson made a big deal of how much he owed me last night at the soiree, and I want to hire Harlon to command the Marine contingent aboard *Haven*...if Harlon's willing. I've already looked into his record and the circumstances of his capture on Oriolis. Sev, I have a job offer for you, depending on how tied you are to Tristan's Gate and the shipyard here. Emily, I have a job offer for you as well. These jobs are not short-term gigs related to the current unpleasantness; they are long-term, 'build something that lasts' jobs that could be considered the challenge of a lifetime. Once we get through this current situation with Sasha's parents, I'd like to sit down with both of you to discuss the offers in depth."

"Care to give us the 'Executive Summary' version right now?" Sev asked.

Cole's eyes flicked between Sev and Emily. "Emily, *Haven*'s designation is 'Battle-Carrier.' I realize the naval term 'carrier' is old school by our experience, but this ship was built to carry a wing of small craft that would've once been called fighters, bombers, and the like back on Old Earth. I want to hire you to be my CAG, which is shorthand for Commander Air Group; you'd be the senior-most flight officer aboard, the Wing Commander if you will. Sev...those fighters and bombers and such? I will need a place to build them. I want to hire you to work with Julianna Painter; she's already signed on to oversee my merchant fleet, and if you accept, you'll be in charge of all system infrastructure."

"Which system will receive this infrastructure?" Sev asked.

Cole grinned. "I would've thought it would be obvious: Beta Magellan. I'll be moving CIE's headquarters from Alpha Centauri to there, just like my father intended."

"But Beta Magellan's jump gate is down; it hasn't worked in years," Emily protested.

Cole shook his head, still grinning. "No. I've been using the system as my personal hidey hole. I only activated the jump gate when I needed to go into the system...but we're getting a little off-topic. The bottom line is this. If Sasha's parents are being held anywhere in the Aurelius system, I have a friend who can find them. Once we have a location on them, we'll drop ground forces under stealth and Electronic Warfare to effect their release...but first, I have to go to Zurich to secure our diversion."

The meeting broke up after that. Sasha took Talia to her quarters. Cole walked everyone to the airlock and messaged Julianna Painter to secure transportation back to Tristan's World for Carl and Lindsey Vance. Once all guests had left, Cole went to the bridge; he wasn't surprised that Sasha wasn't there.

The moment Cole stepped onto the bridge, Mazzi stood from the command chair and said, "Captain on deck!" She moved to the weapons console as Cole headed straight for the helm.

"Jenkins," Cole said, "get us immediate departure clearance with a clear transit vector out of near-station space. We will be leaving the area at speed."

A few moments later, Jenkins announced, "We're clear to depart, Captain. All station traffic in our vicinity is holding position."

"Thank you," Cole said, "and pass my thanks to Station Control, please."

Cole fired a burst of the engines to push the ship backward out of the docking slip. Then, he disabled the vector control system to allow the ship to maneuver through any orientation while maintaining its direction of movement. With the VCS off, Cole then rotated the ship 180° to port, flipped the ship end for end so that the bow now pointed *away* from the station, and rotated the ship back to be parallel to the plane of the docking slip. The sensor display showed him a clear corridor out of near-space with no movers anywhere close to his heading, so Cole locked in that heading and set the sublight engines to seven-tenths' of lightspeed. Despite its immensity, *Haven* shot out of near-station space like the projectile from a gauss cannon. Once they were free to navigate, Cole locked in a destination of Zurich and brought the ship in a sweeping turn to point toward the star in question. A little over thirteen hours later, *Haven* vanished from Tristan's Gate.

———

System Periphery

Zurich System
13 October 2999, 00:37 GST

Haven appeared on the periphery of the Zurich system a little under two days after they reached the periphery of Tristan's Gate. Cole sat at the helm, alone on the bridge, and regarded the sensor display for several moments before he chose the destination and set the sublight engines to half-lightspeed.

Star systems are huge, and the star system named Zurich was larger than most. According to the ancient main sequence spectrum developed before Humanity ventured beyond its own moon, Zurich was an A-type star in the process of transitioning to an F-type star. As such, the goldilocks zone—which allowed for the potential of a habitable, life-giving planet—was much farther into the system than the goldilocks zone for Old Earth, and the planet the founders of Zurich settled on occupied a position in the solar system similar to that of Saturn in Sol.

Three massive stations orbited the settled world in Zurich, and Cole selected Zurich One as the destination before setting the engines to half-lightspeed. It was 85 AUs to Zurich One from the periphery, five AUs longer than the diameter of the entire Sol system, and it would take a little over twenty-three hours and thirty minutes to make the journey. Cole programmed the computer to alert him of any anomalies or problems and went back to bed. After all, it was the middle of the night.

Even as he laid in bed, though, Cole couldn't sleep. He felt using himself as a distraction in Aurelius was the best option, but stepping forward after all these years and admitting to the galaxy he was Heir to the Coleson Trust was unsettling. Someone had massacred his family in Beta Magellan, and whoever it was must've had a *very* powerful reason to commit mass murder. Was the reason no longer valid, or was Cole about to put the largest target in Human space on his back? Only time would tell.

And if he was being honest with himself, his potential fate wasn't the sole reason this course of action unsettled him. Stepping up and claiming the Trust would put him in his father's shoes, and looking back over his life, Cole felt certain beyond any doubt he wasn't worthy. Not worthy at all.

––––––

In Transit to Zurich One
    Zurich System
    13 October 2999, 12:47 GST

"Captain," Jenkins said, "we're being hailed by a destroyer off our port side attempting to keep up with us."

Cole grinned. "Put the call through."

The speakers chirped as the forward viewscreen activated and displayed a young woman looking immaculate in the green and gold colors of the Zurich Defense Force. Her expression implied a certain level of both determination and dedication.

"Attention, unknown vessel. I am Lieutenant Commander Caitlynn Hendry of the Zurich Defense Force. State your intentions in this system."

Cole smiled and gestured for Jenkins to transmit. "Hello, Commander Hendry. I am Bartholomew James Coleson, aboard the Battle-Carrier *Haven*, and I need to visit the headquarters of Credit Suisse. I have banking to do."

"It is most uncommon to see a capital ship without screening elements, and with all the unpleasantness occurring in this region of the galaxy, I'm sure you can understand why we might observe a heightened state of alertness for any encroachment in our system."

Cole nodded. "It's very understandable. Zurich's neutrality is legendary, and sometimes, extra vigilance is necessary to ensure it."

"Thank you, Captain, for your time. We'll transmit a record of our conversation to Defense Command."

The speakers chirped once more, and Cole leaned back against his seat. He was afraid it was only a matter of time before more partisans were pulled into the conflict spiraling around the flailing corpse that was the Aurelian Commonwealth, and Cole wondered how many innocents would get caught in the crossfire.

Twelve hours later, *Haven* docked at Zurich One. While the headquarters of Credit Suisse were open and operated as a branch of the bank, the officers Cole needed to visit did not return to the office until 08:00 later that morning. Cole announced liberty for the crew with the provision that all hands were subject to recall at two hours' notice.

———

Cole entered the Credit Suisse offices to see the same level of understated elegance he'd seen in other branches. Wood paneling on the bulkheads, area rugs in warm welcoming colors, soft lighting that struck a happy medium between too bright and too dark...Cole felt an immediate welcome, and he hadn't even spoken with anyone yet.

"How may I help you, sir?" the young man at the reception desk asked when Cole approached.

"I need to speak with an officer overseeing the Coleson Trust," Cole said. "I carry a sealed writ from the Tristan's Gate branch, and I'm afraid I must hand-deliver it."

"Of course, sir. If you would please have a seat, I'll see that the proper individuals are notified. May I offer you some refreshment?"

Cole smiled. "I appreciate the offer, but I finished breakfast about thirty minutes ago."

"Of course, sir."

After a few minutes, Cole noticed movement nearby in his peripheral vision, and he looked up...and froze. Standing a short distance away was a man Cole remembered from his childhood, when he came to the bank with his father. He was older now, his hair almost all gray with more of a midsection than Cole remembered, but there could be no mistake. Cole was looking at his father's close friend and personal banker, Leland Graf.

If Mr. Graf recognized Cole, he was astute enough not to show it, offering Cole a pleasant welcoming smile. "I believe you have something for me, young man. If you would follow me to my office, we can discuss the matter there."

Mr. Graf maintained his polite indifference all throughout the trip to his office, but once the hatch sealed, all that changed.

"By the stars, boy, it's good to see you! Did you know you have your mother's eyes and your father's chin? Seeing you sitting there in the lobby damn-near stopped my heart," Leland said as he took Cole's hand and pumped it in a fervent handshake. "So...how have you been these long years?"

Cole shrugged. "Some years have been better than others, sir."

"Sir? What am I, some random soul you met in the corridor? You used to call me Uncle Leland, but I suppose there's so much reaction mass out the thruster nozzle we should just go with Leland. Thank you for visiting Beta Magellan every so often. Those visits allowed me to ensure the vultures on the Board of CIE didn't force the Trust onto one of your unworthy cousins...not that they deserve to be called cousins, no matter how entitled they act. What am I doing? Please, have a seat; have a seat."

Leland grabbed one of the two chairs placed for guests and spun it to face the other, sitting without delay. Cole sat in the other guest chair and produced the sealed writ, extending it to Leland.

"Here. Ms. Obrist in Tristan's Gate said I'd need this."

"I'm sure she did, but she didn't know my history with your family. Still, though, I should file that to establish your bona fides with the bank. I wouldn't want anyone thinking I'd slipped a ringer into the system. What made you come forward after all this time, if you don't mind me asking?"

"The Aurelian Commonwealth is coming apart," Cole said, "and in their death throes, the Provisional Parliament has violated its contract with Coleson Interstellar Engineering. They are blockading the jump gates and have declared them off limits to most civilian traffic, being restricted to government and military use only. They need to learn the error of their ways, and I feel I have no other choice than to be Majority Shareholder of CIE when I educate them."

"If they've blockaded all the jump gates, lad, how are you going to reach Aurelius to educate the Provisional Parliament? That seems to be a small hole in your plan."

Cole grinned. "Not at all. I discovered an ancient alien starship back in June and claimed it for myself when I was stuck between the proverbial rock and a hard place. It doesn't have jump engines, so I don't need the jump gates to reach Aurelius."

Leland adopted a thoughtful expression for a few moments before he nodded. "You're the Lone Marine people are whispering about."

Cole shrugged. "It's almost impossible to see inside heavy armor, Leland. It could be anyone."

"Oh, naturally...naturally." Without warning, Leland shot to his feet. "Well, let's get the unpleasantries over with and get you access to your family's Trust."

Leland moved to his workstation, opening the writ and dropping the data card into a reader slot in his desk. He worked for several minutes, humming a tune to himself while he tapped away at his workstation.

"And there we are," Leland said at last. "We must confirm your identity to be sure it matches with our records and the sealed writ, but you and I both know there won't be any deviation."

Another thirty minutes later, Cole left the headquarters of Credit Suisse in total control of assets worth more than the GDP of several star systems. The account Leland called his 'petty cash' held more credits than *Haven*'s ship account by at least a couple orders of magnitude. Leland fired off a notification to CIE that the Heir had stepped forward and claimed the Trust and would call on them when time permitted, afterward providing Cole another sealed writ containing records of every identity verification he'd undergone. That writ would come in handy if the Board of CIE tried to contest his identity.

What Cole also had, though, was authority to speak for CIE, because the company charter was written in such a way that the Coleson Heir became the CEO upon accepting the Trust and ownership of the shares. Cole felt rather certain whoever served as CEO might find that unsettling, but his family's company was a matter for another time.

CHAPTER FORTY-NINE

Docking Slip 12, The Gate
  Tristan's Gate
  17 October 2999, 04:53 GST

Haven slid back into Docking Slip 12 and engaged the forcefields to create—or at the least simulate—the hard seal a traditional docking collar would produce. Not for the first time, Cole wondered if Docking Control saved the slip for them. He never let himself ask them, though, because he didn't know whether it was good or bad if they did.

Just as the helm station reported docking complete, two messages dropped into Cole's queue. Cole accessed the first; it was from Sev, and it was a report they were rush-constructing four dropships using the best stealth technology available and that they could retrofit the three dropships Cole carried if he brought them over as soon as they docked. The second message was from Emily; it contained only two words: We're on. Cole couldn't escape the feeling that things would move *very* fast from that moment forward.

Cole stood up from the helm, turning to the bridge. "Jenkins, put me on ship-wide address."

The speakers chirped once, and Jenkins said, "You're on, Captain."

"Attention, all hands; this is Cole. We have docked at the Gate after a whirlwind tour of Zurich. To answer a question I'm sure is on someone's mind, yes, you'll be getting liberty. However, all hands are subject to immediate recall, so I will ask you not to pursue some of the more raucous entertainments spacers can be known for on liberty. We're on a timetable, and when everything comes together, we will be lighting out of here like we're two steps ahead of Station Security...except I'd better not learn any of you *are* two steps ahead of Station Security. Once we're underway, I'll inform everyone as to what's going on and why the liberty this time is more restricted than usual. As of this moment, liberty rotations begin. Cole out." The speakers chirped as the ship-wide address channel closed, and Cole turned to Sasha. "You have your pilot rating?"

Sasha shook her head.

Cole nodded and pivoted to Mazzi. "Mazzi, I need two pilots rated for the dropships. If they're part of the first liberty rotation, tell them they'll be allowed to run over an amount of time equal to what I use. Have them meet me on the flight deck in ten minutes or less."

Cole and his two shadows that were masquerading as dropships had just departed *Haven* when text appeared in Cole's field of view.

Incoming Comms Call: Battle-Carrier *Haven*
[Wink left for 'Accept.' Wink right for 'Ignore.']

Cole winked his acceptance and chose the following option for his implant to route the call through the dropship's audio system.

"Cole here."

"It's Sasha, Cole. The people leaving the ship are reporting something odd. They're saying there's a military checkpoint just inside the airlock with additional personnel recording everyone's name, picture, and biometric identifiers, and here's the weird thing. The checkpoint isn't intended to keep our people *out* of the station; it's set up to block general access to our airlock. Do you have any idea what's going on?"

"No," Cole said, shaking his head even though Sasha couldn't see it. "I have no idea. Are the SDF hassling our people at all?"

"Not even a little. Everything is pleasant and smiling, and they're even exchanging jokes."

Cole frowned. "As long as they're not hassling our people, I'll track it down once I leave the dropships at the shipyard and talk with Sev. Call me at once, please, if anything changes."

"Roger that," Sasha said.

"Thank you for the heads up. Cole out."

The speakers chirped again as the comms call ended.

Twenty minutes later, they approached the shipyard, and the shipyard directed them to a hangar separate from the main section of the ship-yard. After Sasha's call, Cole felt a twitch between his shoulder blades. The two dropships followed him into the hangar in perfect formation —which made Cole smile—and once the dropship's systems reported pressure in the hangar bay, Cole saw the personnel hatch open to admit Sev and five people wearing Tristan's Gate SDF ship-suit uniforms. Cole now felt certain something was *not right*.

Cole shut down the dropships and activated the maintenance codes that would allow the shipyard's people to move them as needed, and he stood from the pilot's console, slapping the control to lower the boarding ramp as he passed it. His two fellow pilots met him at the foot of his boarding ramp, and it was only after they were half-way to the 'welcoming committee' that Cole realized his pilots had adopted a chevron formation with him on point...one step behind and to either side of him.

Of all the many things running through his mind for what was about to happen, Cole was not prepared in the slightest when the woman in SDF uniform standing in front of and closest to Sev called out, "Atten-SHUN!," at Cole's approach, and all five snapped into a rigid stance and performed a parade-ground-perfect salute. Cole blinked, his mind locked. He knew how people *used* to respond to such things from watching ancient documentaries with his grandfather and since, but he had no idea if that was still appropriate.

Cole's eyes flicked to Sev, and he saw an almost-contained grin trying to curl the man's lips.

"I'm sorry," Cole said, "but I'm not sure as to the proper response. Thank you and as you were?"

The five SDF people seemed to accept that, the senior-most dropping her salute with which prompted the other four to drop their salutes.

"Sev," Cole said, his eyes locked on Sev's, "I think we need to talk. Do you have someone here who can ferry my pilots over to the station? They're overdue to start liberty."

The woman beside Sev turned to the man at her right side, saying, "Petty Officer, can you see these men to the station and get them on file?"

"Aye, ma'am," the man said.

Cole wanted to ask them right there what in all the stars was going on, but he held his tongue and nodded to his pilots, who left with the petty officer.

Sev waited until the two pilots and the petty officer left. Then, he smiled, saying, "Cole, let's go to my office. We can talk there."

Cole took a deep breath and shook his head. "No, Sev. We can talk right here. I've had a twitch between my shoulder blades ever since I landed, and I'm about two seconds from telling Srexx he can have fun."

Sev understood Cole's last statement for the threat it was and nodded. "Look. We're so swamped right now, I had to go to the system leadership to get them to release the military yards to make your drop-ships. They agreed but wanted *Haven* as reserve SDF. Julianna and I discussed it and thought you'd be okay."

Cole sighed. Yeah...not giving Julianna one of Srexx's implants with its quantum comms had been a mistake.

"I'm not wild about surprises, Sev...and I'm not much of a government drone, either. I go where I want when I want and do what I want. I'm not one to ask a whole lot of permission."

"You step in and defend people who can't defend themselves?" Sev asked.

"You know I do. Hell, man...that's how I picked up my first thousand crew. They almost begged me to take them after I'd pulled them out of whatever nastiness they'd gotten themselves into."

Sev shrugged. "Then, I don't see what the big deal is. The terms Julianna and I arranged were that you had to agree for you and your people to be activated; Tristan's Gate can't just call you up like regular reservists. They weren't too happy about that, but Julianna held firm."

"Fine," Cole said, sighing. "I'll accept it for now, but I didn't ask for this. They shouldn't count on me for any long-term planning." Cole turned to the woman standing at Sev's shoulder. "Forgive me for not observing proper social niceties. I don't take surprises well. I'm Cole."

The woman nodded. "Lieutenant Commander Brianna Vance. I'm to be your liaison with SDF Command."

"Vance?" Cole asked, putting forth effort to maintain a straight face. "This wouldn't happen to be Uncle Sev, would it?"

"No, sir," Brianna said. "He's Dad."

"So, what does an SDF liaison do?" Cole asked. "What are your orders?"

"I'm to make myself useful to you while being on hand to assist you with any SDF-related matters that may arise."

Cole nodded. That may have been what she was told *or* what she was told to say. He'd have Srexx discuss the matter with SDF's computers to find out what was going on before they shipped out for Aurelius.

"Well, Lieutenant Commander, I don't know what your dad has mentioned, but things are moving a little fast for us right now. We'll have to sort this out in a week or so. Right now, I need to get back to *Haven*."

"Of course, sir," Brianna said. "We have a shuttle waiting."

"Your dropships will be retrofitted with the stealth coatings and emissions reduction by the end of the week," Sev said, as he fell in beside Cole. "It would be sooner, but I'm running triple shifts to finish the *other* three dropships you need."

"I thought those dropships can carry up to two-hundred-fifty soldiers plus all their gear," Cole said. "Why in all the stars do I need *five* of them?"

Sev stopped and looked at Cole. "You haven't spoken with Emily yet, have you?"

———

Cole stared at the mass of people before him. They were in one warehouse Julianna had purchased for Haven Enterprises, back when she was overseeing the salvage of the Aurelian frigate's wreck and the freighter *Beauchamp*...because the station had no other space large enough for everyone. The only other time Cole had seen a mass of people so large was the one time he'd had the entire crew muster on the flight deck, and he wasn't sure but what this group was larger.

"What is this?" Cole asked, turning to Emily. "Who are all these people?"

Emily shrugged. "Well...word got out that the Lone Marine was hiring. This is the result."

Cole turned to look back across the crowd and said a few words one shouldn't say in polite company. He turned back to Emily. "Emily... I wanted you to hire ground forces people. Doesn't Harlon know the people he needs for Aurelius?"

"Oh, he does, but you also told me and Dad you wanted to hire us for 'build something that lasts' jobs. I figured you wouldn't mind a few extras who happen to have cross-training in fields you need."

"Really?" Cole asked. "What kind of cross-training do you think I need?"

Emily smiled. "Every person in this room has both military experience and time doing zero-g construction...and demolition."

"So, I guess this means you and your father have accepted my job offers?"

Emily's smile shifted to a grin. "You could say that."

"Where's Harlon?"

"He's trying to explain to his grandfather why you won't hire *him*."

Cole blinked. "His grandfather...isn't that Jeb Hanson?"

"Yep. Harlon made the mistake of mentioning what we'll be doing next over dinner the other night, and ever since, Jeb's been all gung-ho to sign on. He takes a very dim view of what the Provisional Parliament did to his good friend's daughter and her family, and he wants his pound of flesh."

Cole sighed. "I have the impression that Jeb can be a hothead."

"You have no idea, Cole. You really don't."

"That right there disqualifies him. I don't want hotheads on my crew...too many mistakes." Cole sighed again. "Okay. I'll get the Kiksaliks and some ship's crew over here, and you can work through all of them. Everyone with Marine experience who passes the interview gets an immediate appointment to the ground forces element aboard *Haven*. If they don't pass the interview, they're out...no second chances." Cole's voice trailed off as he shook his head. "This is insane. All this because they heard *I* was hiring?"

"What can I say?" Emily said, shrugging herself. "You're building a reputation."

———

It turned out not to be so simple as sending over the Kiksaliks with members of the ship's crew. The Kiksaliks took one look at the milling mass of people and refused to enter the warehouse. To solve the issue, Cole rented an office complex for two weeks. The complex had a hundred offices, and Cole put one Kiksalik, one member of the ship's crew to conduct the interview, and an Igthon and Ghrexel from the ship's crew in each office. The Igthon and Ghrexel acted as security on the off chance someone didn't pass their interview and contested the result. Cole rotated personnel every four hours.

After six days, they'd worked through the whole group. Out of 16,834 applications, there were 239 rejections...meaning 16,595 passed. Cole filled out the ship's complement, what he called his aircrew, *and* the ground forces element, and he still had a rather impressive amount of people left over. Cole spent almost eighty-three million credits in sign-on bonuses alone.

———

In the end, Cole called a general command conference aboard *Haven*. All fifty-seven captains from the ships that came with *Haven* from Oriolis were in attendance, along with Sasha, Sev, Harlon, and Julianna.

"I called this conference to make sure everyone is on the same page and to get a few things started while Sasha, Harlon, and I go handle something. As of today, Sev Vance has put in his notice at the shipyard and will transition to the Director of System Infrastructure for Haven Enterprises. Once *Haven* returns, we will shift all our personnel to Beta Magellan, where we'll build a system infrastructure centered on a ship-yard and mining facilities. Sev, please find and hire a reputable company that can build a station in Beta Magellan. It doesn't need to be anything fancy. I'm thinking residential space for fifteen thousand with massive docking facilities and massive manufacturing decks. Leave the manufacturing decks vacant. We'll be installing recyclers and fabricators ourselves; I don't want random construction people seeing them. The station will be our staging area that will go away once we're capable of building our own station; don't let them put it anywhere that would be prime real estate for what we want to build."

"Yes, sir," Sev said, nodding once.

"Julianna, find me personnel transports. We need to ferry the six thousand three hundred thirty-three people I don't need on *Haven* to Beta Magellan somehow...once we find someplace for them to live. You know what? Work with Sev, and see if the company we contract to build the station wants to use any of them for labor. They have their own crews, but if throwing more people at it gets our temporary station online sooner...well...we have a surplus of people. That is not to say I consider any of them expendable; I want to be clear on that point."

"What will we be doing?" The senior commander of the former Aurelian Navy ships asked.

Cole smiled. "Some of you will be running escort for personnel transports. The rest will be making *very* sure no one enters Beta Magellan that we don't want to enter Beta Magellan. Eventually, we'll be scrapping your ships for new construction...but I expect each one of you to save a section of the bridge bulkhead for name plaques on the new ships."

"You should be aware, Cole," Sev said, "that it's still going to be a while before several of the ships are ready for duty. The cruisers, especially; you shot them up pretty bad."

"They *were* trying to kill me and my people at the time," Cole said. "I'm not expecting miracles. What I'm saying is the kind of thing that takes months if not years."

"I don't know about that," Sev said. "We should be able to have your station online and ready to accept those fabricators and recyclers by the middle of next year. At that point, we can begin construction of the shipyard; now, *that* will probably take a year, but I'll see what I can do to streamline things a bit. I know how much you want your air wing."

Cole grinned. "Sure, but that's not *all* I want. *Haven* should have proper screening elements, don't you think? And let's not forget that Beta Magellan will need its own system defense force. Oh...and before I forget, the headquarters for Coleson Interstellar Engineering will join us in Beta Magellan. My father and grandfather believed the rate of innovation within the Solar Republic to be on the decline and thought the next great advancements would come from the Human expansion zones; they wanted CIE to be positioned to both foster *and* profit from the new centers of innovation when they developed. But that's more of a long-long-long-term thing, rather than something that needs to be at the forefront of anyone's mind."

"Why would CIE move their headquarters to Beta Magellan?" the senior commander from the former Aurelian Navy ships asked.

Sasha, Sev, Harlon, and Julianna all shared a grin but kept their silence. Cole took a deep breath and said, "I've always introduced myself as Cole. My full birth name is Bartholomew James Coleson. My father was Jack Coleson, and as of a few days ago, I became the CEO of Coleson Interstellar Engineering when I claimed the Coleson Trust in Zurich."

The former naval officers' eyes grew wide.

"Okay," Cole said. "Is there anything else?"

No one said a word.

"Very well." Cole stood and scanned the faces around the table.

"Julianna and Sev are in charge until I return. If you need anything, see them. Let's get started, people."

————

At 19:44 on the 24th of October, *Haven* requested clearance to depart from Station Control. They were granted immediate clearance, and all near-station traffic was ordered into a holding pattern. *Haven* undocked and, the moment she cleared near-station space, ramped up to half-lightspeed on a course for the system periphery. A little over fifteen hours later, *Haven* vanished from Tristan's Gate.

CHAPTER FIFTY

System Periphery
    Aurelius System
    29 October 2999

Cole, Sasha, and Mazzi stood in the center of the bridge, staring at the tactical plot of the system. The hologram hovering above the decking showed all contacts in sensor range, which seemed at least as far as the star...some 52 AUs away.

"I don't get it," Mazzi said at last. "Shouldn't there be more ships?"

"I would have thought so," Sasha said. "With everything they're doing in the outer regions of the Commonwealth, I didn't expect them to leave the home system so uncovered. A light cruiser, two destroyers, and four frigates seems to be their standard jump gate picket; at least, the three jump gates we can see only have those ships each. I was expecting Aurelius to be the most militarized system we've seen so far."

"We're at full stealth, right?" Cole asked.

"Yes," Wixil said from the weapons station. "All decks have reported that they are rigged for stealth."

Cole chuckled. "Sasha, how set are you on confronting the Provisional Parliament?"

"I want my parents back," Sasha replied. "I'm indifferent to the so-called Provisional Parliament. Why do you ask?"

"Given what we did at Iota Ceti, part of me says we should try to slip down to the planet, retrieve your parents, and depart with no one the wiser. Unless they have a substantial fleet on the far side of the system, I'm not seeing anything that could take us in a straight-up fight."

"If we get discovered before we have my parents, though," Sasha said, "their lives could be counted in minutes...if not seconds."

"It's your call," Cole said. "We'll do this however you say."

Sasha took a deep breath and released it as a sigh. After several more moments, she said, "Let's stealth to the planet and see if Srexx can locate my parents. We'll go from there once we know more."

———

It was late on the 31st when *Haven* slipped in close to Calliope, Aurelius's third moon. Like all of Aurelius's moons, Calliope was tidally locked between the planet's gravity and that of the star, with the planet spinning on its axis 'beneath' it and its two fellows. The other two moons bore colonies and various industrial or commercial facilities, but as of yet, Calliope possessed none of that.

"Well, Srexx? Can you access anything?"

"Cole," the AI said through the bridge speakers, "the latency is atrocious."

"Really? What is it?"

"Two and a half seconds."

Cole blinked. "Is that one-way or round trip?"

"Round trip."

Cole sighed. "Srexx, buddy...do you realize if you were operating on our communications technology the latency to the planet from here would be upwards of six minutes?"

Silence.

"I...I feel sorry for you and your datacenters, Cole. No computer should have to wait so long for data."

Cole fought his sudden urge to grin. "So, are you finding anything?"

"Oh, yes. I've found many things. For instance, General Lindrick departed the system two days ago with the bulk of the forces that would have been here. I have yet to find any record of where they were headed. From what I can discern, the Provisional Parliament is little more than a puppet for General Lindrick, along with someone named Admiral Edom Sedmon."

"Say again, Srexx?" Sasha asked, halfway rising out the command chair. "Admiral Sedmon is part of this?"

"Based on the data I am accessing, Admiral Edom Sedmon yips when Lindrick says, 'Bark.'"

"That...that can't be right. Admiral Sedmon is one of the most respected and decorated officers of the past five decades, maybe longer."

"I am sorry, Sasha," Srexx replied. "I can present the data to you for your own evaluation. It is possible that my relative unfamiliarity with Humans is affecting my analysis. Ah...and there we are. Sasha, your parents are being held in the administrative segregation unit of Corenthal Prison; it appears they have already been convicted of treason and sedition. They have been sentenced to life without parole. Ah, and it appears I might have good news for you. Your brother Nathyn occupies a cell in the next block over from your father; he is part of the administrative segregation unit as well."

Sasha gaped. "Nathyn's alive? You're sure he's alive, Srexx?"

The viewscreen activated and displayed a picture along with an incarceration record.

"Is this your brother?" Srexx asked.

Sasha held her lower lip between her teeth to maintain proper bridge discipline and keep from cheering. "Yes, Srexx. That is my brother."

"Srexx, get everything you can on this Corenthal Prison. I know I said we'd proceed however you wanted, Sasha, but I'm calling it. We're going down there for them. We'll try a stealth job, but we'll be outfitted for assault if we're discovered."

Harlon, his executive, and the personnel performing the operation gathered in a briefing room on Deck Four. Once everyone was seated, a hologram appeared at the front of the room.

"This is Corenthal Prison," Srexx said via the briefing room's speakers. "It is a civilian prison under the authority of the Commonwealth Division of Corrections and Rehabilitation. We will retrieve three people: Paol Thyrray, his wife Mira, and their eldest child Nathyn. Paol and Nathyn are incarcerated in the maximum security, administrative segregation unit of the men's half of the facility, while Mira is incarcerated within the equivalent unit in the women's half. The individuals responsible for operating the fabricators are putting the finishing touches on a jammer that should block all radio communications across the facility. While the jammer blocks all radio communication, I will infiltrate the data network and ensure no *other* forms of communication are possible."

Srexx fell silent, and Harlon stepped forward.

"Okay, people," Harlon said, "this is a stealth job. The facility is a civilian prison, and as such, it is designed around the core purpose of keeping people in; it was never designed to withstand an assault from outside. The goal is to be quick and quiet. One dropship will descend on the facility and land just after local midnight. Srexx will shut down all lights, hardline comms, and the emergency generators just as you're coming in to land. When you depart the dropship to begin the assault, Srexx will take control of all access points to the facility and remove all staff privileges; the prison personnel will effectively become inmates with no authority to open any doors or access any systems. You will move through the facility, establishing only those zones of control necessary to achieve the objectives. Once you have retrieved Paol, Nathyn, and Mira Thyrray, you will return with them to the dropship and proceed back to *Haven*. Questions?"

"What kind of backup will we have?" one person asked.

Harlon grinned. "As many of you know, the captain has conducted certain activities in the past that have earned him the nickname of 'the Lone Marine.' I will not discuss the amount of negotiation and discussion I had to go through to keep the captain from being part of the initial force entering the facility. That said, three dropships will be warmed up and filled with a quick reaction force outfitted in heavy armor and lethal weapons. If the situation spirals out of control and stealth is no longer an option, you are free to call for reinforcements, and the Lone Marine will deploy to secure the situation...but he won't be so 'lone.'"

"Did he really drop a dropship thirty meters on Oriolis VI, sir?" another voice asked from the middle of the room.

Harlon nodded. "Yes, he did, and the flight logs corroborate that. The dropship the captain piloted to the detention facility sat in a concave depression a little over half a meter deep, and its landing struts were buried in the concrete the better part of fifteen centimeters. Captain Vance, *Haven*'s CAG who has her own reputation as a combat pilot, told me later that she'd never been so terrified in her life as she was during the descent to Oriolis VI."

Silence reigned as several of the personnel looked to one another.

"Anything else?" Harlon asked.

More silence.

"All right. Grab your gear and suit up. Muster on the flight deck ASAP."

———

The dropship descended on Corenthal Prison. Everyone aboard was glad it was an overcast night; heavy cloud cover meant less ambient light. As the dropship neared its destination, the jammer magnetically secured to its dorsal surface came online. As the dropship touched down in the exercise yard—the only space large enough for it to land— Srexx locked out the prison's data network, ensuring no internal or external comms could be possible, and shredded the personnel database, ensuring no one possessed any credentials that might permit a local override. Then, Srexx activated a full security lock-down and turned off all lights in the facility, even the massive perimeter lights.

The people broke into three groups as they departed the dropship, named Blue Team, Gold Team, and Red Team. Blue Team's objective was to secure and retrieve Paol Thyrray, with Gold Team responsible for Nathyn Thyrray, and Red Team securing Mira Thyrray. Srexx opened every door or access point they needed as they progressed through the facility, leaving four people at every intersection along their path. Any guards...that is, corrections officers...were stunned and secured.

The teams moved quick and silent, little more than shadows in the already dark night. Just over an hour after touching down in the prison's exercise yard, all troops plus Sasha's parents and brother were aboard the dropship, and it lifted off, slipping away into the night.

———

Cole sat in the pilot's seat of his dropship, his mind drifting between the operation on the planet below and how the Provisional Parliament was violating the contracts between the Commonwealth and CIE. Cole thought about how he'd used Beta Magellan, activating the jump gate into the system for just long enough to allow him entrance, and an idea came to the forefront of his mind.

Cole shifted to the pilot's console and used it to access the ship's comms systems. He opened a channel to the closest jump gate, using the ship's powerful point-to-point laser transmitter, and smiled when the jump gate requested his identity. Cole activated the DNA scanner on the master panel of the console and tied it into the comms channel, soon transmitting an encrypted digital signature of his touch DNA.

After a few minutes, the comms channel displayed the full command console for the jump gate's systems. Cole selected 'Schedule Command Script,' from the menu, built the script to be executed, and set an execution time of sixteen hours from that moment. He uploaded the script to the jump gate and queued the script for distribution to all other jump gates in the system. Then, he closed the channel and went back to waiting.

———

While supporting the extraction teams as they moved through Coren-thal Prison, Srexx continued browsing the various digital storehouses around the planet, focusing on any data related to General Lindrick or where the massive fleet might have gone. While there didn't appear to be any records to be found about the fleet's destination (beyond its departure through the jump gate to Diamond system), Srexx did find information he evaluated required significant further processing in the most unlikely of places...General Lindrick's personal cloud storage. Srexx copied the data to a protected archive in his tertiary cluster and returned his full attention to the extraction teams.

Cole and Sasha arranged for Talia to join them on the flight deck while they waited for the dropship to return. They didn't say a word to Talia about Nathyn being alive; Talia had been a little down ever since seeing the video, and Sasha thought the surprise of seeing her older brother would be a good push to get her out of it. Besides, Sasha was the mischievous one of the two, and she hadn't surprised her sister in a while.

They already had the quick reaction force out of the dropships and the flight deck clear. The heavy armor and gear was back in the armory, and the dropships were resting down on Hangar Two.

"It felt weird," Cole said as he stood beside Sasha, "being here on the ship. I should've been down there."

Sasha turned to look at Cole, a small quirk at the corner of her mouth. "That's the hardest lesson of command, Cole. You give orders that might very well send good people you respect and value into harm's way, and when that happens, there's always the chance one or more of them won't come back. We've been lucky in that regard so far, and I think it is the surprise the hyperdrive allows us that has been a significant factor why...well, that and no one has ever been crazy enough to drop a dropship thirty meters into a prison compound. You have a certain flair about you."

"I feel like I owe it to them to be there with them," Cole said. "Something my father told me once...show those around you the person you expect them to be by living that example every day. Well, it was something like that; I think I paraphrased a bit."

The quirk at the corner of Sasha's mouth grew into a full smile. "Do you think there was ever a moment that the people on the incoming dropship doubted you'd be bringing three dropships full of people in heavy armor loaded for war down to them the moment they called for help? They watched the quick reaction force load the dropships, Cole, and they saw that ridiculous heavy armor of yours sitting right outside a dropship cockpit with a rotary cannon at its feet and a plasma caster beside the cannon. I promise you...they knew you had their backs."

Cole was silent for a few moments before he said, "We need to come up with colors for our ship-suits and a ship's crest, don't we?"

Sasha nodded. "We do...but we have time. We'll want to be sure we get it right; the ship's crest isn't something one throws together."

Just then, a black craft passed through the aft forcefield of the flight deck, and Cole smiled. He accessed his implant and placed a call to the bridge.

"Bridge, Mazzi here," Cole heard his weapons officer say in his right ear.

"Mazzi, we have the dropship. Stand down on overwatch and prepare to depart. As soon as the flight status shows green for maneuvering, put us on a heading for Tristan's Gate and take us out dead slow."

"Aye, Captain."

"Thanks, Mazzi. Cole out."

By now, the dropship was touching down almost even with them. Cole knew they'd have to move the dropship forward or aft to access the lift mechanism for the hangar decks, but that was a small matter compared to the moment that was about to happen.

Cole watched the boarding ramp lower and touch the flight deck. Moments later, he heard the low-frequency hum that indicated the dropship was now magnetically anchored to the deck. Three people in Aurelian prison uniforms stepped down the boarding ramp and walked to the two young ladies waiting for them.

Then, Cole heard it.

"Nathyn?" Talia gasped, barely above a whisper. Then, she almost shouted, her voice edging toward a high-pitched squeal as she took off toward her brother at what looked like a full sprint. "Nate!"

Talia didn't *quite* tackle her brother, but from Cole's perspective it looked like a near thing. He saw the smiles and sheer bliss in the expressions of whom he assumed were Sasha's parents, and Cole looked to his left where Sasha still stood.

"What are you still doing here, Sasha?"

"I'm the first officer, Cole; there's a certain decorum that must be maintained."

Cole turned to face Sasha full on. "Bullshit, Sasha. If that was my family, I'd be on my knees crying like a baby. This one time, decorum be damned. Go."

Cole knew he'd broken through 'the officer' when he saw a single tear escape Sasha's right eye. Then, she was off. She didn't sprint like Talia, but she wasted no time in joining her family.

Cole held his position, maintaining a silent vigil to ensure them as much time as they needed...or wanted. The personnel from the dropship filed across the flight deck almost unnoticed by the five people gathered halfway between the dropship and the starboard hatch. The flight crew approached Cole, while the ground forces team disappeared through the starboard hatch beside the traffic control overlook.

"Captain, what should we do about the dropship?" the pilot asked.

Cole shrugged. "Leave it for now. We can move it to Hangar Two some other time."

The pilot nodded and led the co-pilot off the flight deck.

A short time later, Sasha led the small group over to Cole. When they approached within earshot, she said, "This is my father, Paol Thyrray; my mother, Mira; and my older brother, Nathyn."

Cole smiled as he shook their hands in turn. "I'm Cole. Welcome aboard the battle-carrier *Haven*."

"Thank you for taking care of my girls, Cole," Paol said at last. "It means a lot to me."

Cole grinned. "Well, when I first met Sasha, she was drifting a bit aimlessly, and I thought I might help with that."

"There's a story there," Mira said. "That girl has never drifted aimlessly in her life."

Cole laughed. "Yes, there is. How about I share it over dinner once everyone has freshened up and relaxed a bit?"

"That sounds good," Paol said as Mira nodded at his side.

———

A little under sixteen hours later, *Haven* was proceeding on course for the system periphery under full stealth, moving slow and quiet, when the scheduled time for Cole's script occurred. At midnight on 2 November 2999, every jump gate in Aurelius shut down and broadcast a text message on repeat, including transmitting the text message to each jump gate's opposite in the far system.

The message read:

For repeated violations of the contracts between the Aurelian Commonwealth and Coleson Interstellar Engineering, specifying the free and unrestricted use of our proprietary jump gate technology, all outgoing jump gates in the Aurelius system will be shut down for the period of one week.

Be advised that Coleson Interstellar Engineering will consider this matter in due course to determine an appropriate long-term response, up to and including the possible revocation of the Commonwealth's license for the use of our proprietary technology.

Thank you, and have a nice day.

CHAPTER FIFTY-ONE

System Periphery
  Tristan's Gate
  5 November 2999

A bit over seven days and fourteen hours after departing the planet Aurelius, *Haven* appeared on the periphery of Tristan's Gate. Cole wasn't paying that much attention to the sensor display while he set The Gate as their destination. He was just about to bring the sublight engines online when Mazzi jerked his attention from the helm.

"Captain, there are Aurelian Navy ships blockading the jump gate to Dante, with a larger force moving deeper in system toward The Gate. Tristan's Gate SDF appears to be mustering to meet them."

"It isn't the force from Aurelius, is it?" Cole asked. "It would take over six days for a fleet that size to arrive here."

"The Aurelian forces in this system may have come from Aurelius weeks ago, but they do not match the records I accessed, regarding the massive fleet movement with General Lindrick," Srexx said. "I have also identified several troop transports in the center of the formation moving in-system."

"It's an invasion force," Sasha said. "The Provisional Parliament is moving against Tristan's Gate."

"Not while *we* have anything to say about it," Cole said. "Jenkins, signal SDF Command. Inform them we just arrived in-system and that we will clear the jump gate blockade before approaching the invasion force from the rear. Mazzi, sound battle stations."

Cole shifted the destination from The Gate to the Dante jump gate and set the sublight engines to three-quarters-lightspeed. *Haven* almost leapt toward the jump gate when the engines engaged. A hair over two hours and forty-five minutes later, *Haven* approached the blockaded jump gate.

"Captain," Jenkins said, "we're receiving a message."

"Put it on, Jenkins," Cole said as he brought the engines back to two-tenths-lightspeed for what he felt would be the upcoming battle.

The forward viewscreen activated, displaying a man about Sasha's age in the ship-suit uniform of the Aurelian Navy. Conceit and conde-scension oozed from his entire demeanor, from his shiny, slicked-back hair to his bored expression.

"Attention, unknown vessel. Tristan's Gate has been annexed by the Aurelian Commonwealth. Until a provisional government is estab-lished, all traffic into and out of the system is prohibited. Turn away, or be destroyed."

The viewscreen image froze on the man's half-sneer. Cole swiveled to look at Sasha, his eyebrows lifted in a silent question.

"I would say I feel sorry for him," Sasha said, "but I know his family and know of him. They're not good people, and he's probably a loyalist appointment by Aurelian Naval Command."

Cole grinned. "Well then, let's respond, shall we?"

Sasha hopped up from the command chair as Cole moved to it and Wixil moved to the helm. She started to step out of the video pick-up but Cole stopped her.

"No more, Sasha. You and your family are through hiding. Besides, isn't a first officer's place right beside her captain?"

Sasha gave Cole a smile he hadn't seen before as she said, "Always, Captain." Sasha moved to stand just off Cole's right shoulder with her hands behind her back.

"Jenkins," Cole said, "record for transmission."

"You're on, Captain."

"Greetings, and welcome to Tristan's Gate. I am Bartholomew James Coleson, captain of the battle-carrier *Haven*. We are a member of the Tristan's Gate System Defense Force reserve, and we do not recognize the Commonwealth's authority to annex a park bench, let alone a sovereign star system that has been a respected trading partner for decades. Furthermore, as Majority Shareholder and CEO of Coleson Interstellar Engineering, I inform you that blockading jump gates violates the contracts that permit the Commonwealth to use our proprietary technology. I offer you one chance to stand down and slave your systems to ours, or we will defend this system with as much force as necessary. Coleson out."

"Ready to transmit, Captain," Jenkins reported.

"Full spectrum broadcast," Cole said, as he returned to the helm. "I want *everyone* to hear that."

Cole sat at the helm console and looked at the sensor display just in time to see the cruiser, two destroyers, and eight frigates pivot and accelerate toward *Haven*. Minutes later, a slew of dots appeared on the sensor display in front of the Aurelian ships.

"Missile launch!" Mazzi announced. "We have two hundred—that is, two zero zero—inbound contacts. Point-defense is online and tracking. Flight time is two minutes and thirty seconds, present speed."

"Sasha, you have the conn," Cole said.

"Mazzi, lock missiles on the destroyers and frigates," Sasha said as she searched her mind for what she knew about an Aurelian cruiser's acceleration profile. "How fast is that cruiser accelerating?"

"They've leveled off at two-tenths-lightspeed," Mazzi said. "They were pushing upwards of 80 kps squared."

Sasha nodded, saying, "Lock torpedoes on the cruiser."

"All targets locked," Mazzi replied a few moments later.

"Fire," Sasha said.

"Missiles and torpedoes launched," Mazzi reported. "Flight time is thirty-six seconds...mark!"

Thirty-six seconds later, Mazzi said, "Our missiles and torpedoes are arriving. I'm seeing multiple hits across the frigates and destroyers. The frigates and destroyers didn't stand a chance, ma'am; they're intact but out of the fight. I'm seeing all kinds of life pods launching. The cruiser...the cruiser's reactor just lost containment; it's gone. Incoming missiles approaching outer point-defense envelope. Point-defense firing. All missiles destroyed."

"Helm, bring us about on an interception course for the invasion force, and set the engines for three-quarters-lightspeed."

Haven reached engagement range at the rear of the Aurelian invasion force just as the System Defense Force reached their forward elements. Cole sent a text message to Sasha's implant asking her to have Jenkins inform the SDF commander that the jump gate was no longer blockaded and that *Haven* stood ready to assist, should that be needed.

In the end, the commander of the Aurelian forces saw reason and surrendered to the SDF. The SDF ships moved to escort positions, and everyone headed in-system...with *Haven* bringing up the rear and serving as a silent promise for the fate of anyone who violated the surrender.

When they reached The Gate, some thirteen hours later, SDF Command asked *Haven* to maintain overwatch until all Aurelian personnel departed the transports and military ships...just to keep everyone honest. Cole saw no issue with that but asked Sasha if it might be best to stand down from battle stations to alert status.

It took upwards of an entire day to remove and process all the personnel from the invasion force, but as soon as *Haven* was discharged from its position of overwatch and moved toward Docking Slip 12, a message came in that Carl and Lindsey Vance had once again rented O'Shaughnessy's for a welcome home party for their daughter, son-in-law, and grandson; all *Haven* personnel were encouraged (that is, expected) to attend.

Cole took command of the ship as soon as *Haven* docked and announced liberty for the crew, with a reminder about the Vances' invitation to the celebration two days' hence. The bridge crew departed in soaring spirits, and soon, Cole was alone once more in the nerve center of what had become his home.

"Cole," Srexx said via the bridge speakers over the command chair, "may I have a word?"

Cole looked up from the engineering reports he was reading and smiled. "Sure, buddy. What's on your mind?"

"I am uncertain I have a mind in the sense that you do, Cole, but you should know I found something while searching through the data grid on Aurelius for any records of where General Lindrick went."

"Oh?" Cole asked. "What did you find?"

"I found Lindrick's personal cloud storage, Cole. It was encrypted, and it has taken me this long to verify the data. Cole, Lindrick has always had a reputation for taking 'off the books' side jobs, and while Aurelian Army Command has always frowned on that kind of conduct, Lindrick's political connections have protected him from their displeasure...until he joined Army Command. Among many other files, Lindrick keeps a journal of sorts, separated into files by year. In scanning the journal, I discovered an account of then-Captain Draketh Lindrick being hired to command the force that...attacked Beta Magellan."

The tablet containing the various ship's reports slipped from Cole's numb fingers and clattered on the decking unnoticed.

"You're certain, Srexx?" Cole asked, his voice raw. "There's no chance of a mistake?"

"Lindrick described the operation in rather graphic detail, Cole, and the writing style is consistent with both earlier and later journal documents. The timestamps do not show the file as having been altered in any way—though they have been read—since it was created. I evaluate the probability of this being misinformation at less than 0.000001-percent. I am sorry, Cole; when I verified the data, I was... unsure...what I should do and consulted Sasha. She said you had a right to know and that you would *want* to know. Was her analysis in error?"

Cole tried to speak but couldn't as he fought to contain his tears. He would've sworn he had dealt with his family's death and nothing could rip open those old wounds, but the tears fighting to stream down his cheeks suggested otherwise.

"No, Srexx," Cole said at last, his voice even more raw. "Thank you. Srexx, buddy...I'm gonna need a little bit."

"Yes, Cole."

———

O'Shaughnessy's, The Gate
9 November 2999

Music reverberated off the bulkheads as people danced and cheered, while servers moved through the crowd like the masters of their craft they were. The opening ceremonies—where Carl and Lindsey Vance announced the safe return of their oldest child and her family and thanked *Haven* and her crew for that return—were already concluded.

Cole stood alone on the balcony that overlooked the main floor while—unbeknownst to him—Sasha, Yeleth, and Wixil engaged in a concerted effort to see that Cole remained undisturbed. He stood in front of the panoramic armor-glass that allowed an impressive view of near-station traffic and deep space beyond, a partially finished drink in his left hand. He hadn't sought out anyone after being able to escape center-stage and the collective gratitude of the Vance clan, and he hadn't noticed that no one had approached him, either...a testament to Sasha, Yeleth, and Wixil's success.

Movement to Cole's left drew his attention, and he saw Garrett draw close to stand beside him.

"Are you okay, Cole?" Garrett asked. "You've been distant the past couple days."

Cole nodded, saying, "I will be."

"What's on your mind? I would've thought you'd be all wound up and raring to get started on what's next, now that Sasha's family is safe and you can turn your attention away from the Commonwealth for a while. After all...for the moment, it's over."

Cole lifted his glass to his lips and drained it in one long swallow before turning to Garrett, saying, "While we were in Aurelius, I came into some information that proves beyond any doubt that someone hired Draketh Lindrick to organize the massacre of Beta Magellan, Garrett. Trust me, old friend. It ain't over..."

WHAT'S NEXT?

The story continues in "...Till It's Over!," and it's available now.

Visit your favorite retailer and search for ISBN:
9780999201299

The Jax Files are a set of companion short stories that I publish via my newsletter.

If you're interested, you can sign up here:
http://kfplink.com/dyq

RATE THIS BOOK

Did you enjoy this story? If you did, please consider leaving a review.

Reviews are the lifeblood of visibility for independent authors, especially on the eBook retailers. The more reviews a book has, the more visible it will be on the retailers' sites.

I appreciate all reviews...good, bad, or indifferent.

If you would like to leave a review, visit this book's product page.

AUTHOR'S NOTE
28 March 2019

First and foremost, thank you for reading...both the novel and these notes! I hope that you've enjoyed reading this story at least half as much as I've enjoyed writing it.

Did you really, really, really enjoy the book? Perhaps—dare I say—*love* it? In that case, please, consider leaving a review. Why? The more reviewed books (especially books with more 4- and 5-star reviews) receive greater visibility. Greater visibility means higher chance of more people discovering the book.

This is the first novel in a new series for me, and I'm very excited about it. My goal is to have the first five books written by the time this novel goes live on July 2nd, but one of my favorite sayings is, "Life's what happens while you're busy making plans." So, we'll see.

As of this writing, I am 33,463 words into Cole & Srexx Book 2, "...Till It's Over!" It's coming along rather nicely, if I do say so myself. However, I'm going to pause my work on this novel to write the short story, "Beta Magellan." A respected publisher of short story anthologies put out a call for submissions, and I can't resist throwing my hat...

er, story...in the ring for consideration. If it is not selected for inclusion in the upcoming anthology, you can expect to see "Beta Magellan" join the Newsletter Stories.

This series is a bit unlike the other novels I plan to write. It doesn't have a defined end-point. While I like to plan a story arc across a set number of books (usually ten), the idea for "It Ain't Over..." and the Cole a& Srexx series as a whole was a very unexpected and impromptu idea. I have no problems saying there will be ten books in the series, but will there be more? I don't know. It depends on a lot of things, not the least of which being reception and feedback. If readers enjoy the series and don't want it to end at #10, those sentiments will go a long way in producing Cole & Srexx #11. :)

Once again, thank you for reading. It's time for me to get back to work.

ACKNOWLEDGMENTS

There's an old saying: it takes a village to raise a child. I don't know if that's true or not, but it certainly seems true where publishing a novel is concerned. You would not be reading this were it not for contributions from several people.

The editor of this work, T. F. Poist, deserves far more than a simple 'thank you' for her efforts with this work. Her time, knowledge, and expertise improved this work beyond measure.

Did you like the cover? The background image was created by Jakub Skop (https://www.behance.net/JakubSkop).

I'm sure there are many who will see this next paragraph and think, "Goodness, he's acknowledging his parents and grandparents *again*?" My greatest regret is that I cannot hand my grandfather, Bob Miller, a paperback copy of my novels. So, yes...the Acknowledgements page of *every* book I publish will have the paragraph that follows. Consider yourselves forewarned.

Without my grandparents, Bob & Janice Miller, I honestly don't know where I'd be today; my grandfather taught me to read and love reading, and my grandmother taught me to develop and exercise my imagination. This novel (not to mention my life in general) certainly would not have happened without my parents, Vernon & Judy Kerns.

ADDITIONAL ACKNOWLEDGMENTS

Many people have provided feedback, thoughts, inspiration, or education in varying amounts. I greatly appreciate their time and contribution, and if you think your name should be on this list but don't see it, I truly apologize for the oversight. If you're curious, the list is alphabetical by last name.

Shanalyse Barnett

Greg Brewster

Lori Carrender

Jay Limbach

John Maxson

Jon Minton

Aaron Radcliff

Brad Reed

ADVANCE TEAM

Whether you use the term 'beta readers,' 'eARC group, 'advance team,' or something else, it's very nice to have a group of people who want to read an advance copy and tell you anything you and the editor missed... because that happens. And it happens with *every* book.

Anyone willing to help me make my books a better product deserve all the thanks I can give them, including recognition here.

Fletcher Hawkins
Rob Law
Marti Panikkar

THE NOVELS OF ROBERT M. KERNS

For a complete and accurate listing of all publications, both currently available and forthcoming, please visit Knightsfall Press.

Knightsfall Press - Books

https://knightsfall.press/books

SO...WHO'S THE AUTHOR?

Robert M. Kerns (or Rob if you ever meet him in person) is a geek, and he claims that label proudly. Most of his geekiness revolves around Information Technology (IT), having over fifteen years in the industry; within IT, he especially prefers Servers and Networks, and he often makes the claim that his residence has a better data infrastructure than some businesses.

Beyond IT, Rob enjoys Science Fiction and Fantasy of (almost) all stripes. He is a voracious reader, with his favorite books too numerous to list.

Rob has been writing for over 20 years, and *Awakening* is his debut novel.

Connect with Rob at knightsfall.press.

- facebook.com/RobertMKerns
- amazon.com/author/robertmkerns
- bookbub.com/authors/robert-m-kerns

www.ingramcontent.com/pod-product-compliance
Lightning Source LLC
Chambersburg PA
CBHW051209120726
47905CB00004B/1038